The Widow of Woodholme

Books by Sharon Allen Gilder

The Rose Beyond
Beyond the Rose
The Widow of Woodholme

Praise for ***The Rose Beyond***..."Gilder has matched her Whartonesque setting with a Whartonesque narrative tone that she manages to carry off almost to perfection. Old family secrets are laid bare and all the Hargrove generations must deal with a series of revelations Gilder deploys with a good deal of narrative skill. She layers her story with such lush period color and unabashed emotion that readers will be swept away." *The Historical Novel Society*

To Corrie - Great to meet you! Best always,
Sharon Allen Gilder

The Widow of Woodholme

A Novel

Sharon Allen Gilder

Maryland

Warren Press, December 2022

The Widow of Woodholme is a work of fiction. References to real people, living or dead, events, incidents, establishments, organizations, or locales are intended only to provide a sense of authenticity and are used fictitiously. All other characters, and all incidents and dialogue, are drawn from the author's imagination and are not to be construed as real.

Library of Congress Control Number: 2022917610
ISBN: 9798354021703
Cover Design: JD&J Design
Printed in the United States of America

"The heart will break, but broken live on."
Lord Byron

Dedicated to Mark
with love

And for Jackie, Nate, Sam, Luke & Noah
with love

And my late parents
Warren Collins Allen and Reid Fussell Allen
with love

So We'll Go No More A Roving

by Lord Byron

So, we'll go no more a roving
So late into the night,
Though the heart be still as loving,
And the moon be still as bright.
For the sword outwears its sheath,
And the soul wears out the breast,
And the heart must pause to breathe,
And love itself have rest.
Though the night was made for loving,
And the day returns too soon,
Yet we'll go no more a roving
By the light of the moon.

I am with you always, until the end of the age.
Matthew 28:20

Prologue

December 1821
In the City of Washington and in Georgetown

As they had since his untimely death, thoughts of her beloved Talmadge rose to greet Imogen each morning upon the sun's rise, disrupting the modicum of sleep she was wont to gain. While she lay miserably alone in her bedchamber, her thoughts, like tiny daggers from the tips of needle-thin pins, pricked at her flesh, inflicting new wounds threatening to spiral her into a puddle of remorseful tears.

Only two months past, under a foreboding and heavily overcast morning sky, her husband Talmadge Cornthwaite Simmonds met his fate in a duel at the hands of his rival, Archibald Howard. Their personal rivalries and opposing political views accelerated their growing animosities toward one another, which grew into increasing insults made public in print by Archibald. His untoward advances Imogen's direction, which rarely went unnoticed by her husband, served to fuel Talmadge's rage. Like a devilish prodding fork, Archibald's flirtations periodically evoked Talmadge's ire while simultaneously stirring the fires of lust burning in Imogen's loins.

Although her love for Talmadge was great, their marriage was not exempt from the quirks of conflicting personalities or the demands on his time while expanding his business ventures among his colleagues in the publishing world. His lengthy absences left her to her own devices. Loneliness became her nemesis. Archibald's charms wooed her to thoughts of ecstasy she could only hope to experience in the realm that was her reality at her grand estate. Surrounded by numerous copse of maples and a long drive lined with ancient oaks, Woodholme was the magnificent manor Talmadge designed and commissioned to be built for his bride many months prior to their arrival in America in late May.

As their friendships and business and political connections rapidly grew, Imogen excelled in her role as the mistress of Woodholme, wearing gowns from her favorite European designers and hosting lavish parties for the social elite. Statesmen, politicians, poets and artists rubbed elbows, mingling for the most part in agreeable conversation, which was quite a feat in the political city. A favorite guest, when he was not abroad tending to publishing or matters of state, was Washington Irving. The writer's charm, talent for enlightening conversation, and handsome personage made him a standout at any function. He had regaled Imogen with stories of his stay at J.P. Van Ness' mansion on E Street. He particularly delighted in his visits with Van Ness' wife, heiress Marcia Burns. He said he found her and her philanthropy most charming.

However, the grand parties at Woodholme ceased when word came of Talmadge's death. Winston Cromley, a close friend of Talmadge's who had witnessed the duel, came late in the afternoon to deliver the news to Imogen. He informed her he had run to Talmadge's side to lend aid only to capture his closing words.

"I am in a most unenviable position Imogen," Winston began as he sucked in a deep breath for the courage to share his news. "It is with great regret that I inform you that Talmadge met his end as the morning haze expired over the horizon. Only moments remained for him to gather his final words, which, although they were directed toward you, I hesitate to repeat for they may evoke additional sorrow."

Sobbing, Imogen looked Winston straight in the eyes, searching his face for the faintest expression of hope that his declaration was untrue but none was revealed. She was unaware of the arrangements her husband had agreed to until she read the note he left on her pillow that morn. She was distraught and felt helpless knowing she could not stop what had been put in motion.

She had feared for the worst and prayed for the best but the best did not come. Denial grabbed at her as she shook her head trying to release its grip on her emotions. *How will I live without Talmadge? He was my champion and the force that held me stable. Why would Winston not want me to hear my husband's last words? Were they words of anger for the saddle of shame he carried where Archibald and I were concerned? Or, were they sweet words of lament at what could have been in our marriage?* She was growing impatient with his delay.

"You must tell me, Winston. There can be no holding back. Talmadge would not have spoken the words publically if he had not wanted me to have a hearing of them."

"As you wish, although I have not put aside my misgivings about the telling."

"Now you trouble me further. Can you not see? My mind is imagining all manner of outcomes. You must put a stop to this downward spiral and share what you know."

"Very well," Winston began as he cleared his throat. "As your husband lay injured, gravely injured I might add, he took my hand and with great force of effort said, 'All will be well for her. I have been a burden for Imogen. She will no longer have to tolerate me.'" Reciting Talmadge's words left a bitter taste in Winston's mouth. He felt compelled to lecture Imogen about her part in Archibald and Talmadge's hate for one another but how could he chasten her in her grief? He had not the temerity to broach the subject at this sensitive time and, he thought, what purpose would it serve? His opinion would indeed not alter the outcome of the day's events.

Imogen could not believe her ears. *Is Winston manufacturing words to inflict more pain upon me? Or, was Talmadge getting his final revenge to drive a wedge between Archibald and me? Did he truly feel that he burdened me?* Either way, she felt riddled with guilt. *Is that it? Is it perhaps guilt that tugs at my heart? How culpable am I?* Hers may not have been the finger that pulled the trigger on the flintlock pistol releasing the lead ball that caused Talmadge to take his last breath but her hands felt tainted none the same.

She stood rigidly still as the thoughts of loss swirled about her waiting for grief to work its gnarly fingers into and under her skin. She remained conflicted about her reaction to the words of her dying husband as she silently questioned,

Perhaps Talmadge's death is my comeuppance for my dalliances with Archibald? She was clutched with uncertainty about her future, her reputation and how she could ever again dare to be in Archibald's presence, yet how could she not?

She looked away from Winston as though to dismiss him from the room and peered through the large window that fronted her home, its wavy panes reflecting the colors of the diffused sky as the onset of dusk worked its magic along the skyline. She knew that while she felt broken, she must remain strong. *I must never forget how fragile is life.* She felt at once as though another power had overtaken her as her mind began to wander aloud.

"I like twilight time. Everything is closing down. You can enjoy seeing a beautiful sunset. Yes, I most delight in that," Imogen rambled, wondering if she would ever again feel joy. She sighed a deep sigh, which threatened to envelop her as she tried to regain the details of her last moments with Talmadge. She feared the memory of him would become a blur like the distant horizon she observed fading into the setting sun.

Chapter One

July 1821
In the City of Washington and in Georgetown

Archibald Howard was a man of few words yet many vices. Men trembled at the mention of his name. Women trembled at his mere presence. His debonair style, lush brown locks, and vast wardrobe of dandy suits, which embraced his physique with unsurpassed precision, called into question his personal preferences, although none would confront him on such matters. He was an avid reader and, when he chose to speak, an entertaining conversationalist. His knowledge, paired with his visage, made securing his appearance at one's dinner soirée a much sought after feat.

When the piece of crisply folded parchment arrived, secured with a dollop of sealing wax stamped with a fancy 'S', Archibald read its contents and smiled as he answered affirmatively to the courier without hesitation. It was an invitation he would not decline. Virginia Sterling's reputation for lavish affairs with conversation that flowed as smoothly as the proffered wine meant he would be among engaging guests of both genders with whom he might become intimate.

Archibald admired the Sterling estate. It was fondly known as Rosedale for its abundance of rose bushes, which provided plentiful color and delightful fragrance in the summer months. The mansion boasted a large octagonal entry similar to property Archibald had visited on New York Avenue Northwest owned by John Tayloe III, the renowned breeder of racehorses and founder of the Jockey Club. Aptly named Octagon House, architect William Thornton, the designer of the Federal City's Capitol building, constructed it. Archibald, with a keen eye for the arts and design, enjoyed frequenting structures of notable interest. He recalled reading about the necessity of President Madison and his wife Dolley retreating to Tayloe's home for their temporary residence after the Executive Mansion was burned in 1814 by, as Archibald hated to admit, the British.

He looked about for familiar faces as he passed through the spacious foyer and entered Rosedale's large ballroom where soft, musical strains from a string quartet pervaded the air. The ensemble of musicians, comprised of two violinists, one violist and one cellist, melded their instruments in beautiful harmony playing the last notes of what Archibald recognized to be Bach's "Air on the G String." The din of voices, laughter and overall gaiety comingled with the music to fill the space with bonhomie.

Across the room, a wave of melancholy visited Imogen Simmonds as she listened to the composition. She could not pinpoint why it affected her in such a way. Perhaps she was missing her homeland. She dabbed away a tear forming in the outer corner of her blue eyes and quickly dismissed the emotion the ensemble's music was evoking, for she was determined to find pleasure in the evening. She and her husband Talmadge had come from London some months prior arriving soon after the completion of the large home Talmadge had commissioned for her.

A mutual friend invited the pair to attend Virginia Sterling's party, at Virginia's request, to introduce them to a fresh entourage of Washington notables. Upon Archibald's first sight of Imogen, he sought to capture her gaze. Slowly, yet with great intent of forward motion, he eased his way through the other guests. Most guests, holding crystal stemware filled with libations, were busily engaged in conversations. As he stood before her, Imogen was curiously enamored with Archibald's demeanor. She offered a faint smile as he took her gloved right hand and placed his lips upon the soft white cloth.

"To what do we owe the pleasure of your company, my dear?" Archibald's eyes danced across her face as he spoke, never breaking his focused gaze.

At once, Talmadge nestled to Imogen's side causing Archibald to release her hand and offer a bow in Talmadge's direction.

"Pardon me sir, if I have overstepped my interest in knowing one so fair of face and form. I believe we have not met?"

"You have neither met my wife nor myself and I would encourage you to await a proper introduction before handling that of which you have no ownership." Talmadge's face took on a red hue as his ire rose.

"You best remain calm for I meant no harm. You have my deepest apologies for any misunderstanding. Let us start from the beginning, shall we? I am Archibald Howard and you are?"

Talmadge was hesitant to reveal their names. He knew nothing of this man who bore an accent far from the Queen's English and, thus far, the first impression he held of the man left him wary at best. He wondered if he was putting them on. His manner and dress denoted one well above the bowels of Liverpool, which seemed to be the dialect he had adopted. At once, Virginia was upon the trio having witnessed Archibald's actions and overheard the tenor of their dialogue. As hostess, she felt every obligation to maintain the decorum of her party and see to it that all guests were not only well sated with food and drink but also duly kept from harm's way. However at times, her tongue overtook her good senses. She had yet to greet Talmadge and Imogen although she was well aware that they would be in attendance. A slight wave of nervousness threatened to overcome her as she approached but she let the sensation pass as she garnered the strength to fully face a vestige of her past. A look of surprise overtook Talmadge's face, which did not go unnoticed by Imogen.

"Oh, Archibald my darling, I see you have found two of my comrades! Please let me introduce you," Virginia urged as she stepped between them forming a human barricade of one. "Archibald Howard, may I present Talmadge and Imogen Simmonds. Talmadge has brought his expertise in the publishing industry to our shores. His sterling reputation at London's *General Evening Post* remained untarnished until its cessation earlier this year, which I might add was not of his doing. It seems a difference of opinion about an editorial, which caused quite a stir among readers and agitated the man named in the piece, resulted in charges of slander being slung about. It was quite the topic of conversation in the highest social circles and ultimately threats of a duel ensued. The only way to appease all was for the newspaper to fold, much to your chagrin, is that not so Talmadge?"

Talmadge was taken back not only to have so much shared in so little time with a person unfamiliar to him but also to see Virginia again. It had been nearly a score and two since they were last in each other's company and he had hoped their paths would nary soon cross. He had heard word that she moved to America but had no idea she had settled in the City of Washington. He was equally surprised to learn that she had kept herself apprised of his position at the *General Evening Post* and the subsequent events that caused its demise. *I wonder if she is privy to my latest undertaking in the publishing world at The Washington Inquirer? Heaven only knows what the woman will disclose next?*

In the same moments, Imogen wondered why her husband had become silent. She was certain he was feeling quite embarrassed by Virginia's revelation. She moved closer to him and took his arm not only to lend comfort and assurance but also to reinforce her place as his wife. A curious tenor had fallen over the room leaving Imogen no longer at ease.

Virginia saw the look of surprise on their faces and realized her error in stating too much information pertinent to Talmadge. Readily, she also witnessed her poor decision to have allowed their mutual friend to add the Simmonds' to her guest list. "Oh, my, my. I do apologize. The excitement of the evening and the glass or two of claret I've consumed must be having ill effects on my judgment. Please ignore my prattle and think nothing of it. The night is young and we have much time to delve into the darker corners of our lives, do we not? For now, forgive me while I greet some of my other guests."

Upon her words, Virginia flitted past Imogen, brushing her arm against the sleeve of her gown. Imogen cut her eyes toward her husband who was fully focused on the departure of their hostess. She gave a gentle shake to Talmadge's arm hoping to bring his focus back her way. Virginia's words, "the darker corners of our lives," swirled in Imogen's head as a question danced in her mind. "*What an unusual thing to say, was it not?*"

Talmadge waited until Imogen was fully engaged in conversation with the gentleman named Archibald. He noted that Archibald's accent seemed to have rallied. He was suddenly quite adept at engaging in conversation with a refined English tone. Talmadge would never have abandoned his wife to another had it not been imperative for him to search out the evening's hostess. He found Virginia uncharacteristically alone, refilling her stemware with a hefty pour of ruby red claret. She startled as he approached her, which broke the sequence of calm she was attempting to establish about herself.

"You have been continuously moving about this evening with the fluidity of a Viennese waltz. However, there can be no dodging the fact that you have brought us together, much to my surprise I might add."

"Is it not my duty as hostess to welcome all of my guests and give them a moment or two of my time?"

"There could perhaps have been a more proper way to announce to me that we are frequenting the same city far across the pond from our mother country than to do so within the presence of my wife."

Virginia held close her glass and fondled its bowl. She dipped her head forward stroking the glass with her thumbs as though reciting a silent prayer. She took a faint sip and looked up to face Talmadge's eyes as she swallowed her liquid courage.

"It has been quite some time since last we set eyes upon one another. Time has served you well, Talmadge." Virginia's emerald eyes danced as they did their best to draw him into a gem-like trance. She shook her soft red tresses free of the tortoise shell hair comb that had held them in a loose chignon. Her locks fell gently on her shoulders as she lifted her chin and closed her eyes for only a brief, flirtatious moment before looking intently at Talmadge.

"And you as well, Ginny Kent. I take it that you still find comfort and no opposition when I call you Ginny?"

"I take no objection to that endearment for it always seemed to serve us well."

"Indeed," reflected Talmadge as his eyes gathered in the intoxicating vision before him. Her wavy, ginger-colored hair and her emerald eyes under the shelter of lush, curled lashes were beautiful adornments to her velvety, smooth skin. The beauty that had first attracted him remained despite the time and distance since last their lives had existed in the same breath of space.

"So, have you become a man of so few words? Although, I take no objection to that for words never held much importance between us did they?"

Talmadge sensed himself being drawn into her snare. She might as well have slipped a noose around his neck to capture and have her way with him. He felt weak and his mind began to play tricks on him as he spiraled into thoughts of their time together years before. *I must not succumb to her wiles. Good god man! You are happily married! Get a grip on yourself!* Talmadge looked away from Virginia as he searched the room for Imogen. Not finding her in sight he shook his head and was determined to rally himself to maintain the decorum necessary to finish out the evening.

"Why, Talmadge my dear. You appear flushed. Is it something I have said or are you feeling overcome with regret for having let me go? I must say I am surprised you and Imogen have remained together for she truly does not hold a candle to me."

"I admire your confidence, however I beg you to refrain from invoking Imogen's name in our conversation. She is an innocent among us and I would never want to disparage her in any way."

"Oh, are you not forever the noble one Talmadge? How grand of you to want to protect the weaker sex! Or, shall I say that, which you perceive as weaker?"

"Enough of that. First and foremost, I would not want Imogen to learn of our relationship. I was wrong to be with you when I had promised myself to her. Our engagement was of some length, which does not however excuse my behavior. Perhaps one could call it a weakness on my part although I did ultimately see the error in my ways. Tell me how it is you came to know about my move from England? And, you were a Kent. When did you become a Sterling? Is your husband about or have you shed yourself of yet another gent from your lair?"

"How rude of you to speak so ill of the dead. And, a weakness on your part? Ha! You give far too little credit to my wily ways that attracted you so. At any rate, after you cast me aside I met Reginald Sterling who took great care of me and provided me with a substantial estate to do with as I wished. Upon his death, I tired of living in the United Kingdom. America seemed an apt choice to pursue my dreams of being a devout socialite with a healthy dose of philanthropy tossed in for good measure and, I must say, I have not despaired with any element of my decision. And, as far as your marriage, rumors travel quickly in my social circles. There was no need to hire a sleuth to track your actions or whereabouts. The answers were as simple as attending a tea with some of my lady friends. It appears there truly is something to be said for the reading of tea leaves," Virginia said as she tossed her head back, raised her nose in the air and began to raise the corners of her mouth in a smile until, much to her chagrin, Imogen rounded the corner and took her place at Talmadge's side with the nesting instinct of a protective mother bird.

Virginia took a step back to observe the woman who had captured Talmadge's heart. Everything about Imogen was thin: her waistline, her flaxen hair pulled into a scalp-tight chignon, her voice and, apparently, her patience for she was nearly tugging at Talmadge's arm to exit. Virginia, although noting Imogen's appearance and manner, could sense that her very being held an allure that attracted members of the opposite sex much like a moth to a flame. *What is it about her? She carries herself with an admirable confidence although her face resonates an austerity, which lacks any sense of levity. I must wonder if she ever fully smiles or perhaps she fears her face would crack?*

As Virginia held her thoughts and sought to sort them through, Archibald maintained a tacit distance while he observed the threesome.

"I think it best that we take our leave," Talmadge said as he took Imogen's forearm to guide her to the door. "Thank you for inviting us, Gin, um, Virginia."

"I had hoped you would remain longer to meet some of my other guests. You know it pays to cavort, so to speak, with others of culture and breeding. And, being new to the country, what better chance for you both to form alliances, which might serve you well in business and in pleasure."

Talmadge felt his face begin to heat up as Virginia taunted him with words that might be poorly received by Imogen. At the very least, Virginia's words might cause Imogen to make inquiries he wished to refrain from answering.

He could already anticipate their carriage ride home, which would either be one in awkward silence or filled with harsh, probing words. He took a deep breath as they exited Rosedale's wide mahogany doors where their carriage awaited and he and the footman assisted Imogen into their conveyance.

Imogen had barely seated herself before she began to speak. "Talmadge, my curiosity has been aroused. There appears to be a connection between you and Virginia Sterling that precedes this evening."

"Whatever do you mean?"

"Please do not play coy with me. The two of you were in an intense conversation until I appeared. As we departed, you began to use a shortened version of her name and corrected yourself. Tell me, have you known one another in the past?"

Talmadge took in a deep breath. *How can I divulge my knowledge of Virginia Sterling? There is no need to dredge up a past that holds no merit now. How can I avoid hurting Imogen?* The questions kept bombarding Talmadge as Imogen patiently awaited his response.

"Well, Talmadge? What do you have to say? You had your eyes on her for much of the evening. And she made a curious comment about 'the darker corners of our lives,' which I found most unusual."

"My dear Imogen, I think it best to postpone this discussion until the morrow when we are well rested and our minds are fresh. Please allow me this accommodation."

Imogen was not pleased but she held back any further inquisition. *I shall have adequate opportunities to pursue this conversation with Talmadge. I shall not be put off henceforth. I shall bide my time but my time will come,* she reasoned as their carriage moved away from Virginia's residence.

Archibald had kept watch as the couple swept their way through the throng of other guests and disappeared from view. He found himself fully enamored with Talmadge's bride. *Any man would be a fool not to want her. She is a woman whose society I hope to keep in the days and years ahead,* he mused as he pondered the steps he must take on the morrow to win her favor.

Chapter Two

End of July 1821

Some might label him a rake. It was a title upon which Archibald took great pleasure and rarely any insult. He fancied himself on finer things, which in addition to his wardrobe, included wine and women. Financially he was very stable, which he attributed to his keen sense when it came to investments. He had numerous assets, which he juggled to raise additional capital to maintain the lifestyle to which he had become accustomed. So, for him, the banking business was a perfect fit.

He had built a solid cartel of men whose beliefs were in tandem with his early Federalist views. Although their party had ceased to exist in name, their mission remained unchanged. Maintaining a strong central banking system was key they believed to preserving not only the economy but also preserving power. He enjoyed their parleys regarding investing and found his campaigning efforts to open a variety of banks in Georgetown and the surrounding region not only suited them all well but also gave their coalition a reasonable amount of clout in the political arena.

He felt competent that although the panic that ensued in 1819 forced the closing of many banks, his had prevailed. Recovery was steady and slow but Archibald's ongoing efforts to monitor and ensure there was sufficient hard currency to extend credit and issue bank notes had kept his banks afloat. He lent a deaf ear to anyone who cast hostility toward the institutions he endorsed. A conversation with one of Virginia's guests after Talmadge and Imogen had departed became rather heated when banking became the topic of conversation.

"Well, Mr. Howard, while we stand here well sated with food and drink in this grand home, it behooves us to reflect on the losses from which many are still reeling."

"I shall not pander to your opinions. I for one know that the banking industry is rebounding with better oversight of practices," retorted Archibald.

"You, sir, must feel fortunate to have survived such a compelling time of mistrust toward the very institutions you endorse and, which provide much of your livelihood. Fortunately for you, pauperism has not come knocking at your door with threats of foreclosure and job loss. Why, there are many in the city who can neither clothe their children nor provide provisions for their sustenance."

"It is no secret that I am a man of privilege and I intend to remain so. My banks do support the work of the churches who are providing assistance and nourishment to those in need," Archibald explained. His altruism had its limits. He also felt a great need for a reprieve from the man's antagonism. He was exasperated with the conversation and, feeling no further need to justify himself or engage in a discussion that seemed only meant to denigrate him, he turned to Virginia's guest and wished him a good evening. It was the least he could do.

When Talmadge sent Imogen off to the Bank of Columbia to make a deposit for *The Inquirer*, he had given no thought to whom she might encounter. It was a decision he would soon regret. As she approached the bank's broad double doors, one door began to open as another patron readied himself to exit. He smiled, tipped his hat at Imogen and bade her proceed through. She gave a small curtsy as she gathered the layers of her gown, lifting the hem sufficiently enough to provide clearance for her feet to enter the threshold without exposing her ankles.

"Thank you, sir," she said with a smile as she proceeded onward.

"I wish you a good day, madam," came his simple reply as he exited onto the street.

The lobby of the bank was bustling with customers. Imogen's eyes panned the crowd as she looked about for familiar faces among the predominately male assembly. Just as she was ready to make her way to the bank manager's desk, she caught the attention of a man recently known to her. His eyes locked on hers as he took steps her direction. Imogen wanted to close her eyes and make him disappear but such was not her luck. He was determined to get closer to her and engage in conversation. As he approached her side, she could nearly feel the heat of his body, or was it her body reacting to his approach?

"Well, if it isn't the beautiful Mrs. Simmonds. You are a most welcome sight. To what do I owe the pleasure of your company?"

"If the truth be told, I am in the company of the bank, not yours."

"Touché, my dear."

"With all due respect, I was not aware that our acquaintance was so familiar as to have you refer to me as such?"

"Perhaps I have begun in too bold a manner. I apologize and ask that you take no offense in my address."

"I do have a question for you. I am curious sir as to why your accent was quite different when first we met at Mrs. Sterling's? Initially, I detected the tongue of the Liverpool region as opposed to this moment when you project the very image of English royalty? How is it that you opted to temporarily shed your refinement?"

"A man must find ways to amuse himself until he has better distractions to warrant his attention," Archibald responded, as a roguish grin crossed his face and made his dark brown eyes glisten in a sinister glow.

Imogen stared back for a moment. She was caught off guard by Archibald's repartee and unsure of the stance she should assume to ward off his flirtations.

"So," Archibald continued. "Our hostess of several evenings past alluded to your husband being in the newspaper business. Is that correct, or has he thought better of it after his experiences in our home country?"

"I would say sir, that he is quite comfortable with his decision to remain in the business of publishing. An area, if I might add, about which he is quite adept."

"Perhaps he needs to adapt his focus rather than have you running errands for him like a common courier."

Imogen's patience was wearing thin as she tried to understand the dichotomy of this man who in one moment was lauding compliments her way and in the next slinging slurs. She took a deep breath and straightened her shoulders to prepare for Archibald's next inquisition.

"What is the name of his publication? Is it the *Centinel of Liberty*?"

"No, that is Georgetown's local paper. My husband's publication, *The Washington Inquirer*, has a much wider distribution. Have you read it?" Imogen replied very matter-of-factly.

"I should say I have. In fact, one day I may want to write my own missive for that publication."

"So you feel you have the talents of a scribe?"

"Madam, I am a man of many talents, which I hope to share with you if you will so allow me."

Imogen felt a swell of heat rush over her face. She was wont to touch her cheeks with her hands but knew her gloves would prevent her from confirming that indeed her emotions had taken on a physical display. She hoped Archibald did not take notice although he had not taken his eyes from her. *This man is absolutely insolent! I must take leave of him at once!*

As Imogen pondered her course of action, Archibald stood his ground. The longer he held her gaze she realized her mood was beginning to change. *What spell does he have over me? This is insane! I must gather my senses!*

"So, how may I assist you today?"

"You? Do you not have more important issues of your own to attend? Do not allow me to distract you from your business with the bank today."

"My business with the bank today is as it is everyday."

"Everyday?"

"Oh, yes. I see. As I recall, Virginia did not share information about my occupation as she so vividly shared your husband's little secrets with perhaps more to come."

Imogen felt ready to stomp her foot in frustration. Her patience was running thin with Archibald's circular conversation.

"Enough about my husband. What sir *is* your occupation?"

Archibald smiled, delighted that she was taking an interest in him. Within a moment, a short man with a thinning pate approached the pair.

"Excuse me. So sorry to interrupt Mr. Howard but the bank manager would like to speak with you."

"Thank you Osborne. Give me one moment and I will meet him in his office."

Imogen wondered what the manager could want with Archibald. *Probably some fine mess he has created for himself from some dubious business dealings. I would not be surprised if the authorities are prepared to take some legal action against him,* she mused. She observed his face. He seemed not the least bit disturbed by the message relayed by Osborne.

"I apologize for the interruption. You were saying?"

"I was inquiring about your occupation but perhaps it is too clandestine to reveal to one of refinement?"

"You do intrigue me. Is that not such a thing to say to one whose company you have been in for so brief a time? If you must know, my occupation is not a secret to those about you. I am the president of the bank. Now, may I assist you?"

"Surely one of your tellers will serve me quite sufficiently."

"With no disregard for the efficiencies of our workers, I am happy to be at your service. Here, let me take that sack from you. A deposit I assume?"

Imogen was certain Talmadge would not be in good spirits if he learned that Archibald had knowledge of his business through the money sack she held in what was becoming a tighter grip lest it be snatched from her. Archibald was taken aback by her hesitancy to relinquish the sack. Imogen tried to buy time while she thought through how best to handle the situation. If indeed Archibald was the president of the bank, then he had within his powers access to the accounts of all of the bank's customers. One deposit would make little difference in the information he could glean from *The Inquirer's* account.

As she tendered the sack to Archibald his hand touched the tips of her glove and glided up to her wrist, which he held for a moment in a gentle lock with his thumb and forefinger before releasing her hand. Imogen raised her right eyebrow in a quizzical, yet warning look. Archibald caught her expression, which delighted him. He was happy to garner a reaction from her, which he hoped to temper with an offer. He stepped away to accommodate her bank transaction and returned with a receipt and an invitation.

"I am just thinking. We two have much in common we could discuss. Would you be predisposed to joining me for a glass of claret or tea if you prefer? There is a charming tavern a short walk away. It would do us good to get to know one another better and I am sure your husband would appreciate your learning more about me to allay any concerns he might have."

"Concerns he might have? You sir, with all due respect, must think rather highly of yourself to assume that my husband has given a single thought to you?"

"Oh, my. You bruise my delicate ego," Archibald declared with amusement in his tone. "I can only be healed by your acceptance of my invitation for a beverage to remedy our parched throats on this warm July day. We would be wise to take advantage of the absence of humidity for we know not what tomorrow may bring."

Something about Archibald was lightening Imogen's mood. She no longer felt like bristling at his presence or his offer. *I cannot imagine that Talmadge would find it irregular for me to take company with this man in a public place. What harm could come?* Imogen reasoned as she nodded in acceptance.

Archibald, being quite pleased, offered his arm to escort her, which she accepted as they made their way from the security of the bank to what she began to ponder might become the beginning of an interesting alliance.

Chapter Three

Talmadge was very specific when he met with the architect for Woodholme. A previous voyage to Georgetown many months before had given him the opportunity to select what he considered to be the perfect site for the residence he would share with his wife. He and the architect discussed the classic features he wanted to be evident in the mansion's façade and interior rooms. With a fondness for England's grand homes and wanting to assure that Woodholme would not only be a standout property but would exceed Imogen's expectations, Talmadge based the home's design on England's Georgian style of architecture, which incorporated magnificent Greek and Roman influences. He poured over pattern books from England based on the impressive work of Sir Christopher Wren whose manuals became the keystone of Woodholme's grandeur.

Even the mansion's name was well thought through. He envisioned a riparian home surrounded by large trees on a wooded lot cleared only enough to view a body of water. He liked to imagine it as their very own 'holme' or islet near the Potomac River and Imogen as his demigoddess, his beautiful muse who would preside over their home and fill it with lovers of art, music and like-minded souls passionate about literature.

With unsurpassed symmetry, the large brick structure, situated on a hilltop above the harbor near Georgetown's northern boundary, featured a hip roof with four dormer windows stationed on the third floor on either side of the portico. The portico's pointed roofline peaked above the manse's bold center. The large mahogany entry door was paneled and topped with a semi-circular fanlight whose panes were comprised of clear sections of leaded glass. The door formed the center of the home and was symmetrically flanked across the front of the manse with large double-hung, multi-pane sash windows dressed with dark charcoal gray shutters.

Fluted white columns in the Doric style were evenly spaced with arches between them. The columns configured the wide front porch, which was equally suitable for accommodating a variety of seating areas for an intimate tête-à-tête or larger gatherings of overflow guests. Talmadge had considered painting the brick white to emulate the Greek temples he had noted during his research but he decided against the stark contrast to nature rather preferring the beauty of the natural hues in the brick. He also considered the large masonry quoins he incorporated into the mansion's design, wanting the sandstone cornerstones to remain evident not only as an additional aesthetic component but also as a nod to Woodholme's strength.

It was important to him that his home be a standout among the other substantial private homes garnering magnificent views of the river and city. He had learned it was Charles Carroll's estate, Bellevue, east of his property, to which Dolley Madison sought refuge when the British troops burned the city. He wished to be among the many prestigious citizens at the west end of the Federal City who hosted lavish social gatherings in their Georgetown homes such as Halcyon House and Mackall Square. He would see to it that he and Imogen reciprocated.

Inside Woodholme, the rooms exuded a grand formality of their own. High ceilings lent balance to the soaring columns. Arched doorways fitted with multi-colored brocade portières held back with large, braided silk cords, softened the architectural details of the space. Pediments over the windows provided a division from the picture rail and crown molding above them. The marble mantel of the drawing room's large fireplace featured an intricately hand-carved grape leaf motif just below the dentil molding on the mantel's shelf. The large surround was flanked on each side by caryatid statues in flowing carved gowns. The female figurines standing on marble blocks each had one arm raised to support the mantel's shelf. Talmadge had on occasion consulted with Imogen about the interior's colors and fabrics. He admired her taste and wanted her to have a hand in the selection of their home's furnishings.

There was to be an architectural surprise for Imogen. Talmadge, who had in the past dabbled in the study of medieval structures, added a turret to the back, south facing side of the mansion. The small tower projected vertically from Woodholme's rear wall. A parapet, a low, protective railing wall the Italians called parapetto, bordered it. Its baluster was constructed of evenly placed, lathe-turned stone columns to support the rail. A narrow staircase rising to the third floor provided access to the unexpected architectural element.

Upon the home's completion, Talmadge stood on the turret and was impressed with the view it afforded of the upper Potomac estuary. He envisioned himself standing there with telescope in hand using the optical device to watch the passage and arrival of ships coming into the harbor. *Yes, it is just as I imagined,* he said aloud and raised his head as though speaking in appreciation to the heavens. He smiled with self-satisfaction as he observed the sun's gleam cascading over the ripples of water. The water's movement created a mesmerizing calm he hoped would be a reflection of his life with Imogen.

Imogen was smitten with Woodholme upon first sight. Talmadge arranged to have the top down on his favorite carriage so she would have no obstructions to viewing the finished mansion. The carriage was a sizeable landau with his family crest prominently displayed on the side door. As the conveyance made its way up the lane under the canopy of mature maples and oaks there, in the clearing ahead, was Talmadge's masterpiece. Imogen's jaw dropped in awe of the sight before her. She nestled next to Talmadge and wrapped her arm in his.

"Oh, my word, Talmadge! You have rendered me speechless!"

"And that, my darling, is no small feat!" Talmadge laughed at his jest as Imogen poked him with her elbow.

"In all sincerity, you have surpassed my expectations! I can only imagine what pleasures the interior will provide! This is gloriously magnificent!"

Imogen's reaction was just the tonic Talmadge needed after all the months involved in planning and executing the construction of their home. He felt giddy as he watched his wife's eyes taking in the view.

"Well, my dear, you need imagine no more. Here, let me help you from the carriage and escort you into our home."

Imogen paused as he held her hand to exit the carriage step and gazed into his eyes. Tears of joy flooded her eyes as softly she fell into him giving no care for their driver's presence. Talmadge's eyes gleamed as he took her against him then lifted her chin and placed his lips on hers. They held their embrace totally absorbed in the pleasure of the moment. The rustling sound of two squirrels chasing one another up a tree trunk and jumping from branch to branch caught their attention.

Talmadge smiled. "Perhaps nature is sending us a message, my dear."

"Perhaps so," Imogen responded in an uncharacteristically demure manner as her husband took her hand, gave it an inviting squeeze and led her through their threshold.

Now, some months past, as Imogen began to slumber, she reflected on that first night under Woodholme's roof with Talmadge. She was enamored with the mansion's splendor and the love she and her husband shared.

"Yes, we will have a great life here," said Talmadge as he took her in his arms, spun her about in a modified pirouette and drew her close to him.

His tender kisses and soft caresses led to an exhilarating night of passion. Force was not his forte although once aroused, there was no holding back his determination to find both himself and his wife well sated.

In the several months since their move from their English roots, they had firmly established themselves in their new environment making every effort to develop relationships in the City of Washington that would serve them well not only in social relationships but more importantly in Talmadge's pursuit to publish the most popular newspaper in the area. It was not an easy task and his time away from home was putting a strain on the tenor of their marriage.

When Imogen awoke, she smiled as her mind replayed their lovemaking. She attempted to call forth tender images of her nights with Talmadge, which were becoming fewer. His work called him away for longer hours and he was often weary at day's end. She pulled the bedcovers up, gripping them with her fingers and snuggled them to her chin then looked to her side to seek comfort from him. Disappointment began to etch its way across her face as she realized he had already risen. She had anticipated enticing him to pleasure them both as he had last evening.

She turned on her side to face his pillow. Her motion caused something resting on the linen pillowcase to slip toward her. *A slip of paper with my name? Perhaps it is a love note from Talmadge? He is so considerate to leave little missives to me on occasion,* she thought as her mood lightened only to be replaced by a look of chagrin as she unfolded the piece of paper and began to read:

My dearest Imogen,

Forgive this short notice. I have received word that my request for an interview with Congressman Barbour has been granted. He wishes to meet with me at City Tavern today and I am asking that you join us. Have Calvin prepare a carriage for you. I will meet you there at noon. We shall all enjoy our midday meal together.

With much respect and love,
Talmadge

Oh mercy! Our agendas are not running the same course this morn. I thought we might have a day to ourselves. It seems my desires will have to wait, she mused.

She recalled Talmadge discussing his wish to meet with Congressman Barbour. The Simmonds' had been in his company at several social events, which prompted Talmadge to suggest an interview for *The Inquirer*. Barbour's political connections were impressive and he was highly regarded among many of his colleagues and constituents.

I suppose I should feel complimented that Talmadge wants me present. What harm can it do for me to learn more about the workings of this city? And, who knows, the day may hold other revelations.

Prior to departing for City Tavern, Talmadge sat at his desk holding his missive to Imogen, which he would quietly place upon his pillow rather than wake her at such an early hour to invite her to join him.

He was an early riser, finding that too much sleep left him feeling lethargic. But today, although having risen well before sunrise, he felt sluggish, like a vessel stuck fast in thick mud needing a good tug to release it from its trappings.

His mind went to the unexpected encounter at Virginia Sterling's. He thought he had buried his past with her but here it was resurrecting itself at a most inopportune time. *Humph,* he mused, *as if any time could possibly be opportune when a woman reappears from one's past with whom one has had a fallacious relationship?* He leaned forward placing his left elbow on the desk, brought his forearm up, bent his wrist and rested his chin on the top of his upraised hand. He stared into the space about him and rocked his head slowly side to side as if to balance the thoughts attempting to resolve themselves in his mind.

He looked through his study's wide doorway, which gave him a clear view of the drawing room's fireplace. Above its mantel was a large portrait of Imogen he had commissioned as a special gift to her painted by artist Rembrandt Peale. Peale had captured so many of the qualities Talmadge admired about her — her beauty, her strength, her independence and her charm, which bewitched him.

How shall I resolve with Imogen the existence of Virginia in my life? I must make her believe that Virginia is but a distant memory, one that serves no purpose in our lives now. Yet, how can I make her believe something that I perhaps do not believe myself? I cannot deny that seeing Virginia aroused feelings dormant for over a score of years. For the sake of our marriage, I must get a grip on these thoughts. Imogen is too important to me. She is my love, my life now and I shall make every effort for her to know how committed I am to our marriage.

Talmadge hoped that speaking such words of committal to Imogen would lend reassurance and comfort that all would be well, albeit deep within he wrestled with self-doubt.

Chapter Four

"Patti," Imogen ordered in a raised voice. "Bring my gown and tell Calvin to ready the carriage. I will be in need of your assistance. I am to meet Mr. Simmonds in Georgetown and must make haste."

Born Patricia Ava McAvoy in Ireland a score and four years ago Patti, as she preferred to be addressed, left her homeland when she was four and ten by order of her parents to work as a domestic servant for a wealthy family. Her parents' motives were less than altruistic. The understanding was that much of their daughter's earnings would be sent to them in Ireland to ease the burden of their daily living.

Now, after a decade in America, she had well established herself as a parlor maid. Her early years in service were as a second girl predominately responsible for the upkeep of an estate's large cadre of sleeping chambers. However, Patti preferred her work downstairs where she could be privy to her employers' habits, discussions, and guests while tending to the daily chores of dusting furniture and scrubbing floors. She came highly recommended to the Simmonds' who were pleased to hire her, although she occasionally required prodding when daydreaming overtook her ability to focus on the tasks at hand.

Despite the workload of her days, Patti had nary missed a meal, a fact that was evident by her ample frame, which served to accentuate her short stature. Her shoulder length hair, pulled together and held with a simple clip, cast a persimmon glow about her freckled face. Her visage was in harmony with her plump torso where the tie on her apron struggled to reach about her waist to form a complete bow.

Noting the urgency in her mistress' voice, she scurried first to the rear of the manse and out the wide door from the conservatory to locate Calvin in the stables to deliver her mistress' message. It would be best for him to have the carriage ready and waiting than to have her mistress dressed and waiting any length of time to depart. On many occasions, patience was not a virtue Imogen could muster.

Calvin Gray came to be in the Simmonds' employ soon after the finishing touches were placed on Woodholme. He was a tall, sturdy man with a well-rounded paunch that tested the tension of the hooks holding secure the front of his driving jacket. His brown hair was cropped and tightly curled, which kept it from flopping in his face and served him well no matter what the weather when seeing to the team of horses and driving the Simmonds' smartly appointed carriages. Talmadge held great respect for his loyal olster who had excellent stabling skills. He anticipated and hoped Calvin would be in his employ for a long time.

Calvin had a particular fondness for their emerald green barouche-landau. It was an impressive four-wheeled specimen of transportation incorporating the better of two carriage styles. With a soft black leather top separated into two sections meeting with a latch in the middle, the carriage could be converted to an open vehicle or closed to protect its occupants from the elements or society's inquiring eyes.

He also was partial to the matched team of Cleveland Bay geldings who were quite accustomed to pulling the barouche-landau. Standing at sixteen hands, the geldings were a matched team considered 'bright bays' due to the slight reddish tint to the hair of their coats. The Simmonds' horses displayed the customary black points coloration and sported black manes, black ear edges, black tails and black lower legs. Affectionately named King and Prince in a nod to the popularity of their breed with England's royal family and having originated in the Cleveland area of Northern Yorkshire in Northeast England, the pair were equally suited for under-saddle use.

Earlier in the morning Calvin had prepared the large carriage for the master of the manse and sent him off to work with Lester Cain at the reins. Lester, who assisted in the stables, was the antithesis of Calvin in form. He was tall and lean yet surprisingly strong, which enabled him to maintain control of the horses, clean and lift tack, and move the carriages in and out of the carriage house with little show of effort.

Calvin prepared to hitch Blaze to a smaller carriage well suited to both the horse and its passenger. Blaze was a handsome Morgan approximately fifteen hands in height with a burnt chestnut coat and striking white blaze from his forehead to his snout. In addition to carriage driving, he was equally suited for pleasure riding, which Talmadge often took to his advantage when he needed time alone in the open air.

"Patti! Where are you girl?" Imogen's patience was growing ever thin.

"It's 'ere I am, mum. No worries. It's jest takin' me longer to get from the stables then I thought. Here's ye gown ye wanted."

"Just get about getting me dressed," Imogen demanded as she prepared her hair for her gown to slip over her head.

The gown was a favorite among the vast array of imported finery in her wardrobe. It seemed weekly that her dressmaker would send word that another gown, altered to her specifications, had been completed and was ready for delivery. Imogen was drawn to varying shades of purple finding the deeper hues especially pleasing in her winter wardrobe and lilacs and lavenders cooling for the humid summer months. The color suited her fair skin and lent her an air of royal splendor.

As she donned her gown she admired herself in the looking glass, the cheval mirror set on an angle in the corner of her bedchamber. Patti brought a simple amethyst and diamond necklace from Imogen's carved mahogany jewelry box and placed it around her neck. The piece glistened as it picked up the rays of sunlight entering the mullioned windows framing the space. Imogen smiled as she accepted the matching briolette earrings from Patti's hand taking pleasure in the shimmer emitted by the play of light on the stones' facets. She ran her hands down the sides of her gown then fluffed its overskirt as she continued to admire her visage. Though preparing to meet Talmadge and their congressman acquaintance, she was halted by a fleeting thought of her drink with Archibald. Feeling quite pleased with her appearance she pondered, *Would he not delight in my countenance today? What if by coincidence he were to be taking a meal at City Tavern?*

She tried to abandon the notion knowing the difficulties that might ensue if Talmadge caught wind of her interest in the man, yet she found herself yearning to be in Archibald's presence again. She fondly recalled as they sat, each with a glass of claret in their hands, his dark brown eyes seemed to penetrate the soft blue of her orbs and as he spoke in soft, glowing terms, she became mesmerized by his voice. She closed her eyes as she relived the memory, which drew a pleasant smile across her face. The sound of nearby footsteps broke her concentration.

"Are ye ready? Will ye be needin' anythin' else from me b'fore ye be on yer way?" Imogen's imagination was interrupted by Patti's words.

"No, I am quite ready to leave. Thank you, Patti. It is time for me to be on my way lest I have Mr. Simmonds waiting for my arrival."

"Very well then, mum."

Imogen gathered the layers of her gown with her fingers squeezing the folds with gusto as she bade her feet move forward. *My mind must remain fixed on my meeting with Talmadge,* she mused. *I must not allow the thoughts of another to secure one more minute of my time. Yet how shall I not?*

Chapter Five

Talmadge's driver Lester Cain and the pair of horses pulling his carriage patiently awaited the departure of several conveyances delivering passengers to the front portal of the popular gathering place on upper High Street in Georgetown. Built in 1796, City Tavern was often lovingly referred to as Semmes' Tavern by locals to identify it due to the number of name changes the site endured over the years. Joseph Semmes had been a frequent proprietor of the site whose owners often boasted of the banquet held there in President John Adams' honor to welcome him when he arrived in the city in June of 1800.

The stately Georgian building was a favored gathering place for dining and lodging; community, business and political meetings for Georgetown's governing body; early stage and mail stops; and the patronage of the city's prominent citizens. Talmadge always anticipated rubbing elbows with those patrons of influence and perhaps building mutually satisfying relationships.

As the way became clear, his driver guided the two-in-hand into position to safely allow his charge to exit. Talmadge peered through the window of the carriage's door and wondered if Imogen had yet arrived.

He deemed her presence to be of great value at his meeting with Philip Barbour who since 1814 had been a member of the United States House of Representatives and a member of the Virginia House of Delegates. The two had always had an ease of conversation whenever in each other's company at social functions. Talmadge not only hoped his interview with the soon-to-be-appointed Speaker of the House of Representatives would go smoothly, he also trusted their meeting would be enlightening considering the conversations he overheard in July at Georgetown's Union Tavern. Barbour was with several colleagues at the Birthnight Ball held there in celebration of America's Independence where there was much talk of Jeffersonian Republican principles. Talmadge was very pleased to hear one of the men quote a passage from a published letter Jefferson wrote in 1786 to physician James Currie supporting the written word. "Our liberty depends on the freedom of the press, and that cannot be limited without being lost," Jefferson had extolled.

Talmadge had considered suggesting he and Barbour meet at Union Tavern for it was a very popular destination not only among Washington's most prominent but, as a frequent favorite of the presidents, one could only hope to be on the premises on such an occasion to be in the company of the political elite, fondly referred to as Washington royalty. Talmadge had learned early on upon arriving in America that relationships in the city meant everything not only for one's social status but also in order to gain the support one needed for elected positions and the latest news so important to his livelihood.

Georgetown's newspaper, the *Centinel of Liberty*, had recently run a full-page story about Barbour's visit to Union, which made Talmadge think better of meeting there. He wanted a different angle to his story and hoped to gather some illuminating news to share with readers of his newspaper, *The Washington Inquirer*.

Imogen waited as patiently as she could, considering her limited tolerance for being at the mercy of others. She peered through the tavern's front window, its wavy panes lending some magic to the street scene as the day's sunlight played against the brilliant glass. She saw Talmadge's handsome carriage standing in wait. It was a conveyance of the highest order. The rich green of its cab nearly glowed emerald in the daylight, which lent particular attention to the Simmonds' coat of arms adorning the doors on either side of the conveyance. Its shield of gray, yellow and black featured three sets of trefoils in the matching green of the carriage. Black and gold acanthus leaves flagged the outer borders of the shield. Talmadge's love of heraldry showed in the bold, silver-gray helmet crested with a spray of black and gold feathers.

He had shared with Imogen that the trefoils were an important addition to his family's coat of arms as they represented longevity and perpetuity, two goals to which he aspired.

She watched as he exited the carriage and paused to give a slight bow to a gentleman passerby who doffed his hat. The two became engaged in a brief conversation before bidding one another adieu.

With her gloved hands she smoothed back her hair, which was so taut it had nearly become a second skin to her scalp. She lifted the skirt of her gown to face the entry as Margaret Coolidge, a current owner of the tavern, nodded to bid her welcome. Lighthearted laughter and congenial conversation filled the tavern.

"Ah, there you are Imogen," Talmadge smiled as he moved to greet her and gave a tip of his head to Mrs. Coolidge who led them to their table. He took Imogen's gloved hand in his and escorted her to her seat. She was particularly radiant. Her cheeks held a rosy glow as though they had been freshly pinched for the occasion. The scent of her cologne floated through the air in a delicate waft as the layers of her gown sashayed to and fro when she made her turn to be seated. Her hair, pulled into a tight chignon, was held snuggly in place with a silk shantung hair clip.

"I was watching from the window and saw you talking with someone?"

"Yes. It was good to happen upon Henry Foxall. You may remember an article in *The Inquirer* about him and his iron foundry in town. Quite impressive he is. He is getting on in years. His term as Mayor of Georgetown ended two years ago but he is most acclaimed for his foundries, which cast the cannons for the War of 1812 among others. But, I deviate. I take it there has been no sighting of our friend from Virginia?"

"No. I have yet to see Congressman Barbour. Perhaps he is delayed with important government business."

"Perhaps. Very well. I was in hopes we would make our arrival before his."

"Why is it important for us to be the first to arrive?"

"I suppose a sense of nervous anticipation has come to visit me but I want to be certain this meeting works to our best advantage."

"Surely you know it will, Talmadge. I have the utmost confidence in you and then, of course, I am here so what more can one ask? With me you have an ace in your pocket so to speak." Imogen smiled and gave a wink as she wiggled a bit to settle herself into her seat.

Talmadge signaled the barmaid to approach and promptly ordered beverages for the table, which she scurried off to retrieve. He smiled and gave a nod of his head, which Imogen thought was directed at her until she looked up and saw that the congressman had arrived. Her ego momentarily dashed, she shook off her need for attention to direct her gaze to their guest. She had always enjoyed the congressman's company and was determined to gain his admiration or fear she was losing her touch with the male gender.

"Well, my good man. Thank you for finding time in your schedule to dine with us. You remember my wife Imogen."

"Of course I do. I remember when first we met at the Sterling residence. That was quite an evening. I recall there was a rather flamboyant guest who kept trying to gain my ear. Fortunately, his interests were diverted to other pursuits."

Talmadge felt a wave of discomfort float over him. He knew full well that Barbour was referencing Archibald Howard. And, he knew it was Archibald who pursued Imogen while he was engaged in a rather uncomfortable conversation with Virginia Sterling.

"Oh yes. I know quite well of whom you speak. Archibald Howard is his name."

"Have you had other occasions to be in his company?"

"I, or I should say, we have. He is an interesting chap but can wear on one's good nature after a period of time."

The return of the barmaid provided a pause in the conversation as she placed the round of beverages on the table.

"I hope you take no exception to my selections. If I may be so bold, I ordered ale for us gentlemen and hot tea for my dear Imogen. If you have another preference, please make it known and I will order it forthwith."

Barbour smiled and lifted his tankard in a salute to Talmadge as he nodded to Imogen and took a hearty sip of the heady beverage before returning to the previous discussion.

"I am afraid I failed to catch the nature of his business here. I believe someone mentioned he held an interest in a financial institution?"

"Ah, yes indeed. Mr. Howard brought with him from his native England an impressive portfolio in the business of banking."

"Banking, you say? That may have been well and good for him before the decline that ensued two years prior. Our country has barely recovered from the recession brought on by the panic. I wonder how he is fairing today?"

Imogen was wont to speak. *After all,* she silently pondered, *Talmadge invited me to join him today. He cannot expect me to remain silent.* She straightened herself and raised her shoulders to enhance her posture.

"If I may interject a moment, I have known Mr. Howard to be a rather savvy businessman with an uncanny grasp of investments. He is conservative by nature and his early Federalist leanings naturally drew him to the world of finance and the business of banking."

Talmadge took notice of the congressman's reaction to Imogen's words. At first, he raised one eyebrow while he simultaneously dipped down his chin, and then cocked his head like a bird awaiting a call from a fellow avian. He pushed back his chair a brief distance as his right hand, formed into a fist, came down on the table's surface like a gavel with no sounding block. Fortunately for all, his action did not garner the attention of the other patrons for the melodic strings of a violin, courtesy of a roaming troubadour, overtook the room with perfect timing. A look of concern washed over Talmadge's face, which did not go unnoticed by Imogen. *Perhaps I should have remained mute? Perhaps I should have kept my thoughts to myself?* She began to doubt the relevance of her presence at Talmadge's meeting. The silence at the table was however not long-lived.

"My wife," Talmadge began with his voice raised a decibel to be heard over the zealous fiddling of the musician, "means no disregard for your opinions, or those of the Democratic-Republicans about the banking industry. Suspicions abound about banks in general and I have even heard the term 'war' bantered about when it comes to challenging the banking system. However, not from Mr. Howard, I assure you."

"No worries, my man," smiled Barbour, which made both Talmadge and

Imogen give a silent sigh of relief. "Without my next comments suggesting that the ugly head of partisanship is raising itself, that information only confirms why Howard and I would have little in common politically. In a city such as this, it is impossible to remain apolitical. One's goal must be to find a compromise that will best serve our country. Compromise ahead of conflict should be our fervent goal."

Imogen was envious of the congressman's capacity with language and the frugality he employed to use the least words necessary to convey his message for the result he sought. *I would do well to mimic his conservation of the English language,* she mused. *Philip and Talmadge might find my presence in better favor if I refrain from imposing too many of my opinions.* It was a generous observation but Imogen knew she was not wont to sit back and halt the sharing of her thoughts whether provoked or not. She aligned her shoulders, straightened her spine and cleared her throat as she let fly a question of paramount concern to her.

"If I may, I would be most obliged to obtain your views on abolition. I understand you and Mr. Jackson are allies in that regard. I understand you are an advocate of the rights of states. Where do you stand on the rights of the people? Do you too continue to stand against abolitionists?"

Talmadge thought he would purge his morning meal. Why Imogen would attempt such a volatile and controversial topic, particularly at a meeting he had arranged, stunned him. He had not intended to sabotage the congressman and was having more than second thoughts for having included her. To his knowledge, she and the congressman had never engaged in such subjects in the past. *I must find a way of diverting this conversation at once,* Talmadge silently screamed.

"My dear, Imogen. Let us not put Philip on the spot when you clearly know his views on the matter."

"I merely want to attempt to understand his views, which are contrary to mine."

"Now, Imogen," Talmadge implored as he placed his hand on hers to subdue her inquiry. "We're here to discuss the business of the City of Washington, the deals and political pacts that are its hub."

"That may be very well but I..." Imogen's words were halted by a stern look from Talmadge as he turned to Barbour and signaled him to continue.

"Thank you, Talmadge. To your point, one needs only study our history to date to note that risk taking and the perseverance to see an idea through for the betterment of our republic are two of the principles that guide us as our union grows not only in territory, but also in independence."

"May I quote you on that, sir?"

"Absolutely, you may."

Imogen watched her husband as he maintained not only his rapport but also his professionalism with Barbour. Talmadge's keen sense of personalities and his proclivity for gathering information aided him in composing an article that would either find great favor with his readers or at the very least provide the facts needed for them to make informed decisions. She was however not satisfied with the topic of slavery being dismissed.

"If I may ask, with regard to risk taking as you note, can that not draw on one's fear of the outcome? How do you confront such fear?" Imogen carefully inquired, posing her question with the hopes of not appearing to challenge the congressman.

"Ah, fear is something that must be confronted and overcome or it will defeat you and set you off course. I must add, one must not be impetuous with his risk taking."

"Do you feel that perseverance might be misconstrued as unharnessed ambition for the sake of promoting oneself amongst the competition?" Talmadge asked as he squinted his eyes hoping the question was not seen as offensive.

"Now, my man. Are we talking about politics or the newspaper business?"

"You have me there. Perhaps both." Talmadge laughed as he readied himself to end his questions and focus on the social side of their meeting.

"I am pleased to note that you are dedicated to maintaining high standards for your publication and you have not stooped to the level of some of your competitors who are hell-bent on hiring pamphleteers to distribute pernicious hypotheses. Such conduct only serves to confuse the public with unsubstantiated opinions. With no basis of fact, how can a government be expected to properly regulate itself for the people it serves?"

Imogen was feeling discomfited by Talmadge's attempts to silence her, yet she was finding it difficult to hold her tongue. Were slaves not people to be equally served? She was not wont to have her opinion go unheard. She abhorred the fact that holding humans in bondage was deemed acceptable by other human beings. She felt the only way to ever witness change was to stand her ground and voice her concerns.

Talmadge had on more than one occasion said, "You must remember your place."

She did not appreciate his admonishment. While marriage afforded her companionship and financial stability it was the entrée into the arena of business and politics that most interested her, which she would not gain as a single woman. Keeping abreast of her interests in business and politics were her way of establishing independence among a male dominated world. Her better judgment told her to dismiss the topic of abolition at this juncture rather than ruin her husband's rapport with Barbour, yet she found it difficult to hold her tongue.

"Sir, or if I may, Philip, with all due respect I beg to differ with…" Talmadge cut Imogen's words to the quick like a candle that had been abruptly snuffed. He sensed she would revisit the topic of slavery and he was wont to avoid the controversial subject.

"Imogen, our time with the congressman is fleeting. We shall have more time with him indeed but for now, let us not delay. We must move on to more pressing topics. What shall we have for our midday meal?" Talmadge inquired with a smile, relieved to end Imogen's inquiry although he knew full well this would not be his last hearing of her opinions about slavery and her alignment with the abolitionist movement.

Although reluctant to end the pursuit of her topic of choice with Barbour, Imogen decided to hold her tongue for the present. She would make it her mission to find a suitable time to broach the topic, share her opinion and hopefully influence his deeper reflection on the matter. For now, she would accommodate her husband's agenda.

Broad smiles and a sense of relief came to the threesome as they turned their attention to the large board on the tavern's far wall chalked with the daily fare. Talmadge and Imogen exchanged glances. Years of marriage aided them in reading their common expressions as each sensed the remainder of the meeting with Barbour would prove congenial even if their carriage ride home might be fraught with a quarrel.

Beverages topped the board's list with options of hot chocolate, coffee, ale, Madeira, claret, mead and the "choicest" liquors. Chowders and stews made from a variety of meats and vegetables were hearty selections. The men chose roasted duckling in orange sauce with green peas, while Imogen opted for a plate of chicken fricassee with herbs, sautéed squash and pickled red cabbage. The trio talked intermittently as they dined.

Imogen smiled at Barbour and proffered, "I have heard tell that you and Mr. Jackson are well aligned in your pursuits. Or, perhaps I should refer to him as General Jackson."

Barbour pushed back his chair the slightest bit to gain a larger breath of space between him and the table's edge as he finished chewing his last bite of duckling.

"You are quite right. Andrew and I advocate for individual liberties, which serve to include the rights of states. His military efforts and recent success with attaining Florida from Spain not only assisted in defending our borders but gave us access to the Mississippi River, which will serve us well for it is a major route of trade," Barbour proudly explained. "From your earlier statements Mrs. Simmonds, which I care not to address at this time, you know our position on slavery. Additionally, the controversy over the Second Bank of the United States has not subdued. I am sure Talmadge, you have kept abreast of the debates surrounding the central bank and those opposed to its use as a repository for federal funds. Some blame the panic two years prior on the bank's mismanagement. Well, we could go on and on about this topic so, keeping the best interest of our digestion in mind, I shall refrain from continuing."

Imogen listened to his words with renewed attention. She was not pleased to be slighted by the assumption that she had not kept herself informed about government issues but she decided to ignore his inference.

"You know I have learned a bit of Mr. Jackson's history since Talmadge and I arrived here. His allegiance to the country began at an early age as a courier in the Revolutionary War and I have heard the word 'hero' associated with his name for his actions that led to the victory over the British in New Orleans in 1815. Sadly, many British troops perished. And, if I may broach a topic of previous discussion, Mr. Jackson has made his qualms quite clear about the credit system and his distrust of banks in general. It would come as no surprise to me if the man ran for president," Imogen opined as she looked at Barbour who nodded with a wink.

Talmadge glanced at his notes as Imogen engaged the congressman in conversation. He realized he wanted to get the congressman's views on the topic of nationalism, a discourse, which grew from the War of 1812 and had become a broadening movement.

"Philip, if I may, one more question. I have heard it said that in an effort to move for further independence, President Monroe, aided by his Secretary of State, Mr. Adams, is strongly suggesting America should keep itself free of the influence of the European monarchies. What are your feelings about the fundamental differences of the Old World and the New World?"

"I see you save the more complicated topics after I have been fortified with a hearty meal," laughed Barbour. "Quiet seriously though, many of us in the House endorse a recurring refrain espoused by President Monroe. There are basic tenets, which must be considered and among those are the facts that economic growth and enhancing our military strength are crucial. Look at the British Navy. That is something we can aspire to match."

A tavern maid presented a large tray of sweets to tempt the three. Barbour declined and used her interruption as his time to bid adieu.

"I have enjoyed our visit and thank you Talmadge for your interest in the workings of our government and your work to report to the public what they need to know to make informed decisions. The wheels of progress can churn slowly with so many opinions and so much opposition. But the rule of law and forward thinking are the only ways to properly change and sustain our democracy."

As Barbour stood, he turned to Imogen, took her hand, bowed and placed a kiss upon her fair skin.

"And, my dear Mrs. Simmonds, it has been a pleasure to be in your company today. I hope there shall not be an elongated passage of time before we are once again united in friendly repartee. I bid you glad tidings until we meet again."

With a quick turn, the congressman was out the door as rapidly as he had made his entrance. Talmadge and Imogen sat silent for a few moments. Imogen was the first to speak.

"So, are you pleased with the information you gleaned?"

"I do feel I have a proper amount of content to construct a reasonably interesting article for *The Inquirer*. Barbour is affable and well-informed. We are in good hands with him as Speaker of the House."

"I would like to see an article where *The Inquirer* clearly lays out the platforms of the states and their representatives when it comes to slavery. This topic is not going to die away."

"Are you hell-bent on driving me insane woman? You are relentless!"

"Forgive me. I suppose I had not realized how staunchly my interests and opinions fell in that regard until I vocalized them. You must understand that I feel a strong sense of duty to continue my pursuit of justice."

Talmadge smiled and took Imogen's hand. He appreciated that their differences of opinion drew them to one another. Parleying their opposing views became a challenge to see who might best influence or wear down the other. Rarely did such encounters end in a stalemate. If anything, their discussions became like a game between two worthy opponents who enjoyed the camaraderie as much as the win.

"Well, I for one cannot let the passing of that tray of sweets go unnoticed or without a tasting," suggested Imogen as she turned Talmadge's attention to a topic to appease their palates.

"What is your heart's desire, my dear? Name it and it shall be brought to you forthwith," Talmadge responded, happy to avert for the time being his wife's fervor for a topic about which she was anything but indifferent.

"The gingerbread cake with caramel sauce looks divine. Oh, and a glass of Madeira," Imogen added with a suggestive smile.

"Then that you shall have," Talmadge nearly exclaimed, as the tension he had built-up about the interview began to lessen. He signaled the tavern maid to bring Imogen her selection and a slice of cranberry-apple pie for his palate's pleasure.

Chapter Six

The desserts served to sweeten their time together until they rose from their seats and observed a couple dining on a small repast at an intimate table for two. The pair was unmistakable. Talmadge and Imogen halted briefly in their exit from the tavern as they set their eyes on the vision before them. Intently engaged in conversation, the pair took no heed that they were being watched. Simultaneously, without the other's knowledge, Imogen and Talmadge felt a twinge of jealousy that Virginia and Archibald would be in one another's company.

He is a rogue, Imogen exclaimed silently, wondering if her thoughts could be read by her husband.

Well my, my. Ginny has wasted no time in setting her sights on a companion. Her judgment is certainly askew where he is concerned, Talmadge thought and then worried his words had slipped from his lips to be heard by his wife.

He hoped the two would look his way as he offered his arm to Imogen who reluctantly placed her cupped hand in the crux of his arm. On this occasion, his was a gesture to indicate possession, to mark his territory, a show of warning to anyone who would attempt to usurp his rightly claim.

Neither Imogen nor Talmadge would look each other in the face. Both were concentrating on the pair at the corner table just as a commotion occurred in the front of the restaurant, which caught the attention of all the patrons. A tavern maid's tray and its contents had gone spiraling to the floor.

"No worries. No worries," assured Margaret Coolidge, as she assisted her employee with the cleanup.

Virginia and Archibald lifted their heads just in time to make eye contact with Imogen and Talmadge who nodded their heads in acknowledgment. Virginia's face took on a sheepish expression while Archibald appeared to relish being sighted by the Simmonds'. Talmadge moved forward encouraging Imogen to follow his lead before Archibald, who had shifted his chair away from the table, had the opportunity to rise and approach them.

Virginia's mind drifted to a distant memory, one where no Imogen existed. One where she found herself enveloped in Talmadge's warm embrace after a night of lovemaking, a night where all rules of decency and decorum faded away only to be overcome by lust and need. She put a hand to her face to see if the heat she felt in her loins had risen to create a rosy glow across her cheeks. *I must dismiss these thoughts, for they serve no purpose other than to frustrate and tantalize my being,* she reprimanded herself as she turned to Archibald with a coy smile. *I am however a widow,* she mused. *And, certain needs come calling from time to time.*

For Talmadge and Imogen their return carriage ride to Woodholme was spent in partial silence as each became immersed in the conversations they had exchanged with Congressman Barbour at City Tavern and the couple they witnessed as they departed. Talmadge felt compelled to remind Imogen of her place. As much as he valued her opinion in most instances, on the subject of abolition he thought it best for her to be seen and not heard. She took umbrage at his thoughts and felt he should heed her words about the tide she believed would someday shift. She fervently hoped to alter the axis of his thinking, among that of others, to her egalitarian views. A task she knew would be hard fought.

"Talmadge, when we know better we should entrust ourselves with doing better. Why is it that some amongst us see no wrong in the cruelty thrust upon other human beings in the name of servitude? Is such bondage not a disgrace? How can one rationalize owning people as property and treating them as human chattel? It is time to amend our thinking," Imogen espoused, hoping to sway his mind.

"There are those who would challenge such radical thinking and those who would accuse you of evangelizing about your cause," replied Talmadge who firmly planted his bottom on the carriage seat dare he budge an inch to accommodate her views.

"I shall not be denied a hearing of my concerns nor shall I have my opinions suppressed," Imogen vehemently protested as she crossed her arms in defiance of her husband's lack of empathy. "You represent yourself to be a man of integrity yet you refuse to acknowledge the inequities slavery places on humanity. Perhaps I must find others with whom to associate who share my trepidations for the future of this country."

"Do as you must. If I am not mistaken, you sound like you were raised by the Quaker faith. The Pennsylvania Society for Promoting the Abolition of Slavery has been receiving much press of late with support from The Religious Society of Friends. As I am sure you are aware, the Quakers support denouncing slavery. Next, I will see you carrying a banner for the rights of animals." Talmadge began to chuckle at his comment before thinking better of it. He looked at Imogen and stifled himself before incurring her ire. "But, at the risk of repeating myself I must say, remember your place. A wise woman would take heed. Just assure me that you will not sabotage another interview of mine."

"It is my fervent hope that my words will not be ignored. I must use my voice. How can I in good conscience hold back? Philip will perhaps be swayed at the very least to rethink his stance and give some merit to my views. I suppose I had not realized how staunchly my opinions fell in that regard until I voiced them."

"Again my dear, with love, yet an abundance of caution, I urge you to refrain from voicing your opinions publicly."

"It might just be these differences that align us one day, for without hearing the opposing point of view how are we ever to understand one another and achieve an acceptable compromise?"

Imogen felt as though her skin was crawling. She closed her eyes, shimmied her head and straightened her shoulders as she raised her chin to gain some control over the sensations that traveled through her body upon Talmadge's words.

"Thinking such as the congressman's is thinking upon which I shall not abide."

"I believe we have met an impasse. Can we not put this topic to rest and take pleasure in the beauty of the day about us?"

Must I be a victim of a latent malaise? Must I keep my discomfort with slavery concealed? Are my thoughts without merit? What is so wrong with the society about me that there exists such a refusal to change the inequities afforded to some among us? Talmadge's dismissal of her concerns fueled her ire, although she knew their differing opinions often were the catalyst attracting them to one another.

Talmadge respected Imogen. He admired a strong woman who was tender in the right places, who spoke her mind in the privacy of their home but held her tongue in public. He wanted a woman who would support his desires, give him attention and love and be devoted to him over her own interests. He knew he had found such qualities in Imogen but compromise would be required on his part in order to harness peace in their home.

"Yes, Talmadge. For the present, let us put the topic to rest because I have a topic that needs to be revisited by us. I have delayed my inquiry about you and Virginia Sterling. Seeing her has prompted the topic to come to the foreground of my thoughts. What is the nature of your knowledge of one another?"

Talmadge swallowed hard and leaned back on the carriage seat. He knew Imogen better than to think she would forget about the awkwardness of the night at Virginia's, although he had hoped she would let the matter go. Since that was not to be the case, he readied himself as best he could.

"What is it you feel you need to know?" Talmadge asked, giving himself more time to determine how he would explain his past dalliances with Virginia.

"I suppose I need to know all there is to know? Please, do not send me spiraling in circles when you can answer my question with a simple response."

"Let me preface my comments with the fact that Virginia and I were known to each other many years ago, well before you and I were married."

"Well before? Was this well before we were engaged?"

Talmadge had not expected Imogen to be so specific. He had hoped to escape a timetable that would put him in the position of having had an affair while betrothed to Imogen. Guilt began to creep over his skin and through his veins. *Why do I feel such guilt now? Youth has an amazing grip on what one's conscience will tolerate,* mused Talmadge. *How could I have forsaken her then?*

"Talmadge, have you entered into a trance? Please answer me."

"Imogen, you must understand that I am forever regretful that I veered from my commitment to you. As 'The Bard' himself wrote, 'What's past is prologue.'"

"You think spouting the words of Shakespeare will deter me from pursuing this? I assure you they will not. So, you have a history with her that has brought us to this day, to this dialogue between us."

"We do, I mean we did, but it is just that, history, in the past, nothing upon which to dwell in the present."

An unexpected sadness came over Imogen. Her eyes began to water and well with tears. She felt secure in her marriage to Talmadge but the disappointment in his past deportment began to flame a jealousy she could not squelch. *How could he dare be with another while engaged to me? Was I not enough of a prize? How could Virginia turn his head? She had no scruples and perhaps still does not! I shall be on my guard and I shall not lose confidence in myself!*

Talmadge reached his hand to Imogen to comfort her. She surprised herself by accepting his gesture. She loved him and knew he loved her. She also knew his love for her and the leverage she now had over him would prove a useful tool when thoughts of Archibald Howard arose. *I shall not deny myself any temptations or pleasures that come my way,* Imogen reasoned as she endeavored to justify the lurid thoughts running through her mind.

Chapter Seven

Lester pulled the carriage with its well-matched team of horses up to Woodholme's front portal. As soon as the carriage slowed, Talmadge was ready to make his way free of its confines. He paused a moment to wait for the carriage to fully stop, then turned to assist Imogen down the single step. She gathered her gown with one hand and accepted Talmadge's hand to exit. As soon as her feet were safely on the ground he quickly let go of her hand, left her side, and began to make broad strides toward the front door, held wide open by Patti who had heard the carriage's approach.

"Talmadge!" Imogen called out. "Has something lit a fire to your breeches? I need to speak with you!"

"We have been doing nothing but speaking. I have work to do. Can your thoughts not wait until this evening?" Talmadge questioned, hoping to escape, at least for the foreseeable next few hours, any additional discussion about Imogen's mission to reform him and society.

Imogen picked up her pace to catch up with him. Fortunately for her, Patti stood in the doorway and began talking with Talmadge, which brought him to a halt.

"Seriously, Talmadge. I only need a few more moments of your time. It helps me to express my views to you. I value your opinions for, since we are not always in agreement, they assist me in having a clearer view of those in opposition to mine. I feel it is beneficial to hear all sides."

Imogen knew Talmadge might accuse her of 'beating a dead horse' when it came to her determination to put an end to slavery. Effectuating change for the betterment of and fairness to all was a driving force that remained with her despite Talmadge's efforts to subdue her. *Enslaved men and women need someone to champion their cause.* She challenged herself, *If not me, then who?* If the enslaved were unable to defend themselves, then she was determined to rally support to ameliorate their conditions, whether Talmadge was in agreement or not.

"Very well, Imogen. But, please only for a short while for I clearly need to work on the article about Barbour."

Imogen was pleased to get her way as the two made their way to the drawing room. Imogen settled herself on a nearby wing chair. Talmadge elected to stand, freeing himself to make a hasty getaway if needed.

"So, Talmadge. I see by your posture that I may not have your full attention so I shall make our time together brief. I am curious. There are those who proclaim animosity toward the enslavement of men, women and children yet they perpetuate the practice. How can we deem them sympathetic to the cause?"

"Perhaps Imogen, they are slow to act or hesitant to eliminate a system they feel is working to their advantage. The cogs of progress can be slow to move."

"That is precisely why I am trying to influence a broader base."

"My friends of influence about the city assure me there are those who align their thoughts with yours," Talmadge noted.

"I see little proof of that. Theirs is merely an opportunity to create a platform for self-aggrandizement, ignoring the painful truth of the perpetuation of generation after generation of chattel laborers. How can anyone justify humans being treated as personal property?"

"I am sure you recall Barbour's declaration, and I quote him here, 'the goal is compromise ahead of conflict.' Such action is evident in the legislation that led to Congress' admittance of Missouri this past year as a slave state and Maine as a non-slave state. A balance was achieved by the North and South."

"And it satisfies you that the goal is to maintain an equal number of slave states and free states?"

"Imogen, achieving balance works to appease the pro and anti-slavery factions. It is a beginning. There is too much opposition, especially from the South to take away their freedom of choice when it comes to abolishing slavery or not."

"I would doubt the North is finding it easy to swallow the expansion of slavery into Missouri. Any soul opposed to slavery would find fault with such expansion."

"When it comes to, shall we say, well established traditions and protecting the property of slave owners, laws are not easily swept away. I applaud your work but you must be realistic. The sovereignty of the states must be respected."

The sovereignty of the states, humph, thought Imogen. She understood and appreciated Talmadge's views, which were decidedly a more realistic approach to the topic, and she understood he was protecting her from the disappointment he knew she would endure if future legislation and sectional conflict between the states failed to meet her goals. *But I shall persevere!* Imogen silently shouted as Talmadge made his way to his study for a much-needed reprieve from his wife's agenda.

Imogen needed to seek calm. The topic of slavery, although her choice, provoked her anger to the point she needed to step away for a period of time and, for her own health, find solace in another pursuit. She knew her cause would not be easily solved but such knowledge would not deter her from seeking opportunities to sway the opinions of others. She would continue to collect the facts she needed to support her views and be at the ready to engage the ears of those in power who could put the proper laws in place. After all, she saw it as a matter of human decency.

She wandered to the conservatory to retrieve the book she had been reading by Jane Austen. The romantic mishaps in *Emma* and entertaining characters in fictional Highbury, England, allowed Imogen to drift into their world, even though she found it not so different from her own world where well-defined boundaries were drawn among the social classes. *Hmm. It seems I cannot escape the hierarchies of society for they exist in fiction and in fact. Perhaps I best focus on the good Mr. Knightley and his fine moral character,* she considered as she turned the page to begin another chapter with a man whose company she enjoyed.

Chapter Eight

Archibald's driver and the single horse pulling his carriage delivered him to the front portal of the Bank of the Metropolis on the northeast corner of Fifteenth and F streets. Archibald particularly enjoyed the presence of the bank in such a prominent location. The building for many years had been home to Rhodes Tavern, a popular gathering place and favored boarding house for members of Congress.

Patrons of the bank often regaled Archibald with the site's history. It had been witness to every inaugural parade since Jefferson's. The building held the singular distinction of being witness to the first city council elections in 1802. James Hoban, architect to the president's home, met there along with fellow citizens to draft petitions urging Congress for representation through an elected city council. Many in the city took pleasure in thinking of Rhodes as the birthplace of democracy.

"Perhaps the bank should institute a higher interest rate on all notes in exchange for the luxury of walking within such hallowed walls," Archibald often teased, enjoying stirring up his pot of prankish humor.

He hoped the location would continue to attract notables who had been patrons of Rhodes, for he knew their presence would serve the bank well as a place to see and be seen. He was quite vested in the bank's ability to thrive, having encouraged several other businessmen to put their money and influence behind its success.

Archibald looked up and down the length of the block of buildings hoping to catch sight of Imogen before entering the bank. Their serendipitous encounter at William S. Nicholls & Co.'s dry goods store in Georgetown prompted him to ask her to meet him at the bank under the ruse that he learn more about her anti-slavery society and perhaps assist in some way. He was thankful his propensity for sweets prompted him to step into Nicholls for a square of their delicious fudge. *What a coincidence for me to encounter another sweet I should like to taste as much as this sugary confection,* relished Archibald.

Imogen was at first hesitant to accept his invitation, but curiosity and Archibald's interest in her abolitionist pursuits encouraged her to accept his request. *We are merely two souls, albeit of the opposite gender and one of us married, who are conducting business.* She had however failed to mention the meeting to Talmadge. She had considered telling him when her better judgment had her dismiss such revelation from her mind. *I need no approval from him. I may do as I wish,* she boldly declared. *Am I perhaps yearning for more to come of this?*

She had also taken great care to select one of her favorite daywear gowns, which had a lovely and flowing French silk overlay in the softest shade of rose. The overlay was in perfect contrast to the crisp cranberry taffeta of her gown, which had a three-dimensional border of button roses around its entire circumference in varying hues of pink and cranberry. Her matching hat's large brim, tilted to one side, framed her face in a soft glow as it shaded her from the day's sun.

Imogen admired the bank's open lobby, which had been converted from the tavern's main dining space. Its history as such was evident in the hairline scratches across the wide planked floor created over the years by the movement of chairs as the tavern's patrons shifted forward and back to settle themselves at their tables. She was startled when a tap came to her shoulder.

"My dear, what brings you to this bank today?"

Imogen did not need to turn to know who was questioning her. She immediately recognized Talmadge's voice. She was expecting to see Archibald at any moment and wondered how she would explain her presence there.

"Imogen, I have asked you a question. Are you quite all right?"

She turned to him hoping the flushed feeling on her face was not evident. She searched for the proper words to explain her purpose, yet none readily came. She was given a moment of reprieve when Talmadge's attorney friend, Winston Cromley, gave a brief greeting to him.

"Talmadge! How good to run into you. Will I be seeing you at the races this week? Tayloe is running several of his blooded horses. With the betting, drinking and quarreling that accompanies the races, it should prove to be quite an entertaining event. Perhaps we will witness a fight or two!"

"You are quite right about that, Winston. Sounds like you might relish obtaining a new client or two. Perhaps I will attend this week. Is it being held at the course at Washington Circle or the course at Franklin Square?"

"I hear the National Course is the place to be. I hope to see you there. Well, I best be going. I have clients awaiting my arrival at the office."

Imogen was thankful for Winston's interruption. It gave her additional time to formulate her response to Talmadge. She decided that perhaps a diversion by lobbing a question to him would serve her well.

"Why Talmadge, I did not expect to see you here. What brings you to the Metropolis? Have you decided to move *The Inquirer* accounts from the Bank of Columbia?"

"That is always a consideration so, yes, I am examining my options. And you? Why are you here?"

Just as Imogen was preparing to speak, a sudden flurry of activity drew their attention as the Baroness Hyde de Neuville swept into the bank's lobby where people hoping to gain the attention of the renowned French watercolorist surrounded her and her entourage. A popular 'guest du jour' at the parties of the city's doyennes of good taste, the baroness was a celebrated hostess in her own right. She was also quite adept with a pencil and watercolors. She created highly acclaimed sketches that captured the essence of many structures in the City of Washington's fashionable President's Square district.

Upon sighting her, Imogen was reminded of the rumor circulating in the city, which speculated the baroness might return to Europe within the next two years. Imogen became distressed when she heard the rumor, for she hoped to commission the baroness to sketch Woodholme. *I must make haste to be in her company before her calendar fills and she has not a moment of time remaining to craft a rendering of our home,* Imogen pondered, as she made a mental note to soon invite the baroness and her husband to a reception at Woodholme.

Imogen's thoughts circled back to the matter at hand. As she turned toward Talmadge who awaited her response to his question, Archibald appeared in the bank's lobby. Talmadge bristled as he saw him. Imogen's initial reaction was fear to have the two men confront one another. *No, I must be grateful that Talmadge is here.* She hoped his presence afforded her the chance, before she returned home, to explain the reason she had been asked to join Archibald. *Yes, this is best. All will be out in the open as nothing more than a meeting of acquaintances.*

Archibald, upon seeing the pair, slowed his pace as he approached them. He knew Talmadge would not welcome his company and he wondered how Imogen would justify her presence in the bank. He gave a nod of his head toward the baroness before continuing on his way to greet Talmadge and Imogen.

"I must say it is good to see you, my man. Do let me know if there is anything with which I may assist you. I asked Imogen to come into the bank today to discuss how I might be of assistance in underwriting some of the work of her anti-slavery efforts."

Imogen looked at Archibald as though to hush him. She was shocked he would tell Talmadge he had requested her to join him. Talmadge's ire would certainly be raised realizing she had kept this information from him.

Talmadge looked at Imogen with raised eyebrows then turned to Archibald. "First and foremost, I am not 'your man' and I question what business you have with my wife. How could she be of any value regarding money matters?"

Imogen was beginning to feel slighted by Talmadge's remark. It was not the first time he had suggested she was of less worth, particularly on the subject of financial dealings. She balked at his lack of faith in her and at times would remind him that she was perfectly capable of running *The Inquirer* should the need arise.

"I would not smear this gentle woman's name. She of course holds great value to all who know her. I appreciate her knowledge and I am thankful she could find time in her day to meet with me."

"You say your interest lies in her anti-slavery efforts? How is it that you have come to know about the cause to which she subscribes? If you ask me, it sounds like a clandestine arrangement, for it seems my dear wife has failed to inform me of your rendezvous," Talmadge replied with a sharp edge of sarcasm in his tone.

"I assure you, there is nothing clandestine here, at least for the moment. But your suggestion does tempt me," laughed Archibald, which only served to annoy Talmadge more. "My knowledge of your wife's interests is essentially of your doing."

"Explain yourself."

"It is you who sends her out like an errand boy. You must have a trusted employee who can make the deposits for your newspaper, do you not? But, pay that no mind. Your wife and I had a lovely conversation after you sent her on one such errand. That happenstance meeting afforded me the opportunity to learn more about the topics that capture her interest and drive a beauty such as herself to inspire others to change."

Imogen felt as though she could not breathe. She had neither made any mention to Talmadge about encountering Archibald when she made the bank deposit, nor made known his invitation and their visit in the tavern. *Now, Talmadge will clearly be suspicious. In hindsight, it would have behooved me to tell him and remove any concerns,* she reasoned as she watched Talmadge gather his composure.

"I see *the beauty* and I have much to discuss," said Talmadge as he turned away from Archibald to address his wife. "Imogen, I have a meeting at the office and must take my leave. I trust you too will find it wise to leave and return home. There is nothing for you here."

"As you wish, Talmadge. I will see you at home for dinner."

"Tell Patti to serve you and not to wait for me. I have a long day ahead at the newspaper." Talmadge delivered his parting words, kissed Imogen on the cheek and quickly exited the bank.

"I thought he'd never leave," smiled Archibald with a furtive glance toward the bank's door.

Imogen felt as though the air had been sucked from her. She knew the evening at Woodholme would not be a pleasant one for this would not be the last she heard from Talmadge about Archibald.

"I too must be leaving," Imogen said with worry in her eyes.

"But you have only just arrived. You shan't be going so soon shall you?"

"I must, but I do hope we will see each other again?" Imogen queried. She appreciated the way Archibald came to her defense.

"I know your husband said there is nothing for you here. I beg to differ with him," Archibald said as he raised his eyebrows and took Imogen's hands in his.

She looked about the lobby hoping no one was witnessing Archibald's advances. Her body tingled at his touch. She wanted more. *It seems I was not meant to live a life of tranquility,* she mused as she released her hands from his and made her return, for now, to the security of Woodholme.

Chapter Nine

Patti was not surprised to see the handsome visitor at Woodholme's door. She had spent the earlier hours with her mistress who seemed to take particular care with her toilette that morn, which included consuming a full glass of claret. She had also perused at least one dozen gowns in her armoire before making *the perfect selection* as she termed it. In a brilliant shade of royal blue styled from the finest satin, Imogen's gown shimmered in the sunlight beaming through the windows of her bedchamber. She smiled as she slipped the gown over her shoulders. Patti quickly went to work to complete fastening the ties in the back. The gown's sleeves puffed at the shoulders, as did Imogen's bust over the snug edge of the gown's décolletage. She turned to the large cheval in the corner of the room and swept herself from side to side and back to front admiring her reflection.

"This shall do quite well," she announced as she continued to appreciate her image. She signaled Patti to refill her glass with the nearby decanter of claret. "Patti, I have a special visitor today and I do not want to be disturbed under any circumstances. When he arrives, please escort him to the drawing room and inform him that I shall join him posthaste. There will be no need to interrupt his visit. Do you understand?" Imogen instructed, as she drank a robust portion of claret leaving her glass half full.

"Yes, mum. You'll find I won't be a bother to ye."

"Very well. Now be on your way downstairs to await his arrival so he is not left to wait in the heat. And, here, take what remains of my glass of claret to the drawing room and place a fresh glass there for my guest."

As Patti departed, Imogen took one long last look at herself. Her hair was pulled back in a chignon. The soft coil lent elegance to her coiffure and provided a layer of depth in contrast to the rest of her hair, which was smoothed tightly to her scalp.

She was glad her invitation to meet at Woodholme had been accepted. If Talmadge only knew his request for her to make another deposit for *The Inquirer*, which she readily accepted, afforded her the opportunity to have a chance meeting with Archibald, he would never have suggested she be his courier. Imogen hoped her calculation would come true, for she was most displeased to see Archibald in the company of Virginia Sterling at City Tavern. It was that very day she became determined to move forward with her plan to have him for herself. Their meeting at the Bank of the Metropolis strengthened her resolve to know him in a more intimate way.

As she had hoped, upon seeing her enter the Bank of Columbia, Archibald rushed to her side. She was delighted to see he had not lost interest in being in her company. He bowed, bade her good morning and asked how he could be of service. Upon completion of her business transaction, he asked if they might dine together one day soon. Imogen explained she had an invitation of her own to extend to him, which she hoped he would deem acceptable.

"I find myself in need of some investment advice and I am very much in hopes you will be so kind to meet with me at my home," she queried with a smile as she moved her eyelids down then up in an uncharacteristic display of shyness.

"Will your husband be joining us?" Archibald asked hoping her response would not be in the affirmative. "I am curious because he is, according to Virginia Sterling, an astute businessman."

"You are correct, however, he will not be joining us. This will be a time for you and me to become better acquainted. I have certain desires that need to be fulfilled and you are the one I choose to satisfy those needs."

Archibald was taken aback. Was he misinterpreting her words? *Am I daft or is this woman suggesting more than a business relationship?*

"I must say I am intrigued by your request," Archibald replied with raised eyebrows.

"Why of course," answered Imogen. "Oh my, perhaps I misspoke. I assure you I meant nothing more than a time for the two of us to meet to discuss matters of interest to us both."

Archibald was intrigued with her words and demeanor. Both produced delightfully suggestive images in his mind. Upon first sight of Imogen at Rosedale he was intent on knowing her better. The fact that she was married did nothing to halt his aspirations. Now, here she was making what he interpreted as verbal advances. *Is she toying with me? Or, are these genuine flirtations aimed my direction?* He contemplated, as he prepared to respond. *No matter, I shall accept her invitation and see where this leads.*

"How kind of you to extend this invitation to me, which I will kindly accept."

"Excellent," smiled Imogen. "Then shall we say tomorrow at 11 o'clock?"

"Agreed. You may expect me at Woodholme promptly at 11 o'clock."

The strike of the pendulum at eleven o'clock on the mantelshelf's timepiece prompted Imogen to exit her bedchamber and begin her dissent of the staircase. There was no question in her mind that Archibald would keep his word and that he would be on time. Everything about him was precise from his attire, to his choice of words, to the manner in which he carried himself. He was the picture of perfect posture in standing and in his approach to business.

Patti swept past her as she entered the foyer and gestured to the drawing room and, as instructed, disappeared from view. The large six-paneled doors had been drawn closed. The outer doorway was framed by rich silk brocade portières that were secured at the sides with boldly fringed tiebacks. As Imogen prepared to enter the room she released the decorative cords, letting the dense brocade fabric fall across the doorway as an extra layer of precaution for privacy.

Immediately upon entering, there he was. Handsome Archibald who stood with great vigor, bowed and swept his hat before him then out to his side in greeting. Imogen smiled as she walked to one of the divans to take a seat.

Archibald walked over to join her then hesitated as he thought better of making assumptions.

"If I may be so bold, may I join you here?"

Imogen smiled and patted the space next to her. Archibald noted there was nothing timid in her demeanor. She gladly accepted his bidding. The divan's size provided the setting for an intimate tête-à-tête. As Archibald took his seat, his trousers' leg stroked the skirt of Imogen's gown. She startled at his proximity, wondering if she had misjudged her readiness for such an encounter with him.

"Are you quite all right? I hope you have no fear of me?" Archibald queried as he slid only an inch away from her side to garner her more room.

"No, no, I am quite well. Perhaps my anticipation of this moment has me feeling a touch light-headed."

"Or, perhaps it is the claret," Archibald chuckled as he observed the crystal stemware half-filled with the purplish red libation. An empty glass stood at the ready next to the decanter awaiting his request for a glass to join Imogen.

"Oh, how unthinking of me. May I pour you a glass or would you prefer a tumbler of brandy?"

"The claret will be quite all right. The dark red wines of Bordeaux are among my favorites. Especially the mature ones with their dry, earthy, mineral qualities blended among the flavors of dark fruits."

"You appear to be a connoisseur of wine."

"I am a connoisseur of many things, which I hope to reveal to you," declared Archibald as he reached for her hands, slid over to regain his closeness to her and looked into her eyes. Imogen, who had looked down when his hands grazed hers, raised her eyes to his as a tingling sensation passed through her loins and confirmed the need to respond to her mounting needs. Archibald read the welcoming look in her eyes. Hers was an invitation to take a step he often dreamed would occur. He placed his hand under her chin and lifted it so their lips would meet. Imogen offered no resistance as their lips engaged. They held their kiss for only seconds before Imogen drew back, her conscience threatening to disrupt her desires.

"My dear, I hope I have not been too bold?"

"Quite the contrary. You are perfect. It is I who must wrestle with my commitment to my marriage and the loneliness that brings me to be so attracted to you."

Archibald flinched. "Now, that is a painful barb to my ego. Is it truly loneliness that has enticed you to my side and your tender kiss to my lips?"

"For whatever reason, I am drawn to you despite your arrogance."

"So, now you insult me? You find me arrogant? What is a man of my stature to think? And, I might add arrogance, when properly employed, is quite an effective tool particularly in the banking business. Without pride in oneself how can one take pride in the success of others?"

Imogen threw her head back and laughed. "You humor me to associate pride, an admirable quality, with pompous self-importance."

"My, my, you are the seeming queen of tossing about insults and at my expense no less. And, here I thought I was meeting with a beautiful woman who would find pleasure in my company?"

"Forgive me if I am not making myself clear. Yes, I want to be with you but we must be discreet. I love Talmadge and do not want to hurt him in any way. He has of late had little time for me, which leaves me aching for companionship and the pleasures that come from the opposite gender. If you are open to such a relationship, then we may proceed with the utmost caution."

"Certainly. Where shall we meet?"

"I think it best to meet at your home. I would not want Patti to become suspicious or for Talmadge to return home unexpectedly. I can always find an excuse to be out and my driver will think I am visiting a friend."

"I have another suggestion if you find it agreeable? Upstairs, above the Bank of the Metropolis' lobby, I keep some private rooms. There is an entrance in the alleyway behind the bank, which would provide the discretion you desire. What say you to such an arrangement?"

"How clever," replied Imogen, nearly purring with contentment. "I think that should suit us quite well."

Archibald was nearly overcome with joy. His attraction to Imogen had not waned since his first sighting of her. She had been so off-putting he thought he had little chance of tempting her away from her husband. *She claims she wants to protect her husband. Humph. I have no such convictions. The man can disappear into thin air as far as I am concerned,* mused Archibald. *I will indulge her for now until Talmadge is but a distant memory."*

Chapter Ten

Imogen and Talmadge's relationship was becoming anything but conventional. As she would silently reflect, perhaps only to assuage her guilty conscience, *we never have been wedded to convention.* That concept may have been true on her part but not for Talmadge, although he still held some remorse for having 'sowed his wild oats' while engaged to her.

Perhaps it was his indiscretions over a score of years ago and his love for her that allowed him to abide her flirtations with others of his gender. He feared he would lose her affections if he limited her freedoms and, although her behavior on occasion hurt him to his core, he did not want his objections to cause her to banish him from her life.

He questioned her need for such attention from other men. *Is it a weakness she possesses that takes hold of her and will not let go? That cannot be, for there is nothing weak about Imogen. I wonder if for her it is the challenge of the pursuit or the risks she enjoys, which accompany such behavior? Or, perhaps it is our difference in age?* Although at two score and eight, which placed him nearly a decade advanced in age to Imogen, he appeared a man of lesser years.

Or, he pondered, *perhaps she is bored with me and I am a burden she feels she must bear? I recall my grandmum's pleasure at reciting an adage, "When you marry, you take the two bears with you, bear and forbear."* Talmadge chuckled at the memory. He knew some in their society of friends might rule her deportment lacking in the purity her station in life commanded. Nonetheless, at present, his greatest adversary was Archibald Howard. He wished he had never met the man. Why he had to make his way across the Atlantic and settle in Washington was a curiosity that plagued Talmadge. The man's reputation for intimidation was superseded by his charm, which continued to make him an ever-popular guest among Washington's elite. *Virginia did me no favors by introducing me to that scoundrel. He has no semblance of decency,* thought Talmadge as he tried to shake the man from his mind — a task that was becoming exceedingly more difficult.

The man is so arrogant! Talmadge exclaimed and looked about, not expecting the words to escape his mouth and be thrown into the space about him. He drew in a deep breath and let it slowly release after confirming that he was alone in his office with no one but himself to consider his comment.

As political foes and competitors for Imogen's affections, Talmadge frequently sensed Archibald's growing malevolence, especially toward him. At times he was filled with trepidation that Archibald would cast an evil spell his way. He feared the spell would come to fruition and fulfill a dire prophecy about their relationship. The thoughts taunted him and consumed their fare share of his waking hours.

He also knew his long hours at the newspaper left Imogen to her own devices to keep boredom at bay. Sightings of her about town with Archibald had begun not only to draw untoward attention from everyday society but also to raise eyebrows among the city's gentry. Talmadge was finding it increasingly difficult to maintain a blithe disregard for the recurring insinuations about his wife.

Some of the neighboring women who were active in the Washington Ladies' Guild took umbrage at Imogen's manner and were rather callous in their comments about her appearance. There were those who joked that her head was held erect by her hair, which was perpetually pulled tautly to her scalp. Imogen was well aware of their denigrations and although at times she was deeply hurt with the knowledge of their prattle, she took little care in the opinions of others where her behavior was concerned.

On more than one occasion, she had heard a hiss from a woman or two as she crossed a street in the city. She was certain the hiss was directed at her. *No doubt the sound from a woman who thinks herself anointed with perceived self-righteousness,* rationalized Imogen. She would neither be corralled by the moral stricture to which they adhered nor allow herself to be censured by them with their rumors and innuendo. To her, their words were willfully exaggerated personal perceptions, which she chose to ignore. She deemed her private life and how she chose to live it as a matter of no concern to anyone but herself. She felt their opinions were petty at best, tainted with jealousy, which pleased her as she most enjoyed being envied. *I believe it was Napoleon who said, 'Envy is a declaration of inferiority.' They wish themselves in my place with the adoration of more than one of the male gender. If they only knew the exhilaration I feel they would trade places with me in a heartbeat,* thought Imogen as she prepared to rendezvous with Archibald.

His private room at the Bank of the Metropolis was more than sufficient to meet their needs. On most occasions, Imogen drove herself in a cabriolet Talmadge kept for short visits about the city. The compact, two-wheeled carriage was easy for Imogen to maneuver from the street through the alleyway where the horse could be safely tethered. The carriage's folding hood provided cover not only for inclement weather but also served to protect her identity as she drove along hidden in the shadow provided by the hood.

She was finding it more difficult to produce reasons for her departure from Woodholme that would appease Talmadge. She could only use her meetings with the Ladies' Guild as an excuse on a limited basis. It would be too easy for Talmadge to verify the Guild meetings. The gathering of the committee she was forming to focus on abolition was beginning to meet more frequently, which also served her well to justify her absence from their home. Both she and Archibald had become very adept at scheming. *I often think the devil's prodding fork is at work on us,* Imogen often murmured into Archibald's ear as temptation continued to have its way with them.

In their most intense moments of intimacy, Imogen cast her austere facade aside. She loosened her hair from its grip on her scalp and fluffed it with her fingers. For her the act was an unleashing, a symbol of freedom from the restrictions imposed by society and any self-imposed boundaries she chose to ignore. The role of temptress fully suited her.

She had felt similar urges with Talmadge prior to their marriage and soon after they arrived in America. But boredom took its toll on her better judgment. Meeting Archibald stirred an excitement in her that she could and would not deny. The thrill of their clandestine arrangement made consorting with him a guilty pleasure she was not wont to end.

She entered the back doorway to the bank as she had on several occasions and climbed the stairs taking great care to step as quietly as she could. Under her cape she wore a gown of deep copper silk, which served to emphasize the golden shimmer of her tresses. A wide band of embroidery above the gown's hemline glistened with metallic threads in gold and silver forming a gay pattern of peacocks interlinked with ribbons of tea stained lace.

The gown's neckline was sufficiently scooped to reveal the soft rounds of Imogen's breasts while its puffed sleeves were pulled just off the edge of her shoulders accentuating her fine bone structure. Patti had pulled Imogen's hair back as was customary of her style but left several tendrils falling to the sides, which softened the edges of her face.

Imogen had barely reached her hand up to tap on Archibald's door when it opened full wide. She nearly fell backward down the staircase at the sight before her and had to quickly grab the handrail to steady herself. She could not believe her eyes. She blinked several times to clear her vision but nothing changed. The words 'fight or flee' came to mind but she knew she could do neither. There was no turning back. She felt as though the blood had drained from her body. *Get a grip on yourself Imogen,* she counseled. *You are strong, you are strong,* she repeated the affirmation over and over.

"Do come in my dear. You are looking quite faint. Perhaps you should have a seat?" he said as he extended his hand to aid her up the last stair and over the threshold.

Imogen took his hand, which felt like it was on fire compared to the frigid cold of her extremities. *How shall I explain this? How?* Imogen looked down, her usual confidence having escaped her.

"Let me help you with your cape."

"I shall like to keep it on. I feel a chill in the air."

"Ah, that is an interesting way to describe the atmosphere in this room."

Imogen's mind began spinning with ways to circumvent the situation hoping to grasp onto something, anything that might explain her presence at

Archibald's private room. She carefully considered her words.

"Yes, I am surprised to see you here."

"As well I bet you are," said Talmadge as he spoke through gritted teeth.

"My surprise rests on the fact that when Archibald and I arranged this meeting to discuss business matters, he mentioned he would invite a colleague to join us. I had no idea the colleague would be you," declared Imogen with a tone of confidence in her untruth as she moved into the room.

"Ah, business matters, you say. I should note that is an interesting description of the business you two are conducting." Talmadge was nearly fuming at her bravado.

"Oh, Talmadge. Please do not take that tone with me. You are aware that I find Archibald's company entertaining and on occasion we meet to exchange financial information that I feel will benefit us. We are friends and nothing more," she offered with as much conviction as she could muster. "I wish you could find it in your heart to accept him as he is for he has much to offer. Where might I ask *is* Archibald?" Imogen awaited Talmadge's response fearing some harm may have come to him at Talmadge's hands.

As Talmadge ruminated the words *he has much to offer,* their repetition left a bad taste in his mouth and only served to increase his ire. *How can Imogen possibly imagine that I would believe such lies from her? Does she think me so lame that I do not see through the deceit playing before me?* He felt at a loss. *Why did I choose to precede her on her path tonight? How could I think confronting her might benefit me?* He shook his head as he recalled the deception he put in place to keep Archibald at the Bank of Columbia to delay his so-called *meeting* with Imogen. He found it rather simple to fabricate the need for Archibald to oversee a review of deposit records for *The Inquirer,* which provided him the time necessary to stand in Archibald's place when Imogen arrived.

"Mr. Howard is tending to other business matters at the moment. He should be along shortly."

"Well, in the meantime, I shall take comfort in your presence," smiled Imogen as she employed her wily ways.

"You may use words to appease me Imogen, however they do not negate the fact that you and Mr. Howard are seen far too frequently in one another's company. It pains me to share you."

"Now, now Talmadge. You would not have me unaccompanied, would you? It would not be proper for me to be without a chaperone."

"The point is, perhaps you need a chaperone when you are *with* Mr. Howard? What say you to that?"

"I say you are wearing my patience thin and I am not feeling well. I think it best for me to take my leave. Since we arrived in separate conveyances, would you be so kind to delay your departure to greet Archibald when he arrives? He will understand." Imogen felt dubious about leaving Talmadge to confront Archibald but could consider no other alternative than to feign illness to exit what could become a confrontational situation she had little energy or desire to diffuse.

Talmadge acquiesced to her request, as was his manner. Although an astute businessman who exercised good judgment and impressive leadership at *The Inquirer*, his devotion to Imogen was steadfast. He had become accustomed to deferring to her not only to maintain the peace in their marriage but the fear of losing her was more than he wished to fathom. His loyalty to her remained untarnished since his misstep with Virginia and he intended to keep it that way.

He moved closer to Imogen and took her hands in his. He looked into her eyes and in a ghost-like whisper said, "Very well, my darling. I shall meet you at home."

Talmadge had no intention of being present when Archibald returned. His gratification would come from knowing Imogen would not be there to greet him. He escorted her to her cabriolet and watched her drive away before making his way to City Tavern to imbibe in a pint or two of ale. Although taking to drink to drown his sorrows was not his style, he took some solace as he imagined Archibald's surprise to find himself alone this eve. *Yes, I shall raise some tankards of the amber colored beverage in a toast to a victory, albeit minor. I prevented a tryst and provided a twist in Mr. Howard's plans. Yes, some ale will serve me well this eve,* he declared as the shadow of sadness followed him up the tavern's steps and through its doors.

He wondered if he was a glutton for punishment to make a visit to the Bank of the Metropolis so soon after the scene of deception he viewed the previous eve. There were several stocks and bonds he had purchased through the bank, which offered more promise than current offerings at the Bank of Columbia. He was keen on monitoring the status of his investments and decided to risk an encounter with Archibald. He only hoped there would be no sighting of Imogen in any proximity to the man.

Talmadge's ears perked up when he overheard two gentlemen discussing an article he ran in *The Inquirer* about the continuing work to construct a canal from the Potomac River to the forks of the Ohio Valley. It always gave him great pleasure to have one of his articles spark discussion among the newspaper's readers. He smiled and gave a tap of pride to the copy of the newspaper he carried under his arm. His high spirits were dampened when Archibald made his approach.

"What brings you to the bank, my man? Is it merely to listen to the conversations of others or do you have bona fide business to conduct?"

"First of all, you might start off with wishing a patron of the bank a good day and secondly, as I have informed you in the past, I am *not* your man. Yes, I have business to conduct and, since I am in the newspaper business, it is always good to note when an article has captured the attention of readers to give them pause to discuss it with others."

"What, pray tell, is your latest dribble concerning?" Archibald snidely inquired as he heard one of the men nearby mention the word 'canal.' "Oh, a piece about the expansion of a waterway along the Potomac to the Forks of the Ohio. That is hardly new news and perhaps it is a huge waste of time and revenue."

To the average observer, on the surface, Talmadge and Archibald appeared to maintain cordial relations. As far as Talmadge was concerned, it was a matter of forbearance. They tolerated one another in public but animosity reigned paramount between them. Their characters and philosophies kept them at odds with one another as did their great vigor and fierce ambition to achieve.

"It surprises me to hear you speak in such an uninformed fashion.

Secretary of State Adams is touting the commercial benefits of the canal. Certainly you do not take exception to that?"

"Benefit me? Other than having coal and other products plentiful for my taking, I do not see what I personally have to gain." *Why does he insist this suits my advantage?* Archibald's loyalty, whether it be to a person or a potential business arrangement, focused on what was best for him.

"Where is your foresight? I would not, if I were you, scoff at the idea. This canal could be just the tonic needed to boost Georgetown's prominence in commerce. You might be wise to invest in this project yourself for the capital and stocks will certainly pass through Georgetown banks. How can you lose on such an endeavor?"

Talmadge's comments gave him pause. *Perhaps it is my animosity toward the man that closes my ears to his opinions,* contemplated Archibald. He began to rethink his position. The idea of additional revenue passing through his banks peaked his interest. "Here, let me see the article," ordered Archibald as he snatched the newspaper from Talmadge's grasp.

The Patowmack Canal Company continues to meet to forge ahead with former President Washington's vision to clear the way for a canal to make the Potomac River navigable to reach the forks of the Ohio River Valley. Progress has been slow with the formidable plans to construct several skirting canals along the Potomac River at Harpers Ferry, Seneca, Little Falls and Great Falls where the more turbulent portions of the waterway, the rapids, produce challenges to building the roads, canals and locks necessary to operate the system, which proves to become a significant artery for transportation.

The project has been met with several obstacles including interstate rivalries; the recurring instability of the economy; and the reliance on government assistance, which has been inconsistent.

> It is most unfortunate our former president did not live to see the locks open at Great Falls in 1802 after the Patowmack Canal Company, working on the Virginia side of the river, successfully blasted the solid rock there. Washington had great expectations for bulk commodities such as coal, wheat and lumber to be transported to markets, maintaining Georgetown's prominence in commerce. Private investors are welcome to contact the Patowmack Canal Company.

He quickly read through the article and thrust it back to Talmadge. "I shall take your suggestion under advisement, although it pains me to even consider a suggestion from you."

"Why shoot yourself in the foot? Is it just to be contrary with me? You can only benefit from this. I have no idea why I waste my breath with you. This is a large undertaking and will require enormous resources of capital. Perhaps you would like to join the private investors?"

"I shall see. There are many factors to be considered. The entire project could fail, or perhaps we will not see the canal completed in our lifetime and, therefore, we shall never reap the reward. I must give this some thought."

"It is interesting to learn that you are not the risk taker I thought you were," taunted Talmadge.

"The day will come when you no longer question me or my motives," warned Archibald as he stepped away to go about the business of his day. *It appears the time has come for me to complete the writing with which I have tasked myself,* he roguishly grinned. *Yes, soon Mr. Simmonds will see for himself that the risks I take have been well-planned and suit my purposes quite well.*

Chapter Eleven

Talmadge held a piece of parchment in his visibly shaking hand. Although the letter was not signed, he knew full well who penned the malicious words meant to agitate him and harm the reputation of *The Washington Inquirer*. Early on, he had found investors to resurrect the fledgling newspaper and he would be damned if one man would bring down all he had worked so hard to achieve.

How the letter came to be in print without his authority was another matter he would soon address. Nothing, especially not editorials submitted by the general public, was to run without his express knowledge and approval. Although he knew he could increase *The Inquirer's* readership with a gossip columnist like Tillie Tattler who was employed by his major local competitor, *The National Intelligencer*, which had recently become a daily publication, Talmadge claimed he chose not to lower *The Inquirer's* standards by serving up rumor and innuendo. Many believed his real fear was how often he would have to edit his wife's shenanigans from the gossip page.

"Gibs!" Talmadge shouted through his office door hoping his managing editor would hear the urgency in his voice. "Gibs!"

Gibson Harris, fondly known as Gibs, was an affable man of short stature with a cherubic face. Talmadge held him in high regard and had always had the utmost trust in him until the scathing editorial appeared. He could only assume that Archibald had conspired, if indeed it was he, with an employee who had the ability to slip beyond protocol and allow an unauthorized article to go to print. He was determined to find the culprit and never let such a deed happen again.

Talmadge looked at the latest edition of *The Inquirer* where the critical editorial was centered on the page and loomed large. Rather than remove his eyes from its view, he was drawn to read it through an additional time to confirm its contents:

The Public Best Beware

It should come to the attention of the public in general, and quite frankly be of no surprise, that a shameful scam of sorts is being played on us by this very publication. The obvious bias of the owner of this essentially mercantile rag would have us all accept as true that there is but one party in which to believe and that we will never fully release ourselves from the panic that devastated so many in 1819. Too many articles published here encourage a heightened hostility to banks, the very institutions we count on for our investments and economic expansion. Those of us who are wise enough to know the truth shall not fall folly to the dribble produced by these presses meant to sway our opinions against all that any man of substance and honor would summarily discard as rubbish. As our territories increase and sectional disputes ensue, perhaps it is time we return our loyalties to resurrect the tenants of the Federalists, and cast aside boyish dreams of a perfect union run by our present party of ill-informed, disparate patriots. Now is the time to rally our forces and put an end to the shame that is this newspaper.

Archibald Howard is such a scoundrel, thought Talmadge as steam nearly rose from his eyes and ears. *The man is nothing but a fop hell-bent on slinging poison my way. No signature! Ha! He thinks I would not recognize the chicken scratch style of his writing? Or perhaps that is just his purpose. He knows I would immediately identify the script and now he awaits my response. Well, I will certainly not disappoint him!*

Talmadge began to pace about, vigorously jabbing his finger at the parchment. He wanted to ball it up in his hand and toss it across the room until he thought better of such action. He needed to preserve the letter and was determined to demand an audience with Archibald if there were to be any chance to thwart the man's spite.

"Gibs!" Talmadge shouted once again, growing ever-impatient waiting for him to respond.

"Mr. Simmonds, Gibs has gone to see Doc Davenport. He had a mishap, cut his finger badly when he came in to look at the press that needed a minor adjustment. He wanted the doc to give it a look. He'll probably be back soon," said Joseph, one of the typesetters.

"Very well. Thank you Joseph. I will speak with Gibs upon my return. Tell him I have some business outside of the office to which I must attend," Talmadge explained, as he opened his valise, placed the letter inside and made his way to the nearby coat rack. Later he would get to the bottom of the flagrant disregard for the proper chain of command that led to the unauthorized publication of Archibald's inflammatory dispatch meant to harm. With hat in hand and his frock coat across his arm, he notified the rest of his staff that he had a meeting to attend and would return later in the afternoon.

He was very proud of his newspaper, its independence, and the editors, reporters, typesetters and pressmen he had hired to ensure the newspaper's motto was something the public could count on, not only for interest and fairness but also, most importantly, for accuracy. The motto: *Delivering the latest news in print* meant keeping abreast of topical news that would continue to draw the public's attention including politics, crime and human-interest stories. Advertisers were the buoys keeping his paper afloat. Without them he would not be able to keep the presses going. And, he certainly did not need the bad press served up by Archibald to impact the rapport he had developed with his advertisers and subscribers. He found his readers looked forward to learning about not only the business of government but also the businesses in the city and the latest wares they stocked whether it be fashions, foods or elixirs.

Talmadge walked the several blocks to Archibald's residence hoping to find him working in his study. Each step he took was fraught with emotion.

He had no idea what the results of their confrontation might be but he needed nary an ounce more provocation to want some element of harm to come Archibald's way. Archibald's letter was full of language directed at Talmadge and his management of the newspaper. His words meant to provoke Talmadge from the missive's opening sentence, which screamed accusations that his publication was biased and laced with partisan falsehoods. Provoke him he had. Archibald knew exactly what nerve to push to render a response from Talmadge.

As he had anticipated, Archibald not only was in residence, he answered the knock at his door where he gave a wary smile Talmadge's direction before ushering him through the vestibule and into the foyer. He held no fear for his safety as several servants were about the premises on which he could call at a moment's notice. Talmadge elected to go no further than a few short steps past the vestibule. He was protecting himself if indeed a hasty exit would necessitate itself. He raised his hand in the air, flapping the piece of parchment back and forth before Archibald's face to both warn and intimidate him.

"Well, my, my. To what do I owe this pleasure? What brings you my way, my good man?" Archibald's face contorted into a smirk as he watched Talmadge become increasingly agitated.

"An attack on my newspaper is an attack on my good name. I take such personal affronts quite seriously and would remind you to mind your words and your back."

"Is that a threat you're wielding my direction?" Archibald inquired. He raised his eyebrows, which allowed creases to form across his forehead.

"It is certainly more than a reprimand. I would urge you to cease your public campaign to disparage my name and my livelihood before justifiable harm finds its way to your doorstep."

"You surprise me, Mr. Simmonds. Rather than discuss this as mature human beings, you essentially have tried me in a court of one. You appear prepared to take immediate action and proffer a sentence that will lead to my demise."

Talmadge was surprised smoke was not streaming from his ears. Archibald had lit a fire within him that showed no hope of relenting. He must find a way to douse the flames of his fury lest his health fall victim to his bullying.

"Mr. Howard, you best stand me with my peers where I shall experience a full exoneration from your accusations. You must not ignore the consequences of your blatant disregard for the status I have rightfully earned."

"Or so you think! *The Washington Inquirer* has become nothing more than a mercantile rag! Void of the news of businesses and advertisements, there would be little left for any reader to read! Your coverage of events and the interviews you post are aimed at *reforming* versus *informing* the public. You sir, are at the very least too unstable and wrought with an unchained ego to properly serve our community at large. Your publication will never have the dominance held by *The National Intelligencer.*"

"I will have you know that we have attracted some of the finest and wealthiest readers and advertisers whose reputations have seen their businesses grow in abundance. *The Inquirer's* subscribers and the public at large have met my newspaper with encouragement. It has been of great benefit to them. But, wait. Why do I even attempt this parley with you? If you were a wise man, you would have hedged your bets and never turned your back on my newspaper no matter what opinion you held of its merit."

"This is the most truth I have heard from your lips! You have finally admitted that *The Inquirer* is a gamble!" Archibald exclaimed as he threw his hands out toward Talmadge as though he were casting a net to gather in an unsuspecting school of fish.

"You sir, and I use that prefix loosely, know nothing of the publishing industry. You have done your utmost to slander and demean all that I have so carefully and thoughtfully built. I find you and your opinions repugnant. It is time that you forego any further communication and contact with my wife and myself. You have no place in our lives."

"Best I remind you of the freedoms afforded to me by this country? I would ask you, as a journalist, to make yourself readily familiar with the First Amendment to the United States Constitution, which provides unalienable rights to me as a citizen. You, sir can neither abridge my freedom of speech nor my right to challenge the freedom of the press if I choose to find disagreement with the publisher or that which is published."

"Trust me, I know full well what constitutes the First Amendment to the Bill of Rights of the United States and need no further lecture from the likes of you." Archibald's impertinence was wearing thin on Talmadge's nerves. "For some inane reason you view yourself as a member of the City of Washington's gentility. You are an elitist at heart! And, I must ask how you were able to convince a member of my staff to run your slanderous opinion? Who complied with you?"

"Certainly you do not expect me to name the man? All I shall say is that it was obviously one of your typesetters. And, it has been my experience that a slide of hand laced with a monetary reward is a sure way to gain one's amenability."

"Gibs and I shall see to it that the culprit is singled out and dealt with properly. There is nary a soul who will benefit from your radical ideas for they seem the rantings of a madman!" Talmadge's voice raised an octave as he felt more heat coming over his face and his body became tense.

"Great heavens man! Calm yourself! You're becoming as red as a beet. It's truly not to your advantage to raise your blood pressure to such a degree. You might rupture a vessel and then where would that leave your beautiful Imogen? Imagine her having to find another." Archibald smirked as he shook his head side to side silently uttering a 'tisk, tisk' as he continued to taunt his nemesis. "Though you may find my missive unsavory to your taste, there are those who appreciate my opinions and long to hear more."

"More of your *lies* you mean? My scribes thoroughly research their stories before they go to press. And they treat the news with equity, which is more than one can say of other publications. None in our midst can attest to such a claim. Nothing is fabricated as you suggest. The truth, if ascertained, is to be revered for it is so very rare, especially in this city."

"It is the very standard by which I live," said Archibald with such conviction Talmadge wondered if he truly believed his words or was intent on trying to convince himself of a personal moral compass that did not exist.

"Humph," Talmadge nearly snorted as he shook his head in disbelief. "Does that moral citadel translate to your private life as well?"

"Perhaps you want to review your principles and policies. My father often said, 'a lie well told is better than the truth.' There is great merit in that. It makes for a much more interesting read," Archibald said as he pursed his lips together and gave a widespread, mocking grin in Talmadge's direction.

"From the very moment we met you became a thorn in my side. My gut instinct should have warned me to steer clear of the enormous wake your sea of deceit cast in my path, certain to toss me off course. I have tried to maintain a professional relationship with you considering your affiliations with our monetary institutions. What my wife sees in you is of great mystery to me yet, what I can imagine brings me great disdain. She has no true feelings for you. You are her paramour and nothing more."

"It is best to leave free of this conversation any mention of Imogen. Additionally, since you continue to disparage me and have called me a liar, you leave me no recourse but to settle this dispute by challenging you to a duel." Archibald's stance became very firm and the muscles in his face hardened as he lifted his chin in a defiant challenge. The two men were formidable foes, a fact that would not serve either of them well.

"It is you, Mr. Howard who have erred. Your blatant disregard for the sanctity of marriage and the sacred bond I share with my wife is cause enough for me to wish you nothing but ill will."

Talmadge's rage and pride had gotten the best of him. He, as a man of honor, could not dismiss Archibald's challenge. His mind raced with the threat before him, which he knew he must accept. Yet, how would he explain his decision to Imogen? Her welfare was of paramount importance to him. He had failed her once before and was not wont to cause her undo distress.

Thoughts of Ginny crossed his mind, which added to the dread churning inside him. He needed to survive to buffer any exposure she and Imogen had with one another. *Why have I allowed my distaste for Archibald to escalate to such a degree that I have found myself in such a threatening position?* It was very like Talmadge to cast blame upon himself, to take responsibility away from another. He had done so with Ginny. He accepted their relationship as a product of his own lust rather than disparage her for her responsibility in their affair. And, then there was Imogen. He was devoted to her despite her roving eyes. He blamed himself for her behavior, reasoning that his failure to award her the attention she craved led to her wanderlust.

Why? What has happened to my life? How have I arrived at this juncture? No answer came to him as he exited Archibald's dwelling and walked the path to his office all the while observing his surroundings and breathing in the air as though it would be his last opportunity to do so.

Chapter Twelve

Imogen worried about Talmadge. When he returned home, he was unusually quiet as though deep in thought. She wondered what cast a cloud of doom and gloom over him. She spotted a copy of *The National Intelligencer* on the hall rack in the foyer. *Talmadge must have left this here,* she assumed. He often picked up a copy of his competitor's publication to review and study what it deemed fit to print. The newspaper was opened to the society page to a missive by Tillie Tattler, the anonymous scribe whose claim to fame was writing titillating, suggestive details about the lives of others. She was infamous for not naming names but her vague descriptions could be readily recognized by her sly innuendos, especially by those who were guilty of her accusations. Imogen took the newspaper in her hands and began to read:

Dearest Readers,

It seems the mistress of a certain estate is finding pleasure in the arms of more than one of the male gender. Her husband would be wise to tether her like one of his stable horses lest she ride into the sunset with another or, will she find another paramour to suit her fancy?

Poor Mistress of Many. You may soon get your comeuppance.

With a reluctant warning,
Tillie Tattler

Imogen was appalled. She held her hand to her mouth as though such action would silence the words that had been spewed to the public. She knew at once the column was about her, about her private life made public by this malicious gossipmonger who was obsessed with spreading scandalous information about private and public figures. "Outrageous!" Imogen shouted, then quieted herself rather bring attention from her staff.

What to do, what to do? Her hands began to shake and she felt sick to her stomach. *Could this be the cause for Talmadge's change in mood? I must find him and hope it is but a coincidence that this is the revealed page. With any luck, he placed the newspaper there without having read Tattler's column. It is my fervent hope that that be the case.*

"Patti," Imogen called to the girl as she descended the staircase. "Have you seen Mr. Simmonds? Was he upstairs?"

"I 'aven't seen 'im mum. Not up 'ere that is. Ye know 'e likes his time in 'is study. I ken go look fer 'im there fer ye if ye like?"

"That will not be necessary. You make a good point. I shall see if he is there."

Imogen proceeded to walk the hallway to Talmadge's study were she came upon closed doors. Patti had not mentioned any visitors, although at times the girl was lax in her duties and failed to alert Imogen to guests. She lightly tapped on the door and waited only a moment before the door opened as if by magic for there was no one in sight. She peered around the door to find Talmadge still holding the doorknob and looking very disheveled. His hair was tousled in an unkempt way, quite uncustomary to his usual impeccable style. His jacket was open and his neckcloth was loose about his neck. He watched the look of surprise consume Imogen's face and then turn to one of concern.

"Talmadge, what on earth? Have you taken ill?" Imogen queried. She had never known her typically well-groomed husband to look in such a manner, particularly on the main floor of their home where staff and visitors might cross his path. *He looks as though I have stumbled upon him in the middle of a rendezvous with another.* She looked about the room, squinting to see into the dark corners of the space. The draperies were pulled closed, fully covering any chance of light entering the room. A lone candle on his desk was providing the only illumination. As its flame flickered back and forth, Imogen became mesmerized by its syncopated sway. She turned her eyes from its hypnotic effect and, having seen no one else in the room, she once again addressed Talmadge.

"Are you unable to speak? Have you gone mad? I have never known you to sequester yourself like this during the light of day. What has come over you?"

Talmadge took a deep breath. He looked up to the ceiling then dipped his head down before raising his chin to look Imogen in the eyes. *Such a lovely face,* he murmured. *I hope I shall see it again and again.* He reached for Imogen and brought her forward against his chest. There was a gentle forcefulness in his actions, which prompted Imogen to accept his advances and not thwart them in any way. He placed one hand on her head and removed the hairpiece that held her hair tight. He swept his fingers through her loosened hair, now free to flow about her shoulders. He ran his hand along her neck and then across her collarbone, dipping his fingers into the crevice between her breasts, cupping the fullness of her chest, and then searching out a nipple. He backed up, the two of them engaged in a slow waltz, moving as one toward the door, which Talmadge quietly closed, then turned the key to lock out any interruption.

His lips went to hers. They began to share fervent kisses, their tongues relishing the intensity as their passion grew. Imogen ran her fingers down Talmadge's torso to his waist where she released the fall front opening on his trousers to free the growing urgency in his loins. He lifted her gown and moved his hand along her pantalettes already wet with anticipation. Imogen gasped as Talmadge deftly reached between her legs and used several fingers to stimulate her as she readied herself for his entry. He could hold back no longer. With her back to the wall, he easily entered her; slowly at first, then his thrusts became more intense as her body grabbed him, encouraging him to give more. Initial moans gave forth to the louder sounds of pure ecstasy as Talmadge completed his ride, leaving them both fully sated. As he withdrew, Imogen's gown fell back around her. Talmadge refastened his trousers and they held each other in a warm embrace.

"You are my greatest love, Imogen. Never forget that."

"You know I love you too, Talmadge. I must ask why you sound so dire? Has something happened about which I should be aware?"

"No. No. I would not want to worry you."

"You worry me by the mere fact you are saying so little, although I can say I very much enjoyed your most recent actions without words," Imogen smiled coyly, which made Talmadge want to take her again.

She decided she dared not mention the gossip column for fear of ruining their carnal interlude. *No, I shall ignore it for now,* she concluded. *Although I know not what tomorrow will bring if members of the Ladies' Guild or any others who choose to read and believe such rubbish begin to whisper in my presence or shun me altogether. I cannot have such thoughts create a cause for concern, at least not at this juncture when Talmadge and I have made love.* Amorous sensations continued to course through her when she was reminded that she and Archibald had made arrangements to meet later tonight. *Oh no, I must get word to him that there has been a change in plans.*

"Talmadge, I am just remembering that I need to speak with Patti about a matter," she informed him as she straightened her gown and pulled her hair back with her hair comb.

"Can it not wait?"

"I shan't be but a minute."

"If you must. I shall miss you every moment you are gone from my sight."

Imogen's face formed a wary smile. There was something unusual about Talmadge's demeanor, which she could not distinguish. His sudden need to make love, his words bordering on poetic, and his reluctance to let her go, made her question his manner. *There must be a deeper meaning, which I am not grasping. I cannot dwell on this,* she determined as she disregarded the concerns her intuition was casting her way.

Slowly, she opened the door to the study and looked about the hallway thankful there was no sign of Patti. *Thank goodness the girl was not lingering outside the study doors!* Imogen quickly stepped through the hallway to the drawing room where she went to her desk. She was just about to withdraw a piece of parchment to write a message to Archibald, which she would have Patti deliver when she saw a letter addressed to her. She recognized the stationery and the untidy script. *Archibald. How did this arrive on my desk? Oh, my god!* She hoped he was not about the home to hear the intimate exchange with her husband. She carefully unfolded the paper and read his cryptic message:

Mrs. Simmonds,

I regret our business meeting has been canceled for this evening. With any luck we will be able to reschedule on another day in the near future. Please accept my sincere apologies for any inconvenience.

Yours respectfully,
Mr. Howard

How peculiar? Yet, how convenient? And, why so formal? *Imogen questioned. Perhaps he thought Talmadge would come upon his letter. It was best for him to exercise discretion.* She read through Archibald's words one more time. *I wonder what he means by 'with any luck'? Well, he has saved me from having to make excuses to him.*

She was unaware of Archibald's dilemma and the torment he experienced making the decision to cancel his plans with her. He had put much thought into whether or not he should see her the night before he was to face her husband in a challenge whose outcome was unknown. *How can I in good conscience make love to a man's wife the night before we settle a dispute with firearms?* He was racked with a rush of uncharacteristic guilt and indecision. Canceling their rendezvous he determined was his best option. Fortunately, Patti was the one to answer the door when he came calling. She invited him in but he declined, handed her the note to Imogen, instructed her to place it on her desk and quickly went on his way.

When Imogen returned to the study, Talmadge was deep in thought. His head was bowed and she could see that his lips were moving but there was no audible sound. She hesitated to disturb him but her inclination to do so prompted her to call out his name.

"Talmadge, are you quite all right?"

It took a few moments for him to respond. When he looked up, she saw sadness in his eyes, which tugged at her heartstrings. Slowly, he stood and walked to her. She thought perhaps he wanted to take her in his arms and have his way with her again but such was not the case. He held her hands in his and then stroked her cheeks, enjoying the softness of her skin.

"I love you, my dear Imogen. I shall always love you no matter the circumstances that come upon us."

Imogen took Talmadge's hands and brought them up against her chest. "Here is where you will always be — always close to my heart whether near or far. I see worry in your eyes. You need not fear the capacity of my love for you –it exists no matter the company I am reported to keep."

Talmadge wanted to erase any concerns he had about Imogen and her *friendship*, as she termed it, with Archibald Howard but he was fully aware of the rumors circulating about the city, which he attempted to quell by assigning them little credence. He knew she would deny the rumors for it seemed denial was her way of delaying the inevitable truths. Such refusal on her part only served to accentuate the turmoil in his mind. *Perhaps I prefer a state of denial myself?*

"Do not concern yourself with the idle prattle of those whose hearts rage with jealousy," urged Imogen. "We cannot live our lives forever considering the opinions of others. You know better than anyone that controversy and disparate opinions drive the newspaper business for the public thrives on debate. It is only human nature. And, some prefer to offer unsolicited advice. I would argue that we must not be influenced by or deterred from living as we wish."

Talmadge was feeling drained. His thoughts were weighing him down and he knew nothing would be served by continuing to discuss gossip and rumors –topics he was quite surprised Imogen brought forth.

"I for one wish to retire early this eve. Will you join me?"

"It will be my great pleasure to do so," replied Imogen, thinking he wished to repeat their lovemaking in the sanctity of their bedchamber. Little did she know the pressing burden on his mind. On the morrow, he would rise early and quietly leave Woodholme –perhaps for the last time?

Chapter Thirteen

October 1821

As he fastened the final hook on his waistcoat, Talmadge pondered whether this would be the final time he exercised such a simple task. He questioned having accepted Archibald's challenge, yet there was little alternative unless he chose to endure public ridicule the remainder of his days. He was a proponent of self-preservation at all costs, thus he worried that his skills with a firearm were severely lacking in contrast to those of his opponent who often boasted about his abilities, frequently tossing the term 'marksman' into his conversations about himself.

There was little time remaining for such thoughts as he mounted his favorite horse, Blaze, for his journey to Bladensburg, Maryland, and the dueling grounds just northeast of the city that would bear witness to his fate. Dueling was illegal in the City of Washington, thus disputes among men, in order to evade the laws of the region, eased their way over the boundary lines into Maryland to an area bordering a creek whose moniker, very suitably, became 'Blood Run.' Discussions in political circles regarding passing a Congressional Act to prohibit such confrontations had fallen victim to the slow moving nature of the legislature. Excuses varied with the majority of the legislative body wanting to exercise prudence to protect the liberties and freedoms of its citizens. The public was still reeling from the death in March 1820 in Bladensburg of naval hero Stephen Decatur at the hands of fellow naval officer James Barron. Only time would tell if such face-offs would go out of fashion but, for now, Talmadge had nothing to hold him back but fear.

He felt it a necessary courtesy to write a short message to Imogen to explain his absence, which he placed on his pillow just before he quietly left their bedchamber. He knew once she read his message she would be prompted to go to him and attempt to stop his confrontation with Archibald but the timing would be lacking and the deed a fait accompli.

My dearest Imogen,

It is with a heavy heart that I must convey that I have kept something from you. I hope you will forgive me. Circumstances have arisen between Archibald Howard and myself, which have warranted a meeting very early this morning to settle our differences in a way only men of honor can. I do not mean to cause you undue worry but I have no knowledge of what the outcome may bring. Know that I love you, will always love you, and hope to soon hold you in my arms again.

Until then, remember me as your loving husband, Talmadge

Blaze was very cooperative under saddle and easily followed commands. *Perhaps it would better serve me to have a wayward equine that would ignore my directions and take me far off course,* thought Talmadge. *Then I would have the horse to blame for my failure to appear.*

He knew his was a fool's folly to even suggest such an alternative. It was time for him to buck up, face his fears and accept whatever lay on his life's horizon. Blaze's regal stature with his head and tail held high lent a royal, yet perhaps stoic, presence to Talmadge as he and the equine made their way to his unknown destiny. *Either way, this meeting can have anything but a satisfactory outcome,* Talmadge contemplated as he imagined himself or Archibald gravely injured and lying on the turf he had traveled so far to build a new life upon.

Leaving his home country was a decision that left him torn between his profession and Imogen's wants and desires to relocate and establish themselves far away from the controversy that encompassed them in England. Imogen felt a fresh start in the publishing industry, especially in the growing territories of America, would serve them both well. Little did Talmadge know that their lives would be fraught with a man like Archibald and his wily ways.

When he first became aware of Archibald's interest in Imogen, he passed it off as a rogue's fleeting fancy to acquire the admiration of as many of the fairer sex as possible merely to stroke his own ego. Yet as time bore on, Talmadge was wont to admit what he dared not want to believe that his Imogen was caught in Archibald's snare. Rather than lose her, he turned a blind eye to their relationship hoping it would be nothing more than a passing phase. *And, now, look what has come of my ignorance! I should never have tolerated her indiscretions! My love for Imogen has tainted my good judgment!* Talmadge nearly screamed aloud as his thoughts bombarded him with regret.

As he and Blaze passed the boundary stone marking their path into Maryland, Talmadge saw an assembly of men standing erect in their dark morning coats mimicking black pawns on a chess board. He squinted his eyes to find his focus on the gathering hoping his opponent had failed to show. No sooner had he held that hopeful thought than a figure stepped forward through the dissipating haze. Talmadge knew at once it was Archibald. He was fully attired in his usual finery, his boots polished to a high shine, as though he were prepared to attend a social event. Upon seeing Talmadge, he tipped his top hat toward him and bowed, not so much as in greeting but more to mock and intimidate him.

Talmadge had neither room nor tolerance for Archibald's contemptuous behavior. He ignored his gesture and looked about to identify the other faces willing to risk being present for the illegal encounter. Doc Davenport, prepared with his medical bag in his hand, stood back from the men. The seconds for both sides, who had arranged the meeting place and established the parameters of the duel, stood at the ready with their gun cases housing the weapons they chose to be employed. Both were in possession of Wogdon dueling pistols. The flintlock pistols were rather simple yet elegant in design, featuring a level top and octagonal barrel parallel to the interior or bore. When aimed and raised to fire, because the weight of the weapon was by design so properly distributed, the pistol became a natural elongation of the shooter's arm ready to wield its fury.

Each leather gun case housed a matched pair of pistols should there be a need for a second shot or a pistol failed to fire. *Perhaps neither of our weapons will properly fire and we can be done with this foolishness! The fact that we have both chosen to risk our lives to settle a dispute may be proof enough that we are brave men of honor and, by the grace of God, we can walk away unscathed.* Talmadge held that hopeful thought as he stepped down from his mount to address his second, Winston Cromley.

Winston was one of the first men he met when he arrived in America. He was an attorney by trade; a profession that Talmadge reasoned could be advantageous if he were in need of counsel pending the outcome of the duel. Winston had agreed to risk being present knowing he could invoke attorney-client privilege to stave off any criminal charges that might find their way to his doorstep.

Talmadge noted the somber look that had overtaken his friend's face as he cocked his chin down in a greeting nod.

"Not the way I had ever envisioned beginning a morning. And you, my friend, what say you about this day?"

"Agreed. 'Tis with great apprehension I appear," Talmadge said as he felt a pang of regret for giving any credence to his dispute with Archibald and accepting his challenge.

"The ways of the world will likely only change with public opinion enforcing such change. Laws can go only so far to eradicate some behaviors. It is up to men, and perhaps the women who in their own ways guide us, to find this method of settling disputes barbaric before it can cease to exist. The idea of resolving differences by being forever haunted with the blood of their victim on their hands is no way for an enlightened society to function."

Talmadge nodded in agreement although Winston's dissertation on dueling and the moral woes of society were of little comfort to him now.

"Alas, I fear the die has been cast," Talmadge said with dismay.

"Oh yes, in the alleged words of Julius Caesar, 'Iacta alea est,' 'the dice have been thrown.'"

The two moved forward toward Archibald and his second, a man Talmadge had never met. *Probably some miscreant from one of his banks, a floor sweeper no doubt, only here for the game of it,* Talmadge surmised. He had no care in being introduced to him or introducing Winston in turn. Anonymity would well serve them all this day.

With the defense of Imogen's honor weighing heavily in his heart, Talmadge stood before Archibald not only to protect his wife's good name but also to put a stop to the slanderous claims Archibald repeatedly threatened to make against his publications. His insults had become more frequent and more public. He had long tired of the intimidating nuances Archibald made suggesting the words he sent to press were mundane and lacked the proper caliber to attract a sophisticated audience.

The seconds led their charges to an opening in the field where they had already measured out 10 paces where the duelists would each stand before turning to take aim and respond to the signal to fire. All had agreed that Winston would issue the sign to turn and fire. The seconds presented them with their open pistol cases for easy access to their weapons. Each selected one pistol from their pair. Then Archibald and Talmadge were instructed to stand back-to-back and walk the predetermined paces that would put them twenty-five feet apart.

As they took the field, neither would admit their apprehension but both felt queasy in their stomachs. The moment of truth had come. There was no retreating. Soon the pistols would be fired releasing a single-shot of black powder and a .54-caliber lead ball. Remaining back-to-back until the signal to fire came added an additional burden, for the men would have no time to face one another to properly take aim.

Step-by-step the sound of boots on turf, at times rustling through the underbrush of twigs and leaves, were the only noises emitted from the space. Even the wildlife was silent as though their intuition foretold of an impending event that would rock their tranquil environment.

Archibald and Talmadge seemed unaware of the silence about them as they ended their promenade and stood perfectly still awaiting Winston's sign. All at once, tearing through the thick band of silence came Winston's voice.

"Turn! Fire!"

It all happened in an instant. Talmadge's pistol fired first followed in moments by Archibald's. The lead ball from Talmadge's pistol raced through the air nearly missing the seconds and Doc Davenport. As the assembly of bystanders checked their clothing for signs of blood, Archibald stood reverently still as he watched Talmadge fall to the ground. Archibald had taken perfect aim.

"Doc! Doc!" Winston called out as he ran to Talmadge's aid.

Talmadge writhed in pain as he gathered the strength to put his hand over a gaping wound in his abdomen. Blood flowed forth saturating his morning coat as its wool fibers became soaked with the crimson fluid so vital to life.

Doc Davenport raced to Talmadge's side. As he expected with but one glance at the wound, his worst fears were to be realized. There would be no recovery from his injuries.

Archibald's face appeared to lose all color. His months of snide remarks and bullying toward Talmadge became suspended in time as he witnessed the scene before him. There were no cruel words uttered or any signs of boasting about the outcome of the duel. He solemnly turned to his second and handed him the pistol to return to its case as the gravity of the scene before him took hold.

The last remnants of fog lifted their eerie hold on the surrounding air as Archibald became enveloped in a fog of his own doing. He felt suffocated by the extremity of his actions. The thought of Imogen and how she would respond weighed heavily on his mind.

Doc Davenport stepped away to allow Winston to kneel by Talmadge who was trying desperately to retain enough strength to speak. Winston leaned closer as Talmadge's mouth began to move with greater control.

"Tell her, tell her," were the repeated words nearly whispered as Talmadge gasped for a breath of air. "Tell her, tell her, all will be well for her," he panted. "I have been a burden for Imogen," he inhaled as best he could to be able to continue to speak. "She will no longer have to tolerate me." Upon those words, like a spent candle with smoke from the tip of its wick weaving its way up into the air, Talmadge was drained of all life.

Archibald remained in a self-imposed stupor as he listened to the words of the dying man. *A death caused by my hand,* Archibald glumly affirmed, as though he felt some remorse for the outcome of his actions.

"God rest his soul," choked Winston as Doc Davenport bent down to close Talmadge's eyes.

"How could his pistol have fired so prematurely?" Archibald inquired as he drifted back into reality.

"It looks to me as though the pistol had a set trigger. That would explain why so little pressure was needed from Talmadge's finger to make the pistol fire. Yours was set in the same manner. Looks like the steadier hand had more control of the weapon," noted Doc Davenport. "Talmadge was very unsteady about following through with this duel. As hindsight teaches us, you both would have been wise to settle your differences with words and avoid the ways of the dark ages. Now he's dead and you will forever have his blood on your hands."

As Talmadge's body was carried away, Archibald searched for a sense of guilt, regret, remorse, yet none readily came to his aid. He was at once alone in a quagmire of circumstances of his own creation with which he must live.

Solace. I must find solace amidst the turmoil roiling within me, Archibald railed within, his insides bombarded by his actions that led to Talmadge's limp body being prostrate before him for all to see. *I have done what was required of me, what was expected. I was issued a challenge and took heed in following it through to its end. I shall take no shame in that. But, Imogen may never forgive me. Yet I must, I must find a way to convince her that these actions, like the determination of a runaway horse, could not be halted. I must find a way.*

Chapter Fourteen

Imogen's mind continued to replay the day not long past when Winston Cromley came to Woodholme to inform her of Talmadge's fate. The stabbing reality of his loss seemed a pain that would not abate as she sought solace on the upper levels of her home.

Her journey ascending the narrow steps to the turret was fraught with angst. Her feet felt heavy as though laden with lead weighting down her every step. A force, seemingly neither of her doing, nor her control, called her forward as she continued her upward trek. Thoughts of Talmadge taunted her, pulling at her every move, slowing her ascent. She lifted the hem of her nightgown to gain more freedom for her feet. The gown's thin, white silk fabric freely flowed about her torso in the stairwell as she rose higher and higher to her destination on the third floor.

She opened the door to the turret and reached out for the parapet's balustrade to steady her. A periodic gust of wind challenged her balance but she was determined to maintain her stability. She gazed out over the Potomac River. Moonlight helped to light the night's sky despite a light mist threatening the clarity of the atmosphere. The moon's beam shown across the river forming a pathway of sorts, like a temptress mapping Imogen's way, inviting her to come forth. The river's current kept the water in motion maintaining its rhythm, offering some tranquility to the thoughts raging in her mind. She held tight to the railing as the gusts of wind became more prevalent and persistent. Her gown was whipped about creating an ethereal display, as though the heavens were calling her forth in a funereal dirge.

Her mind drifted as though lost in a memory from which she cared not to retreat. *Oh, Talmadge. How have events brought me here? How shall I go on without you?* The ripples created along the moon's reflection as the current made its way downstream mesmerized her. *Come to me, come to me,* rang in her ears. She heard the words but questioned whether they were coming from her voice. *Is that you Talmadge? Have I lost my mind? It has been a while since I have heard your voice. I fear I don't know it anymore.* Tears welling in her eyes became whisked away by the wind as she continued to grip the railing to retain her stronghold. She was impressed by the precision of design implemented by the architect as she bent forward and closed her eyes to feel the full force of the wind on her face. The words 'come to me, come to me' floated in the night's air. She tried earnestly to recollect her husband's sound to no avail.

Talmadge's voice may have faded from her consciousness but his facial expressions were pinned to her memory. She recalled the way his eyes lit up when she entered a room, the way his slightly crooked smile lent an air of contentment when they sat and shared the news of their days, his warning look laced with the utmost care if he questioned her intentions, his pensive gaze when deep in thought and the playful, alluring ways he employed to tempt her affections.

A look of melancholy framed her face. She was wont to end her grieving, to relieve herself of the pain of his loss and the guilt that tugged at her heart but how? As she considered the actions she could take to do so, a heavy cover of cumulus clouds floated across the indigo sky obscuring the moon, erasing its ghostlike reflection on the water. The hypnotic spell of the current's water dance, forming beckoning fingers attempting to signal her forth, could not compete with the sheer will to survive that engulfed her.

Intermittent droplets of rain began to awaken her senses. A welcomed period of calm washed over her. She felt cleansed of the worries that had become entwined, threatening to dismantle and render her a pile of useless pieces no longer fit for her or any man. *I must shake off these latent feelings of weakness that are manifesting themselves. I am stronger than that. I must muster the confidence to believe in myself,* Imogen spoke aloud nearly begging for someone or something to confirm her declaration.

"Here ye are! Forgive me but ye 'ave no business bein' up 'ere on a night like this!"

Imogen was so startled by the sudden admonition she nearly lost her balance. It took her a moment to catch her breath. *Oh my God! Am I now imagining this voice of warning? I must be going mad!* She thought the sound came from behind her but she could not be certain. Grasping the railing, she turned to see what appeared to be a cherubim angel, with a human face and hands, its wings flapping in the wind.

"Come now. Follow me before ye fall," called out the angel who reached her hand out to Imogen.

Imogen blinked her eyes several times as she focused them on the image before her. She pondered, *Who is this spiritual messenger?* The clouds began to shift and once again expose the moon's glow, which illuminated the form. Imogen closed her eyes and shook her head in an effort to make sense of the vision she held in her mind's eye. As she exited from her stupor, she was relieved to see a familiar face, yet embarrassed that she had allowed herself to become so unsettled by grief and succumb to her imagination. *Many would not believe my reticence for my voice is usually strong. It is that air of confidence that fools them but the truth be told, I may have a bold voice but I do not always feel self-assured,* Imogen reasoned as she wiped her face with her fingers in a dual effort to remove the moisture from her wet cheek and wipe away the thoughts of weakness infiltrating her mind. *But, who am I to care what others think about me? I always rise above their petty declarations. Their envy and jealousy invigorates me,* Imogen rationalized.

"Come to me, come to me," spoke the angel with her hand outreached.

Patti's night cover billowed at her shoulders as the wind filled the cloth, lifting the sides of her robe up and out to create the appearance of wings. Imogen took Patti's proffered hand.

"It seems you are my guardian angel, Patti. For that I must thank you," Imogen shouted above the sound of the whipping wind.

"It's me job to see to yer welfare, mum," said Patti, as she urged her mistress to come along with her.

A verse from Psalm 91:4 entered Imogen's mind, which she silently recited as they descended the stairs. "God will cover you with his feathers, you will find refuge under his wings; his faithfulness will be a protective shield…for He will give his angels orders concerning you to protect you in all your ways."

Imogen was grateful Patti brought her back to her senses. She returned Imogen safely to her bedchamber, freshened her night's attire and tucked her under the bed's plump, down-filled cover.

I pray for God's protection. But who am I to make such a request when my actions have been less than pure? Imogen mused, her thoughts fraught with conflict tinged with guilt. She questioned her choices, her lifestyle, and her reason for being.

This too shall pass, Imogen silently announced as she drifted off to sleep waiting to face the challenges of a new day on her own terms, in her own way while a new, biting missive of gossip went to press for all to read:

Dearest Readers,

It scares many of us to know that certain premonitions have come to pass for the poor Mistress of Many who now holds the title of widow. You know who you are dear.

Poor woman of many titles. Ah, Mistress and Widow. You have our sympathy for a while until we learn of your new transgressions, which we are certain you will have. How could you not?

With a wish to mend your ways,
Tillie Tattler

Chapter Fifteen

Imogen had always appeared, for all intents and purposes, to flourish in her role as mistress of Woodholme. Talmadge gave her full rein to run the large household at her discretion. Each piece of furniture, artwork and a variety of exquisite accessories had been carefully selected by her and expertly placed at her direction. She was forever asked by friends to assist in the décor of their homes. She took great pleasure in establishing colors, curating fabrics, and selecting appointments and light sources to cast the most efficient yet ambient glow to maximize a room's affect on its occupants.

She equally excelled as a grand hostess. Dinner parties were her forte. An invitation to an event at Woodholme was a much sought after and not to be missed event. On more than one occasion an uninvited guest would appear at one of the Simmonds' receptions where by shear numbers he or she thought they would blend in and not be found out. Talmadge enjoyed repeating the story of an uninvited female guest whom, when he approached her about her presence, smiled and exclaimed, "Oh, Talmadge. I knew you would want me to be here, so here I am!"

Such pleasant memories were cut short as they floated through Imogen's mind only to be met by thoughts of darker days, which tormented her. Upon the loss of Talmadge, austerity had not only become her manner, it had infiltrated her persona to such a degree that friends, family and household staff were hard pressed to find a soft edge to penetrate her tough façade. In the past, as would suit the occasion depending upon whom she was wont to impress, her voice remained demure, softly spoken like the proper lady she was trained to be yet, another side could also evoke itself. On those occasions, the lamb in her forsook its meekness and emitted the fierceness of a roaring lion.

Now dreams, albeit bordering on nightmares, interrupted the tranquility of Imogen's sleep. Talmadge played a leading role in the scenarios that came into view causing her to toss and turn. She and her husband were not void of times of conflict where unkind words were exchanged only to be later forgiven but not always forgotten.

In her fitful dreams, Talmadge appeared, standing tall and wearing one of his best suits. He held his arm out in exasperation exclaiming in a tirade to Imogen, "Your behavior is that of a feral cat! How desperate for your affections do you imagine I must become? I am troubled by your reckless and bold behavior. Why must you give me cause to doubt your commitment to our marriage?"

The images Imogen saw were in vivid color. A massive fireplace with an ornately carved cherry mantel framed the firebox, which held a roaring fire. The hot glow of the fire flickered in Talmadge's eyes. *What does this mean?* Imogen wondered as she tried to sift through the significance of his words and conduct, which forced her to engage in conversation with him.

"I am troubled by your accusations. How can you question my good name and intentions? I am disappointed you hold me in such low regard. You must know how it grieves me to hear you speak in such a way. You know I hold a great fondness for you." Imogen offered hoping to calm Talmadge's ire.

Talmadge picked up an iron poker, which was among other necessary tools for tending the firebox. He waved it in the air as he continued his rant.

"Fondness! Fondness!" Talmadge was becoming increasingly enraged as he cast the poker back preparing to hurl it toward Imogen.

"Please, Talmadge do not wish me any harm. The fondness I have for you goes deeper and far greater than love. I like and respect you. That alone should cause you to put down that weapon before undo harm at your hands comes my way."

"Your allegiance my dear appears to be to none other than yourself! You know I am fully aware of your affections for Archibald. He is a scoundrel!"

"Talmadge, you of all people have repeatedly said we must seize that which brings us the greatest joy. Having you both in my life brings me satisfaction."

Talmadge was becoming impatient. "I wonder what my place *is* in your life? Perhaps you would do best without me?"

"No, no. If I fear anything at all, I fear losing you. Ours is an abiding love."

Imogen's movements became more restless as she tossed and turned trying to extricate herself from the images interrupting her sleep. She heard a knocking sound but disregarded it until it became more intense. Slowly, she opened her eyes grateful to have awakened from the unpleasant dream. She felt anxious and conscious of her heart's rapid beat, both trying to remember and forget what transpired as she slept. She looked up to see Patti drawing back the draperies and preparing her toilette.

"There ye be, mum. I've a nice mornin' meal fer ye. Let me help ye get ready for yer day. It looks to be a fine one, yes indeed," announced Patti as she made her way to Imogen's bedside.

Imogen looked at Patti and wished she felt the same sense of calm the girl did as she went about her daily routines. *I know not how fine the day will be but I will face it none the same,* thought Imogen as she sat straight up, stepped from her bed and rallied herself to accept her widowhood. *It is 'time to till the soil' as my mother often said,* thought Imogen. *It is time to cultivate a new chapter in my life. But how do I turn the page on all that is past?*

Chapter Sixteen

In solitude, where we are least alone.
—Lord Byron

Imogen brushed aside a small cluster of leaves gathered along the base of Talmadge's tombstone as she prepared to lay a spray of carefully selected flowers atop his grave. She admired her choices for the aromatic bouquet of calla lilies, roses and carnations, which she had enhanced with wisps of leather leaf and eucalyptus greens. *Yes, Talmadge would be pleased with my selection,* she mused.

Lending a blind eye to her conduct, she had carefully thought through the symbolism behind the medley, especially the calla lilies, which spoke to marriage and fidelity. She accompanied the cluster of lilies with white roses, a symbol of purity, along with several white carnations representing remembrance. She swept her hand over the fragrant tributes to Talmadge as though such action would serve to ease her conscience and dismiss any indiscretions on her part regarding her wedding vows.

After Calvin prepared the cabriolet for Imogen's outing, she chose to drive herself on her pilgrimage to Rock Creek Cemetery. She preferred to walk its grounds in solitude and reflect on the residents who had been laid to rest. She looked about her at the monuments, mausoleums, sculptures and markers adorning the burial sites. They rose like otherworldly structures among groves of trees. She read the names, birth and death dates and the many tributes etched on the memorial stones. *Mothers, fathers, and children all gone to eternal life,* she noted. She shook her head and once again stroked her hand over the lush bouquet on Talmadge's grave. Many of the nearby graves were also embellished with flowers. *Lovely remembrances placed by loved ones missing their departed,* she lamented. *It is as though I am in a garden, albeit a garden of the dead.*

She lifted her eyes to Talmadge's grave marker and read the inscription carved into the light gray stone: "Though he sleeps, his memory doth live." She felt a tear come to her eye but quickly rejected it with a swipe of her glove. Theirs had been at times a tumultuous relationship, more of her doing than his. He loved her so intensely that he forgave her transgressions though they hurt him deeply. And, ultimately, Archibald had the final revenge. *Code, code, code. How can men of intelligence abide a code that results in the maiming or death of another? Honor, honor, honor. What honor is there in snuffing out a life? Men have got it all wrong and leave us, the women, to suffer the aftermath of their actions.* She shook her head attempting to dismantle thoughts that would neither sooth her now nor change the outcome before her.

She wanted to be free from the weight of the angry thoughts that rushed over her like a dark wave hell-bent on keeping her down. Experience taught her that wounds, whether old or new, fester when not allowed to heal. She wanted desperately to heal yet, thus far, time had not served her well. *I shall have to find a way back to happiness. Perhaps it is time to let forgiveness be my guide and exonerate Archibald for his actions. Heaven knows the courts have, so why not I? Who am I to beleaguer my judgment upon him? Who after all is Archibald? Is he but what I choose to see?* She was perplexed by the dichotomy between herself and Archibald. *Or perhaps,* she thought, *are we of the same ilk? Cut from the same cloth? I am so confused and torn. Perhaps I should continue my estrangement from him? What shall I do, what shall I do?* She looked to the sky for guidance.

Once again she found herself in conflict with herself. As she wrestled with the confusion in her mind, she slowly walked to the bench she had commissioned to be placed near Talmadge's grave. She read the words inscribed in the dark gray stone. *"Forever in my heart and the air I breathe."* She took in a deep breath. The bench and its inscription were her way of keeping him immortalized. *Ours was not a perfect union*, she mused. *Few are. Would you not agree Talmadge?* She sighed. She knew her lasting tribute to her husband was cast with sincerity however, she was not so certain about the candor she might employ if she chose to meet with Archibald. *Talmadge, I always thought my time with you was unlimited. Alas, I now see it was folly for me to believe so.*

A series of words from Ecclesiastes 3 filtered through her head — 'For everything there is a season, and a time for every matter under heaven' — before she settled herself on the memorial bench, looked to the sky and spoke aloud.

"I know I failed you in many ways Talmadge but I too was a victim of sorts, albeit a victim of my own doing. How can I possibly be held responsible for the effect I have on men and the advances they make upon me? I am not always so able to repel them. Must I not be excused for that?" Her thoughts hummed about her like a swarm of impatient gnats waiting to bite an unsuspecting victim. She swatted at the empty air as she considered her next course of action.

A sudden breeze approached her back placing a brief, chilling puff of air upon her exposed neck. The sensation caught her off guard. "Is that you Talmadge come to scold me? I assure you I have endured enough scolding from others. Would you believe there are those who say I wished you dead? How absurd and what a wretched thing to say! Never would I wish you gone from my life. Leave it to the jealous old biddies to make such vile statements about me. I shall ignore their insults and find a way to go on without you for I must," Imogen declared as she shifted to a more comfortable position on the bench.

Tears once again welled in her eyes as a story published about the composer Beethoven's letters to his beloved came to her mind. She had taken to heart the composer's heartfelt words, and began to recite portions of one letter to the best of her memory: "What tearful longings for you…Oh continue to love me…never misjudge the most faithful heart of your beloved. Ever thine. Ever mine. Ever ours."

"How have we come to this? How have I?" Imogen sniffled and reached for Talmadge's handkerchief. She was thankful that no one had intruded upon the privacy of her visit to her husband's grave. *For now,* she silently mused, *I shall sit alone and take in the quiet around me. It is peaceful here and sometimes alone is the best company.*

Chapter Seventeen

As Imogen entered the foyer, there was no mistaking the person before her. Although her visitor's head was bent down and loosely covered with a soft hood, Imogen fully recognized the ginger-colored locks that encircled the woman's décolletage and rested along her collarbone. *Why would Virginia Sterling have the audacity to cast her shadow on my doorstep? There can be no good to come of her visit,* Imogen thought as she shimmied her body to ready her countenance for their encounter.

Since the fateful day when Talmadge lost his life, Imogen had worked diligently to build a fortress about herself at Woodholme. She was comforted in the plush surroundings they had created together and felt no immediate need to change her circumstances. In recent days, she had gladly swept away Archibald's attempted intrusions on her period of grieving for she was in no mood to draw forth the wagging tongues of her critics. Her dalliances with Archibald had become more than a whisper among her social circle, although those closest to her knew better than to breathe a word of reprimand her direction if they wished to remain in her good graces. It seemed with Talmadge gone, the rumor mill felt exceedingly obliged and free to spin yarns about her reputation. She knew she certainly was not the first of her married peers to engage in a relationship with one of the opposite gender that offered benefits beyond congeniality. *Let he who is without sin, cast the first stone,* Imogen mused as she paraphrased a passage from the Bible.

Upon hearing Imogen's footsteps, Virginia raised her head in greeting. Imogen's ebony satin gown shimmered as sunlight from the transom window over the doorframe cast soft beams across the cloth. As Virginia pulled back the hood covering her hair, Imogen had to admit there was no question that Virginia's beauty had not faded, as was the fate of many matrons. Her sense of style served her well, making her ever popular with the City of Washington's social elite. Both facts did much to irritate Imogen who felt in competition with her upon their first meeting despite the fact that Virginia was her senior. Only six years separated the two. Imogen was two score, while Virginia was two score and six. Still, curiosity about her visit prompted her to be respectful and invite her to sit in the drawing room. Initially, no words were exchanged, only an acknowledgment with a nod of their heads, as Imogen held forth her hand and motioned for Virginia to follow.

As they entered the drawing room, Imogen took a seat on one of a pair of tufted divans covered in a deep purple shade of cotton velvet. The divans sat opposite one another in the spacious room. Patti, who had just completed plumping several down-filled cushions, looked to her mistress who tartly announced, "There is no need to fuss." Then, with one wave of her hand promptly dismissed her from the room. As Patti exited, Imogen motioned for Virginia to take a seat opposite her but Virginia elected to stand as she began to speak.

"You see Imogen, I have lost him too. You know he was my first love. Perhaps I should spare you that detail of my life but I think it is important that you know," Virginia shared with little expression. She held her place, her posture erect as she awaited Imogen's response.

"Seriously? Have you truly come calling to pay your respects or to unburden yourself from a lifetime of regret for letting one so important to you slip away? Or, perhaps you wish to unleash some additional level of trauma upon me? Do you feel that I have not suffered enough with the loss of my husband, which remains so fresh a stain on my soul?" Imogen was trying to project the best version of herself that she could muster but her efforts were becoming a struggle.

She took the handkerchief she held in her hand and gently dabbed at the tears beginning to spill down her cheeks. Like the handkerchief that accompanied her to the cemetery, it was one of Talmadge's linens, which bore his monogram. Since his passing, its use comforted her and lent a reminder of his scent. Despite numerous washings the citrusy fragrance of his favorite cologne, Caswell Number Six, never seemed to fully dissipate the soft fibers of the cloth. It was one of Caswell-Massey's most invigorating scents with an aromatic blend of orange blossom, bergamot and rosemary. Imogen would periodically raise the linen to her face and breathe in the fresh, familiar scent that was as much his signature as was his written mark.

She was determined to gather her senses. *How can I lay bare my emotions like this with this woman? I must regain my own good senses,* Imogen pondered as she carefully folded Talmadge's handkerchief and held it securely in her hand.

"I have no ill intent I assure you," Virginia emphasized. "I have spent the time since word reached me of Talmadge's passing pondering the actions I should take. For me, as with many who remember their first love, there is a sense of 'what if?' What if things had taken a different direction? What if we had not gone our separate ways? There are so many questions that keep one longing for what might have been and with that comes the regret of not knowing."

"So, it appears we both have a significant sense of loss? Is that what you wish to convey to me or again, are you merely here to unburden your sorry soul?"

"I wish I clearly knew what is in my heart. I would like to think that I come to you merely to say that whatever the future may bring, we were both fortunate to have had such a man in our lives."

"Why are you sounding so mysterious? What do you mean about the future? Are you now proclaiming yourself a soothsayer ready to spill forth revelations of what lies ahead? You best be mindful for there are those who would call you a witch. Perhaps it is time you release the bonds holding you back with your list of 'what ifs' and face the world in all your deceitful glory. Lies simply beget more lies. We all have secrets. Perhaps it would behoove you to search your soul for the truth and lay it out now to simplify your life?"

"I have heard it spoken about you," Virginia began, and then thinking better of it left her statement unfinished.

"Go on," retorted Imogen. "Do not let me hold you back from the slur you wish to cast my direction. If you are referring to anything that Tillie woman has attributed to me you must remember such allegations are not fact! She writes whatever she wants to sell the newspaper. The more scandalous the story the better! I cannot help that I have drawn her interest." Imogen was livid to think Tillie Tattler continued to supply her loyal readers with rumors purportedly associated with her. *Has she no shame to throw aspersions on a widow?*

Virginia looked at Imogen's expression. Her raised eyebrow said all there was needed to say. She realized she was on tenuous ground at best and should most likely take her leave. Had it been folly for her to face Talmadge's widow? *What was I thinking? How could I possibly have thought Imogen would welcome me and see me as a true mourner with respectful thoughts on her behalf? No, she sees me as nothing more than a woman scorned and an interloper on the relationship she built with her husband. There is little more to be said at this juncture. Time will lend its hand in what comes to be.*

"I fear I have only made things worse between us. That was not my intent. I think it best if I leave for now and perhaps in time we will be able to find a common ground on which to meet."

"This is perhaps the wisest thing that has been uttered from your mouth since you arrived. I bid you good day."

Imogen's words carried a sharp edge. Virginia knew to say no more. She equally knew that secrets always had a way of revealing themselves and hers would hold no different outcome.

Virginia stepped into her carriage and settled in her seat as the horse drew her carriage away from Woodholme. She reached into the pocket of her cape and removed a letter from the small satchel that rested there. It had come to her unexpectedly just days before. Upon receipt, she immediately recognized the seal. The deep crimson shade of sealing wax was stamped with the crest of a notable family whose name she knew well. A large 'C' was centered in a heraldic shield. It was without a doubt from the Carlyle family of London.

She had anticipated sharing its contents with Imogen. Had their visit taken on a warmer tone she would have been inclined to do so. She was surprised to receive a letter from Frederick Carlyle. His words stirred a memory in her that brought much regret and pain. She was speechless as she read his letter and learned that what she thought had been forever sealed in secrecy, was secret no more.

Chapter Eighteen

Upon Talmadge's passing, Imogen had assigned herself the burden of being the reigning 'keeper of the flame' of his memory. She felt duty bound to regale him in the presence of her social circle, though most suspected Archibald's attention's toward her were never pure and had ultimately resulted in Talmadge's death. *Perhaps it is guilt, which taunts me? If so, I shall not allow that to be my guide,* she rationalized.

She was feeling the urge to put an end to the words of adoration she felt compelled to spew about Talmadge, although she was periodically reminded of Winston Cromley's declaration that it was her name Talmadge uttered before all sound was snuffed from his lips. Such knowledge led to the pangs of guilt thwarting her resolve to move forward. She was determined to squelch the flames of gossip that spun together in guarded whispers among her lady friends, like the rising steam from a witch's cauldron. The time had come to release the weight of the torch she carried for Talmadge. It was a symbol of the past, which left her powerless to provide the comfort and warmth she craved. *I must cast off the vestiges of the past and return to that, which brings me pleasure today.*

Her selection of clothing for the day befitted the subdued mood she chose to reflect. Her gown was of the purist shade of petal pink –a soft blush, which cast a subtle, rosy glow about her visage. She enjoyed the demure status the delicate chiffon fabric provided in sharp contrast to the widow's weeds she had donned for far too long. Her period of mourning may not have passed but she cared not what others thought. She felt no obligation to observe such arbitrary customs, which she deemed archaic at best. *Black clothing does nothing to lift my mood. I shan't wear it another day!* Imogen declared with great gusto.

She feared she would now and forever be known as the Widow of Woodholme, the sad proprietor of a large manor filled with costly possessions but empty of the trappings that spoke of love and belonging. She was more than receptive to abandoning the worthlessness spinning an isolating cocoon around her. *No, I will no longer languish in this role as Mistress of Woodholme. Today is my day. Today I pledge to free myself from this numbness that consumes my mind and limbs.*

No sooner had her words left her lips than Archibald appeared in the doorway. The decorative bullion fringe bordering the edges of the portières adorning the drawing room's entryway graced the shoulder of his waistcoat like an officer's epaulet.

"Please forgive me not only for my unannounced return to Woodholme but, my lovely, for the sadness I have placed upon your countenance."

Imogen was appalled. She stood rigid and frozen in place like a marble monument to a time in the recent past when she was a wife, not a widow. *How can he enter my home, this sacred place I shared with Talmadge, and perform as though all can be forgiven? His audacity infuriates me!*

"Forgive you?" Imogen shouted so loudly she thought her lungs might burst. "You speak of forgiveness? What? For you, who have so brutally slain my husband? Why, for you to expect a shred of consideration from me is the folly of a fool!"

"My dear Imogen. There is no need for a tart tongue. You are a wise woman and well aware that Talmadge and I had no other solution to settle our differences. We merely administered an honor code by which we live. Why, by its very tradition, it has served us well to have those who have wronged us atone for their misdoings. A tradition, I remind you, that the great bard himself acknowledged when he lent to Brutus the phrase, 'Slaying is the word; it is a deed in fashion.' How can you chastise me for merely following a code that has existed throughout history? Men have been throwing down the gauntlet for centuries to avenge their differences. Surely, you are amenable to an act upon which your husband was most agreeable?" Archibald held his position in the doorway with much hesitation about approaching Imogen who appeared ready to do battle with him.

She held back her fists fearing they might not wield the leverage she desired to bring him down. She had been taught to use words, not force, to effect influence on others. *I must muster all efficiencies of vocabulary if I am to come to terms with Archibald's conduct.* Imogen took a deep breath before she began to speak. "You should have used your good senses. Could you find no other manner of reconciliation? With honor as your unwavering guidepost you have stripped me of my title as wife, leaving me to wallow in widowhood!"

"I found this act to be my only recourse to repair the injustices slung at me time and again by Talmadge. I guess I was sorely mistaken to think you would find me virtuous and worthy of your affections."

"Virtuous? You taunted and incited Talmadge to a duel. You have an assassin's heart. You were fully aware that day that your skill with pistols far outweighed that of his. Sometimes it is as if I were with you holding the weapon that took him down. I feel his blood is on my hands as well as yours."

"Does that bring you comfort to think we were aligned in our actions?"

"What a twisted thing to say to me. No, there is no comfort in such thoughts. I never wished my husband dead!"

"My dear Imogen, you know I have great affection for you. Can we not come to terms that will be agreeable to us both?"

"Terms? Under what conditions do you think I would forgive you? You are unworthy of my affection, let alone my love and devotion. Your apology does little to remedy the pain you have inflicted."

"But you must understand that this is the way of gentlemen. We have our honor to uphold. Even the court of law has acquitted me. Why must you remain so steadfast in holding me guilty of an act not deemed a crime by our peers?"

"Gentlemen! Ha! A gentleman would not resort to harm but instead settle his differences with words and a courteous bow to appease his challenger. You could have but struck Talmadge across the face to hold your honor in tact. There was by no means reason enough to settle your dispute by force. I find your act and you repulsive!"

"The date, time, and place had been set. There was no turning back from our mutually agreed arrangements."

"The thought of calling it a draw never crossed your mind? And, why pistols? He may have been spared had your weapon of death been a sword."

"We were obliged to use the weapons chosen by our seconds and you are well aware that neither of us were skilled in parrying. And, sadly in Talmadge's case, he was no better at brandishing a pistol than he was at wielding a pen."

"There you go, continuing to slander his good name and reputation. How dare you poke fun at such a dire time in my life."

"Imogen, look at me. The person I am and have always been has not changed. You have never questioned my motives and I ask that you refrain from doing so now. It's time for you to put this to the past."

Imogen drew in a deep breath. Her options had narrowed to few. One thing about which she felt certain, she would neither languish in the loss of her husband nor be forced to assume the role of a lonely dowager. *Oh, why am I so confused? This man muddles my mind. I need a sign from the heavens to guide me or, at best, release me from the grief that has consumed my days.*

Archibald's charm surpassed her capacity to deny him. He was a picture of good health and style. *Any woman would be grateful to have his attention, so why am I so hesitant to renew that which gave me much pleasure while Talmadge was alive?* Imogen was torn by her conflicting thoughts. Remorse threatened to capsize her emotions as she questioned her motives. *How might I honor Talmadge's memory yet satisfy my own needs?*

The tangled web of thoughts she was spinning for herself were suddenly silenced by the sound of a knock at the manse's front door. Imogen could hear voices, which ceased as her servant approached the drawing room's doorway.

"Excuse me mum, there be a man 'ere who's wantin' to see ye. Says 'is name is Mr. Frye, Mr. Sawyer Frye, that is. Should I be showin' 'im in?"

"Give me a moment Patti. In the meantime, please show Mr. Frye to Mr. Simmonds' study and inform him that I will be along shortly."

Patti gave an acknowledging dip of her knees as she turned to follow her mistress's orders.

As Patti took her leave to attend to Woodholme's latest arrival, Imogen turned her attention to Archibald. She recalled the words she would have said to her husband if she had known he had not only been challenged by Archibald but that he was determined to accept his challenge. *My darling, you must cast off his aspersions as nothing more than the ravings of a dissatisfied soul.* Her unspoken words lingered across her lips. Yet, such recurring thoughts were moot for she realized neither of the men would have come to a mutually satisfying resolution, for neither would apologize nor forgive the other. Their opinions of one another had reached an unavoidable stalemate, one that would end in a draw of weapons.

"Archibald, your insistence that the duel was a necessity has led us to this unforgiveable outcome. For you, it meant you would maintain your rank in society as a virtuous gentleman. However, as it has turned out, I am left a widow with a man before me who thinks I must let bygones be bygones and allow the memories of my life with Talmadge to fade away like the writings on a sundrenched piece of parchment. I insist that you become well aware that there exists in my heart a place that will never heal." Imogen's eyes began to well with tears, which she promptly stopped as she drew her shoulders up and regained her composure. "I am but a withered woman and I ask that you take leave of my presence."

"Why would I forsake you at this time when the consolation from a friend seems so necessary to your happiness, your perseverance?"

"Because I so beg your compliance with my request, which a true gentleman would neither question nor deny."

"Then perhaps I must proclaim to be neither a gentleman nor the cad you make me out to be. Why yes, I can see the headlines now, '**The Withered Widow of Woodholme Languishes in Her Garden of Despair**,'" proclaimed Archibald as he shimmied his body to replicate a withering bloom. Perhaps I should rescue you from your garden of despair. In the words of Hosea 2:14, "Therefore, behold, I will allure her, and bring her into the wilderness, and speak comfortably to her."

"If your words are meant to humor me in some way, please know they do not. You are poking fun at me at a very delicate time in my life," sniffled Imogen. It is at the very minimum refreshing to witness your nod to religion.

And, if you truly wanted to win back my favor you would consider a topic, which you know is of great importance to me."

"Please do not tell me you are going to bring slavery into our conversation at this time. That topic has no place here."

"It assuredly has a place. Look at your own home. Look at your house servant Harrison. You could release him from servitude in your home and let him live as a free man. Why are you in opposition to this?"

"Harrison lives a very good life in my home."

"According to you. If he felt free to tell you his true feelings, you would hear a different story, of that I am certain. I suggest you explore your conscience, if it can be found. There was a time when you drew me into your company indicating you wanted to discuss ways to underwrite my work on this topic."

"Another example of wanting to get into your good graces, so to speak," said Archibald with a devilish expression. "Actually, I am certain Harrison appreciates the benefits he gains from the good charity he receives in my home."

"Ah, so you consider yourself a benevolent master. Next, you will tell me you expect adulation for the inferiority and dependence you impose upon him and the rest of those on your land," Imogen said with frustration testing her nerves.

"Yes, perhaps you are correct. I am performing a kindly service with harm to none."

"Cruelty comes in many forms, Archibald. You best take time to assess that which you think to be so kindly."

"It appears our conversation has met an impasse. You know my opinion and it shall not be changed. It is my opinion that you are fighting an uphill battle that will not soon be won."

"Why are you such a skeptic? It is not an admirable trait," Imogen implored.

"I am not so much a skeptic as a realist. It might serve you well to adopt my viewpoint. You will be wasting far less of your time if you do."

Archibald's opposing views only served to sharpen Imogen's resolve to continue to persuade and recruit others to join her committee's cause. She knew she should never have broached the subject in her emotional state but she wanted to quell Archibald's teasing tone about her widowhood.

"My hope is that on the morrow you will have a change of heart and come to see the rationale behind all that has occurred," Archibald nearly begged as he reached a hand to Imogen, which she unequivocally declined, although she felt an unexpected tug at her heart.

Without motion, she tried to shake away the feelings attempting to thwart her resolve to shed Archibald from her life. *I must dismiss this hold he has on my emotions and not allow him to cast a spell over me. Why, oh why, am I drawn to him still? I must maintain a grip on my good senses!*

"Why are you so pompously certain that one day will make a difference in my feelings? You speak of hope. What a word, for it carries with it no plan, no direction, only an idealized vision of something desired and perhaps never to be accomplished. I cannot dwell another minute on your hopes. Silencing our words at this time would best suit us both. I have a guest to whom I must attend and therefore bid you good day."

Imogen reached for the skirt of her gown. Lifting it slightly to offer her feet freedom of movement, she swept it back then forward as though whisking Archibald and his aura from the room. With her head held high she left him standing alone as she walked to Talmadge's study to see who awaited her behind the closed doors.

Chapter Nineteen

As she pushed open the heavily carved double mahogany doors to Talmadge's study she was pleasantly surprised by the vision before her. She gave him an abbreviated nod in greeting before she spoke.

"Mr. Frye, I presume."

"Indeed. It is a great pleasure to be in your presence Mrs. Simmonds."

Imogen was impressed with his polished English accent. It lent itself to the tone of one with a refined upbringing as did his attire and well-kept, wavy brown hair. Like a cavern of darkness, his deep brown eyes added a depth of intrigue as she watched him study her face. The hint of a smile lent an upward arch to the sides of his mouth as he made his observations. Imogen was caught off guard by his perusal. She felt transparent as his dark eyes roved downward and returned upward to meet her gaze, leaving her blind to interrupting his intentions.

"I suppose I shall say thank you to that, however I am curious about your visit. If I may be so direct, who are you and what do you want?"

Mr. Frye smiled, revealing a dimple on his lower right cheek, which did not escape her gaze. There was a playful nature about him, which drew her attention. He admired her beauty and was equally enticed by her desire to get to the point of his call on her residence.

"I am Sawyer Frye," he stated with conviction.

"Of that I am fully aware, as you surely are aware, and are merely having some fun at my expense. I wonder Mr. Frye, what is your purpose here?"

"I apologize for any hesitation. I was not certain that your staff announced my name so I thought it proper for me to do so. Merely a formality on my part, I assure you."

"Well then, it seems an apology from me is in order, although I did greet you by your name. That said, there is no excuse for my rudeness, but I have had a rather harrowing time of late for my husband is recently deceased."

As the words slipped from her tongue, she wondered what brought her to reveal something so personal to a perfect stranger. Sawyer's reaction caught her attention. He seemed unusually affected by the news. *Is it possible he knew Talmadge? Why has the look of shock consumed his demeanor?*

"He is deceased? Oh my goodness, no. I must say I am caught off guard with this alarming news. Allow me to express my most sincere condolences. I was completely unaware. I only recently arrived from the United Kingdom and such news had not crossed my path. In fact, your husband was the one that encouraged me to come to America and pursue my journalism career. I was so in hopes of meeting with him and perhaps continuing to hone my skills under his tutelage."

"How did you meet? It is odd that your name never arose in my conversations with him. And, please allow me to say that I do not mean that in a callous way. I fear my ability to grasp the proper words has escaped me this morn."

"Think nothing of it. I fully understand. Perhaps I should take my leave. I have arrived unannounced at a difficult time."

"I would ask you not to do so. I would like to learn more about your friendship with my late husband. Talmadge always had an eye for talent, especially when it came to writing," Imogen offered as she gestured for him to have a seat on a nearby leather wing chair.

Being in Sawyer Frye's presence had leavened her mood. *He has an air about him that I find both comforting and quite pleasant to view*, she pondered. *And, considering my current circumstances with the burden of a newspaper to run, he might be the answer to filling the void of managing editor vacated when Gibson Harris was promoted to Talmadge's editor-in-chief position. Yes, I think it very wise of me to consider the option suddenly upon me. On the heels of Talmadge's death, perhaps this Sawyer Frye is a gift from the heavens.*

"So, might I ask? What is your preference as to how you are called? Do you prefer Sawyer or, is there perhaps another name to which you prefer to respond?"

"It actually is quite interesting that you would pose that question to me. There is another name by which I am known."

"Well, cease the mystery and share that name at once," Imogen nearly demanded as her curiosity and short temper got the most of her. "Again, I apologize for my tone. I have had a difficult start to my day and should not lay the burden of that on you. So, this other name?"

"Duke."

"Excuse me? What is that you say? Duke?"

"You have that quite right, Mrs. Simmonds."

"And how is it that you have come about that title?"

"I should say it is an interesting story to be sure."

"Well then, spill it out," Imogen ordered, still unable to gain control over her surly mood.

"Perhaps we should become more acquainted before I share the innermost details of my life. Since Mr. Simmonds held close to his vest information about me, perhaps I should maintain a similar stance and hold in close reserve such knowledge. What say you?"

Imogen shook her head, not to disagree or to reject his proposal but to gain a few moments to study his demeanor, which she was finding intrigued her to her core. She sensed a refreshing playfulness in Sawyer's style and sought to pursue it further.

"Am I to understand from the shake of your head that our conversation has come to an untimely end?"

"If you are to understand anything, it is that I shall not be made a fool. You appear to enjoy taunting me like one would tease a cat with a fine piece of herring. I have asked a simple question about the royal title you espouse to hold. It seems the least you could do is explain how this came to be?" As she continued to study his face, she felt she could bathe herself in his smile.

"I assure you, I mean no harm," Sawyer replied, trying to placate her vacillating disposition.

"Well then, the title I shall use to address you for now will be Mr. Frye until you care to divulge your history in regard to being addressed as 'Duke.'"

"With all due respect, your husband and I were accustomed to calling one another by our first names. I would be most pleased if you would do so as well, if that is not too forward of me to request?"

"I think perhaps I shall need some time to reflect on how you and I shall address one another until we have had more time to become better acquainted. For now, we will maintain the formality of our surnames. That said, in the meantime, I would like to receive some samples of your work. With the passing of Mr. Simmonds, I find myself as publisher responsible for overseeing his newspaper. He was quite devoted to *The Washington Inquirer* and I would like to see it continue to flourish, which is no small matter with competition from other publications. The ongoing goal of the newspaper, first and foremost, is to remain afloat. Secondly, we wish to rival the *Saturday Evening Post's* weekly newspaper that launched in August, which is no small task for any print media. Pardon my expression, but I will be damned if its owners Atkinson and Alexander will drive *The Inquirer* out of business. Georgetown's *Metropolitan* and the *Centinel of Liberty* are also ongoing threats to our readership."

"Additionally, I have moved *The Inquirer's* managing editor to the position of editor-in-chief. Gibson Harris is his name, however he answers to 'Gibs.'" Imogen watched as Sawyer listened intently to the information she shared. "I will need to find a replacement for Gibs."

"Without appearing presumptuous, I have samples of my work with me," Sawyer said as he reached for his valise and extracted several papers, which he presented to Imogen.

"Ah, a man who is prepared is always a refreshing sight," noted Imogen as she nearly cooed her reply. Her attraction to Sawyer was softening her mood and titillating her spirit. *His mere presence is the tonic I have needed since Talmadge's passing and the absence of Archibald.* She mused, *I can only hope his writing is suitable to the standards Talmadge set in place at The Inquirer.*

As Imogen read the articles with Sawyer's byline she was impressed with the felicity and fluency of his writing. His skill with words captured her attention and engaged her to know more. She smiled as she imagined how his talent would be a welcomed addition to *The Inquirer* and how refreshing it would be to frequent more time with him.

"Your writing is superb! I am most impressed. Please do not think my actions hasty but I would like to offer you the position of managing editor, which will of course require you to not only assign stories but also to cover the latest news in Georgetown and the City of Washington. How does that sound to you?"

"I am honored by the dispatch to which you present this offer to me. There will be the matter of salary to discuss and I must secure lodging. I understand there are several boarding houses from which to choose. I shall look into that straight away."

"By all means. I assure you, the offer will be most agreeable for us both. Let us talk the terms of your employ on the morrow. That will give sufficient time for me to notify Gibs and perhaps have the two of you meet. And, on the matter of lodging, there are several rooms above *The Inquirer's* newsroom, which I can make available to you. There is a fireplace in the main room with ample furnishings among the other rooms to suit your needs."

Without awaiting a response, Imogen pulled open the top drawer in Talmadge's desk, removed a key and placed it in Sawyer's hand.

"Here, I shall not take no for an answer," Imogen smiled. "Consider the lodging part of your compensation."

Sawyer was not wont to deny Imogen her offer of lodging for fear she would rescind her offer of employment.

"Thank you. You are most generous," he replied. *She is certainly an interesting woman*, thought Sawyer as he bowed to leave. *I wonder what other offers she has on the horizon?*

Chapter Twenty

Imogen was quite pleased with herself for envisaging the idea of Sawyer working for *The Washington Inquirer*. She felt he would add the youthful presence the paper was lacking and his placement there would also afford her the opportunity to keep him close at hand. Gibs informed her that Sawyer was settling in quite nicely as managing editor. It had been only two weeks past when he assumed his position however, that had given Imogen ample time to rendezvous with him at the office and establish a growing attraction, which had become mutually agreeable.

"Patti!" Imogen called out in a tone the girl had come to recognize whenever her mistress was determined to see something through without hesitation. "Patti!"

As Patti entered the drawing room, she saw that her mistress had dressed for an outing without her aid. *Perhaps she got one o' the other girls to 'elp lace her. She must be in a 'urry like a bee's got in her drawers!* Patti silently reasoned.

Imogen's lavender chemise gown flowed with tiny wisps of pale pink petals scattered about its skirt. She wore a pair of her favorite briolette earrings. The 15-carat amethyst drops where in the softest shade of lilac and their facets reflected the light from the morning sun emanating through the drawing room's windows. Her aubergine velvet cape lay on a nearby settee waiting for assistance to don it and be on her way. Patti observed her mistress's determined face. Those who did not know her well might term her expression stern but Patti was not unnerved. She had observed the very same look on the occasions when her mistress had a mission to complete to which her mind was firmly set.

"Oh, there you are. I shall be going to the office for a few hours. Please inform Calvin and have him bring the carriage round for me posthaste. I should like to leave shortly. And Patti, should visitors come calling, have them leave a card and I shall see to them at a later time. Also, it is of no one's concern as to where I am, so you may keep a tight lip on my whereabouts."

Patti was quite accustomed to Imogen's secretiveness. She was actually surprised to be told her destination. *The newspaper's certainly been more than a wee bit on 'er mind e'er since Mr. Simmonds' passin',* Patti mused. *I wonder what has 'er goin' there today? Seems like a man would be better suited to oversee that business if ye ask me but, then again, none of it be me business and nobody's asked me, of that I be sure. Oh, Saints preserve us! Maybe it be a man that draws her there?*

"Patti. I am in need of some reading material and have reserved a book at Davis & Force's bookstore. The title is *Pride and Prejudice* by Jane Austen. You know the shop on Pennsylvania Avenue? It is not far from Center Market and next to Brown's Indian Queen Hotel, which is somewhat between the President's House and the Capitol. You should have no trouble finding it. While I am out, please make your way there and retrieve the book for me. You might also find time to select some fresh produce at the market."

Imogen tilted her head toward her cape indicating to Patti that she needed to assist her. As soon as the outer garment was correctly placed, Patti scuttled away toward the back of the manse and exited to the stables at the rear of the property to deliver orders to Calvin that the carriage was needed.

Sawyer was fully engaged discussing an article at his desk with Gibs when Imogen entered the newsroom. She was glad Gibs accepted the position of editor-in-chief and pleased he agreed that Sawyer was the perfect candidate to assume the position of managing editor. Imogen knew Gibs would be an outstanding mentor for Sawyer.

She continued her promenade in Sawyer's direction. She bid Gibs hello and was pleased to see him gather several pieces of paper and exit the room. *A wise man,* Imogen chuckled to herself. She was well aware of the whispers that circled the newspaper and beyond its walls about her newfound *friendship* with her young, handsome managing editor.

Imogen was not dismayed by such banter. She had established a lifestyle that suited her needs, both physically and emotionally, with an emphasis on her physical needs, which were sated by her lust for the men in her life.

Her coterie of loyal friends although few, served her well and rarely, if ever, questioned her rationale. For that she was grateful. Even when vestiges of her past filtered into conversations, her circle of friends knew better than to dwell on Talmadge's passing, even though many wondered if Archibald would return to her companionship. Now, however, their loyalty was sure to be tested whenever she appeared on the arm of Sawyer Frye.

The title of duke suited him well although his link to nobility was fictional at best. His stature, erect posture, and gait garnered the attention typically attributed to one of hereditary peerage. His peers enjoyed the fact that he found no folly in answering to the sobriquet "Duke" and, actually, he rather enjoyed the moniker. Imogen enjoyed his narration of how he acquired his royal title when the two met at City Tavern for a midday meal earlier in the week.

"So, do tell me about your noble name," grinned Imogen anxious to know if heredity played a role in his title.

"I assure you it came about quite casually," noted Sawyer as he lifted a fork full of roasted venison to consume before continuing his tale.

"So, you are without a duchy?" Imogen queried with disappointment mounting.

"Ha," laughed Sawyer. "My dukedom is of the non-royal variety although it holds the name of one of importance. King George III bestowed Arthur Wellesley with the title the 1st Duke of Wellington. I met a peer of Wellesley's brother Richard, named Edward. Edward, out of sheer foolishness, began to call me the Duke of Wellington because he learned that my father's name was Arthur. Since dukes inherit the title from their fathers, Edward thought it was a great way to poke fun my direction."

"Ah then, you are not a member of the peerage?"

"Absolutely not. There is no royal blood running through my veins, at least not to my knowledge. And, I sincerely hope the 1st Duke and any further Dukes of Wellington are not offended by the occasional peer who addresses me as such."

"Perhaps I should call you 'Your Grace,'" laughed Imogen as she stood and curtsied.

"I think Sawyer should be quite sufficient," he smiled wanting to add "my love" to his words for his attraction to Imogen was growing very strong.

Whispers about the handsome young man, who at seven and twenty was Imogen's junior, were becoming more and more prevalent. When she entered a gathering of her lady friends, conversations abruptly halted to a hushed silence. She was well aware of the turn their allegiance was taking and would soon make it well known that she would not tolerate their two-faced behavior. She looked at them and saw the faces of hypocrites. She knew there were those among them whose conduct was no more lily-white than her own. *Must I quote from the good book to stop their campaign to belittle me? Perhaps they need to be reminded of Jesus' words, "He that is without sin among you, let him first cast a stone at her."* Imogen found it most useful to make reference to the Bible whenever she felt a reading from the "Good Book" exonerated her from her behavior. She was determined to withstand her most fervent critics come *'Hell or high water'* as her grandmum would often profess.

"I hoped you would find your way here today," smiled Sawyer as he stood to greet Imogen. She beamed as he put his arms about her waist. "Look at you in this lovely frock, which only enhances the beauty inside it."

Imogen blushed as his adoring words resonated in her mind. He pulled her closer and placed a kiss on each cheek before centering his lips on hers. She embraced the warmth of his lips and welcomed the slip of his tongue as it made its way into her mouth. Their relationship had moved quite swiftly much to her great pleasure. His first advances had happened late one afternoon when they were alone in the newsroom. Sawyer thanked her for hiring him and praised her abilities to oversee the running of *The Inquirer* since it was a task fairly new to her. He knew she was a bright woman, which intrigued him all the more. *Beauty and a good mind,* he grinned. *I shall have to see if there is room in her heart for another love interest.*

As she held several pages in her hand preparing to read them through, Sawyer put his hand on hers, tilting the pages toward the oil lamp to gain better light. She looked at him questioningly then smiled, which was all the encouragement he needed to lean forward and kiss her on the cheek. The two found themselves unable to resist the mounting feelings raging within. Her lack of resistance bade him continue his pursuit of her fancies as he ran his fingers along her neckline then down into the folds of her gown's bodice. She arched her back as his fingers massaged her nipples. He began to place kisses up and down her neck until he released her breasts, cupped them in his hands and suckled them softly.

He returned to her lips, as their kisses became more eager, which led to more bold fondling and the undoing of their garments. Their passion was beyond control. Imogen found the firm surface of Sawyer's desk no deterrent to their lovemaking as he lifted her up to place her on top. Stripped of his trousers, Imogen viewed his body fully ready to engage with hers. He massaged her thighs and spread her legs as he found his ease within her. His thrusts deepened and their bodies writhed in unison to a glorious rhythm that became their own.

Dearest Readers,

It seems this widow is not one withering on the vine like a spent grape. She has taken to a certain duke and he to her. Will this be a royal match? And, what of her other gent? Is he still in the running for her affections? Time will only tell if the duke tires of her or if a worse fate befalls him.

With concern for her lovers,
Tillie Tattler

Chapter Twenty-One

Virginia held Frederick Carlyle's letter in her hand. She could not let it go. The parchment was becoming slightly crumpled with her frequent handling of the missive, which made a crisp crinkling sound at the touch of her fingers as she read his words over and over. *I must go to Talmadge's widow again. I cannot let any more time pass us by.* Virginia sat at her desk and wrote a note, which she sent by courier to Imogen encouraging her to meet with her and hear her out this time. She was grateful to soon receive a reply accepting her request.

As she stepped onto Woodholme's spacious portico, she was pleased to note that the draperies were drawn back, an indication that Imogen was open to letting the outside world back into her domain. With some trepidation, she lifted the brass doorknocker and guided it to make several strikes against its backing plate. Patti greeted her and led her into the drawing room where Imogen stood with a fresh pot of tea on the table before her and two cups waiting to be filled.

"Thank you for agreeing to see me. I hope this is a sign that we can be civil with one another?" Virginia questioned, wondering whether she perhaps should have chosen more suitable words to win Imogen's favor.

"Virginia, it is not as though we are any manner of friends and I cannot guarantee that we shall ever be." Imogen remembered that her conduct toward Virginia on her last visit to Woodholme had more than bordered on rude. She hoped to keep her behavior in rein during this visit but so far Imogen was not warming to her. "But, please have a seat."

"Very well, Imogen. However, that said, I must insist that there will be no manner for us to move forward or reconcile our animosities toward one another without my sharing a truth, which may be difficult for you to hear." Virginia spoke as her nerves threatened to get the better of her.

"Well, it appears that since you have requested another visit with me, your truth cannot be escaped by either of us. It seems it is following you and perhaps at times it haunts you therefore, the truth be told, you have no alternative but to choose to set it free. I hope the hearing of it does not haunt me as well," Imogen warned as she cast a stern look Virginia's way.

"You speak as one with the experience of truth telling. Or, perhaps with you it is withholding the truth, or telling the best version of the truth that you can muster?" Virginia retorted, dead set on holding her ground with Imogen. She would not be made to feel inferior by her.

Imogen was doing her best to hold back her anger but her wrath had become a potent adversary ready to strike with the venom of a poisonous snake. Archibald had on occasion accused her of speaking with a serpent's tongue. Perhaps his assessment was accurate, although Imogen liked to think not. *People just do not understand my motives,* she would muse to herself, as though such thinking would absolve her from any unfortunate outbursts exercised by her tongue.

Virginia removed a piece of parchment from the small satchel that rested in her lap. She felt it best to begin her explanation to Imogen by reading Frederick Carlyle's letter to her. In some ways she felt that putting the telling of her secret under his authority lessened the burden of her part in the charade under which she had long lived.

Imogen listened intently as Virginia read from the letter. She heard the name Savanna and learned that she was a young woman of two and twenty who was adopted by the Carlyles. She learned that the young woman had become aware of the fact that she was not of the Carlyles' blood. She learned that the young woman was given as an infant to the Carlyles and adopted by them. She learned that the young woman was seeking more knowledge of her birth mother, her birth father and her heritage. Imogen shifted in her seat as she endured Virginia's reading wondering what any of the information had to do with her. As Virginia paused, taking a deep breath to continue, Imogen could hold back no longer the questions brewing in her mind.

"Virginia, the question begs to be asked why you are reading this letter to me? How is it that you would have any interest in this young woman named Savanna? Why are the Carlyles finding it necessary to contact you?"

"I will answer you with a very heavy heart. Please prepare yourself for what I am about to share with you." Virginia tucked down her chin, looked at her abdomen and placed her right hand there. She took a deep breath then raised her chin and let out the calming air. "I am the woman who gave birth to Savanna. I am the woman who gave her away."

"And, you think you are the only woman to have done such a thing? Again, why have you requested an audience with me to share this information that is so many years past?"

"I will tell you but this is the part of the story that will not settle well with you."

"Enough delay. Spit it out!" Imogen shouted to the rafters, startling Virginia whose eyes began to flow with tears.

"Talmadge sired Savanna."

"What?" Imogen questioned as she began to stand, then sat again when she realized her legs felt too weak to support her. "This is absolutely incredulous! You said you were here to speak a truth. Why are you lying to me? Have you gone mad?"

"No. I have not gone mad. This can no longer remain a part of my past and, because Frederick tells me that Savanna is soon arriving in the City of Washington, I can no longer hide my past."

"I am not wont to believe a word uttered from your mouth. Talmadge would have told me if his dalliance with you sired a child and he never would have abandoned his responsibilities. He longed for an offspring. Is it because he is no longer here to defend himself or answer to your accusations that you feel free to throw such sludge against his good name?"

"Talmadge did not tell you about the child because he was unaware of my condition. You two were betrothed by the time I learned I was with child so it behooved me to keep silent. No good purpose would have been served to soil our reputations and keep him from marrying you. He made his choice and I made mine."

"A choice you seem to regret, or is that only because that past is knocking on the door of your present?"

"How can you be certain that Talmadge is Savanna's father?"

"Until I married Reginald, Talmadge was the only man with whom I had ever been. He knew me as Virginia Kent and affectionately called me Ginny."

"So, you had us attend the party in your home under faulty pretenses. You cared not that we meet the elite of society. You had the single purpose of rekindling your relationship with Talmadge! How dare you!"

"Of course, it was wonderful to see him again and I wanted to meet his wife. I had heard much about you and wanted to see for myself if the rumors were true. When I later learned of your affection for Archibald, which appears to have bloomed from your meeting at my party, I thought perhaps there was a chance, though remote, that Talmadge would once again turn his affections toward me."

"Alas, I suppose you were quite dismayed to have him turn away from you."

"You were his love, Imogen. Anyone could see that. He was such a good man, a loyal man and very devoted to you no matter your dalliances. Somehow, he turned a blind eye to your indiscretions."

"So, now you judge me? You, the woman who had an affair with my husband and bore a child out of wedlock? How dare you!"

"I will not justify my actions although I do ask you to remember that you and Talmadge were not yet married when he and I were together."

"You knew he was courting me."

"Imogen, I would say we have more in common than we ever knew. Savanna will soon arrive and I am certain she will want to meet with you. We must wrestle with how we tell her about Talmadge?"

"Let us leave that discussion to another day. I have heard all I can stand to hear for now. Let me gather my senses if that is even a possibility," Imogen said, as she gained enough strength to stand and usher Virginia Sterling out of the halls of Woodholme.

Dearest Readers,

It seems Merry Widow has a new reason to rejoice. Sources close to the mistress of you know where, say she may have a child coming her way. Oh, do not dismay. There will be no need for a midwife. This child is arriving full-grown. We shall soon see if she is a beauty to rival the attention usually bestowed on her stepmother? Poor Merry Widow. You may have to share the attention of your suitors.

With reluctant tears of joy,
Tillie Tattler

Chapter Twenty-Two

Alone in Talmadge's study, she felt a presence among the bookcases and other objects filling the handsome space. *Why is peace so hard to achieve?* Imogen mused. *I, and I alone, am responsible for my future, my happy tomorrows.* As she reflected, she felt a puff of air graze her shoulder, then slip away along the length of her neck. She looked toward the window for the source of the breeze but the sash was shut tight. *Now, all I need to do is lose my mind,* she feared as she continued to look about the space for an explanation. Soft and swift came another puff across her shoulder and along her neck like a delicate feather left to float in the air. Then, the ethereal sensation was gone as fast as it had come. *Is that you Talmadge? It would be quite like you to come to my aid with one of your gentle whispers to sooth and guide me.* She felt at once not only shaken but a wave of guilt engulfed her as the sensations threatening to unnerve her danced about in a glorious taunt.

So, is this how you shall extract your revenge upon me for dallying with another? You must know I loved you dearly. I feel I cannot be held responsible for the urgings of my soul. My heart always beat for you, although perhaps not in the purist of ways. I know, I know, we said our vows and promised to forsake all others. Yet, we both know better than that. There are ghosts from your past that have revealed themselves of late. And to think, no heir was born from our union. I know you wished for one, yet it was not to be. And, now I am to meet the child you never knew. I am sad you will never know her and I am so confused and tangled in a quagmire of self- doubt. Come now, Talmadge. Help release me so I suffer no further guilt of conscience, she begged in her one-sided dialogue, hoping he could absolve her from above.

Imogen gathered the skirt of her gown and sashayed around the large mahogany desk that had been the site of so many across-the-desk meetings with aspiring journalists. She slowly swept her hand along the desk's leather top with its gilt tipped edges. *Perhaps Archibald was right that I have arrived at a crossroads. Perhaps it is time,* she pondered. *It is time I put an end to the hurt I am inflicting on myself by keeping Archibald from my life. Am I going mad? I am well sated with Sawyer, so why do thoughts of Archibald come calling? Why can I not be satisfied with one man in my life?*

Determined to follow through on her first instincts no matter how confusing, she took a seat in the burgundy executive desk chair, its leather cushions studded on all sides with brass nailhead trim. She opened the desk's center drawer and removed a piece of parchment bordered in black, a requirement of her station as a widow. She reached forward for the black pen sitting in the fully stocked inkwell and began to compose the words she hoped would bring Archibald to her door and end the estrangement they both suffered, although she was not without worry about the possible outcomes of her action.

Archibald,

Time and considerable conscious efforts have prepared the path necessary for me to consider forgiving you. The weight of your actions, which have forever altered the life I knew, is a burden I must dismiss if I am to find the peaceful life I seek.

I, upon this writing, am requesting an audience with you posthaste. Although we cannot assure that the outcome of our meeting will be mutually acceptable, I feel we must at the very least make an attempt to find a common ground on which we can both agree.

With respect and best regards,
Imogen

She blew a breath of air across the parchment and waited a moment for the ink to dry, then carefully folded her note and placed it in a matching envelope. On the outside she simply wrote, "Mr. Howard." She heated the tip of her stick of sealing wax with the flame from the candle lamp on Talmadge's desk. Its deep rose color dripped into a small puddle on the envelope. A smile with tightened lip came to her face as she elected to forego black wax, which would have been more appropriate for her station as a widow. It gave her pleasure to abstain from the mores she felt so confined her since Talmadge's passing. She waited a moment, then stamped her monogram into the substance and waited for it to harden. She walked to the doorway and reached for the tapestry bell pull to signal Patti who arrived within moments.

"Here, Patti. Take this envelope and deliver it to Mr. Archibald Howard's residence at once," Imogen said as she thrust the envelope toward Patti's outstretched hand. "Let there be no dilly-dallying on your part. Make this your only mission then return to Woodholme. Have Calvin prepare the sulky for you to make your way to Mr. Howard's and back. That will expedite your travel. Oh, and be certain that this envelope is given directly to Mr. Howard and not another soul."

Patti was accustomed to her mistress's demanding tone, which was more prominent when she felt threatened or heavily burdened by an event or person with whom she found no favor. She made a brief curtsy as she exited the room and headed to the rear of the mansion to inform Calvin of her departure. She smiled as she welcomed the thought of riding in the carriage rather than having to advance to Mr. Howard's on foot.

Archibald's houseman answered Patti's knock on the door. He observed the envelope in her hand and immediately reached to retrieve it. Patti drew back her hand and shook her head, which caused the servant to step back.

"I 'ave this 'ere delivery fer Mr. 'oward."

"I see that from the name written on the envelope. I will give it to him."

"Oh, no, ye see. I'm to deliver this to 'im meself. Them is the orders I got directly from me mistress."

"Very well then. Let me see if Mr. Howard is available to see you."

Patti waited only a few moments before Archibald appeared in the hallway.

She recognized him from his visits to Woodholme, which had been significantly reduced in number since the passing of the master of the manse. He smiled as he approached her.

"Ah, Patti it is, if I remember correctly? What brings you to my doorstep?"

"This 'ere envelope is fer ye," Patti offered as she looked down, a sense of reticence overtaking her.

"And from whom might it be?" Archibald inquired with every hope it was from the girl's mistress.

"Why, Mrs. Simmonds sent me with it so I best be assumin' it be from 'er."

"Very good then. Thank you. I shall read it with great fervor. Good day to you."

As the girl took her leave, Archibald looked at his last name written in the familiar and lovely cursive he immediately recognized as Imogen's. He lifted the envelope's flap, removed the parchment and unfolded it to view the contents. His eyes lightened as he read her request to have him call on her. *This is what I have hoped for. Finally, she will see me again,* Archibald mused as he imagined being once again in her presence.

He had visited *The Inquirer* on several occasions in hopes of seeing her only to be disappointed by her absence. However, he was introduced to her new managing editor whose youth, handsome face and dapper clothing caught his eye. Archibald's proclivity for women did not exclude his interest in some of the male gender. He felt at times a misfit when such propensities found their way into his desires. For now, gaining back Imogen's favor was at the top of his agenda, which meant he must dismiss any thoughts of himself and Sawyer Frye. *I must find a way to make the most of this visit so she will accept me back into her life and discard the young Mr. Frye! Oh, how word of them together has pained my heart. I must not falter in proclaiming my love for her but I must do so with the precision of a surgeon's knife, lest I lose any chance of properly mending our wounds.*

Quickly, Archibald set about writing a simple letter in response and dispatched his houseman to make the delivery.

Darling Imogen,

Thank you for your invitation. I look forward to seeing you on the morrow. Please expect my arrival at one o'clock in the afternoon.

Yours,
Archibald

Morning clouds, which had cast a gloomy gray over the city, gave way to bursts of sunlight as large white cumulus puffs slowly moved across the sky adding brilliance to the afternoon's atmosphere. Archibald felt the warmth of the sun's rays and saw them as a hopeful sign that today would offer a fresh start, a new beginning for his relationship with Imogen.

As his carriage rounded the bend in the lane leading to her front door, he drew in a deep breath, closed his eyes and looked upward as though calling on a higher being. *Why the good Lord would have mercy on a rascal like me, I cannot say but, Lord, I hope I receive the favor of your good graces this day.* Archibald felt strongly about redemption and hoped this was the time for his. He stepped from his carriage and walked the few steps under the portico to the front entrance. As he raised his hand to lift the large doorknocker formed of heavy iron molded into the shape of a lion's head, the door slowly opened and Patti greeted him. She looked down and smiled as she stepped aside to bid him entry.

"Good afternoon, Patti. I am here to see Mrs. Simmonds. Please announce my arrival," Archibald spoke softly attempting to control his tenor lest Imogen find his approach too gruff and demanding.

"Yes, sir. Please follow me, sir. Mrs. Simmonds is waitin' in the study fer ye." *The missus surely be keepin' this door busy with the men folk,* smirked Patti hoping no one could read her mind.

Archibald waited a moment before he took his first step forward. He needed to gather his thoughts and a healthy dose of courage to face the one he had so wronged. Along with his bowler hat, he had donned his best chestnut brown breeches and frock coat with an exquisite white shirt boasting ruffles down its front and along the edges of its cuffs. As he approached the study he bade himself pause before the richly paneled mahogany doors. There she was. Sitting with her back to the doorway, she appeared to be intently observing the amber glow of the embers spitting and spurting in the firebox. She turned to face the sound of his footsteps, which had ceased just before he entered the room, as though there existed an unmarked line he had not been invited to cross. Her tongue was mute as she looked him up and down, dipped her head toward her hands and fondled a handkerchief, which he could see held Talmadge's monogram. Slowly, she stood, nodded her head in greeting and signaled Archibald to enter.

"It has been some time since last we were in each other's presence. I am glad you have come. I feel we have much to discuss." Imogen spoke with guarded emotion for she was uncertain how their meeting would unfold.

"I am relieved to see that your time of self-pity has safely passed," Archibald said, but at once regretted his choice of words lest they place a deleterious effect on their meeting.

"I am not so certain it is self-pity that has consumed my days but rather the need to absolve myself from any part I may have played in the ire you and Talmadge felt for one another. I have decided that our relationship, yours and mine that is, was not what drove the two of you to draw yourselves into a duel. Your business conflicts and perpetual mudslinging far outweighed our personal indiscretions."

"How fair of you to grant me a pardon," Archibald said, as he removed his hat and bowed at Imogen who smiled as he regained his stature and moved closer to her. "It would seem you have granted yourself one as well."

"Spare me the sarcasm, Archibald. I am issuing an olive branch of sort. You know I have forever found favor with your wily ways. In fact, it might be said I have missed your propensity for developing schemes that work to your advantage much to the chagrin of others. I hope God will not strike me dead for thinking so."

"My dear Imogen, we have a bond that forsakes all sense of reason. Perhaps we are far too similar in our views of right and wrong. Or perhaps we both live without a conscience to burden us. We have like minds. We cannot be bound by the prattle of others. We have only one life and must live it to the utmost for our pleasure without regard to society's mores," Archibald rationalized, as images of Sawyer Frye came into view. He feared Imogen was garnering too much pleasure from the man.

"So, you are essentially saying that we have no shame?"

"I am saying that we must keep the faith that we can weather any storm. If one is willing to risk all, then nothing is unattainable." Archibald looked to her with longing, hoping his words would not fall silent on her ears.

"Perhaps we are in this for the adventure, the danger that comes with infatuation? Perhaps the lack of commitment draws us together?" Imogen queried as she tried to fathom excuses for their attraction to one another. "So you feel we may impulsively cast aside convention with, as the French so eloquently say, a 'je ne sais quoi?'"

"There is much to be said for the French. Their accent alone is worthy of romance. Perhaps we are the ones guilty of making our situation a 'l'amour compliqué?"

"How could it not have been complicated with the heart of another involved?"

"My dear, we could go on and on reliving the past. It appears that you have arrived at a crossroads. You may continue to mourn and find yourself forever consumed by a past with me you cannot alter, or you may choose to live now, in the present. We must focus on what we have, not on what we have lost." Archibald spoke gently, but his words were edged with an urgency to renew his relationship with Imogen.

She stepped away from the protection Talmadge's desk provided, thus decreasing her distance from Archibald. Her closer proximity to him was like the forces of a magnet finding opposite poles, drawing her to him with greater intensity. She thought of shaking off the attraction but was drawn to him even more. She closed her eyes and took a deep breath to gain the strength for her next steps. She feared she was weakening too quickly to the spell he so ably cast over her, like a fisherman's net entrapping its catch. She opened her eyes to find him extending his arms to gather her in his embrace.

"I caution you Archibald to allow me more time. The relationship between us is complicated especially in light of your actions, which resulted in my husband's demise."

"Oh, Imogen. Will you ever forgive me? I have pleaded with you. And, you must have read my avowal in *The National Intelligencer*. I know little more I can do to win back your affections. I sense you need to hear more from my lips before you will exonerate me. A pardon from you is of paramount importance to me."

Imogen had indeed read Archibald's avowal. Its simplicity was in stark contrast to the resulting magnitude of his actions:

> I, Archibald Howard, hereby affirm as follows that Talmadge Cornthwaite Simmonds and I agreed to participate in a duel. It was a mutually agreed upon solution to settle our differences, which resulted in Mr. Simmonds' death.
>
> I, Archibald Howard, further declare and swear under penalty of perjury that the information I have provided is true and accurate to the best of my knowledge, information and belief. Signed by my hand and seal on this the 30th day of October 1821.

Archibald's open declaration duly served to put his reputation at rights with the public-at-large and surprisingly worked to soften Imogen's heart. His was an honest admission, claiming his culpability in Talmadge's death. The court granted him leniency, finding no discrepancies in his statement, which aligned with those of his seconds, and the testimony of Doc Davenport. He told the court he accepted his part in the actions upon which both men had agreed. With his sworn avowal and the fact that he sought no mercy from the courts, all charges were waived in his favor with the caveat that he never place himself or another in the position to settle a dispute with such force. Such restraint on Archibald's part, of course, would remain to be seen.

"You might have chosen a different publication for your avowal. Why did you elect to have your missive run by *The Inquirer's* competitor?" Imogen queried still miffed that her competitor got the exclusive run of the avowal.

"I feared *The Inquirer* would never put my sworn statement in print. It was imperative to me that the truth of the court's findings be placed in the public view. The court has granted me leniency and it is my greatest desire that you will see fit to do so as well. While I cannot apologize for my actions, I can apologize for the pain my actions placed on your being. For that I am eternally sorry."

Unable to quell the desire running through her veins, and weary from the sadness she had endured, Imogen inched closer to Archibald. She was drawn in by the fresh scent of the tonic that cloaked his skin, his handsome face and attire. She had been celibate, at least with him, far beyond her liking. Archibald became jubilant as he watched her approach and observed the glow washing over her face. She felt the stroke of his hand across her neck, which stirred carnal desires.

"This moment has been my fervent wish these many months," Archibald sighed as he took her heartily into his arms. "I have missed your touch, your embrace," he whispered in her ear.

"As have I," Imogen responded, nearly purring like a hungry cat as they drew back and gazed into each other's eyes.

"The challenge of having you is worth every measure of my time," murmured Archibald.

"Challenge? To what do you refer?"

"I was merely referring to another whose company you have been known to keep of late."

"Please do not ruin this moment for us," Imogen whispered. "I am with you and that is all that matters."

With great thought of motion, slowly and methodically, Archibald brought her lips to his, relishing every moment of their engagement. When the kiss was done, their eyes met once again. They pressed their foreheads together, creating an alignment that spoke to the affection they felt for each other. *I can only hope the desire I feel and witnessed in her eyes will not relinquish itself on the morrow. Maybe Mr. Frye is no match for her attraction to me?* Archibald felt he could only hope that the passage of time would help expel

Imogen and Sawyer's affections for one another. Such was his wish but he expected it would take some actions on his part to assure the end of their liaison.

Chapter Twenty-Three

Imogen was finding it quite a challenge to juggle her relationships with Archibald and Sawyer. Keeping the two men apart was becoming increasingly more difficult since many of their social circles intersected. Their shared acquaintances were also more aware of the time each was spending in the other's company. Women were more likely than men to openly share their views about her behavior. Before she had barely exited a room, tongues would start wagging with unsolicited opinions. Imogen, although not deaf to such banter, gave it little heed. She would do as she pleased and as pleased her. She would not succumb to the opinions of others and was determined to exude the utmost confidence when in the public view. She stood straight, no slumping, with her head held high.

"I am Imogen Simmonds," she would boldly announce when she arrived at a dinner party, maintaining a dynamic posture as she moved about the room.

As much as she exuded confidence when in public, there was a voice inside her that questioned her choices. It was as though a mercurial muse sat on her shoulder pushing her forth and pulling her back. She hated when reticence overtook her, leaving her lacking the confidence she desired. Some days it was a challenge to overcome thoughts that left her vulnerable to what she perceived as weakness, so she determined herself to fight those thoughts and rise above them.

Her most pressing matter was how to temper Archibald's rising ire about Sawyer. His jealousy seemed to be affecting his state of mind. His visits to Woodholme were not only increasing, his time there was becoming more sustained.

Upon a recent visit, Archibald became very agitated when he saw a hat resting on a nearby table, which he knew to be Sawyer's. He immediately thought the young man was hiding about and began to leave the drawing room in search of him. Imogen tempered his fury by placing a hand on his shoulder, which caused him to pause.

"Archibald, please allay your worries. You are allowing your imagination to run away with you," pleaded Imogen.

"My imagination? My imagination? How can that be when I have all the evidence I need that young Mr. Frye has been with you? And, the man would not leave his hat so he must still be about and I shall find him. It is about time we settled…" Imogen cut his words short as she moved closer to him and took his hand in hers.

"You have nothing to fear, Archibald. We had a meeting about the newspaper today and neither I, nor Patti observed that Mr. Frye forgot his hat. I shall see that it is returned to him on the morrow."

"Ah, another excuse to be in his presence!"

"We are colleagues. Of course there will be many times when we are together. You must understand that?"

"I understand what I see and hear. It is a picture that paints you two as more than colleagues!" Archibald nearly roared as he jerked his hand away from Imogen. "Perhaps it is the splendor his youth brings to your business relationship that entices you to him!"

She was distressed to see him exhibit such hostility toward Sawyer. She had no intention of ending her relationship with him. Sawyer was for her a refreshing complement to Archibald's bold and demanding ways. Sawyer was vibrant, respectful and trustworthy. He was mature beyond his years and she always felt comfortable in his presence. He listened thoughtfully when she felt the need to garner his views and he never judged her. She knew she could count on him professionally and personally, the latter being of utmost comfort to her.

Archibald remained a source of stalwart companionship and opened the doors for her to the men of power in the city with his many connections in the banking business. Those connections were proving useful as she worked to gain support for her movement against slavery. His moral principles may have been lacking but who was she to question such ethics? Their compatibility when intimate was full of sensations she was not wont to lose.

What am I to do? Imogen silently questioned. *Must I make a choice?* She was torn as to which of the men she most preferred, for each offered qualities she desired beyond companionship and carnal pleasures. She was not wont to dismiss either from her life, nor was she disposed to rein in her promiscuous behavior.

I need guidance, for my prayers seem not to be heard. I hope God will forgive me for thinking in such a way, she sighed as a wave of dreaded helplessness rushed through her. *Ah, the Taylors. I must make a call on the sisters,* she assured as she forced another silent prayer for God to mend her ways. She squeezed Archibald's hand hoping to calm him and looked into his eyes.

"How might I sway you to forgive me?" she smiled as she led him from the drawing room, through the hallway and toward the staircase.

Archibald smiled and followed her lead, knowing he could not deny her, nor would he choose to do so.

Chapter Twenty-Four

Gertrude Taylor was the most full figured of the three sisters and the eldest. Her chest, well-padded with ample breasts, was a fond place for wee babes to nestle who came to visit. The homely trio consisting of Gertrude, Hazel and Mabel, lived together in a large, predominately stone and masonry home inherited from their parents. Their father Elias, who owned a fleet of clipper ships, made his fortune in global trade where the success of his business was dependent on the vagaries of the weather, the stamina of his crews and the cargo he bought and sold. He and his wife bestowed every amenity toward the care and deportment of their daughters thinking their refinements and dowries would attract wealthy suitors despite their plain visages. Their father had sorely miscalculated their abilities to entice those of the opposite gender leaving Hazel and Mabel spinsters and, although only Gertrude found true love, her father was never pleased with her choice. Gertie, as her family chose to call her, fell in love with a sailor whom she met while visiting the shipyard docks with her father.

His name was Theodore Smallwood and he adored Gertie. His moniker was "Tea" for all the tealeaves he sourced from China and the fondness he held for the hot beverage. He felt a calm about Gertie the moment they met, which served him and their household well, especially after her father threatened to disown her for marrying beneath her station. Theodore did not balk when Gertie held fast to her maiden name, never adopting Smallwood in deference to her father. She felt it was the one concession she could make to soothe her father's disappointment.

Tea was of moderate stature but built strong with solid arms and legs strengthened from his years of sailing and managing cargo. His brown hair, lightened by the sun's rays and flecked with gray, curled and peaked out below a small brimmed, flat-cap made of dark navy wool felt, which had in recent years become a popular head cover with mariners. The cap also served to hide his receding hairline about which he liked to quip, "I have wavy hair, it's waving goodbye."

When he returned home from the shipyard, Tea often sat with the trio of sisters when a visitor came calling. If the need arose, the Taylor's sizable parlor could accommodate a large number of guests. Although seating was ample for large groups the room's design allowed for several intimate clusters of settees and chairs, which were placed about the space for personal conversations.

A brand new Chickering & Sons pianoforte held a prominent placement in the parlor between two double-hung windows. The instrument was a recent gift from Elias' friend Jonas Chickering who was to distribute the pianofortes from his warehouse in Boston in a year or so. He wanted to garner opinions about his product before placing it in the marketplace. Chickering was aware that Elias' daughter Mabel was adept at playing the instrument. She was typically called upon to pleasure guests with several tunes. On occasion, Hazel and Gertie accompanied her with vocals. Although Mabel had an ear for music, her skills on the keyboard failed to extend to her voice, which was known to make listeners cringe with her off-key, high notes. She meant well none the same and put her heart into delivering a tune to the best of her ability. Mercifully, guests who were hard of hearing were spared the eye wincing notes achieved by the tenor of her voice.

Imogen enjoyed her visits with the Taylors whom she had come to know and trust. She met them through her ladies' guild where they immediately felt a mutual sense of bonhomie. Their family's deep roots in the city and affluence further spurred her to gain their association. She often sought their counsel and could trust that their discussions would be held in confidence. Above all, she valued their opinions although, true to her temperament, she ultimately enlisted her own views to remedy the quandary in which she found herself. Such actions did not always serve her well.

She considered Tea an eccentricity. His cap never seemed parted from his head. His habit of taking tea with his wife and her sisters and his doting nature would imply to some that he was a man with idle time who was adverse to more important pursuits, which was not the case. Upon the death of his father-in-law, he took over the management of his shipping business. Imogen found the touches of whimsy associated with Tea odd in a charming way. She appreciated his sensitivities and never let his presence halt her from airing her mind or concerns.

As the door opened to the Taylor mansion, there they were, lined up to greet her like four regimented peas in a pod. They bade her enter and within moments of settling in their seats Imogen stated the reason for her visit.

"I come to you today with a heavy heart. I have recurring dreams of Talmadge. It is as though I am haunted by him," she shared as worry spread over her face.

"Perhaps that is the prodding of your conscience," noted Hazel.

Gertie and Mabel cast sharp, reprimanding stares at Hazel.

"Yes my dear," said Gertie as she took Imogen's hands in hers. "Hazel's words may be blunt but she makes a necessary observation. Forgive me for saying so but Talmadge was not unaware of your, shall I say, *friendship* with Mr. Howard?"

"Gertie, you are correct. However you know I loved Talmadge although I may not have shown it in the most formidable manner."

"I think I am justified in saying that we three, and I will include Tea in this too, are concerned for you if you engage in keeping company with Mr. Howard," Gertie spoke, as she searched Imogen's face for any essence of guilt or remorse.

"I understand that you want the best for me but who is to say that does not include Archibald?"

"Yet, Mr. Howard has made you a widow. How can you return to what I shall in Gertie's words characterize as a *friendship* with him?" Hazel queried.

"And then there is the matter of the younger gentleman, a Mr. Frye I hear?" Hazel added, which brought raised eyebrows from Gertie, Mabel and Tea.

"Yes, are you not afraid of what others might think? I mean, you were not guided in this fashion by your parents where you?" Mabel inquired.

"We can leave my parents out of this discussion. They are long gone and left me to my own devices for much of my formative years. I am only concerned with what I myself think. I am repulsed by the scrutiny of others."

"So, although you have come to us for our opinions, they hold little value as you move forward?" Gertie inquired, as she shifted her bottom on her chair and smoothed the skirt of her dress.

"The old biddies who chastise me might delve into their pasts, or at the very least their hearts' desires, to measure the purity of their thoughts. The infernal buzzing of their voices is like a swarm of hornets waiting to choose a victim and go in for the sting. I can be nothing if I cannot be myself. I am so weary of pretense," Imogen nearly shouted, then thought it best to lighten her tone for her audience.

"Now, now Imogen. Would you speak of them in this way if they stood before you in this room? You must think before you speak and consider the harm that can be done with words. They can become unwieldy weapons in an arsenal that might better serve you if you determined yourself to speak ill of no one," said Gertie.

"Gertie is quite right. You of all people should know the harm of words, for your reputation has been called into question on several occasions by that disgraceful Tillie Tattler," noted Mabel with a playful gleam in her eye for having mentioned the columnist whose gossip often garnered her rapt attention.

Imogen was not pleased. Her face became sullen and her eyes vacant. *Speak ill of no one? Why that idea goes against all I stand for!* She felt as though she were being lectured to rather than heard. She usually was in the mood for their sage advice but today was a flagrant exception.

"I can see from your expression that we have lost you to your own thoughts. Perhaps we should abandon our topic and be thankful for our time together. Here, let me replenish your tea cup," offered Gertie as she reached for the porcelain teapot decorated in a sweet pattern of petite pink and red rosebuds. "I see our beverage is nearly spent. Tea, would you be a love and freshen the pot?"

Tea showed no hesitation in honoring Gertie's request. He was pleased to take leave of the conversation if only for a few moments. He would hold his comments for now, thinking it was perhaps more appropriate for the women to have their say.

"What if I take great pleasure in criticizing the others in the realm about me?" Imogen queried. "I have certainly endured enough of their barbs thrown in my direction. I would rather chew nails than acquiesce to their standards."

"I would guess you would need to ask yourself how well that serves you? Does the task of bringing others down assist in any way to bring you up?" Gertie queried. "We want you to be happy. We fear the loss of Talmadge has left a bitterness in you that will take time to dissipate. You must give serious consideration to your code of conduct. You are privileged to have the wealth that places you in an enviable position in society. With such wealth comes responsibility."

Imogen knew Gertie's words held much merit but she was not willing to relinquish her ways. *Maybe it is the thrill and danger of having two men compete against each other that feeds my self-worth?* Imogen shook her head to discount her thoughts.

"Yes, let us know dear what we can do to help," Mabel asked as she stood to leave their intimate circle and walked to the pianoforte. *Perhaps a lively tune will shake her from her dire mood,* she mused, as she settled herself on the piano's bench and placed her fingers on the keyboard.

Hazel was wont to continue the topic with Imogen. She felt their friendship necessitated a further probe into lessons that one was never too old to learn. She wanted Imogen to understand the consequences of her actions.

"Mabel, please wait a few more moments before you begin your composition. I want to address Imogen," she said as she turned her way. "And, I must add that I hope you will hear me out."

Imogen sighed and a deep huff exited her open mouth. She closed her eyes and shook her head, not so much as to decline Hazel's request but to prepare herself for the lecture to come. She leaned forward with some trepidation, like a naughty school child about to be disciplined by its tutor with a sturdy hickory switch.

"Imogen, you have no need to fear what I am about to say," noted Hazel. "I know you are a grown woman and you have every right to your opinions. However, I must say that each of us must exercise discipline in our daily lives. Just because you feel something about someone does not mean that you must express your feelings. Words can cut like a knife and leave scars that perhaps never heal."

"You are suggesting that I tame my tongue?" Imogen questioned as she thought to herself, *I shall, out of respect, refrain from dismissing their views. They want nothing but the best for me. Of that I am certain, yet I shall not fully yield to them.*

"I am suggesting that you give thoughtful consideration to your words before you utter them. You certainly may think as you will but when you speak, speak that which is proper, that which neither condemns nor demeans," explained Hazel to an unyielding Imogen.

"I am in agreement with Hazel," noted Gertie.

"Me too," chimed in Mabel. "Do not let your chastising of others be among your regrets one day when you are called to answer before the Almighty."

"Civility is always the best choice," said Tea, his eyebrows lifting to the rim of his cap as he entered the room with a fresh pot of English breakfast tea and a plate of scones. "Remaining unapologetic can only serve to feed the bitterness forming itself about you like the barnacles on a vessel of the sea."

"And," Tea noted. "I for one would not take lightly the ruminations of the gossipmongers for gossip has ruined many a reputation. If I may quote scripture, which suits this conversation, I would cite Proverbs 22:1, *'A good name is rather to be chosen than great riches.'*"

"Yes, Imogen. What would your mother say? Surely she raised you to be a proper lady," Hazel responded, as she glanced to her sisters and Tea to find them nodding their heads in agreement.

"As I mentioned, my mother is a longtime gone. I loved her but I never understood her choices. She found little time for me. I created a number of imaginary worlds with my dolls that brought me comfort in her absence. And, my father's idea of praise was silence. I so wanted to feel noticed and appreciated by him. Perhaps my pursuit of men is the result of his inability to provide me with the proper nurturing."

"I think there comes a time when we must move past that which harbors darkness in our souls. What good can come from reliving things that cannot be changed? This may be presumptuous on my part but, I dare say, the words of Edward Gibbon in his work *The History of the Decline and Fall of the Roman Empire* are some that have remained with me, especially with my love of the sea: 'The winds and waves are always on the side of the ablest navigators.' Consider yourself well able, Imogen. As the infamous Captain Lawrence said less than a decade ago, 'Don't give up the ship!'" Tea gave Imogen a heartfelt smile.

Imogen took Tea's words to heart. She knew he and the Taylor sisters wanted the best for her. She would not oppose his advice or his guidance. She placed her hand on his shoulder and said, "Thank you my friend."

Gertie reached for a green velvet pouch resting on a small round pedestal table next to the settee. She looked at her sisters for approval before handing the pouch to Imogen. Imogen was at first hesitant to take the offering, wondering why the pouch was being handed to her. Curiosity got the best of her as she started to untie the satin ribbon, keeping its contents safely inside. Just as she loosened the soft strand of ribbon, Gertie reached forward and placed her hand upon Imogen's.

"Wait just a moment, my dear. I must preface this presentation with a word about its origin," Gertie spoke as she looked about and registered her eyes on each of those present. "The item enclosed is of particular significance to us. One might question why we would choose to part with it? However, the answer remains simple — there are three of us, and one of you. We have collectively decided that rather than select one of us to inherit the enclosed, we have chosen you as its benefactor and hope you will cherish it as much as it was valued by its previous owner."

Imogen's interest was piqued. She stroked the soft pile of the emerald colored velvet pouch. She looked up at the adoring sets of eyes surrounding her and observed a tear slowly falling from Mabel's eye, its glassy sheen revealing itself as tears built up in Gertrude's and Hazel's eyes. *What could this be?* Imogen pondered.

"If I may speak for all of us, we want you to please accept with all our love the enclosed remembrance of our mother Agnes. It was her most personally worn piece of jewelry and among the things she left behind," noted Gertie.

Imogen completed the loosening of the satin ribbon strands. With her fingers she reached inside to retrieve its contents. In her hand she held a simple but lovely, sterling silver fragrance vessel in the shape of a small, slightly flattened flask with a stopper, its hinged sides attached to a silver chain. She held it for a few moments then raised it to her nose where the faint essence of what must have been the Taylor sisters' mother's cologne remained in the vial. A floral scent with hints of roses, orange flowers and jasmine danced about her nostrils. It was a pleasant but not luxurious scent. Perhaps its full essence had faded over time.

She was surprised the sisters would want to part with what was perhaps the last remnant of the scent that was a part of their mother's persona, her self-definition, something that would, upon discovery, bring to mind her presence.

"I am moved that you would entrust this to me and gratified to know you think so highly of me to have me be a steward of this heirloom. Of course, I will treat it with the utmost care and treasure it always," said Imogen as she carefully placed the personal artifact back in the pouch.

"Mother was clear as a bell when she died. She was wearing this piece of jewelry and among her last words were instructions for us to 'share it at the right time with someone with whom you hold much care.' We have chosen you to be the recipient," smiled Hazel.

"Our mother was a very wise soul. She imparted great wisdom to us. It is our hope that you will seek out her counsel by prayer and by the very smelling of this piece of jewelry. Its lingering scent, we feel, is her way of communicating from beyond. Please do not think us insane for believing so," Gertie voiced as she took Imogen's hand and gave it a gentle squeeze.

"It will remain among one of my most prized possessions," acknowledged Imogen. She took her hand and one-by-one laid it on top of the hands of each of the sisters as a seal of acceptance and solemn promise. "And, no, I do not think any one of you to be insane. Our faiths and beliefs are the very foundations that bind us to one another. I welcome your mother's presence in my life and will happily seek her guidance," Imogen acknowledged as she stood to leave.

The sisters shared a collective smile. As Imogen made her exit, Gertie, Hazel and Mabel stood in the doorway and held hands as they watched her carriage fade from view.

"I hate to be a skeptic but perhaps we should not be wasting our breath on her," sighed Mabel.

"Oh, come now Mabel. We mustn't abandon her. It is times such as these when someone needs us to lend all the support we can," noted Hazel.

"Is it not true that we all tend to be creatures of habit? Perhaps she is a compulsive sinner and cannot be swayed from her indulgences? You have heard the same rumors as I. I felt it necessary to mention Mr. Frye lest she overlook the fact that she has had two men in her life since Talmadge's passing," noted Tea. "Maybe a few visits with the 'good book' would serve her well," Tea laughed as he imagined Imogen engaged in reading the Bible.

"My hope is that she can be honest with herself as she grieves the loss of Talmadge and considers the place, if any, Archibald will hold in her life, not to mention the young man at her newspaper. I worry about her confusion for she is not clear about her choices. Oh my, I wonder how her story will unfold?" Gertie shook her head in dismay.

"It depends on the story she chooses to tell," declared Tea as the sisters turned to him with a questioning glare.

Dearest Readers,

Thankfully, our widow has taken to her confidantes for counsel. We can only hope their advice is sound and sets our widow on a more righteous path than the one she has been trodding.

With respect for secrets and sordid truths,
Tillie Tattler

Chapter Twenty-Five

February 1822
In the City of Washington and in Georgetown

Standing on soil in the City of Washington, Savanna Carlyle studied the scene before her, feeling confident in her resolve to leave the United Kingdom and all that was familiar to her, although the Federal City was not as she had anticipated. She had pictured America's seat of government as being an imperial city, a place resplendent with fancy structures and lush landscapes. On the contrary, although parts of the city were cultivated, there were large, unkept spaces much like a wilderness with shabby houses scattered about dotting the landscape. She saw before her a confused montage of rustic pastures amid natural lawns — some ornamented with cows and chickens, unbuilt streets and buildings much further than a stone's throw from one another. Nonetheless, the young woman of two and twenty, was determined to see her mission through. She boarded a carriage and as it jostled her to and fro, her mind was threaded with anticipation laced with uncertainty. *I have little choice now that I am here. I must overcome any hesitancy and go forth with confidence*, she asserted, hoping to gain additional strength from her words.

As her destination came into view and her carriage slowed, she admired the grounds surrounding the stately home. Its property was in stark contrast to much of the landscape among the city's buildings. The home, which she had learned was called Rosedale, was well surrounded with mature oak and maple trees, although the season had left them void of their lush leaves. She studied the architecture of their bare branches and was reminded of the empty feeling that led her away from London. She wondered about her destiny and what role fate might play in this new world, so unfamiliar from the one where she was born and raised.

Before she took the final steps that would put her at the threshold of a truth, which could only be confirmed by the mistress of the mansion, her mind drifted to her charmed life on the outskirts of London with her doting parents, Frederick and Louise Carlyle. The Carlyles and their ancestors had for centuries been placed among British notables. Most grew their dynasties through hard work and perseverance. Along the way they made enormous contributions to the arts, which put Savanna in the unenviable position of having to be alert to requests for her company at social events. She would muse, *Is the invitation being extended solely for my philanthropy or perhaps it is my engaging character that prompted the invitation? Perhaps both?*

Her parents answered her every whim and, due to their wealth and its accompanying social status, left her wanting for nothing, except perhaps a man who could accept the challenges she posed for herself.

Her desire was to excel in a calling other than wife and mother. Not that she was opposed to the norm of domesticity but she found great comfort in meeting societal needs, especially needs she witnessed that would aid and improve the health of society. On her walks through Chelsea she often visited the Royal Rose Apothecary owned and operated by Nigel Yates. She imagined herself well ensconced at the apothecary as 'Doc Carlyle' since apothecaries, as was the practice, were not required to have a medical licensure to compound medicinal remedies. So, the men, and occasionally women, were commonly referred to by the appellation 'Doc' or in Nigel's case, 'Doc Yates.'

Savanna found herself drawn to the smells of the shop where a variety of medicinal herbs and powders attracted her senses. She was not repelled by the scents, as was the case for many who entered. Mortars of thick, yet translucent, purple glass with white marble pestles were neatly arranged on a shelf behind the sales counter. The purple glass lent a royal air to the space, seemingly apropos for the shop's noble name. Below their purple counterparts sat more substantial mortars fashioned of gray granite. They lined the lower shelves of the glass front cabinets. The granite mortars were the most used and efficient vessels for crushing and grinding compounds into powders.

Savanna sighed as she drew herself away from thoughts of the Royal Rose Apothecary. *All of that will have to wait for now. I have a more pressing mission of which to attend.*

Savanna's decision to leave her homeland was triggered by a private conversation she overheard the year past between her father and his brother.

The two men were having what began as an innocent parley about their inheritance. As they smoked finely rolled cigars and consumed tumblers filled with well-aged brandy, their conversation became heated and their voices grew louder. The commotion drew Savanna's attention as she passed along the hallway. They were unaware that she stood only a few feet away from her father's study where the door was left ajar. Their discussion escalated into name-calling and the exposure of a long-held secret.

Stunned, Savanna reached for the doorframe to stabilize herself. Her legs felt weak. She wondered for a fleeting moment if she had misunderstood and not heard her uncle's words correctly. *Can this be true? Am I imagining this like a mad dream that has no bearing on the truth? I must gather my senses*, she whispered, as the men continued to throw barbs at one another.

"Owen, you are a scoundrel to bring any mention of my daughter's birth into this conversation! How dare you use your own insecurities to threaten my relationship with Savanna!" Frederick's voice quivered with rage.

"Ha! I will use any means necessary to assure myself that you will not alter the arrangements our father declared for us upon his passing. How dare you suggest that you can remove my name from his list of beneficiaries when you have, living under your roof one, not of your blood, whom you fully intend to benefit from your wealth! I shall not allow the bastard child you adopted to have what is by birthright mine!" Owen shouted as he lifted his glass and swallowed a heady portion of his libation.

"You are being made bold and fortified by the drink for, I would hope, you otherwise would never reveal something that Louise and I have held in your trust. You know full well that I will not take any action against you. I was merely teasing when I said it would do you well not to disparage me in any way lest your name be stricken from our father's designation of beneficiaries. Do not attempt to turn this *discussion* into a rivalry over our inheritance. The documents our father signed bind me to ensure you receive your fair share of his monies and properties. Good Lord man! Can you not take something said in jest? Our father has barely been in his grave and here you are tossing accusations my way. Get a grip on yourself and lower your voice."

Savanna felt numb. She feared her legs would not support her if she attempted to move away from the study door. *Adopted? How can this be? I should have put this together years ago when friends of my parents would try to determine if I looked more like my mother or father. I should have questioned my dark hair when they both had flaxen hair. It just seemed an oddity that perhaps crossed over a generation. What am I to do?"*

Savanna took a deep breath. She held her head up and shook her arms, then her legs. She placed her hands on her shoulders and drew them along to her neck where she rested her hands and used her fingers to massage her neck muscles. *I have not changed, yet have I?* She knew this was only one of many questions she must ask her parents. *Why would they keep this from me? How could Uncle Owen know, yet I have been kept uninformed?* Her thoughts became angry ones. *If this bears truth then I have been lied to all these years! I hate them for this! They have made a fool of me!* Her mind screamed with thoughts of the treachery her parents had willingly bestowed upon her.

She stepped away from the study's doors to retreat to her room. In so doing, the crinolines beneath her gown rustled, alerting her father and uncle to someone's nearby presence. She quickened her pace. Both men looked to the doorway and recognized her form as she swooped away. Frederick raced to the door and stepped into the hallway only to see Savanna with the front of her gown raised to allow her feet clearance to quickly and safely access the full flight of stairs. Briefly, she paused on the landing to catch her breath as her father called out to her.

"Savanna, wait!" shouted Frederick. "I must speak with you."

With tear clouded eyes Savanna turned toward him. He knew in an instant that she had overheard his brother's declaration. She looked down the staircase at her father's face contorted in worry. He looked so small from her vantage point, or perhaps that was how she was feeling about him at present. She decided to halt her retreat and confront her father for an explanation about her uncle's pronouncement. Within moments, Owen stepped into the hallway. As he began to approach his brother, Frederick turned and put his hand out to halt him.

"It would be best brother for you to take your leave now."

"But," Owen began when his words were cut to the quick by Frederick.

"Take your leave now. You have imparted enough damage for one evening. I will talk with you on the morrow."

Reluctantly, Owen retrieved his hat from the hallway rack, placed it on his head and gave a modest bow toward Savanna. She remained silent, neither acknowledging his departure with a word nor a gesture.

The hinges on the massive, carved front door seemed to wince as Owen made his exit, then all was painfully quiet. Frederick cleared his throat and shook his head in an attempt to stall the inevitable. He wished his wife were not away visiting relatives. He knew he could use her gentle ways to bring calm to the situation he found upon him. Savanna waited without any movement, determined to force her father to have the first word.

"Savanna, I question your haste. Has something caused you distress?"

"With all due respect, *Father*, if I may still call you such, my world has been forever changed."

"Changed? How so?"

"How so? I heard what Uncle Owen said."

"Oh, Savanna. You mustn't take seriously what a man says when he is enjoying his brandy."

"You shall not evade my inquiry! You owe me that much!" Savanna shouted. Her need for answers was unequivocal.

"You have no cause to talk to me so."

"No cause? No cause, you say? I have every right to demand the truth of my birth. Why have you and Mum held this from me? Your brother is aware of something about which I have been kept in the dark. He spoke with such authority. It may have been the drink that loosened his tongue to reveal a fact known to him and kept from me. What precipitated his declaration is of no importance. What was said was said! And, heaven knows how many others have such awareness. I am owed an explanation!"

Frederick grimaced and took in a hearty breath. He knew there was no escaping Savanna's request for the truth. "I beg you to please come down from the landing so I may tell you what should have been revealed years ago," Frederick urged. Savanna complied with his request. He put his hand out to assist her down the stairs as he thoughtfully and carefully explained how she came to be adopted by them.

"This information is not easy for me to share. Your mum and I have remained very discreet. Everyone about us, with the exception of your uncle, is of the belief that you are of our blood. Your mum went away for a period of time and returned with you, which abated any questions about your conception and birth," Frederick explained and cleared his throat as he continued. "A young woman, Virginia Kent, found herself unwed and her reputation compromised with a pregnancy. When we, who were seeking a child of our own, learned from the local doctor that the mother was unable to keep the child, we did not hesitate and readily agreed to take the baby in as our own."

Savanna began to cry for which she was thankful. The shock of what she was hearing had nearly frozen her to the bone. The tears welling in her eyes and beginning to fall onto her cheeks lent realization to the fact she was still capable of performing normal functions. She wiped at the tears with her hand. Her father offered her a handkerchief, which she did not decline. She was torn between her affection for him and her disgust.

"I am so sorry you have found out this way. You are so dear to us Savanna," Frederick spoke with a tear in his voice.

"Tell me. Tell me about this woman who gave birth to me. This Virginia Kent. Do you know her whereabouts? Is she still alive? Who sired me? It is imperative and, quite frankly, I feel you are duty bound to hold nothing back from me."

"I can honestly tell you that your mum and I know nothing of the man who 'sired' you as you say. I did learn from one of my associates in investment banking that Virginia Kent had married. I believe the man's name was Sterling. Actually, that was his surname. I am forgetting his first name at the moment. It is of little consequence since I believe he has passed on."

"Could it be that this man whose last name is Sterling, could it be that he is my biological father?"

"I would have no way of knowing that. I would say that truth lies with Virginia Kent."

"You mean Virginia Sterling for she must have taken her husband's last name?"

"I would suspect you are quite right."

"Do you know where she is living?"

"Word has it that after her husband died, she left our shores for America. That is the last I heard her name come up in conversation. However, that said, on the morrow I shall inquire about her location and inform you posthaste. Savanna, I know this is all so very hard to hear. My heart aches for you and what you must be feeling. I am so sorry that we kept this from you. We have never thought of you in any way other than as our daughter. You were born of our hearts and we would not take back any part of our decision to bring you into our lives. When your mum returns home I know she will say the same."

"It is difficult enough to think that you have led me astray about my beginnings. I am equally angered and hurt that Mum has held this secret. Were the two of you never going to disclose the truth to me? What were you thinking?" Savanna queried with disbelief and anger brewing in her mind.

"Perhaps we were not thinking as clearly as we should have. In hindsight, this is something we should have shared with you as soon as you were able to understand. Perhaps it was selfishness on our part, selfish pride to be more exact."

"So there you have it. More concern about the reaction of others than to the consequences of betraying my trust once the truth came to light as it always does."

"Again, I am eternally sorry for keeping this from you however, it does not in any way change the love your mum and I have for you. Please know that and hold that close to your heart."

"I will need some time to come to grips with this knowledge. My first instinct is to take some time for myself. I am at odds with who I am. I am Savanna Carlyle and yet I am not. I need time, I need time," Savanna repeated as she contemplated her next steps. She felt her future sanity held no alternative but to travel abroad in search of the truth. *I must travel any path in search of the truth, in search of my history, in search of my roots,* she rationalized with conviction as she attempted to gather her senses and bid her father adieu.

As she ascended the staircase to retreat to her bedchamber the word 'roots' pounded in her brain. She held close to the banister to steady herself. *Roots, roots, roots! Oh, how I wish I could be satisfied with all that I have for I have so much. But, if there be another part of me, a branch that makes my family tree complete, then I must pursue it with the full measure of my strength,* she reflected and readied herself to prepare for her journey.

Chapter Twenty-Six

As unsettling as was the letter Virginia had received from the Carlyles, their follow-up correspondence left her equally fraught with angst and foreboding. *How shall I cope with meeting her face-to-face?* Virginia paced the floor of her bedchamber holding tight to the latest correspondence. She wanted to collapse into a puddle of nerves, close her eyes and bid her past to make a hasty retreat into an unknown realm, one where she would not be obligated to explain her choices.

Alas, she knew such thoughts were but a fantasy. *I must gather my senses and strength to face the demons of my own doing that are coming before me.* The Carlyle's letter was unequivocal in indicating they were not able to hold back their daughter's determination to travel to America. She insisted on meeting with Virginia and would not be denied. Virginia bolstered herself for what lay ahead as she exited the sanctity of her bedchamber and proceeded to make her way step by step down the curved staircase.

As she approached her waiting visitor, her sashay through the foyer seemed unusually long, as though time were standing still, or at the very least slowing her pace. She stopped several feet away from the young woman, taking in the beauty of the stranger before her who was of her own blood. The two women looked at one another, each carefully studying the other, searching for something to connect them, to make the unfamiliar familiar. Savanna's raven tresses were bold just like her father's thick black hair, the father whose identity she was unaware, but her eyes were a mirror image of her mother's. Virginia marveled at the sparkle in her green eyes like the facets of a fine gem.

"Welcome to my home. I hardly know where to start," said Virginia with a tear caught in her throat.

"From the beginning might be best," came Savanna's reply.

She was curious to know what this woman, this mother she had never known had to say about abandoning her to another family. Virginia was struck by the young woman's composure, or perhaps it was a protective wall she had constructed to shield herself should meeting her birth mother not elicit the results she desired.

"Here, please come into the drawing room where we can sit and I can hopefully provide answers to your questions," Virginia said, as she motioned Savanna forward, knowing she soon might have to face the grim reality that her daughter would want nothing to do with her.

Virginia began to explain the predicament in which she found herself, being unwed with child. She, in delicate fashion, explained the great love she felt for Savanna's father whom she could not wed for he was betrothed to another.

As tears came to her eyes, she apologized for her improprieties. "I am so sorry for my, shall I say, lack of moral standards when it came to men, or I best say, one man. I was young, yet old enough to know what I was doing was wrong. As it turned out, I was given a gift that I felt I could not keep. Too many would be hurt by my actions and lives would be changed if I did not let you go. In hindsight, that is exactly what has occurred. You have come to me to confirm the truth of your heritage and I hope you will find room in your heart to forgive me."

"Forgiveness may take some time. I am not opposed to forgiving you. I just need some time to absorb all that I have learned in the past few months. The Carlyles are the only family I have known until now. I must ask, who is my birth father, that is, if you know?"

Virginia was taken aback by the slight implied in Savanna's question. It was not as if she had had relations with multiple men. *If she chooses to insult me perhaps I need not tell her whom her father is for what does it matter now? The man is dead,* Virginia reasoned. *She has no need to be the wiser. On the other hand, how can I* deny *her the full knowledge of her heritage?* Virginia was trying to come to terms with her own history and her decisions of the past, which she knew she would have repeated without question. *Now, here is this beautiful young woman wanting to know who her father is and I will have to tell her that he is dead. The poor thing has to deal with one blow after the other.*

"I assure you Savanna, I know exactly the identity of your birth father. I want to also assure you that I was only promiscuous with one man before I married my late husband Reginald Sterling and that one man was your father. There is no question about this. However, I have the sad news to share that," Virginia paused a moment before completing her sentence, "he is deceased."

"Deceased? Oh my goodness, no. What happened? What is his name? How can I know more about him?"

"He died only a short while ago. He unfortunately was the victim of a duel. It is all very sad how this came about. His name was Talmadge Simmonds. I, of course, can tell you about him but you may also want to meet his widow, Imogen Simmonds. She lives in a large mansion known as Woodholme. She and her home are quite well known. Upon receiving the letter from your father, that is, Frederick Carlyle, I made a call to Mrs. Simmonds' home to announce your existence and your relationship to her. I hope the words I have chosen here are not deemed as harsh. I merely choose to be as direct as possible. She was unaware that she had a stepdaughter and after the shock of losing her husband, I felt it was only reasonable to take care in presenting her with this news. I can tell you that on my list of regrets, failing to inform Talmadge about you is high among them."

Savanna sat very still and remained quiet for several contemplative moments before she gathered the strength to speak. Her mind was bombarded with a tornado of spinning thoughts. She was enveloped with extreme sadness that the opportunity to meet her birth father had been taken from her. *If only I had the knowledge of the truth of my heritage months, if not years before! Why did the Carlyles keep this from me?* She determined herself that the bitterness threatening to take over her thoughts would not prevail. She was in the United States on a mission to know her birth parents. *I must give Virginia an open mind to know her better and come to terms with her explanations for giving me away. I must remember most importantly, I came to be out of love.*

"Mrs. Sterling, I shall make arrangements to meet with Mrs. Simmonds since you have informed her of my 'existence' as you say, and I would like to meet with you again so we may know one another better."

"Please call me Virginia or Ginny if you prefer. Ginny is the name your father called me so it is an endearment that keeps him near to me. Our close relationship became strained years ago upon his marriage to Imogen, which I am sure you can understand. Do give her a chance to adjust to the news of you. She has a heart, although it sometimes is difficult to sense on first meeting."

"Understood. I think for now that I am most comfortable calling you Mrs. Sterling. Let us see how that might change over time," Savanna said in a firm but graceful way.

"Where are you staying?"

"I have a room at the Union Tavern and Hotel. The accommodations are quite satisfactory and the proprietor has provided a coach from his stable for my transportation as needed."

"You are most welcome to stay in my home, if you wish. I have more than ample room as you can see and staff to assist your needs."

"How kind of you. Let me see how the agenda for my time here transpires. For now, I shall remain at Union but hope you will keep your kind invitation open if the need arises for me to reconsider my living arrangements."

"Very well then. I have another thought. I wish to host a dinner party in your honor and hope you will accept my invitation to do so? I feel it will be a further way for us to become familiar with each other and for you to become acquainted with my friends."

"I should like that very much."

Virginia determined herself to thwart the rumors, which were certain to ensue, about her connection to Savanna by introducing her publicly. Her party would be a debut for Savanna and a way for Virginia to bare her soul and bring closure to her hidden past. *Some may change their opinions of me. I must accept that but not be deterred,* she reasoned. She had an additional agenda in mind, which was devious at best. She would invite Imogen to attend with an escort and hoped she would accept the invitation with the ruse that she could meet Savanna. *This should make for an interesting night,* schemed

Virginia. *Archibald is sure to attend for he never misses an opportunity to put himself on display and rumor has it that Imogen is quite smitten with her new managing editor. There may be no need to light the fireboxes in my home for sparks may be flying with the tension in the room!*

Chapter Twenty-Seven

"I long for warmer days when I can escape to the garden. I am most alive during the blooming season," Imogen reflected aloud to the glass walls of Woodholme's conservatory. "The promise of renewal and rebirth is forever evident in the tiniest of buds waiting to burst open and display their glory for our viewing pleasure. There are days when I feel all of nature abounds in me and those are by far my happiest of days." Imogen smiled and seemed to wallow in a trance, as she closed her eyes and imagined a garden laden with her favorite flowers. Visions of roses, dahlias, sunflowers, daffodils and pansies filled her mind's eye, as did butterfly bushes embraced by winged fairies such as monarchs, swallowtails, Baltimore Checkerspots and cottons.

"Is it possible you have lost your mind?" Archibald queried, while he hoped against hope that he could convince her to see the error of her ways and forego her relationship with the young man who had become her constant companion.

Imogen opened her eyes wide. "Good Lord, Archibald! You nearly scared me to death. Patti has once again failed to announce your entry and, who may I ask, are you to question my sanity? If I have gone mad it is solely of your doing. I did not fire the shot that took Talmadge's life."

"I am speaking of Mr. Frye. I think you are completely mad to continue taunting me with your provocative association, which we both know full well goes far beyond the purviews of an employer and employee."

"This is truly none of your concern. Sometimes one must travel a different path just to remain sane. That said, if I choose to engage my time and attention with someone who brings me pleasure, then so be it," Imogen retorted, with anger building in her voice.

"You women are so emotional. You don't think with your head. Anyone can twist your arm or heart and that's precisely what this man Frye has done! He's nothing but a second rate journalist. A hack at best."

"Oh, so now you purport yourself the arbiter of good taste? How can you possibly criticize one so widely read? His presence at *The Washington Inquirer* has increased our readership threefold. I doubt you can make the same claim of any of your business dealings."

"You have placed this gent on a pedestal. He is no paragon and I would remind you that objects placed on high have a tendency to take a fall from grace. I warn you to beware…"

"Oh, is this the evil spell of jealousy rearing its ugly head? Am I not allowed to have a friend of the other gender? Do you expect that I shall be tethered to you like a prized horse?"

"We have an understanding, or so I thought?" Archibald queried.

"An understanding you say? To whose advantage is this understanding of which you speak? It sounds rather one-sided?"

"You know full well what I am saying. You and I have a bond, an agreement."

"I know of no formal agreement between us."

"It may not be in writing, and perhaps unspoken, but it is a bond just the same."

"Again, you appear to take ownership of me."

"As of late, I doubt any one man could take ownership of you. In point of fact, it baffles me how Talmadge was able to tolerate your behavior. His manhood must have been cut to the quick by the axe that is your tongue."

"What a nasty and shrewd choice of words, Archibald. And, all because you cannot contain your jealousy," Imogen nearly shouted, as their simmering differences reached the boiling point.

"Jealousy? Jealousy? Why would I be jealous of a young man with no experience in the ways of women who is merely playing with your affections to maintain his position at *The Inquirer*? You are blind to the obvious. And, you allow him to refer to you by your given name! That is outrageous and unprofessional! You and the newspaper would best be rid of him. Perhaps I can help you in that regard?"

Archibald's haunting words sent a chill through her torso as remnants of the dark and bloody day when Talmadge met his death echoed in her mind. Was Archibald just having a momentary spell and fit of anger, or was he threatening Sawyer's well-being?

After seeing Archibald off in his carriage, Imogen felt the urge to return to the calm of her home's landscape. She layered her gown with a warm cape and stepped outside where she carefully managed her footing on the stone steps leading from the back of Woodholme to the path toward the rear gardens. She lifted the skirt of her gown as she maneuvered the steps and continued forward. She hoped to find renewed solace among the evergreen shrubs and desperately needed to gain a sense of peace in the midst of the recent peaks and valleys she was enduring. She felt weary although she knew such ups and downs were a part of being alive.

A gust of wind swept through the remainder of a large butterfly bush entangling its branches in a swift to and fro waltz. Its lavender flowers, mostly well spent from winter's fury, barely held their attachment as another wind gust came upon the shrub. She watched the chaotic movement of the foliage, which served to remind her that among chaos beauty could emerge.

I need to see Sawyer. I must warn him of Archibald's potential wrath toward him. The man seems to have lost all sense of reason when it comes to my friendship with Sawyer, worried Imogen.

Imogen's thoughts had no sooner turned to Sawyer's safety than she heard footsteps approaching from behind. She swiftly shifted her body around, fearful that Archibald had made a return. To her great comfort it was Sawyer. As he caught her gaze he picked up his pace and quickly came to her side.

"Hello, my lovely Imogen," he whispered as he took her in his arms in a warm embrace.

She welcomed his arms and felt like melting into his chest. He was the tonic she needed to wipe away her toxic meeting with Archibald. As they released their hold on each other, much to Sawyer's chagrin Imogen began to cry.

"What is it my lovely? What brings you such sadness?" Sawyer stroked away the tears running down her cheeks. It was uncustomary for him to see her in such a state. He took her hands in his and drew her closer, as he placed a kiss on her cheek.

"It is Archibald. I fear he has such jealousy and hatred for you that harm will come to you at his hands. I cannot bear the thought. It pains me to my very soul to imagine any injury coming to you."

"Concern yourself not, for I have little concern for Archibald's threats my direction."

"Sawyer, must you pay my warnings no heed? He is assuming more moments of irrational behavior. Quite frankly, I am concerned for your well-being. I beg you, you must take extreme care."

"Dear Imogen, Archibald may be a master at wielding words but with me he may have met his match when it comes to brandishing a weapon."

"It seems you exhibit a blatant disregard for my feelings and a lapse of memory when it comes to Archibald's ability to engage in ruthless acts." Imogen knew her words were harsh but fear kept her from holding them back. "Do not be fooled by his charms. I have been duped by him time and time again," Imogen begged, as she turned her head to wipe away another tear.

Sawyer moved closer to Imogen and placed a hand upon her shoulder. She could feel the heat of him as he moved his hand along her shoulder until his fingers touched the bare skin along her collarbone. He turned her toward him and lifted her chin so their eyes could meet.

"How might I best quell your fears? You know I mean you no distress."

Imogen sensed she could melt upon his gaze. As his dark brown eyes met hers, her orbs felt seared by their intensity.

"Please excuse me for my weakness. I feel so unworthy. I fear I have displeased you with talk of Archibald, which was not my intention." Imogen's voice was nearly begging as she pleaded for his forgiveness. "Perhaps it is I who need to heed my advice and examine my contact with him. I know you are well aware of our relationship. I do not mean to pit you one against the other. Please forgive me if that is what has come to pass."

Sawyer was not in the least concerned about Imogen's relationship with Archibald. The benefits he gained from being in her favor far outweighed any jealousy he could muster. He was content to continue to be in her employ and mutually enjoy the pleasures her fancies aroused.

"Let me erase the worry from your mind," offered Sawyer. He had an inimitable way of reaching to the core of Imogen's needs. His youth, energy and lack of fear were characteristics she admired. Desire raced through her body as he took her hands and kissed them. "You are more than worthy, and you must know that I am at my best when in your company. Let's return to the house. I shall show you what I mean."

Chapter Twenty-Eight

The throng of elegant carriages lining the driveway with horses turned out in their finest harnesses and tack were an immediate indication of the wealth and finery to be found within the walls of Virginia Sterling's estate this evening. She had included an illustrious group of friends and acquaintances on her guest list to showcase the daughter about whom none of them were aware. The evening would be a debut for them both. Guests would meet the young, beautiful debutante and learn of the woman who bore her. Virginia felt prepared for the ridicule she would undoubtedly receive, knowing she might lose some friendships, where loyalties were more attached to their own good reputations than to longstanding relationships.

Virginia walked about the rooms of her home with nervous excitement. This was among the most important evenings she had ever hosted. As she greeted her guests who began arriving in droves, she looked about for her daughter. *How unusual and at the same time wonderful to be welcoming my daughter to my home,* reflected Virginia.

It was not often that Savanna's entrance into a room went unnoticed. This evening would be no exception. Savanna Carlyle had been turning heads for much of her life. Having advanced to a score and two years, she had yet to find a man to meet her fancy. Many had tried, but all had failed to win her heart.

The empire waist of her chemise-lined gown lent unmistakable form to her petite frame while its scooped neckline accentuated her firm and alluring bust. She gathered her gown's subtle train in her right hand as she slowly swept about the room. Of the palest turquoise, the gauzy cotton fabric moved with a mesmerizing ebb and flow enthralling the men in her wake. Making initial eye contact with them and then demurely glancing away, she drew them into her spell.

Her long raven tresses fell in cascading waves about her shoulders. The candlelight emanating from the chandeliers caught each silky strand of her locks, making them glisten as she turned her head to and fro. Her ineffable beauty was unsurpassed. Her emerald eyes gleamed like the finest stone in the gem family, attracting the admiration of the men in her presence, much to the chagrin of the young women on their arms. She had on many occasions heard someone exclaim she was a 'gem of the first water' and it was obvious that many in the room would attest to the validity of that appellation.

Imogen initially enjoyed observing the effect the young woman's arrival had on Virginia's guests who filled her ballroom until one guest took particular interest in the young woman's presence. As he politely nodded and stepped away from his conversation with Congressman Barbour, he bent his right arm and, in a rolling gesture with his hand, made a slight bow to bid the beauty a warm greeting. *Surely he is simply wishing to make her feel welcomed and will soon abandon his focused attention on her,* Imogen fumed hoping her thoughts remained silent and her expression blank so others would not sense her raging jealousy. *Who is she? Could she be the result of Virginia and Talmadge's tryst for I have never laid eyes on her?*

Savanna smiled as she cocked her head and casually dipped it to the side to acknowledge the handsome stranger whose approach brought her pleasure. He appeared to be only a few years her senior. His wealth of wavy brown hair was well kept. His dark brown eyes held a friendly gleam as he smiled to reveal a single dimple on his lower right cheek. *Ah, I often heard my nanny say, 'One with a dimple was kissed by the angels when he was born,'* Savanna thought fondly, as she returned the smile, then looked away to see Imogen's fast approach.

Having observed Imogen's proximity to Savanna, Virginia was soon upon the two nearly knocking the young gentleman to the floor.

"I beg your pardon, but I must make an introduction, which has been a long time coming," Virginia apologized as she caught her breath. Her heart was racing as she stepped to Savanna's side. "Imogen Simmonds, I would like to introduce my daughter Savanna Carlyle. I might add, I am happy to do so."

Virginia took Savanna's arm while the two awaited Imogen's greeting. Imogen stood stoically still, letting her eyes take in the young woman before her. *Talmadge's hair,* thought Imogen, *she has her father's lush black hair.* She looked from Savanna to Virginia noting their identical eye color. *Like that of twins blessed with glistening emerald orbs. The resemblance is remarkable,* observed Imogen. She held her focus a few more moments before words spun onto her tongue.

"It is interesting to meet you, Savanna. Virginia has told me much about you. You can only imagine how I took the news of your existence. I am still trying to find a path to acceptance," Imogen stated with clinched teeth. She wanted to be easily swayed, at the very least, to like the girl, but the roving eyes of the men in the room as Savanna made her promenade had not pleased Imogen.

"Oh, and this young gentleman is Sawyer Frye," said Virginia with a devilish smile.

Leave it to her to annoy me further, thought Imogen. *The woman knows exactly how to raise my ire. She saw Sawyer's advances Savanna's direction and wishes to throw his attentions to another directly in my face!*

"Mrs. Simmonds, Mr. Frye, I am pleased to make your acquaintance," said Savanna with a nod of her head. "Actually Mrs. Simmonds, it is my hope that we might meet one day soon in a more private setting where we can discuss matters important to us both?"

"Yes, I shall welcome such a meeting. I can arrange my schedule tomorrow to have you visit around noon, shall we say? Virginia can give you details about my home. Woodholme is known to most in the city so it shan't be difficult for you to find. And, we will meet alone," added Imogen as she gave a warning look to Sawyer.

Archibald, like a cat waiting to pounce on an unsuspecting mouse, suddenly sprang from the shadows. He had been lying in wait, having witnessed the exchange between his hostess and her guests. He had noted the look of affection in Sawyer's eyes when Imogen was near and the return issued forth by her. He knew that look well and equally knew it did not bode well for him. He could barely contain his jealousy seeing Sawyer near her but he felt the presence in the city of this new young woman held promise for his cause to remove Sawyer from Imogen's affections.

"My goodness Archibald! You nearly scared me to death! You should have made yourself known in a less dramatic fashion!" blurted Imogen as she gave him a chilled stare.

"Forgive me my dear if I am anxious to meet Virginia's daughter, and you know I am a great proponent of drama both on and off the stage. Virginia, you will find no shame from me in your revelation. I quite fancy news that deters us from the daily business of greed and politics in the city."

Imogen closed her eyes and shook her head. Leave it to Archibald to find a silver lining in a sensitive topic at the expense of someone else.

"So, Miss Carlyle is it? If I may be so bold, how did you come about that surname?" Archibald inquired much to Virginia's chagrin.

"Surely, Mr. Howard, you can understand the need for privacy in such matters," answered Virginia as she gave a look at Savanna. She assumed Imogen would comply with Archibald's inquiry upon their next rendezvous and apprise him of all the details.

"Why, I meant no harm. It seems curiosity got the best of me. Do forgive me." Archibald replied as he threw his head back with a laugh. "Perhaps I might try a different line of inquiry, if you have no objection, Miss Carlyle."

"It seems that would depend on the nature of your inquiry?" Savanna responded much to Archibald's delight. He enjoyed her spirited demeanor and pluck to answer his question with a question.

"I guess I am curious as to how long you intend to remain in the City of Washington and, if for a prolonged stay, what you might do with your time?"

"How lovely of you to be concerned about my itinerary, although, with all due respect, I am not certain how what I do is of any importance to you?"

"Please do not take offense. I am learning, albeit it slowly, that some women are seeking resources outside of their homes for, shall we say, independence from their daily domestic routines. You appear to be well educated, so I thought you might have such professional aspirations?"

Savanna was beginning to soften to Archibald's charms. While she questioned his interest in her, she appreciated his assessment regarding women and their abilities beyond their homes.

"I see," replied Savanna with a smile. She looked at the faces of those surrounding her who seemed to be keenly awaiting her retort. "I am pleased that you asked. Pharmaceuticals are of great interest to me. In fact, I am preparing to visit an apothecary in Georgetown in hopes I may work there. The shop is Dr. Litle's Drug Store. I have a letter of introduction to present. We shall see what comes to pass."

"Do let me know if I can be of any help in that regard," offered Archibald with a bow.

"I, as well, may be called upon to assist you in any way needed," added Sawyer who thought better of it after the words escaped his mouth. If Imogen had been a horse she would have been stomping her front leg to indicate her irritation at Sawyer's offer. *What on earth is he thinking? Is he so easily captivated that he might brush me aside in public?* Imogen was not pleased. *I shall have to set her straight when we meet tomorrow. She will soon learn those for whom I care are not to be shared.*

Despite Imogen's reaction, Sawyer found himself gravitating toward Savanna. In addition to her beauty, there was an air about her, a confidence he appreciated.

"It seems I have stirred a hornets nest," chortled Archibald. "Miss Carlyle, it appears you have many willing to come to your aid and, I am certain Mrs. Simmonds will lend any hand necessary to make your time here comfortable. Is that not correct, Imogen?"

"Quite so, Mr. Howard," Imogen formally responded as she cut her squinted eyes toward him in warning.

"What say you that we leave Miss Carlyle and Mr. Frye for a few minutes. Excuse us, will you? I have a matter to discuss and Mrs. Sterling, I would think you have other guests with which to visit?" Archibald declared as he firmly took Imogen by the arm and guided her away. He was determined to accomplish his goal to further engage Savanna and Sawyer with one another and separate Imogen from Sawyer's company, if only temporarily until he could devise a permanent solution.

Chapter Twenty-Nine

William S. Nicholls & Co. was a popular stop for Gertie when she shopped in the city. She enjoyed walking among the aisles of dry goods and household necessities and could rarely keep from looking at the latest trinkets the Nicholls' had imported from abroad. Brooches were among her favorite finds even though they held essentially no worth other than to enhance one of her gowns or shawls. She cared little that there was no significant monetary value attached to them unlike the fine jewelry she had inherited from her mother and grandmother. Those were gems she and her sisters would always cherish as they had the silver fragrance vessel they gifted to Imogen.

"Good afternoon, Gertrude," said Lydia Cromley, her mouth forming a mischievous grin. The wife of Talmadge's good friend Winston, Lydia reveled in her reputation as a gossipmonger. She was delighted to have her path cross with the Taylor sister for she knew of her strong kinship with Talmadge's widow and hoped to gain some new details, or at the very least spread her own toxic tales about the Widow Simmonds. There were many who suspected her to be the voice of *The National Intelligencer's* gossip columnist Tillie Tattler, though no one had been able to prove such a claim.

"Good afternoon to you, Lydia," responded Gertrude with a slight irritation in her voice. She preferred to remain guarded whenever in Lydia's presence. The woman was known for asking probing questions, which curiously often showed up in print.

"I am so delighted to see you. It has been far too long. I suppose you have been busy trying to cope with the nefarious activities of your poor friend who has taken to wayward ways."

"What my friends do or do not do should not be of importance to you," said Gertrude trying to maintain her decorum.

"Ah, then you do not deny the allegations about the Widow Simmonds?"

Gertrude held back a retort while she gathered her thoughts. She wanted to remain objective about Lydia and refrain from having her physical appearance contribute to her attitude toward her. Lydia was a homely woman of short stature. Her coarse hair was dry with no sheen to brighten the strands of gray beginning to form about her temples. Her ruddy face lent some color to her otherwise drab appearance. Even her eyes, which were a mousey brown, had no sparkle. Her skin was dull with no glow. It was as though she had scrubbed away the natural oils that might have delayed the spread of wrinkles that had formed about her mouth, the edges of her eyes and across her forehead. She was no beauty by any stretch of the imagination. *If Lydia is responsible for the gossip column, perhaps her mean-spirited missives have sucked the youth from her skin,* thought Gertrude with satisfaction.

"May I be brutally honest? I prefer not to engage with you in such conversation. If you have questions about Imogen, I strongly suggest you approach her with them directly rather than trouble me with your inquiries."

"You surprise me, Gertrude. Are your manners something of a forgotten past?"

"My manners have not waned, nor do they have any bearing on this conversation. If anyone needs to examine her conduct at this juncture you have but to view your image in a dressing glass. Since you are not here to bid me glad tidings Lydia, I suggest that one of us remove herself from this store or at the very least take to a different aisle," Gertrude urged as she began to step away.

"I understand how difficult it must be to watch someone for whom you care make such an uncertain and, quite frankly, inappropriate and frivolous use of their lives."

"Do you not have a better place to focus your scrutiny? None of this should be any of your concern and I would warn you to avoid slanderous statements.

I am sure your husband, as a respected lawyer, would advise you the same," Gertrude replied as she turned her back on Lydia and exited the store.

Dearest Readers,

Your friend Tillie has it on good authority that the Merry Widow's friends are trying their best to protect her reputation. 'Tis a difficult task she has handed them. They are not issuing a peep about her. In fact, they appear embarrassed to discuss her behavior. This writer truly doubts the Merry Widow will be able to alter her ways. We shall see.

With titillating prospects on the horizon,
Tillie Tattler

Chapter Thirty

Late February 1822

The clocks throughout Woodholme struck the noon hour, one slightly behind the other. The amalgamation of their lack of precision created a cacophony that startled Imogen from her thoughts. Less than twenty-four hours before, she met the beauty named Savanna and invited her to come to her home.

Savanna, Talmadge's offspring and my stepdaughter, Imogen acknowledged with some chagrin. *I must keep an open mind about her. Talmadge would want that of me. Were he alive, I know he would embrace the knowledge of her and want her in our lives.* Imogen may have been saying the words but the mere speaking of them was not convincing her to believe them. She placed her hand on her abdomen and gave it a gentle pat, imagining what it would be like to be with child. Such was an opportunity not afforded to her, yet it was one to which she had never been opposed. She and Talmadge had discussed the desire for children early on in their marriage but try as they might, she remained barren and they resolved themselves to the fact that parenthood for them was not to be.

Just think, Imogen muttered to herself. *Virginia was able to give Talmadge something I could not. But, he never knew, he never knew,* she lamented as the sting of her infertility seared her ego.

Before making her way from her bedchamber, she took one final look into the cheval glass. She issued forth an approving smile. Her gown was the perfect complement to her flaxen colored hair and blue eyes. It was fabricated of cotton in a soft shade of jade green with satin embellishments of quilted leaves along the hemline, creating a raised pattern in a trapunto style. She wore a choker length necklace with a large pear-shaped aquamarine drop and briolette earrings to match.

This will do quite nicely to greet her, voiced Imogen. *And, being in our home will give her the opportunity to see how prosperous and successful her father was. I do wonder what she will want to know of him?*

As she descended the staircase, she paused on the landing to take in the opulence around her. *Yes Talmadge,* she looked to the ceiling as she addressed him. *You and I have been quite fortunate. We may not have created a child together, but we have always had much for which to be grateful.*

"There ye are mum. Yer visitor is in the drawin' room. Is there anythin' I ken be getting' fer ye?" Patti announced with raised decibels breaking Imogen's concentration on her surroundings.

"For goodness' sake, Patti! You nearly scared the wits from me! Lower your voice or our guest will think you crass. You may bring us tea and a plate of sweets but please give us a few moments alone before you do so."

"Yes, mum. Of course, mum," Patti replied softly, adding a brief curtsy before going on her way. Imogen shook her head, then set her eyes on the doors of the drawing room. With a moderate degree of nervous anticipation she opened the doors, prompting Savanna to stand to greet her. If it were possible, Savanna was even more beautiful than she had been last evening. Imogen held back a gasp as she took in her beauty. *Talmadge would have had difficulty containing his joy in her presence. The knowledge of her would at first, I am certain, have caught him off guard until he warmed to the idea that there was someone on this earth whom he could call 'daughter.' Oh, how he would have relished this moment. I must make the most of this for him and treat her warmly.*

"Mrs. Simmonds, thank you for your kind invitation to your home and for receiving me this day."

"The pleasure is mine. Here, please sit. Make yourself comfortable. My house girl will bring along tea but in the meantime I suspect you have questions, which I will try my best to answer."

"First let me say, your home is magnificent. There are so many special touches where it appears great care was taken at every turn to accommodate the size and use of the rooms."

"How kind and thoughtful of you to observe. My husband gave me carte blanche to do as I wished, almost literally, as though Woodholme were an unblemished piece of white paper. I had a blank slate upon which to design the contents of each room."

"Well, without the fear of repeating myself, it is magnificent."

Imogen sensed an awkward silence forming between them, which she hoped to halt. Although she had not scripted the young woman's visit, she had decided to use the latest edition of *The Inquirer* as a starting point to conversations about Talmadge.

"So, if I may, I shall refer to my late husband as your father unless you take discomfort in such appellation?"

"As you wish. It will take some time for me to become comfortable with the revelation that I am not of the blood of the mother and father forever known to me. Meeting with Mrs. Sterling has given me some comfort and has helped in understanding the circumstances that brought her to make the decision to have me raised by others. Please do not misunderstand, for I love the Carlyles. They are the only family I have ever known. However, I wish they had been forthright with me. Their secretiveness has created a wound that will take time to heal. In the meantime, I wish to learn more of Mr. Simmonds. I understand that you have no children of your own?"

"That is correct. Your father was generous, kind and loving and would have thoroughly embraced you as his daughter. He was a very proud person and I might add, very handsome. He was also a very determined man who was highly respected not only in business but in the social circles he frequented. He was passionate about the newspaper industry and you can see from the quality of the content of this edition of *The Inquirer*, his pragmatism was a good match for the high ideals he lent to his craft," Imogen shared. Her eyes filled with tears as she handed the newspaper to Savanna who turned several pages before speaking.

"In addition to publishing, what were his other interests?"

"He enjoyed traveling, social events, the outdoors, especially time in our gardens, and he had a keen interest in architecture. He worked very closely with the architect on the design for Woodholme. In fact, the architect said he found it refreshing to work with someone who was not ignorant of the arts. He said there are those who think they have good taste but clearly do not. Talmadge had a great design sense. He was very adept at writing and enjoyed arranging interviews with the city's elite as well as ordinary citizens such as shopkeepers, stable hands and any order of interesting souls whose stories he felt would be of interest to his readers."

"I wish we could turn back the clock and he could be sitting with us right now. But alas, that was not meant to be."

"I share your wish," Imogen sighed. "He is often in my thoughts and will always remain in my heart. You know you favor his features in many ways and those of your mother. Upon meeting Virginia, I am sure you witnessed her green eyes that are a match for yours? Did she tell you that you have your father's lustrous black hair? I can show you. Let us take leave to your father's study where there is a small painted portrait of him."

"I should like to see that," said Savanna as she looked over the fireplace mantel and acknowledged the large portrait of Imogen. "Yours is quite impressive."

"As I mentioned, your father was very generous. It was his idea to commission a portrait of me. Some might find it ostentatious however, if you have great wealth and great taste, why not display it?" Imogen laughed as she led the way to Talmadge's study. A knock at the front portal brought Patti scurrying along the hallway.

"Oh, Patti, after you see to the door, please bring our tea and sweets to Mr. Simmonds' study. We shall partake of our refreshments there."

"Yes, mum," she answered with a touch of annoyance to be given two tasks to complete simultaneously. *Good Lord! I'm only one person, I am. 'ow can I be gettin' the door and gettin' the tray of tea?* Patti shook her head with a scowl on her face until she opened the door and saw a face that always brought her pleasure.

"Well, if it ain't Mr. Frye. 'ow are ye sir? Was the missus expectin' ye?"

"Thank you for asking, Patti," Sawyer replied as he stepped into the foyer.

Patti noticed he took care not to answer her question and he was determined to enter whether he was expected or not.

"The missus already has a visitor," noted Patti.

"Well, now she has two," retorted Sawyer.

Imogen heard the voices in the foyer and then the sound of footsteps coming toward the study. While Savanna admired the portrait of Talmadge, Imogen stepped to the doorway and was surprised and somewhat annoyed to see Sawyer.

"Good morning, Imogen!"

"What a lively greeting, Sawyer. Do you come bearing some exciting news?"

"Not at all. I thought we could review some ideas I have for the newspaper?"

Imogen stepped further into the hallway making every effort to keep Sawyer away from her other guest. "Actually, now is not a good time. I have a visitor, as you are well aware. Did I not convey my wishes clearly enough last evening when I said I wanted to meet with her alone?" Imogen was doing all she could to maintain her calm and keep her voice down.

"Indeed you did. I thought I might at the very minimum award her a friendly 'hello.' She is new to the city and would most likely appreciate more who will make her feel welcome here."

"And you are suggesting that you should be assigned that task? If I did not know better, I would think you had an ulterior motive? When you say *more* do you mean admirers?"

"Imogen, surely you are not insinuating there is more to my visit?"

Just as Imogen readied herself to respond, Savanna appeared in the doorway and smiled at Sawyer. For a moment he seemed to have lost the ability to speak. He was captivated by her beauty, which sent him into a momentary trance until she spoke and broke the spell.

"Mr. Frye. How pleasant to see you again," Savanna declared softly, her voice almost like the purr of a kitten.

"Yes, thank you Miss Carlyle. And you as well."

Imogen felt suddenly invisible. The two had locked a gaze on one another. It was as though she did not exist in their world. *I was determined to like this girl, especially for Talmadge's sake, and treat her like the daughter we never had, but my better instincts are telling me that she is going to be trouble where Sawyer is concerned.*

"So, Miss Carlyle, I take it you have found suitable lodgings?"

Imogen was aghast at Sawyer's inquiry. *Why would he find her lodgings of any interest? Perhaps I should offer her a room at Woodholme so I can keep a watch over her comings and goings? That might however limit my privacy. Why would I want to put myself in such a position?* Imogen was in a quandary. *I can always make other arrangements for myself. Yes, it might be best to have her under my roof.*

"I have. They are quite sufficient for my needs."

"And are your needs many?" Sawyer inquired much to Imogen's chagrin.

"My, you are a curious sort are you not, Mr. Frye?"

"Merely wanting the best for you during your visit."

If Imogen were a fowl, her feathers would have been fully splayed, especially around her neck, which was feeling thick and warm. She had had enough of what she deemed the flirtation initiated by Sawyer. *I must put an end to this conversation at once!* Imogen silently shouted.

"If I may interject, Savanna you are most welcome to reside here at Woodholme. It will give you the freedom to come and go as you wish, for I can provide transportation for you and your daily meals will be ample. My staff will see to your comfort and the walls that meant so much to your father will embrace you. What say you to my offer?"

Savanna hesitated to respond too quickly. She had rejected Virginia's offer to stay at Rosedale and did not want to offend her by accepting Imogen's proposal. *My father's connection to Woodholme may help me feel his presence. To walk the same halls, reside in the same rooms and visit the gardens he enjoyed may bring a needed ease of comfort.*

"Yes, Mrs. Simmonds. I shall accept your kind offer to stay in your beautiful home. I shall arrange for my belongings to be brought from Union tomorrow morning, if that arrangement is acceptable to you?"

"Wonderful. I am delighted. You will be welcomed here and it will give us the opportunity to know one another better. Your father would be most pleased to have you here."

Sawyer's ears perked to learn Savanna had taken a room at Union Tavern and Hotel. He knew it well. It was a favorite spot to stop for an afternoon glass of ale and small repast before returning to *The Inquirer*.

"Miss Carlyle, I assume transportation from Union that brought you here was dispatched elsewhere. Please allow me to escort you back to your lodgings. My carriage is at the ready, so there will no need to have Mrs. Simmonds' man Calvin prepare hers. I am happy to be at your service."

Imogen was beginning to seethe. *All the more reason I need the girl to stay with me so I can keep an eye on her. What is Sawyer thinking? His 'welcoming' Savanna to the city is becoming a bit too familiar for my liking.*

"How kind of you, Mr. Frye. Yes, I shall accept your offer."

"Very well then, after you. Good day, Imogen. I shall speak with you later," Sawyer said as he gestured his hand forward for Savanna to precede him through the foyer and out the door.

Imogen stood stoically still. She wanted to scream but held back her emotions. "Speak with me later! Humph! Oh you certainly will," Imogen declared aloud as Patti came around the corner with a tray of tea and sweets.

"Where'd ye like me to be puttin' these refreshments, mum?" Patti asked as she looked around to see no one else in sight. "'ave yer visitors gone?"

Imogen knew what she would like to reply but it would not be very ladylike. "You may put them in the drawing room Patti. It appears I shall be a party of one," Imogen replied sadly. She was beginning to feel as she had when the news came of Talmadge's death. Joy had drained from her face. She feared she was losing Sawyer. *Will I ever feel felicity again?* Imogen questioned, as she sat alone with nothing but a cup of tea to bring her comfort and warmth.

"You have a wonderful laugh," Sawyer said to Savanna as they rode along through Georgetown. "I hope it not too bold for me to say so."

"Not at all. It is much better for one to be told something pleasant about herself than to be scolded for a less welcoming trait."

"I am glad you have joy to express. When Imogen told me of your story it would only be natural for one such as yourself to be overcome by the truth that has been withheld from you all these years."

Savanna laughed. "Firstly, I refuse to let bitterness prevail and secondly, you make me sound ancient when you say 'all these years.' I would guess you are the senior statesman here, although it is probably not proper of me to discuss age with you."

"I have no reason to hold back my age. I am six and twenty."

"I guess then, I am surprised you would want to accompany me to Union since you apparently prefer to be in the company of a woman some years your senior?" Savanna noted with a dubious grin.

Sawyer was caught off guard. He wondered what she was implying. "What an interesting statement. May I inquire about the basis for such a comment?"

"I have eyes and they rarely deceive me. Only an imbecile would not see the way you and Mrs. Simmonds look at one another. It was quite apparent to me at Mrs. Sterling's party when first we met. And, Mr. Howard was very anxious to part the two of you. And, there is today when you offered to drive me to Union. I say, that would not have been Mrs. Simmonds' preference."

"You have only freshly arrived in the city and have formed some interesting assumptions. Imogen is my employer and we enjoy a mutually agreeable friendship."

"Ah, is that what it is being called in this country these days?"

"My word. Have manners been discarded like rubbish?"

"Pardon me if you find my words acerbic but I prefer to get right to the point of things. If you have an *agreement* with Mrs. Simmonds that pleases you both, then by all means you should pursue it."

"What if such pursuit put me at risk of losing another *agreement* of which I might take great pleasure?"

"What on earth are you suggesting?" Savanna queried, taking pleasure in their repartee.

"Perhaps it is best for me to refrain from responding. Here, we have arrived at our destination. You were wise to seek lodging in Georgetown. Many who reside in the City of Washington spend much of their time enjoying the amenities the town has to offer. Here, let me help you from the carriage."

Sawyer stepped down and lent a hand to Savanna. As she looked up to take his hand, her shoe caught on the edge of her gown causing her to lose her footing, which thrust her forward into Sawyer's waiting arms. Her body came hard against his chest. The side of her face rubbed against his warm cheek, which sent unexpected, tantalizing shivers throughout her torso. As she turned her head to free herself from his face, her lips brushed against his, producing a fleeting moment of bliss. She put her arms around his shoulders as he guided her down his body to rest her feet on the ground. It all happened in seconds, which she knew she would relive over and over in her mind to extend the pleasure of the moment.

"Are you quite all right?"

"More than quite," Savanna replied as she focused on his dark brown eyes, rich with random flecks of gold.

Sawyer mirrored her gaze, taking in every facet of her emerald orbs. *What is happening?* The question circled about his confused mind. Little did he know, the same question was running about Savanna's mind. Their skin-to-skin encounter left them both at a loss for words, while the need for more was creating a mounting desire within them. A whinny from the horse and stomp of his foot startled them to attention.

"I guess I best be on my way. My mission is accomplished. I have gotten you safely here and my horse has become impatient."

"I thank you for the drive and for catching me. I am typically not so clumsy," apologized Savanna as she turned toward the hotel.

Sawyer touched her arm, his gloved hand to hers. "No worries. Will you be in need of transport to Woodholme in the morning? I can circle round before I begin my work day. It will be no trouble."

"How kind. Perhaps it would be best for me to have Union's driver get me there. It might be best for Mrs. Simmonds to see that too."

Sawyer appreciated her concern for Imogen's feelings, although he wondered if he would be showing the same concern. His initial interest in Savanna had turned to more. Riding with her in the carriage, watching her laugh and then, the near kiss created an accumulation of delectable sensations inviting his imagination to soar.

"Very well, I understand. However, no falling into the carriage driver when you disembark. You must reserve such actions for me," laughed Sawyer as he hopped into his carriage and commanded his horse to move along. "Step up son," he ordered as the horse with its charge moved along Bridge Street toward High Street to *The Inquirer's* office. The clip clop of the horse's hooves held Sawyer's focus, tuning out all the other sounds about him as he rode along with visions of Savanna whirling in his head.

Virginia was not overly dismayed when she learned Savanna had taken up residence at Woodholme. She understood how she might be drawn there to be nearer to her father's life, staying in his home around the objects he saw and touched. Imogen had been kind enough to suggest Virginia could call on Savanna from time to time if she so desired, which Imogen saw as a way to keep Savanna occupied and away from Sawyer.

Savanna's accommodations at Woodholme were exquisite. Her bedchamber in warm shades of lavender, green and rose held every amenity. The large four poster bed was plump with linens; small chests with oil lamps on top flanked each side of the bed; a double-door wardrobe left ample room for her clothing; and a writing desk did double service as a dressing table replete with a sterling silver brush, comb and hand mirror. A full-length cheval looking glass stood to the left of the fireplace whose richly carved marble mantel featured wisps of vines and leaves. In a far corner was a basin and pitcher with soap and linens awaiting her morning toilette.

She found it easy to settle into her surroundings and Imogen had been very gracious inviting her to use the home as though it were her own. Imogen's manner was not what her appearance suggested on first impression of an austere, rigid, self-righteous person. She could be genial and warm when circumstances moved her to be so, and not the evil stepmother Savanna had met in some of the novels she read.

Imogen greeted Savanna in the conservatory for their morning meal where a dining table and chairs sat before a wall of windows providing a magnificent view of the gardens. Winter's chill left the gardens devoid of much color. The few stubborn leaves holding onto the branches of deciduous trees would be no match for the strong winds, rain and snow that was sure to come. Savanna liked to imagine the gardens full of bloom, and trees with lush canopies providing needed shade from the heat and humidity she had heard were typical of the summer season. *I wonder if I shall be in the City of Washington come spring?* It was as though Imogen read her thoughts.

"Tell me, what are your plans?"

"I should like to make a call on the apothecary in Georgetown to inquire about work there."

"Actually, I meant beyond today. You, of course, are welcome to stay here as long as needed," Imogen offered, thinking better of her statement as soon as the words left her mouth. *What if she remains in the city and becomes a distraction for Sawyer? I must see to it that such an outcome does not occur. Ah, I could ask Gertie and her sisters to play matchmaker and find a suitable gent for her.*

Imogen enjoyed Savanna's company and was initially pleased with her decision to have her as a guest in her home. Her resemblance to Talmadge comforted Imogen and along with the traits she inherited from Virginia, Savanna had the best of both parents. She was a beauty full of grace.

Imogen had grown fond of her but feared someone else in her life was leaning in the same direction. *I feel so conflicted!* Imogen raged as her mind toyed with ways to possibly rid herself of Savanna without causing undue harm.

"At Virginia's party, I recalled your revealing an interest in pharmacology, which drew my attention to a newspaper story about the Philadelphia College of Pharmacy formed earlier in the year by a group of pharmacists there. Perhaps you would find great appeal in pursuing your interest in pharmaceuticals in the Philadelphia area where there is a very passionate contingent of pharmacists. In fact, in a tip of their hats to America's founding fathers, they met in Carpenters' Hall in February one year ago to devise a constitution for an association to protect the sanctity of their profession. The resulting Philadelphia College of Pharmacy opened in early November. It seems it would behoove you to inquire about applying for entrance."

"How kind of you to offer such a suggestion. It is something I shall consider, for I am not opposed to entering a field not typically held by my gender. Of course, of that fact you are aware, or perhaps you know I quite like a challenge?" Savanna slightly tilted her head and fluttered her eyes as her mouth formed a mocking grin.

"Ah, I see you misinterpret my suggestion. I am merely looking out for your best interests. I am aware that the medicinal herb industry is expanding thanks to a group of whom you may not have heard considering your limited time here. The United Society of Believers in Christ's Second Appearing is harvesting an enormous variety of herbs for use by physicians and those of your ilk."

"My goodness that is quite a title. From where I stand, it appears you have been quite busy learning about my area of interest. Is that true?"

"It is never too late to educate oneself, even in areas upon which one has little or no interest."

"Perhaps there is an elixir for your affliction," Savanna laughed as she watched Imogen's face roll into a scowl.

"Well, have you amused yourself? There is no need to exhibit a hostel attitude toward me. I should think you would want to maintain your reputation as one with certain refinements considering those who sired you."

Savanna had not been the recipient of a verbal lashing by Imogen until now. She questioned what had spawned her indignation. *It seems my attempt at humor was misplaced. Probably best that I let it go for now,* Savanna wisely contemplated, deciding not to engage in a war of words with Imogen.

"And yet, maybe I will be satisfied with a possible apprenticeship in the pharmacy in Georgetown. I have a letter of introduction from Doc Yates whom you may have known in Chelsea? His Royal Rose Apothecary is quite well respected, and I am certain that his recommendation on my behalf will be well received here."

"When you say *here*, of where do you speak?"

"Why the apothecary in Georgetown at the corner of Water and Falls Streets, of course. I recently learned that due to the ownership for many years by the druggist John Ott, the shop has gained an excellent reputation for the compounds it dispenses. Dr. Litle's Drug Store is its current title. I intend to call on him within the week. In fact perhaps today."

Imogen held her tongue as thoughts whirled through her head. *Perhaps I shall call on Dr. Litle before she does and discourage him from hiring her. I want her out of the city.* A faint smile crossed Imogen's face as she relished in the idea of her preemptive measure to sabotage Savanna's employment.

"You hesitate. Is there something I must know about Dr. Litle before I approach him with my request?"

"Oh no, my dear. I was merely giving thought to another matter."

"Well, if Dr. Litle will have me, I am certain I will excel under his tutelage."

"Time will tell, time will tell," quipped Imogen.

"You asked about my plans beyond today. As I just mentioned, if Dr. Litle will have me and I find my position there acceptable, I may extend my stay. There is no reason or rush for me to return to England."

Fast approaching footsteps broke the cadence of their conversation as Sawyer entered the conservatory, pulled up a chair and joined the ladies at the table with Patti in hot pursuit.

"It's sorry I am mum. 'e rushed right by me an' be givin' me no time to announce 'is arrival," puffed Patti as she caught her breath. "Well, Mr. Frye, I'd be offerin' ye to 'ave a seat but looks like ye 'ave already invited yerself. Would ye be wantin' some biscuits to go with the tea ye be pourin'?"

Sawyer laughed. He was not one to stand on ceremony, or worry about proper etiquette in Imogen's home. He knew he would be welcomed there or, so he thought until he looked at her expression.

"What Imogen? Have I done something to warrant your reprimand?"

"Let's see. You come barging in during our morning meal when the timepiece on the mantel indicates you should be well on your way to the office. I am afraid to ask what brings you here?"

"I can think of no better way to start my day than in the presence of two beautiful women."

If Imogen were not looking directly at Sawyer as he spoke she would have thought it was Archibald uttering some of his flagrant flattery. Sawyer knew full well why he was there. Resisting being in Savanna's company was becoming unbearable, which racked him with guilt. He knew his allegiance was to Imogen not only for his employment but also because he enjoyed being in her presence and pleasuring her, something that filled lustful needs for them both.

"I believe I may speak for Miss Carlyle and say we are moved by your kind salutation," replied Imogen, hoping it was not the chance to see Savanna that spurred his visit.

"Speaking of Miss Carlyle, how are you this fine day?"

"Very well, thank you. Imogen has made me very happy here."

"Ah, Imogen is it? So you are finding comfort in addressing her less formally?"

"Indeed I have, Mr. Frye," smiled Savanna.

Sawyer was not certain whether a twinkle came to her eyes when she used his surname or he was seeing a reflection off the wavy glass of the windows. Either way, her voice warmed him and he could only hope she would find comfort and choose to refer to him by his given name. Then again, he was afraid if that should happen, he might be so delighted he would not be able to control his glee. In Imogen's presence, that would be an enormous error of judgment on his part. *For now, Mr. Frye it must remain,* Sawyer rationalized.

"What do you ladies have on your agendas?"

"Miss Carlyle was just telling me she hopes to make her way to Dr. Litle's Drug Store to inquire about employment."

"Here I am once again at your service. My carriage awaits and, if you would like, I will be happy to deliver you to his doorstep."

"Sawyer, Miss Carlyle may not be ready to depart just now."

"Ah, are you speaking for the two of you again or shall we allow her to answer for herself?"

Savanna was sensing the beginning of a sparring match developing between the two. She wondered if they needed a moment without her in the room. She did not want to decline Sawyer's offer yet in the same breath she did not want to annoy her hostess.

"If it is agreeable Mr. Frye, I have only to retrieve my reticule from my room. My letter of introduction from Doc Yates in Chelsea is within. I shan't be but a few minutes if you are not opposed to the delay?"

"By all means, Miss Carlyle. There is no rush on my end."

When Savanna stepped into the hallway and Imogen heard her footsteps on the staircase, she turned to Sawyer with a glare.

"What exactly are you up to? Of late, you have found more and more reasons to make unannounced visits here. Are my visits to *The Inquirer* after hours not enough for you? Or, is it someone else's company you seek?" Imogen was beginning to feel short of breath as she continued her reproof. "I am well able to provide transportation for her, yet you keep stepping up and volunteering your services. Pardon me if I am feeling suspicious, which seems justified!"

"No need to worry, Imogen. It always brightens my day to see you in the morning, however, since Miss Carlyle arrived, those mornings have become fewer and fewer. So, here I am," replied Sawyer as he stood and moved to Imogen. He took her hands in his and lifted them up, encouraging her to stand. "How about a kiss to start my workday?"

Sawyer had a way about him that soothed and calmed Imogen's disquieted spirits. Perhaps it was his youth that contributed to his playful demeanor? Whatever the cause, she was delighted to oblige him. But first, she looked through the windows to ensure none from her staff were about the grounds to witness their intimate display.

Imogen moved forward. Sawyer put his hands about her waist and pulled her close. He brushed his hand along her cheek before placing a tender kiss there and then moved his lips along her jawline to her mouth. She welcomed the warmth of his lips with an immediate response that spoke of desire. Neither was intent on pulling away. Sawyer moved his hands upward about her bodice as she moved her hands to his neck and pulled him closer. Their kisses became more intense until their good senses warned them to await a more appropriate private setting free from intrusions. She wanted him to ravish her but she knew that would have to wait. They ceased their embrace and moved apart just in time as Savanna reentered the conservatory. She observed the look of guilty pleasure on their faces. *Had I expedited my return,*

I dare wonder what I might have encountered? Rumors about her father's widow and suspicions about the company she was keeping had come her way on occasion with a guest at Virginia's. She had hoped it was Archibald Howard who sated her desires, however one look at Imogen and Sawyer confirmed an attraction beyond that of employee and employer, which Savanna was dismayed to see. *Why am I having these thoughts about him?*

She was not alone in her thoughts. Savanna's arrival in the city was causing a distraction for Sawyer he had not anticipated. He also was finding it more and more difficult to avoid Archibald's wary eye. Archibald's suspicions and jealousies were mounting to the point Sawyer felt threatened merely being in the same room with him. Imogen attempted, whenever possible, to suppress Archibald's fears about Sawyer much as she had with Talmadge when he became aware of her association with Archibald. She was worried their relationship was eroding.

Her mind turned to Archibald and then to Sawyer and Savanna. *Can it be that Archibald cannot see his way to share me with another? I have seen the glances he gives to members of his own gender and have not called him out on it. Perhaps I feel no competition with them? No matter, for my main concern is Sawyer. Am I imagining his interest in Savanna? Am I the one exhibiting jealousy? Surely I have more confidence in myself than this, or do I not?*

Imogen's thoughts were making her weary. She was wont to be free of self-doubt but as she watched Sawyer assist Savanna into the carriage for their trip to Dr. Litle's, she closed her eyes and prayed her intuitions were unjustified.

Chapter Thirty-One

Agnes Taylor's fragrance vessel had become an amulet of sorts for Imogen. She found herself wearing it as part of her daily wardrobe, or at the very least carrying it in her reticule, the handbag's drawstring keeping the piece secure. She was enchanted with fondling its smooth silver surface. To be entrusted with the stewardship of the heirloom was an honor she was well apt to receive. She hoped there was truth in the belief that the charm of such ornaments was the protection they provided the wearer. She wondered if there was an incantation she might evoke to ward off any evil or harm threatening to come her way? *It is as though my world has become a large kettle with its contents ready to reach the boiling point and melt me away*, Imogen worried.

She was reminded of the taunting chant of the three witches in the couplet from Shakespeare's MacBeth: 'Double, double, toil and trouble; Fire burn and cauldron bubble.' As she recited the words, she shook her head to ward off any dire predications. She wished not to follow MacBeth's fate as he had with the prophecies of the witches whose callings to him reminded her of the sirens of the sea in Greek mythology who lured impetuous sailors into their watery lairs.

She held the vessel and rubbed it between her thumb and forefinger to gain solace and erase her thoughts of witches and evil. She captured a waft of the comforting scent of Agnes' cologne, which remained evident having withstood the passage of time. *A call to the Taylors would be best advised,* she reasoned, as she prepared for her visit. *After all, I do owe them an explanation for my failure to enlighten them about the secret of which Talmadge was unaware.*

Her voice began to catch at the mere mention of his name. *Is it residual guilt worming its way into my thinking? Oh no,* declared Imogen. *I will not allow myself to become mired in guilt's sadness and regret.* However, the sting of grief and self-doubt lingered as Imogen awaited the opening of the Taylor's portal.

"Gertie, I find myself so confused," explained Imogen as the senior Taylor greeted her. Hazel, Mabel and Tea, in their customary receiving line, led the way to a cozy seating area. Imogen drew comfort from her visits, which were met with kindly reception. She was susceptible to their thoughts and took value in their guidance.

"It is your advice I seek. It seems I am not succeeding when it comes to making the best choices for myself, particularly where the male gender is involved. Once again I find myself in need of direction."

"What is it, my dear? You know I am most obliged to assist you in any way, although my experience with men is very limited. Tea has always been my true love and my sisters did not bless me with brothers-by-marriage, so I have a very small realm of understanding when it comes to men," said Gertie with a playful sigh as she looked at Tea.

"Many might deem you fortunate in that regard," Imogen observed. "My world would be much less complicated but for the men in my life. It is an attraction from which I cannot seem to waiver."

"Well, in one area you have got it right. Life embodies many choices. We know you prefer to disregard some of society's norms and mores however, there are standards to which we must adhere if we are to live in peace with not only others but more importantly ourselves," Gertie remarked, trying her best not to sound like she was preaching to Imogen.

"Why would I listen to them? Who are these people to determine what I desire, what my best choices might be?" Imogen bristled.

Tea and the Taylor sisters looked at one another. They were feeling the weight of revisiting Imogen's inability to budge from her wayward ways and suspected she had more to reveal that was burdening her.

"I know you, as am I, are a student of Shakespeare," noted Tea. "His character Iago in *Othello* makes a statement very apropos to our conversation. Without presenting myself as a thorn in your side I will share it with you: 'Who steals my purse steals trash; But he that filches from me my good name robs me of that which, not enriches him and makes me poor indeed.' Wise words to be considered."

"Thank you Tea. I appreciate your astute assessment of my situation, yet I shall not relinquish my independence to my prudish peers."

"What most is troubling you today?" Hazel and Mabel spoke in unison.

"You always have the uncanny ability to see through me. Such skill must go hand in hand with being wise. I must admit to you that I was remiss or, shall we say, less than forthcoming on my last visit. However, I prefer to think of myself as being guilty of omission," Imogen announced as the four pairs of eyebrows facing her became raised.

"You have us intrigued. Please do go on," encouraged Gertie, as the others nodded in affirmation.

"I hope you will not think I am speaking ill of the dead but this is about Talmadge," revealed Imogen as she proceeded to slowly tell the Taylor sisters and Tea about Virginia Sterling and everything Virginia had disclosed about Talmadge and the child the two had created. Her audience sat in silent reverence as she spoke, never interrupting for any inquiries to be expressed.

"There you have it," said Imogen as her voice began to falter and tears welled in her eyes. "I held close this information because I did not want to ruin Talmadge's reputation in your eyes."

"To say we are stunned is an understatement. We never suspected, we never suspected," repeated Gertie as she shook her head in disbelief.

"The news was quite disturbing to me as you might well imagine," shared Imogen. "And now, the child, young woman actually, is in the city. Her name is Savanna."

"Have the two of you met?"

"That we have. I have such mixed emotions about her. On the one hand she is the daughter Talmadge and I never had, yet on the other hand she is finding popularity with someone dear to me, which does not settle well with me," Imogen sighed. She enjoyed the gentle rapport Gertie, Tea and the sisters lent her and felt at ease in their presence. Their understanding of her was as harmonious as the chords and notes Mabel played on the family's Chickering. They provided calming voices of reason, which she appreciated and respected.

"Are we to surmise the one dear to you is Mr. Frye? I only cite him because of his age. It would seem he and, it is Savanna I believe you said, have a proximity of age that might draw them to one another?"

"Yes. You once again correctly perceive the situation in which I find myself. I truly do not want to lose him."

"Maybe there are unspoken words the two of you need to address to understand the place you hold in each other's lives?" Hazel suggested as her sisters and Tea looked on contemplatively.

"I remember Mother often saying, 'We all have our druthers,'" noted Mabel. "I think that might have been the way she addressed the choices or preferences we make in our lives. Would you 'druther' lose Mr. Howard than Mr. Frye?"

Imogen had not considered losing either one. *I expect to keep both men in my life. Why would they go elsewhere when they have me?* Even as the words went round and round in her mind, her confidence receded, as the fear that she might lose Sawyer to another threatened to paralyze her.

"It seems you must ask yourself what is the force that drives you? Is it the challenge to win, to be the victor at all costs? Or is it love, or the need to be loved?" Gertie asked as her concern for Imogen mounted.

Imogen was feeling bombarded as the sisters pelted her with questions. If she truly understood her motivations she would have a better grasp of her behavior and not feel the need to seek their advice. She felt a twist within her torso. Their words were heartfelt, of that she was certain but deep within she was not disposed to rein in her promiscuous behavior. She would bid them leave for now. She had shared the news of Savanna. There seemed no more to be gained at this juncture. *Maybe an ending is what I need no matter how painful? An ending would offer me a new beginning? Heaven knows I have endured loss and survived. No, I cannot think that way. I always get what I want, and I shall not be denied now or in the future.*

Chapter Thirty-Two

March 1822

The soles of her shoes moved slowly along the flagstone path covered with the latest remnants of nature's bountiful release. The scattered foliage, its vibrancy long past, had become crisp, making the leaves rustle together with Savanna's every step, creating a swish, swish, swish sound. She enjoyed her much needed moments of solitude where a visit to the extensive gardens at Woodholme provided the respite she needed from thoughts of how she came to be and the new people in her life she was coming to know.

Breathing in the cool air refreshed her as she proceeded deeper into the garden where an ornate iron gate awaited her entry. She lifted the latch and pulled the gate toward her, its rusted hinges seemed to protest as the gate opened full enough to permit her through.

She passed under the arched iron arbor covered with lush vines of English ivy. The verdant perennial canopy was a welcomed contrast amidst the barren branches of the deciduous trees whose buds were beginning to show, ready to wake-up, like a wink to the promise of the future. She enjoyed observing the architecture of the trees, made more obvious with their absence of foliage, each having their very own unique design. Of particular interest was a rather gnarly old oak; its branches crooked and bent like an old witch's fingers. It stood firmly grounded where the path diverged toward a rose garden. Void of their robust blooms, she imagined the rose bushes in the coming months with their velvety petals filling the space with shades of crimson. Lingering nearby was the evidence of several zinnias, the majority of their stems crisp and brown. Savanna bent to sniff the dried flowers to see if perhaps some fragrance lingered, but they too had succumbed to the change in seasons.

She recalled sowing large zinnia seeds as a child, first cultivating the soil then scattering the seeds, covering them with a thin layer of soil and a fine sprinkle of water. She remembered her excitement when only one week later the first sprouts began to show their heads. *Ah, the joys of childhood. Simple and carefree,* she mused as she continued her journey.

She saw a large patch where a field of dahlias had been. She knew their foliage would not tolerate the freezing temperatures of the winter months. She recalled being captivated by the flowers, which the Carlyle's gardener tended, typically in May. She envisioned the delicate petals of the pompon and peony shaped cultivars in soft pink shades, which resembled perfect orbs, encircling a yellow core at their head. Another variety she remembered from home was more cactus-like with long, spiky petals pointed at the end, extending like a ray of sunlight. Savanna was enthralled by the symmetry of the petals during the warm months and the ability of the tubers to endure winter in preparation for early spring.

A sudden robust rustling of leaves interrupted her sole promenade. She had become absorbed in the sights surrounding her, finding succor in the soothing marvels Mother Nature provided when she was startled by the sound making its way closer to her. She turned to locate the source, fearing a wild animal was bold enough to make its approach. She squinted her eyes to focus on something moving in the near distance. She held her breath, then released it when she saw the figure was that of a man. His familiar gait put her at ease.

"I hope I am not a bother? Patti said I might find you here."

Savanna smiled. Sawyer's handsome face was always a welcomed sight. He removed his hat, placed his arm across his abdomen and gave her a bow, which she returned with a slight curtsy.

"I must say, I was at first alarmed, for I feared a wild beast had come to ravage me," Savanna teased. "What brings you here?"

"Not what you were thinking," laughed Sawyer. "Although, the idea does perk my interest."

Savanna felt her face taking on a rosy glow as heat radiated across her cheeks. She was enjoying their repartee, especially since it was free from Imogen's ears. She had announced she would remain ensconced in the drawing room to work on her latest needlework.

"The good news came to me that Dr. Litle has seen fit to hire you. Have you begun your work there?"

"That I have."

"And, what say you? Is the place a good fit?"

"I feel very comfortable there. Dr. Litle is quite knowledgeable and is willing to continue to educate me about the variety of compounds available as well as how to operate his drug store."

"I am certain he finds you more than capable," beamed Sawyer.

Savanna felt a fresh blush cross her cheeks. Sawyer's compliments were about to be her undoing. Propriety prompted her to resist the urge to embrace him, although she sensed he would find favor in her doing so.

"If you do not mind my asking, what brings you to Woodholme today? Surely Imogen informed you of her schedule?"

"You assume we have a daily dialogue that keeps us abreast of each other's events?"

"I apologize. Perhaps it was too bold of me to suggest such a thing? I best not speak of your time away from the newspaper. There is no need for me to be privy to such things."

"I find nothing prying in your questions. You have an innocence about you, which I find most refreshing. It is always a pleasure to see you and I was in hopes we might enjoy a midday meal together one day soon at a tavern of your choosing? For its convenience, I might suggest A.P. Rodier's Oyster House on High and Bridge Streets adjacent to your place of employment. That is, if Dr. Litle is kind enough to let you take leave of his store for a short while?"

"I think that should be quite lovely as long as Imogen takes no exception," pondered Savanna thinking she would like to retract her inclusion of Imogen in the decision-making process. *Why should I care to have her permission for me to be in Sawyer's presence? She has no claim on him.*

Sawyer smiled and moved closer to her. His emotions were beginning to surge as the urge to kiss her nearly overtook him. She returned his smile and looked into his eyes as she stepped closer to him. He took her hands in his and prepared to bring their lips together when the grating creak of the iron gate's hinges sounded a warning alarm that they were no longer alone.

Chapter Thirty-Three

The sight of Sawyer and Savanna in the garden in such close proximity to one another sent titillating sensations throughout Archibald's body. Upon seeing them, he quickly turned and made a hasty exit before they were able to clearly identify who had happened upon them. *This is perfect!* Archibald boasted. *Seeing them together confirms what I have suspicioned and gives me renewed hope that Mr. Frye may resolve the concerns I have about his hold on Imogen's affections. Nonetheless, Imogen may feel challenged to heighten her pursuit of Mr. Frye, which will not serve me well. I must devise a plan to assure he has no further place in Imogen's heart. I think it best I see Imogen and ascertain her true feelings for me.* He worked to clarify his plan as he made haste and returned to Woodholme's front portal.

Patti answered Archibald's knock and upon his inquiry confirmed that the mistress of the manse was alone. Patti ushered Archibald toward the drawing room where Imogen busied herself completing a small needlepoint piece she intended to frame and place in her bedchamber. It was a lovely composition of flowers in varying shades of pink and deep rose, forming a bountiful bouquet held in a cobalt blue vase. As she moved the threaded needle through the cloth, Archibald entered the room with robust flair. His voice boomed out her name, startling her and causing her to stick her finger with the needle.

"My word, Archibald! Are you trying to frighten me to death? Where is Patti? I shall admonish the girl later for not announcing your presence before your entry," Imogen scolded him as she placed her tongue to her finger to ease her discomfort and remove the drop of blood that formed.

"Imogen my dear, I do apologize for my unannounced visit however, one day is turning into the next and I am feeling at a loss when it comes to our alliance. I want passion restored to our shared bond," said Archibald with notes of pleading in his voice.

"You might look elsewhere," Imogen stated bluntly, still examining her finger, although there was a lilt of playfulness in her tone, which went unmet by Archibald's ears.

"Why has your desire for me waned? Are you so enamored by the mere idea of being in the presence of royalty that you allow a false title to rule your emotions? Perhaps I should take on the title of earl or marquess, or at the very minimum apply viscount or baron to my name? Would that produce more passion in you to issue forth in my direction?"

"So you have heard about his title? How did that come about?"

"The *farce* of a title you mean. Quite some time ago, Gibs visited the bank and happened to mention *The Inquirer's* managing editor was the Duke of Wellington. I knew that could be anything but the truth. And, I knew you would never be so gullible. Gibs laughed, and upon my inquiry explained the story to me. Quite a tale, I might add. For all I know, Frye believes he is a duke!"

"He believes no such thing."

"Perhaps he could be royalty for his wandering ways."

"Archibald," Imogen said with an exasperated breath. "What are you implying?"

"Do you not believe him to have roving eyes?" Archibald held his ground as Imogen's annoyance with him grew.

"Why do you want to taunt me so? He is a man and he has eyes. Whether they rove or not does not concern me unless the roving takes a serious turn."

"Well, you might want to sound some bells of alarm for he appears to be sharing his affections with another," said Archibald, as he smiled smugly, quite pleased with himself for placing concern in Imogen's path. He hoped his efforts would end her affair with Sawyer so he could put an end to the evil thoughts formulating in his increasingly wicked mind.

Archibald's demeanor and reputation as a refined, social dandy had begun to take a nasty turn soon after meeting Imogen and Talmadge. Imogen noted that his propensity for malicious behavior was becoming magnified not only in his actions but also in his words. She initially was attracted to his sense of style, his associations in the city, his strength of conviction and the attention he awarded her. Since the outcome of the duel with Talmadge, Archibald's threats were to be taken seriously. She questioned whether Archibald was trying to form a wedge between Sawyer and herself so he could have her solely to himself.

Perhaps I should abandon Sawyer and dismiss him from my life to protect him from Archibald's wrath? She was in a quandary as to the actions she should take. *No, all the more reason to keep Sawyer close and protect him. It is Archibald I should not have welcomed back into my life. Why is it that I cannot resist him?* She continued to want both men in her life and could not imagine herself without either of them.

"Marry me." The words exited Archibald's mouth more as a command than an ask. Imogen was taken aback. Archibald had never suggested such a thing. She always supposed he was satisfied to be free to choose another should their arrangement and his interest in her wane. *I wonder how I would respond if it were Sawyer making a proposal of marriage to me?* The thought brought a smile to her face, which was short lived when Archibald took notice.

"I see my suggestion brings you pleasure?"

"Quite the contrary," Imogen quickly replied. She felt unsettled by his proclamation to be fully committed to her. She knew it was a ruse to sever her ties to Sawyer. "Why do you wish to tantalize me with any discussion of Sawyer Frye? Whom he chooses to frequent his time with is of no concern to me."

"Well, that is certainly good to know since the woman in question is none other than your stepdaughter. My goodness, Imogen! They are courting one another right under your nose!"

"I am well aware of the kindnesses Mr. Frye extends to Miss Carlyle."

"Kindnesses? Is that how such affections are being addressed? I am surprised you are not asking her to remove herself from your home!"

"Why do you persist in turning our time together into a tempestuous argument? You are spewing accusations around trying to capsize my thinking, like an ill-fated boat on stormy seas. I shall not continue this discussion for it does not benefit either of us and, in answer to your proposal, albeit it was weak at best, my answer is an unequivocally firm 'NO!' You are harassing me and causing worry where none exists in what appears to be a lame effort to cause a rift between my employee and myself. You must cease this now!"

"Employee? Employee? You must think me totally daft to believe such a claim! We both know he is far more than an employee to you!"

"Archibald, please refrain from shouting," Imogen said mustering as much calm as she could.

"I shall lower my tone when I feel you have heard me. Mr. Frye is engaging too much of your time and must be dealt with immediately!"

"Are you suggesting that I release him from my employ?"

"That would be a beginning. He needs to disappear and the sooner, the better!"

Imogen was becoming concerned about Archibald's menacing tone. His suggestions that Sawyer had affections for Savanna, while concerning, were challenging her to keep Sawyer in her grasps and see that any dalliance between the two was no more than a simple friendship and interest in one another's welfare. *No, I shall not be taunted by Archibald's ramblings. They are his desperate attempts to limit my freedom to choose whose affections I wish to enjoy. Surely no merit can be found in his intimidating words?*

Her thoughts had no sooner ceased rallying about in her head when Savanna and Sawyer appeared in the doorway. Archibald raised his head with squinted eyes as though needing to view the two through a pair of spectacles that had slipped down his nose. Imogen took note of his posture. *He thinks himself so smart,* thought Imogen wishing she could wipe the smug expression from Archibald's face. *So, the two are together. What of it? Savanna lives here and Sawyer has come to see me. I have no need for concern, or do I?*

Chapter Thirty-Four

Imogen was feeling rattled from Archibald's unannounced visit. Their time together was becoming more and more unsettled. She was glad he took his leave soon after Savanna and Sawyer appeared. She was quite surprised he chose to leave Woodholme before Sawyer. *A wise choice on his part,* thought Imogen. *He senses my displeasure with him and, since he fully believes Sawyer is courting Savanna, he was comfortable leaving the three of us together.*

Her concern and disappointment became elevated when Sawyer barely gave a wink of attention to her. There was no kiss on the cheek, no holding of hands and no intimate gaze, which she could return. She excused his lack of advances thinking he was exercising discretion with Savanna in the room. However, he made a hasty excuse that he was needed at the office, offered a simple bow to both women, and quickly turned, making a swift exit. Imogen was left in the rare position of being speechless. She did note the extra glance he lofted in Savanna's direction, which Savanna captured, then looked away out of respect for Imogen. *Perhaps there is some merit in Archibald's appraisal of the two of them. Am I remiss in casting off what is before me? Is ignorance bliss as poet Thomas Gray penned?* Words from one of her favorite poems by Gray, *'Ode on a Distant Prospect of Eton College,'* which she had memorized, came to mind. *Ah, yes, so it goes, 'where ignorance is bliss, 'tis folly to be wise,'* she reflected.

Savanna looked about the drawing room for a piece of needlework she had begun. Imogen, having completed the small needlework for her bedchamber, went to the table where the book she had selected to read awaited her return. As she picked up the book, she remembered a letter that had arrived earlier that day addressed to Savanna.

"There is a post for you on the entry hall rack," Imogen said to Savanna as she lifted her eyes from the book she was preparing to read and pointed to the foyer. "I took the liberty of looking at the source. It seems your parents, adoptive though they may be, have finally found it necessary to contact you." She regretted her words as soon as they left her mouth. She did not mean to diminish the bond Savanna had with the Carlyles for, after all, they had raised her as their own, yet there was a part of her that continued to feel conflicted about the girl. *Could it be jealousy?* Imogen wondered.

She had taken Savanna into her home to assuage the guilt she felt that Talmadge never knew of her existence and the fact the girl never met her father. He would have wanted Imogen to extend a welcoming hand yet, on the other hand, in addition to Archibald's warnings, Imogen too was sensing a growing friendship between Sawyer and Savanna. She preferred to ignore his foretelling of the future. *He thinks himself a wise soothsayer but his predictions only serve to stir my emotions and confuse me. Oh, so many emotions! Jealousy, guilt, shame, anger to name only a few. I guess I should throw love into the mix, for my conscience tells me I should have a speck of care for the girl.* Imogen's thoughts scurried about. There was a part of her that wished Savanna would return to England and she would be done with her. *I wonder what the post from the Carlyles has to say? With any luck they will insist she come home. Would that not be a lovely solution?*

"Thank you," offered Savanna. "Their letter is most likely in response to the post I sent them to announce my safe arrival and give them my location in the City of Washington. I am sure they are most pleased that you have given me every consideration and that I have found work in Georgetown."

"Oh yes. I would imagine they miss you terribly. Have you given any thought to providing them with your homecoming?"

Savanna laughed. She sensed on occasion that Imogen was merely tolerating her presence, that she felt a duty to provide food and shelter for her. Many of their evenings together in the drawing room rendered pleasant moments of camaraderie as they conversed and worked with needle and thread on canvases to complete needlepoint scenes, which Imogen said she intended to have made into pillows to accent the room's divans. Savanna enjoyed getting to know her better for she could catch glimmers of the softer side of her stepmother. She admired Imogen's intelligence, her management of *The Inquirer* and her dedication to her committee's cause but, in the same breath, she was leery of Imogen's motives and her lack of ability to rein in her anger. She reasoned that she would absolve her of her outbursts as traits necessary for a strong businesswoman.

"I see I have humored you?" Imogen questioned.

"Yes, to a degree. That is, if I did not know better, I might be inclined to think you were ready to have me gone. Perhaps I am overstaying my welcome and best return to Mrs. Sterling's if her offer remains open for, at this juncture, I have no intent on returning to my homeland."

Ah, pondered Imogen. *Yes. Returning to Virginia's is a distinct possibility. I can imagine she would take no exception to having Savanna reside with her. She is after all her daughter.*

"Well, let's wait and see. You have not read the contents of the letter from your parents. Perhaps they present a good case for you to return to them? I am somewhat surprised that curiosity alone has not prompted you to open their correspondence at once? There is no need to answer. For now, I am happy to have you here and hope you feel the same." Imogen hoped not to choke on her words. It was true she could keep closer watch over the girl if she remained at Woodholme but keeping her from Sawyer's view was becoming impossible. *At least I added 'for now.' Should the tide within my mind change, I may see her ebbing away to Rosedale.*

"Yes, indeed. I am most appreciative of your hospitality," Savanna replied, although she had certain suspicions about Imogen's sincerity.

Patti, who lightly tapped on the doorframe to the drawing room and waived an envelope before her as though she were a spectator brandishing a small flag during a parade, interrupted their conversation.

"What is it, Patti?" Imogen queried with annoyance in her tone.

"Pardon me, mum. I was jest dustin' is all and thought it be best for me to be givin' Miss Savanna this letter before I knocked it to the floor and it got lost is all."

"How thoughtful and kind of you, Patti. I appreciate the care you take with my possessions," Savanna praised as she reached to take the letter proffered by Patti.

Patti gave a fleeting curtsy as her cheeks blushed with pleasure to be given a compliment for her actions. She gave a glance to her mistress and seeing her stern expression, she swiftly turned to return to her duties elsewhere in the mansion.

"I will leave you to your reading," Imogen said as she stood to depart. "I will be home the remainder of the day if you have the need to discuss the news from your parents?"

"Oh please do not leave on my account. I am happy to go to the conservatory or the garden rather than have you take leave of your reading."

"No worries. I have tired of the book for now. In fact, I think I shall retire to my bedchamber to refresh myself before our evening meal."

Savanna nodded in acceptance as Imogen walked toward the foyer. *I am curious as to what the Carlyles might be requesting of Savanna. I cannot say I hate to pry, for needing to be in the know has always served me well, but I do not want her to think I am nosey enough to directly inquire about the contents of the letter. Maybe she will want to share it with me. Or how lovely it would be if she carelessly left it in the public view and I happened upon it!* Imogen's face lit up with delight at the very thought.

Savanna looked at the wax seal stamped with a script 'C.' She knew it well. She could envision her mother sitting at her father's desk composing the letter, folding it, slipping it into an envelope, dripping the heated wax onto the envelope's flap, and then impressing the wax with the finishing touch of the embossed 'C.' She ran her fingers over the seal and closed her eyes as her fingers traced over the monogram. *Carlyle. I am a Carlyle or have always thought I was until of late. Would it have been easier for me to accept having been adopted if I had been told from my earliest years? I shall never know. I was forfeited that opportunity. I am trying my best to believe my parents meant no ill will toward me. But how could they truly believe the truth of my birth would not rise up like a great wave ready to swallow me whole? In their efforts to protect me they have failed and caused me undo angst.* Savanna shook her head back and forth as she readied herself to open the envelope. She removed the single piece of parchment fully laden with her mother's beautiful cursive and began to read:

Our Dear Savanna,

We miss you greatly. Our home has an emptiness it has not ever known. We thank you for your post informing us of your safe travel. We were comforted that you seem to have been immediately welcomed by Virginia Sterling and Mr. Simmonds' wife. We share your sadness at the news of Mr. Simmonds' passing and in such a tragic way. His fate has caused him to be gone too soon.

Alas, we want you to know that we hope you will return home and give us a chance to talk all of this through. There was little time before you left to properly share our feelings and apologize for the way you learned of your birth parents. We feel no differently about you now than we would if we had had the good fortune to be your birth parents. You were born of our hearts and you must never forget our great love for you. We hope you can come to have such feelings again for us and oppose any resentment you feel toward us. You will always have our support.

In the meantime, please write to us from time to time and continue to inform us about your work as an apothecary.

We are very proud of you and remain always your loving parents,
Mum and Daddy

The wells of Savanna's eyes filled with tears. She held the parchment to her chest and felt her heart pulsate against the letter making it appear as though it had a life of its own. She could feel her parents presence and devotion in the words, which she would savor as she read them over and over again.

Chapter Thirty-Five

Sawyer pulled his carriage to a post in front of Dr. Litle's Drug Store where he secured his horse. He paused to give the chestnut brown thoroughbred a rub and parting pet on his forehead before moving to enter the store. His conscience thought better of his being there but his heart held a stronger sway over him.

Savanna was creating an unfortunate distraction for him. Unfortunate only in the way thoughts of her diverted him from and made him question his affections for Imogen. He was torn. It was as though his mind and heart were engaging in a tug-of-war where there would be no designated winner. He also knew the frequency of his visits to Dr. Litle's were proving to be more than the need for the goods and services the drug store provided.

He looked at the storefront's window with its name boldly displayed in black letters alongside the symbol denoting a pharmacy, which featured a snake coiling around a chalice. He recalled one of his conversations with Savanna when they discussed her interest in pharmacy and she explained the Greek roots of the medical symbol. The chalice was known as the cup of Hygieia, named for the Greek goddess of health. Hygieia was a relation of Asclepius', the ancient God of Healing who was typically depicted with a wooden rod wrapped with a snake. Savanna further explained the origin of the word pharmacy from the Greek word 'pharmakon' meaning remedy and poison. "That might explain the representation of the snake," Sawyer commented at the time. "I think of those who fear the reptile's venom yet how, throughout time, snakes have held fascination, particularly in medicine and worship." Savanna had smiled at his knowledge. Their shared interest warmed her.

Through the window a collection of mortars and pestles lined a ledge running the window's full width. He peered deeper through the glass hoping to catch a glimpse of Savanna before venturing inside. He spotted her behind the counter talking with a patron who appeared mesmerized by her every word. He knew the feeling well.

He turned the doorknob ever so slowly to avoid interrupting her work, quietly stepped over the threshold, and guided the door closed to keep it from slamming shut. Despite his caution, Savanna caught sight of his entry and her face ignited with delight. She turned her attention back to her patron after giving a nod of welcome to Sawyer.

"Thank you, Doc Carlyle. Thank you so much. Your advice is always sound and has helped me in immeasurable ways," acknowledged the patron who bid her good day as he gathered his satchel in his hand and exited the drug store.

"Hmm, Doc Carlyle. My, my, I am impressed to hear you given such an appropriate and worthy appellation," reflected Sawyer with pride ever evident on his face.

"Why thank you sir. How may I be of service to you today?"

"That is a very leading question," Sawyer teased, hoping he was not overstepping his familiarity with her.

Savanna chose to ignore his retort, although she was gaining much delight from their exchange.

"I would hope there is nothing ailing you?" Savanna said. She wanted to add, *for you seem quite fit,* but she refrained from being so bold.

"Perhaps we could find something to cure a condition that has begun to plague me of late."

"Do tell? Are there symptoms you might share?"

Before Sawyer could utter a response, Dr. Litle returned from the storage room in the back of the store, bringing an end to Sawyer and Savanna's flirtations. The pharmacist loudly cleared his throat to be certain he had made his presence known.

"Dr. Litle, may I introduce Mr. Sawyer Frye. I am not certain the two of you have met. Mr. Frye has been a customer of the store of late but, if my recollection is correct, you were out making calls on some of your other patrons, or should I say patients, on those occasions. Mr. Frye is the managing editor for *The Washington Inquirer.*"

"A pleasure to meet you sir," acknowledged Dr. Litle who reached out his hand to Sawyer who obliged him with a hearty handshake. "*The Inquirer* is my source for the latest news. I hold a strong confidence in the newspaper's ability to inform without prejudice for one's politics. And, the store's advertisement we post there is always well received by our patrons, especially when I feature a new elixir that may be of benefit."

"Thank you. It is a pleasure to meet you as well. I shall relay your fine words to Mrs. Simmonds and Mr. Harris, our editor-in-chief. It is always gratifying to hear favorable reviews, of that you can be sure."

"Oh yes, both of them have visited my store. They find it a convenient stop after doing business at the Bank of Columbia next door. Mrs. Simmonds is a charming woman. So sorry about the loss of her husband," Dr. Litle said, as thoughts of seeing her in Georgetown and the city with Archibald Howard, and the rumors he had heard from patrons who read Tillie Tattler's column, reminded him that she was apparently not suffering the throes of a lonely widow. "And, Mr. Harris, I believe he goes by Gibs, is a good natured man. Both of them are always welcomed patrons," Dr. Litle added as he went about replenishing supplies on the shelves.

Sawyer pulled his timepiece from the fob in his vest pocket and gave it a quick glance. He had desired more time to visit with Savanna but he knew Imogen would question his whereabouts if she arrived at *The Inquirer* and found he had gone missing. *No, it is best I take my leave now. There will be other occasions for me to be in Savanna's company for I shall make certain of that,* he reasoned as common sense dictated his decision.

"I am just noticing the time. It appears that duty to the newspaper calls. So, I must bid you both good day. I hope to see you again soon," said Sawyer as he nodded to Dr. Litle and gave a wink of his eye to Savanna who gladly captured it by drawing in a deep breath of air.

Archibald was just turning the street corner when he came to an abrupt halt. He watched and listened as Sawyer commanded his horse to 'step up son' and the carriage and its charge went on their way up Bridge Street. He observed the storefront of the business from which Sawyer's conveyance pulled away and recalled its association with Miss Carlyle. *Ah-ha! It seems Mr. Frye has made a call on the fair Savanna! She announced at Virginia's her desire to work at an apothecary, Dr. Litle's if my recollection is correct. That certainly explains young Mr. Frye's visits to this establishment. Why Imogen refuses to believe what I see with my very eyes is beyond me! If she continues to ignore my warnings, perhaps I need to employ another tactic, for it seems my words are having the opposite effect of my intentions and have only served to draw her closer to young Frye. Think Archibald, think,* he reprimanded himself. *Perhaps Mr. Frye would consider returning to the United Kingdom? Perhaps I could persuade him to encourage Miss Carlyle to go back to her homeland and he could accompany her? If they refuse, I may have no other recourse than to permanently eliminate him by some manner.* A scowl formed on Archibald's face. His expression and the sudden darkening sky cast an aura of foreboding. A menace was in the air and readying itself to be revealed.

Imogen tossed and turned in bed. She was experiencing increasing nights of fitful sleep. She was unable to pinpoint the roots of her unrest. Upon her waking hours, the remnants of a recurring dream depicting her reaching out to an ungraspable apparition that floated about before her and then vanished into the mist remained with her. The nighttime visits from the unexplained hosts appeared sometimes to be that of a man, then perhaps a woman, then a child. *Is this Talmadge? Me? Savanna? Virginia?* She wrestled with the fantastical hallucinations trying to make sense of the images as she stirred about in a self-imposed delirium.

If I were to share these dreams with Gertie, what would she make of them? Would she and her sisters think I have lost my mind? I have put myself under too much pressure of late. Losing Talmadge and keeping the newspaper afloat would be enough to wither most of the women I know. In addition, there is managing my anti-slavery committee, renewing my relationship with Archibald, accepting Sawyer into my life, and now Savanna. The list goes on! Oh, Savanna. I have so wanted to accept her as the daughter I was never able to have and to do what is proper, as Talmadge would have wanted, but she is a temptress. She is threatening my affections from Sawyer. Why must I feel so conflicted about her?

Imogen found comfort in her discussions with Savanna about Talmadge. She wanted the girl to know all she could about the father she never knew. Speaking of him brought back the many reasons Imogen loved him and the privileged life he maintained for them. Talmadge's success allowed them to live on a grand scale in a grand home. He provided her with every amenity from household staff to her wardrobe and furnishings. He loved her deeply and accepted her needs beyond the walls of their domesticity. She pleasured in their intimacy but somehow felt she never had enough. *Perhaps that is the source of my dream, the reaching out for more and more, yet never finding satisfaction.*

"Enough of these worries," Imogen said aloud. She called for Patti to ready her toilette and prepare her wardrobe for the day. She remembered Virginia had sent word she intended to call on Savanna before she left for Dr. Litle's. Imogen considered being present for their visit but then thought better of it. She expected Virginia wanted to befriend Savanna and become better acquainted as had been part of Imogen's plan, in addition to keeping a watch over her chance encounters with Sawyer.

With Patti's assistance, Imogen slipped into a beautiful day frock in a shade of deep tangerine. The bodice featured an empire waist with a scooped neck and sleeves puffed at the shoulders. Gold trim accentuated the cuffs of the sleeves, waist and full hem of the gown. Imogen selected one of her gold chains with a large, oval smoky topaz pendant, which Patti fastened at her neck and handed her the matching oval drop earrings. The colors of the gems and her gown were perfect complements to her flaxen hair, which Patti brushed and then pulled together into a loose chignon. Imogen was beginning to tire of her signature tight-to-the-scalp coiffure and felt the chignon softened her appearance and, on occasion, her mood.

She admired her image in the looking glass. *Yes, this shall suit me quite well for Virginia's visit and,* she mused with a large grin forming, *and I may call on*

Sawyer at The Inquirer or call on Gertie. I have any number of things to occupy my time today.

"Patti, please go see that Miss Savanna is prepared for our guest. I would expect Mrs. Sterling to arrive very shortly."

"Actually mum, I looked in on Miss Savanna before I be comin' to yer room jest to see if she needed me 'elp with anythin'. She said she was doin' jest fine so I let her be."

"Very well, but in the future you must see to my needs first. I am the one who pays you and you should know by now that you best cater to my needs, not those of others."

"Yes, mum. It's sorry I am mum," Patti apologized with a dip of her head and a brief curtsy before she went on her way.

Savanna made her way downstairs and was the first to hear the knock at the door. Looking about for any sign of Patti, Savanna proceeded through the foyer and into the vestibule to open the door for their visitor. The two women hesitated for a few moments as they took in each other's beauty. Virginia was ever elegant in a layered gown of embroidered silk in a rich green, lush like the verdant fields of Ireland. The color served to enhance her green eyes and paired beautifully with her fiery red hair. Savanna's dark raven locks fell deftly over her shoulders and onto an equally lovely gown of silk taffeta and satin in a vibrant shade of cerulean blue. The bottom of her gown was rimmed in three layers of matching ruched fabric, which provided the fabric extra sway as she moved about.

"Please come in," requested Savanna as she invited Virginia over the threshold. "Your gown suits you well. I have admired your selections for they seem to rival those of our French counterparts. You appear quite aware of the latest in fashion."

"Thank you, Savanna. I can say the same for you. You have a keen sense of style."

"I shall say thank you as well. Here, please follow me into the drawing room," Savanna said as the expression *like mother, like daughter* came to mind.

Patti came scurrying toward the pair. "Looks like I jest made it in the knick of time! Is there anythin' I ken be gettin' the two of ya?"

Savanna and Virginia nearly laughed at Patti's hasty arrival. She had turned the corner from the staircase so quickly she nearly slipped to the floor but caught herself on one of the portières hanging on the doorframe, which helped to slow her pace.

"You best catch your breath before you bring us a tray of tea and sweets," suggested Savanna. "We would not want you to take a spill with Mrs. Simmonds' fine china. Nor, of course, would we want to have you injure yourself."

"Yes, Miss Savanna. Yes. Thank you miss. I'll be gettin' the tea ready and right to ye. Please go on in and have a seat. It won't be takin' me long."

Virginia and Savanna smiled broad smiles but, in courtesy to the girl, held back the laughter her behavior provoked. They settled themselves on opposing divans with a table between, ready to accept Patti's anticipated refreshments. Virginia clasped her hands in her lap and drew them together against her body as though she were preparing to pray.

"It is so good to see you and have this time to truly visit. My parties at Rosedale are not conducive to our having a private conversation, and any time together seems to be fleeting. Thank you for seeing me today," Virginia smiled a bit timidly for she was wary of the conversation to follow.

"I agree we have needed more time to speak with one another," said Savanna. "I was very pleased when I heard you wanted to call on me. If I may be so bold to say, to see you is to see someone whom I resemble. Not our hair color but our eyes and the way we carry ourselves. I often looked to find myself in the Carlyles. I thought it odd that I resembled neither of them. And, it saddens me greatly that my birth father is deceased. I suffer with the truth that I have essentially lost him twice. Imogen has made every effort to speak of him and describe his appearance and his manner to me, which aids in soothing the questions that linger in my mind about who I fully am."

Savanna's words to Virginia were heartfelt and poignant. She sometimes felt her thoughts became a confluence of emotions merging to cause her angst. Getting to know Virginia and expressing her feelings served to ease her toward acceptance of the hand dealt to her by the elders in her life.

"Learning that I have an identity that has been unknown to me for all these years has filled me with a wealth of turbulent emotions. I fear my words may cause you pain but I must release them to gain some semblance of order," Savanna continued as her voice became more urgent. "I struggle with the feelings of having been abandoned at birth, and then again by the Carlyles, for their failure to be forthwith about my adoption. Essentially, I was lied to and betrayed," Savanna declared as she looked to Virginia for answers and comfort.

"I wish your father knew about you. I wish he could see you," Virginia lamented.

"Is that not of your doing?"

"As I explained when we first met, my decision seemed to be the best choice at the time. Your father was betrothed to Imogen. There was no changing that. I could not raise you alone. We both would have been shunned. I knew you would have a good life with all the amenities with the Carlyles. I hope you will find comfort in the fact that your father is forever part of you, and you are forever part of him. Nothing shall change that."

Virginia continued to hold her hands together although a strong urge was building within her to stand and sit close to Savanna, to take her hands in hers, to beg forgiveness. "I can never *know* how you feel but I can *imagine* how you feel. I can imagine the grief and sense of loss that pervades you. I can but ask for your forgiveness. I never realized the vast ramifications of my lapse in moral character and how it would have bearing on you, the resulting child. I hope that knowledge will serve, if only in some small way, to ease the burden upon you."

"Tell me how you would feel under the circumstances? Tell me if you would find trust in your elders?"

"Again, I can only imagine your feelings when the truth was revealed by your father and your uncle. I can only imagine your thoughts when that shroud of secrecy was lifted. Please trust me, and trust that I only want the best for you. I feel I have been given a gift to have you reappear in my life. You are a blessing that has been apart from me for far too long," Virginia's voice began to falter as she stood and moved to stand before Savanna.

Savanna rose from her seat to come face-to-face with Virginia. The two looked into each other's eyes. It was as though they were held in suspension where nothing could interfere with their moment in time. The bond severed by circumstances so many years ago was finding its way back to a place of healing. Virginia leaned forward to embrace Savanna, which she accepted with open arms.

"To know me, who I fully am, is to know you, the woman who gave me life," said Savanna as tears filled her eyes.

Virginia's eyes were equally wet with tears as she asked, "May this be a new beginning for us, for you, my daughter?"

"Yes, Mum, yes it can."

Fortunately, Patti's timing was perfect. Her ability to be easily distracted from her duties served Virginia and Savanna well. The two were ending their embrace when Patti entered the room with the tray of tea and a small platter of assorted sweet buns. Savanna observed three cups and saucers and wondered if the girl oddly intended to join them.

"Are you having tea with us Patti or is someone else about?"

"Aye, but it not be me, Miss Savanna. The mistress is about and...," Patti cut off her words. She feared she should not have used the word mistress. She had heard rumors from other housemaids when she went to the market about her employer, and a few tales about the widow Sterling where the moniker 'mistress' was used. She did not want to offend the women or have them think she was part of the rumor mill circulating in the city.

"Patti, why has your tongue gone silent? It appears you were about to inform us of another visitor?" Savanna inquired, actually hoping Sawyer was on the premises.

"No worries, no worries. I was jest wantin' to say that Mrs. Simmonds will be havin' tea with ye."

Patti had no sooner made her announcement than Imogen appeared in the doorway.

"Everything I take it, has gone well? I trust the two of you have been engaged in a good visit?"

"Yes we have," Virginia and Savanna responded in tandem.

"My, my. If I am not mistaken, I would say your bond has grown for you are responding as twins might. You are making quite the pair it seems?"

Virginia and Savanna looked at one another and smiled. Savanna reached out and took her mother's hand in hers. "I feel I may speak for both of us when I say that today we arrived at a new understanding. Today, we both gathered the wisdom of forgiveness, which shall do much to serve us well."

Imogen, though pleased for Savanna's newfound acceptance of Virginia, felt a twinge of jealousy that Virginia's relationship with Savanna would exceed hers. She witnessed a show of affection between the two, which she had yet to feel coming her way from Savanna. *I know I sometimes have been received as having an aura about me that repels others from advancing in my direction, which I find curious since those of the male gender are quite drawn to me.* Imogen mulled the thoughts over in her mind, particularly fancying the images she conjured of men finding interest in her, as she contemplated ways to draw Savanna closer to her. *What am I thinking?* Imogen's mind nearly roared. *I must maintain a reasonable distance in order to keep the girl from my personal life. I fear Sawyer will reject me for her, yet it is essential that I feel confident about him, hold my trust in him. I must trust him, must I not? Why should this be so confusing? For now, I shall ride the tide of change for I have no choice but to face that, which is inevitable. Change is looming.*

Chapter Thirty-Six

April 1822

Archibald spent a restless night imagining how he might rid himself of Sawyer Frye. *The young man has stolen Imogen's heart and attention!* Archibald shouted into the air as his thoughts surrounded him with reckless abandon. He could not let his hurt remain one-sided. If he was to suffer, then he was to inflict the same on others whether they be friend or foe. He was fuming with jealousy and, although he knew he could challenge Sawyer to a duel for stealing the affections of the woman he loved, he felt he needed more to assure the outcome of a duel would go in his favor.

You must remain rational, Archibald advised himself. *You need a plan that will have every element of success. There can be no room for failure or mishap.* As he batted about potential options attempting to find balance in his thoughts, a vision suddenly sprung to mind. *The Carlyle girl may be the answer to my needs. I shall make a call on her at Dr. Litle's. Her knowledge may prove quite useful. Yes, she may be my best resource,* he reasoned as he conjured ways to sway Sawyer from Imogen.

He selected his favorite wool suit in a creamy shade of beige, which was in contrast to the majority of his wardrobe comprised of deep shades of forest green, navy, cocoa, and charcoal. The suit featured a pair of full-cut 'cossacks' in a style popularized by trousers worn by Russia's Alexander I. Pleats gathered at the waistband created a fullness in the body of the trousers that tapered to his ankles, exposing a proper amount of the top portion of his leather shoes.

He added a vest and a matching frock coat whose waistline seam was tightly fitted to his mid-section with full panels extending in a cut-away style from the sides of his waist to the back of his knees. His shirt of ivory colored linen was topped off at the collar with a white neck scarf.

He stood before the looking glass in his bedchamber and, emulating the late French leader Napoleon I, he tucked his right hand into his vest and admired his countenance. *Yes, this is my homage to you in remembrance of your recent passing,* acknowledged Archibald whose associates would say his hand-in-frock-coat was an unnecessary gesture in tribute to a man who many considered an ill-tempered tyrant. If others knew the 'reign of terror' Archibald was planning, they would deem his gesticulation very apropos. He picked up his hat, placed it on his head and said, "Nice work, my man."

He stood before the front window of the apothecary and paused to read some of the posters on display advertising ways to avoid the infirmities of old age. A testimonial was printed nearby with a headline that read, 'Avoid an early entrance to the gates of death.' The words caught Archibald's attention. *Hmm death. I do hope to avoid an early grave at all costs.* He continued to read through the patient's testimonial, 'With but one bottle of Dr. Litle's Restorative Cordial I was symptom free and restored to improved health.' *Humph, who would be fool enough to believe such exaggerated claims?* Archibald grumbled, making a mental note to himself to seek out a bottle of the cordial before leaving. *I must say, Litle has excelled himself with this tempting display.* Several bottles of soothing balms in the store lined the windowsill along with a variety of other tonics claiming to be aphrodisiacs. *Hmm, another purchase I might consider. I take no exception to something that boasts of increasing desire!*

The wave of a hand caught Archibald's eye. He looked more closely and saw that it was Savanna acknowledging his presence on the street. *I guess I have no reason for hesitation now that she has seen me. Archibald, this is your chance. Make the most of it,* he said, referencing himself by name — the narcissist in him never far away for his ready retrieval.

The bell above the doorway tingled as Archibald stepped inside. He tipped his hat to Savanna as he advanced to the counter.

"Good morning, Mr. Howard. To what do we owe your visit today? How may we be of help?" Savanna asked, maintaining her professional stance.

"Why, thank you for asking, but first I must say how lovely you are looking today."

"Thank you for your observation. However, is that to say *today* is an exception to all other days when you have seen me?"

Archibald was taken aback by her response. *She has a bit of a tart tongue, does she not? The ladies usually become enchanted by my allure. I was not aware of her bold nature. I shall have to find a way to charm her despite her ways, for she may be my only hope.*

"Certainly not," chuckled Archibald. "It would probably be best for me to be more general in my declaration and thus encompass all the days of the year."

Savanna cast a wary smile, pleased she had made Archibald adjust his statement. Her exposure to him had rarely been without others present, usually at one of Virginia's parties or his calls to Woodholme. She found his behavior very self-centered with an edge of abrasiveness. This was one of her first opportunities to speak with him alone. *I wonder if my father would approve of Imogen's ongoing friendship with the man who took his life. That is certainly of no consequence now, for Father is gone and God knows Imogen allows no man or woman to control her decisions. She is a free spirit – perhaps as much a rascal as Archibald,* she nearly laughed aloud at the thought.

"Your presence leads me to wonder how we may help you today?"

"We? Is there someone else about?" Archibald inquired, hoping they were alone and no other customers would happen in.

"Actually, Dr. Litle has left me to manage the store today. I say 'we' because it seems all whom I have encountered in the medical profession use the term 'we' rather than 'I.' They are probably referring to their colleagues in the profession as a way of suggesting their diagnosis or treatment has the support of others in addition to themselves."

"That is an interesting analysis, which brings me to the purpose of my visit. We are seeking knowledge about noxious substances."

What a rogue he is, thought Savanna. "*We?* Are you making fun of me for I see only one of you?"

"I could not resist saying the word, however the 'we' is in reference to myself and my staff. We need to rid ourselves of some vermin and my mind immediately went to you."

"You don't say? How lovely that you thought of vermin and me in the same breath," teased Savanna as she fiddled with a bottle stopper resting on the counter.

"Oh my. Here I go again starting off very badly. It would be better for me to say I thought of you and your expertise in the field of compounds. Surely the knowledge of poison was among your studies?"

"Of course. But you confuse me. I thought death by duel was your weapon of choice and, yet now, you show a suspicious curiosity for the elements of poison? And, you ask me of all people. Have you no one else to call upon to do your bidding?"

"My dear, I had hoped to be afforded a kindly reception from you of all people."

"From me? Why should I bestow any courtesy upon you? As I recall, you have been nothing but a thorn in my side since I arrived in America. We have little in common other than our homeland, a fact I would as soon dismiss."

"I dare say you forget your ties to the Simmonds clan or, perhaps tribe is a more apt description, for your kith-and-kin leave much to be desired when it comes to class, where I know I severely outrank you."

"What a curious choice of words on all counts. Your words merely lend credence to what others say of you and your so-called rank. Perhaps you meant to say 'bank' rather than 'rank.' You continue, by words and actions, to diminish your station among colleagues and acquaintances."

"My goodness! That is quite a lashing you have given me. We have gotten off to the wrong start. Let me apologize for any misgivings you have about sharing your knowledge with me. I am merely trying to rid my home of a family of mice who have taken up residency."

"Why am I not surprised that rodents would take great comfort in your domain?" Savanna threw her head back with a laugh. "Perhaps you should consider bringing on a cat or two to manage the population?"

"Why do you choose to stain your tongue with such distasteful words?"

"If this is your way of coaxing me to assist your endeavors, I suggest you follow a different course," urged Savanna. She was growing tired of his presence and the vigor he was applying to glean information from her. *Why is it that his inquiry holds with it so much suspicion for his intent? Then again, what harm can come from sharing my knowledge of compounds with him?* "What exactly would you like to know?"

"Ah, thank you my dear. I appreciate your consideration to enlighten me with the facts of your trade. I would specifically like to know about the very best, most effective poison to purge my home of the vermin that disturb me."

"There are several compounds, which you may find useful," said Savanna as she pointed to the jars clustered on a shelf specifically designated for noxious substances. "Thallium sulfate is a rat poison. It is extremely toxic and therefore quite effective, as is strychnine," she shared as she moved along the shelf. "Death by strychnine is not particularly pleasant, actually it is considered quite inhumane by many. And then, there is potassium cyanide, which is very fast-acting. It is a toxic chemical asphyxiant rendering a rapidly fatal result to the recipient. It interferes with one's ability to normally saturate oxygen. Potassium is a white granular solid. Sodium cyanide, with a close resemblance to sugar, is a colorless crystalline salt. If it is a liquid you desire to spread, the mixture is highly soluble in fluids such as water," she explained. "Lest I forget, there is arsenic, which I would not recommend for the variety of horrific symptoms it produces prior to death. There are any manner of toxic berries and shrubs such as Atropa belladonna. Merely a few of its berries and the juice from the perennial herbaceous plant can take an adult's life."

"My goodness. That is much to remember. You impress me and you have enlightened me. It appears you have made my choices very clear."

"If you are a student of Shakespeare with a fondness for *Romeo and Juliet* as am I, you may recall the apothecary's words to Romeo: 'Put this in any liquid thing you will, and drink it off; and, if you had the strength of twenty men, it would dispatch you straight.'"

"I see, potassium cyanide you say. And, may I further ask, what the effective dosage might be?"

"If your intention is for the dosage to be lethal, then one hundred to two hundred milligrams with a median dose of one hundred forty milligrams would serve your purposes well."

"Again, you impress me with your ready knowledge. Have you had first hand experience with this poison?"

"Since I am here to tell you about it, I obviously have neither tasted of it nor ingested it but, during my studies, I heard tell it produces a burning sensation leaving an acrid or bitter flavor on the palate. There truly is nothing redeeming about it, lest the desired result be death. I must add that you will assure me these substances will not be misused."

"I assure you, when the time comes they will be put to the intended use." Archibald had heard all he needed to hear. He trusted he would remember the proper dosage when the need arose. For now, he needed to distract Savanna.

"May I have a closer look at the two there, the potassium and the cyanide?" Archibald asked so politely Savanna decided to accommodate him. She removed the respective jars from the shelf and rested them on the counter. "I will also be wanting to purchase several bottles of Dr. Litle's Restorative Cordial. I see two bottles in the window display and hope you have more."

"How many bottles would you like?"

"Six should suit me quite well."

"Let me see if Doc has any more in the storage room. Excuse me while I look for them."

Archibald was elated that his ploy to have Savanna leave the counter worked in his favor. Quickly he removed the stoppers from the jars of poison. He reached into his frock coat and removed two jars. One was empty, which he swiftly filled with the powdery substances. The other jar was filled with sugar from his home. He poured the sugar into the apothecary's jars and replaced the stoppers. With the jar of poison securely in his frock coat, he perused the countertop to be sure there was no evidence of his tampering. He was relieved to see no signs of lingering powder. He took a deep breath and let it out followed by a hefty sigh just as Savanna returned to the counter.

"A rough day?" Savanna inquired.

"What do you mean?

"That was quite a sigh."

"Oh that. I was just thinking of all I have ahead of me."

"Like killing mice?"

"Oh yes, killing a rodent."

"*A* rodent? I thought you insinuated you had an infestation? Which brings me to ask," said Savanna, as she placed her hands on the jars of poison. "Will you be wanting me to prepare a bottle for you with these substances?"

"That will not be necessary. I think I shall wait and see if my staff can remedy the situation by other means. I do want to be as humane as possible even though they are vermin. I shall just take the six cordials," Archibald said as he gladly handed over payment for his purchases and bid Savanna good day.

Savanna looked out the window and shook her head. *All the curiosity about poison, yet he leaves without purchasing an ounce. Very odd, and it makes me question his intent. He is obviously concerned about self-preservation with his interest in Doc's curative cordial. The cordial seemed to take precedence over any sinister motives he had toward the mice population at his home. I really should not give a care, but I hope he has what he needs to remedy all that ails him.*

Archibald stepped onto the street and patted the chest of his frock coat. It was as though Savanna's words had traveled through the air into the street as Archibald whispered, "I have everything I need right here."

He felt elated to have successfully obtained what he needed. "I have some time before I need to make a call on Frye. This is time for celebration. Yes, Archibald you need to reward yourself with a drink or two," he announced to his best-loved audience of one and began to walk down Bridge Street to the corner at High Street where he entered Union Tavern to fortify himself for the drama he intended to play-out on the streets of Georgetown.

Chapter Thirty-Seven

Sawyer's frequent visits to Dr. Litle's were always met with delight by Savanna, and for Sawyer they were a welcome diversion in his day. His attraction to her had become a temptation, which he could not deny. In his heart he knew he was being untrue to Imogen. He feared hurting her but he could not go on suppressing his feelings for Savanna that were continually tugging at his mind and texturing his heart with desire.

"Well, if it isn't the dear, fair Savanna," announced Sawyer with a chuckle as she returned to the front counter from the storage room. She acknowledged him with a broad smile and demure dip of her head.

"To what do we owe this visit from you Mr. Frye? And, so late in the day."

"My work kept me from stopping here any earlier. I regret my late arrival and I shall have to return to my duties but I felt an urgent need to come here," said Sawyer with a dip of his hat.

"Without making too personal an inquiry, is there a malady that plagues you, which we may try to remedy?"

"Indeed there is," smiled Sawyer, delighted that Savanna had given him the perfect entrée to extend the invitation he had in mind for her.

"Please, kind sir, do not leave me in suspense," teased Savanna.

"Ah, so you have become an impatient maiden have you? Very well then. I shall not tarry a moment longer. I, Miss Carlyle, desire the pleasure of your company at the theater on Friday's eve."

"Pray tell, where?"

"The Washington Theatre."

"Oh, the theater on Louisiana Avenue. Yes, one of our customers informed me that it had been rebuilt after it caught fire nearly two years ago. She said it was originally on C Street nearby Carusi's Saloon. I have so centered myself in Georgetown that I feel somewhat confused with the streets in the city. She mentioned that Carusi's Assembly Rooms were a lively place to gather. I should like to attend sometime for apparently the political satire is most entertaining, as are the dramatic performances and musical revues."

"Yes, and there have been several troupes of professional players strolling about to various other establishments for candlelight performances. McGrath's Company of Comedians performed The Beggar's Opera at Union Tavern some weeks ago. I have been told they have been performing well over a score of years with no sets, and their costumes are of limited description, but the shows are great fun despite the lack of embellishments. However, that said, I have two tickets for *Hamlet* at The Washington Theatre. Junius Brutus Booth is performing to much acclaim. I understand he is quite good."

"Well, how presumptuous of you to purchase tickets before knowing my response?"

"I feared you might say that. I made no assumptions," laughed Sawyer. "I merely wanted to assure that, if indeed you did accept my invitation, I had secured the tickets lest we lose the opportunity to see the play. The theater is quite popular, and although the new building has expanded its seating to 700, I wanted to be certain to have reserved seats. Additionally, the theater has instituted a new mandate that no cigars may be smoked within its premises, which will at least eliminate one of the noxious smells one endures when in such close quarters."

"Good to know, indeed. I would be sorely remiss to turn down your invitation for I so enjoy the theater. The Carlyles were large supporters of the arts. It was important to them as part of my education to have such culture in my life."

"Is it only the theater that sways your acceptance or could it also be that you find enjoyment by being in my company?"

"Why, Mr. Frye, how bold of you to make such an inquiry," teased Savanna.

Sawyer threw back his head with a hearty laugh. Merely being in her presence brought him joy. He was grateful she had come into his life, although he was finding it more and more difficult to keep his feelings for her at bay while he wrestled with his relationship with Imogen. Balancing his time with the two women was becoming arduous. *How am I to explain to Imogen my time with Savanna?* Sawyer questioned. *And, Archibald has become a menace, an albatross. He is a weight I need removed. Ceasing my time with Imogen may benefit me two-fold. I will be free to devote myself to Savanna and remove Archibald's jealous concerns.*

Savanna loved Sawyer's laugh. It filled her with delight. The attraction she felt toward him had not waned. He made her feel desirable. *To be the object of his desire is a dream come true. I have spent many a waking night with him paramount in my thoughts,* reflected Savanna.

"I shall be enormously pleased to be in the company of thespians and, of course, that pleasure includes being with a character such as yourself."

Sawyer was ready to add a retort when the bell above the door jingled as Dr. Litle entered and broke the cadence of their conversation. It was just as well for Sawyer needed to return to the newspaper. He hoped Imogen had not come around yet to find him missing from his duties. Gibs was usually very good about covering for him with reasons Imogen would typically accept as true. Once, when she questioned Sawyer's whereabouts not feeling secure in Gibs' explanation, she told Sawyer and Gibs that she could not abide liars. *Interesting,* thought Sawyer as an old idiom came to mind. *The pot seems very comfortable calling the kettle black.*

Chapter Thirty-Eight

Archibald lingered in the shadows of the store next to Dr. Litle's waiting for Sawyer to exit. He hovered like an angry hornet waiting for an unassuming victim to sting. He had begun his pursuit of Sawyer at *The Washington Inquirer's* office where he had hoped to engage in conversation with him, but Sawyer seemed to be on an urgent mission and left too quickly for Archibald to keep pace. *I would have preferred to have my discussion with him in a more private setting but, perhaps, it is best to air my complaint publicly to have witnesses to our differences,* reasoned Archibald, who was feeling bolstered with the whiskey he had consumed. He waited until Sawyer was well away from the storefront before he approached him.

"Mr. Frye! Mr. Frye!" shouted Archibald. "Just whom I need to see! May I have a word with you?"

Sawyer shook his head. He had had a long day with numerous story deadlines requiring him to place much pressure on his staff to complete their assignments. He had little patience for Archibald on a good day. Engaging in conversation with him at this late hour would challenge him to maintain his composure. He only hoped Archibald was not there to incite him. Sawyer raised a hand up to acknowledge him, then looked away hoping he would disappear but Archibald moved forward and stood so close before him that the tips of their shoes nearly butted up against one another.

An angry look had taken over Archibald's face. He smelled of whiskey and, contrary to his usual style and good taste, his wardrobe was somewhat disheveled.

"What, man, is your problem? Lately, I tend to find you at my every turn. Is the business of banking going so poorly that you have idle time to pursue me? And for what purpose?"

"You, sir, know full well why I am watching your every move!"

Archibald's voice was becoming louder and louder. It was as though he wished to draw attention to the scene he was creating. His efforts were having the desired effect for a group of people halted in their daily routines and stopped to listen to the engagement of the two men.

"I have no such knowledge."

"Well, let me educate you then!" Archibald's voice boomed. "You have placed the reputation of the woman I love in jeopardy. I implore you to put an end to your relationship with her at once! You have taken advantage of a widow and should be sorely ashamed of yourself for so doing."

"Mr. Howard, you sir, are out of line. You also are creating a scene," Sawyer noted as the number of onlookers grew. "Perhaps you should either cease your commentary at once or, if you persist, we should remove ourselves from the public display you seem intent on propagating?"

"Oh, no! This shall do quite well. You are a cad. A gentleman would never stoop so low as to cause the reputation of a fine woman to be defamed!"

"I would warn you Mr. Howard to hold your tongue. You are the cad, not I," Sawyer declared, his voice rising in anger. He was thankful the commotion was far enough away from Dr. Litle's that it did not draw Savanna's attention.

"A cad? You sling such accusations my way? You have just caused me to challenge you to a duel. There will be no other way to settle the shame you heave upon me to restore my honor as a respectable gentleman and to restore the reputation of the woman I intend to take as my wife!"

Murmurs from the crowd began gaining velocity. The word duel could be heard circulating among the men and women in the street.

"I have no interest in a duel. You are the one who first called me a cad. Such an affront was unnecessary and uncalled for. Perhaps you called me such because you see yourself as such?"

"You may think you can distract me with such ridiculous details. The fact remains that you have caused slander to fall upon me as well as the woman who is very important in my life. It is her honor that I am compelled to uphold against the disgrace you have brought against her. I advise you to readily select a second to meet with mine to set a date to resolve this matter."

Sawyer closed his eyes for a scant moment wishing he could make Archibald disappear in a puff of smoke. He knew he could not refuse Archibald's challenge, not only on the basis of the code of honor, which society placed upon them, but there were numerous witnesses to their exchange. Soon word would spread. *How will I ever explain this to Savanna? I can only hope I live to have that opportunity.*

Chapter Thirty-Nine

Tea got more than he bargained for when he ventured into Georgetown for some flour and sugar at William S. Nicholls & Co's dry goods store. His satchel was beginning to weigh him down as he came upon the heated exchange between two men on Bridge Street. Curiosity caused him to join several other spectators whose rapt attention prompted him to see what the commotion was about. The men seemed familiar to him but he could not say they had ever met. He turned to a man near him to question whether he knew their identities.

"Only know the one, a big banker. Archibald Howard is his name. I cannot name the other one, though I have seen him here on occasion," shared the man who kept his eyes on the men as he spoke to Tea.

Archibald Howard? The name is familiar. Imogen has spoken of him in our home, Tea thought as the name awakened his memory. *Oh, my god! If my recollection serves me correctly, he is the one who challenged Talmadge to a duel, which certainly did not meet to Talmadge's advantage.*

Tea wondered who the younger man was. He watched as the two men turned away from one another. As they did, Archibald shouted, "You will soon hear from my second, Mr. Frye! The time has come to settle our differences once and for all!"

Mr. Frye? That name is known to me as well. He too has been the subject of conversations with Imogen. Oh my, there may be no other way for these men to come to terms with their dispute for in this case, I fear the accusations are true, Tea surmised with sadness mounting in his mind. He watched as the man known as Mr. Frye continued down Bridge Street. *He is probably headed to Union Tavern for a hearty mug of ale. That is the action I would take under the circumstances,* reasoned Tea whose heart weighed heavy on whether or not he should breath a word to Imogen about what he had heard and witnessed.

The scene Tea encountered in Georgetown two days past remained with him. His sleep had been interrupted by fitful dreams, which he felt were his due for keeping to himself what had transpired between the two men known to Imogen. *In good conscience I have no recourse but to inform her,* he rationalized. *And, if I do so, with any luck I shall get a good night's sleep tonight! Some force lingering deep within my mind has held unnecessary power over my waking and dozing hours.* He made his way in his carriage to the corner of Washington and Water Streets in hopes of finding Imogen at *The Inquirer*. He tethered his horse where he could find a space several storefronts down, then walked the short distance to his destination.

As Imogen approached the front entrance to *The Washington Inquirer*, she caught sight of a familiar face. He came upon her hurriedly, wanting to engage her attention before she set foot inside the newspaper's offices.

"Imogen, I am glad to catch you here. I wonder if I might have a word with you," he looked around nervously finding the street clear of other pedestrians.

"My goodness, Tea. How unexpected to see you here but a pleasure I might add," Imogen smiled and cocked her head in a dip of greeting. "Is all well? You seem somewhat agitated? Nothing is amiss with Gertie or her sisters I hope?"

"No, no. All is well with them. However, all may soon not be well with others in your life."

Imogen did not like Tea's tone. His ominous bidding was causing her alarm. He continued to look about the street to ensure others would not hear his words.

"What is it that you know? You have gained my undivided attention but please speak up for you are scaring me."

"I feel compelled to share with you what I overheard. I have thought long and hard about whether I should burden you with this information but I feel I cannot in good faith keep it from you."

Imogen thought she would jump out of her skin. *Why is it that so many people I encounter, especially men, find it such a task to release words from their mouths? Such delay is not only annoying it is worrisome!*

"Tea, I assure you I would rather know what it is you have to share rather than wallow about with worry and wonder."

"Very well then," said Tea as he stopped looking around him and took Imogen's gloved hands in his. "There was talk, more like an angry shouting match between Mr. Howard and Mr. Frye and I am afraid it resulted in a challenge being called by Mr. Howard toward Mr. Frye," Tea spoke so quickly he became anxious and Imogen thought he might lose his breath.

"Tea, please slow down. This news you wish to share is taking a toll on you. There is no rush. I have time to hear you out. What is the challenge of which you speak?"

Tea took in some deep breaths, swallowed hard and blurted out, "A duel!"

"What? My ears must be mistaken? Please tell me that what you said is not so," pleaded Imogen as she released her hands from Tea's. She placed her right hand to her mouth and briefly closed her eyes as she thought through what she had just heard. *This cannot be. I must put a stop to this foolishness.*

"I can do no such telling, Miss Imogen. The two men apparently agreed to settle their differences in a duel. There is no denying the words I heard. The threat and challenge were real."

"When is this to take place?"

"That was not said. Mr. Howard asked that their seconds speak with one another. I suppose the date, time and place will be set by them. They are most likely keeping any details to themselves to avoid interference and prosecution. I can only say that I am very sorry to report this to you for I know it has caused you dismay."

"Dismay is the least of my emotions. No good will come of this. All I can think about is having suffered through this with Talmadge. I am still recovering from his loss and certainly do not need to repeat the past. I shall talk with them and try to reason with them."

"You will do, I know, as you wish, however I feel that any efforts on your part will do little to dissuade them, for their threats were heard by others. You understand the honor code and they will not divert themselves from it."

"Honor code? Honor code? Yes, I know the words but understanding them is another thing entirely. I have made my feelings about that very clear with Mr. Howard. It is as though he has gone mad with his bitterness toward Mr. Frye."

"I would agree there is no love lost between the two. I hope I have not overstepped our friendship by giving you this news?"

"Not in the least, Tea. Now it is I who must decide how I shall approach Mr. Howard and Mr. Frye," Imogen said as she looked to the door of *The Inquirer* and prepared herself to face Sawyer with what she knew.

"Gibs?" Imogen queried as she looked about *The Inquirer's* offices in search of Sawyer. "Gibs!" Imogen shouted, her nerves getting the best of her. In a few moments, Gibs came around the corner wearing a canvas apron, its pockets filled with type.

"Good day, Mrs. Simmonds. I had not expected to see you here today."

"And why is that? I rarely have a set schedule that I follow."

"Oh, I mean no harm by that. It is just that you are rarely here if Mr. Frye is not about."

"Not about? Are you saying he has stepped out somewhere?"

"No, actually, he told me he would not be coming in today. He said he was caught up on his work and he hoped to see me on Monday next."

"How unusual for him not to be inundated with deadlines on a Friday. And, he said he *hoped* to see you on Monday next? Why would he not?"

"I guess that is for him to know. All I can say is what he said to me."

Worry lines began to form on Imogen's face. *Could this be the day of the duel? Is that what is keeping him from work? Would I not have heard something by now? Would I not be informed?* Imogen's thoughts were making her feel queasy. Gibs took notice and rushed to get a chair, which he placed behind her.

Imogen declined his kind offer by waving him away. He was not taken aback, for he was accustomed to being dismissed by her at other times. *Patience is not her virtue,* Gibs muttered silently to himself.

"I am going to return to Woodholme. Should Mr. Frye grace you with his presence, please inform him that it is of the utmost importance that I speak with him."

"Of course, Mrs. Simmonds, of course," replied Gibs, happy to have her take her leave so he could return to his tasks.

Imogen kept a look out for Sawyer as her carriage made its way through Georgetown. She hoped he was not lying injured somewhere, the victim of the foolish challenges men made to one another. *Why am I going home? I need to see Archibald. If he too has gone missing, then I have every manner of reason for grave concern.*

Her mind swirled with the possibilities of *what if* and *if only*, which she realized she had no leverage to control. On the carriage ride home she reconsidered sharing Tea's news with Savanna. *What purpose would it serve? The news will only scare the girl, as it has myself. And, I will suffer the experience of watching her reaction clothed with concern for Sawyer. I think I shan't say a word about this to her. I shall bear the repercussions of my decision, if needed, when the time comes. Hopefully, there will be no bad news to share. Perhaps what Tea heard was merely an angry exchange among threats that would not come to fruition. I shall ready myself to call on Archibald at once to appease my mind.*

Patti was looking out the window when her mistress's carriage arrived. She quickly scurried to the front portal and opened it wide for her to enter. Imogen came in with a flourish.

"Patti, is Miss Savanna at home or has she gone to the apothecary?"

"She'd be tellin' me she'd somethin' special planned fer today and would not be returnin' 'ome until later this evenin'."

"Where was she going?"

"That I do not know. She looked very pretty in 'er gown like she'd be goin' somewhere after 'er work in Georgetown. And, she 'ad a big smile on her face," beamed Patti with such zeal that Imogen wanted to wipe the smirk from her face. It was as though the girl wanted to taunt her with suspicion about Savanna's plans.

Chapter Forty

It was a rare occasion for Imogen to visit Archibald's home. The two found their trysts at his private quarters at the bank to be a satisfying habit, free from the watchful eyes of the gossips who kept their sights set on his home on the chance she were to appear. Since Talmadge's death, she felt she deserved the freedom as a widow to see whom she cared to see when and wherever she chose, although she wrestled with the thinking of the women who wanted to shun her for her escapades. Many still sought to hiss her, thinking it their duty as proper society, but their curiosity outweighed removing Imogen from their lists of invitees to their dinner soirées. They felt a certain sense of celebrity about her reputation, which allowed them to live vicariously through her dalliances. *Their opinions show little mercy for me,* she sighed. Imogen was determined to become numb to their persecution. She would let their petty minds think as they wished for she had more important matters in which to attend.

As she raised her hand to knock on the door, it began to open. She was surprised to see Archibald and not Harrison performing the duties of greeting a guest. Archibald took note of the questioning expression on her face.

"Why the look of surprise?"

"Oh, Archibald, I did not expect to see you at the door."

"Well, it is my home. Am I not allowed to manage the door from time to time?"

"You know what I mean. I expected to see Harrison."

"When I received word of your visit, I sent him off as I have also done with the rest of my staff. The time has come for us to have a serious discussion and I wanted the benefit of silence with no distractions to disturb us."

Imogen hoped he was not intending for them to be intimate. She smelled the strong stench of whiskey on him. He rarely overdrank but when he did he was not a pleasant drunk. She had taken note of his increased rendezvous with spirits resulting in a marked change in his personality. She was concerned their discussion might turn hostile and the only way to subdue Archibald would be to relent to his advances and let him have his way with her. She regretted having acquiesced to his desires on other occasions when their conversations had become heated. Rather than feel like his lover, she felt she was his whore whom he thought he could treat as a paid trollop. She did have to admit that although his advances were forceful, she garnered some pleasure from how hard he entered her, thrusting himself deeper and deeper until he was fully spent. She questioned why she allowed herself to be treated in such a way. *Is there some punishment I feel I must endure because of my wayward ways?* She shook off the idea that there existed any weakness on her part. She had other matters of concern and would not relent until she aired her concerns with Archibald.

"Here, come in," Archibald said as he motioned with his hand for her to come forward. "I have a wonderful decanter of claret for us to enjoy."

Imogen entered his study. As Archibald poured their wine, she looked to his desk where a small bottle rested close to the desk's edge. She walked closer, put her hand to the vessel and picked it up. When Archibald turned and saw her, he moved with great speed and wrested it from her grasp. He opened a drawer and placed the bottle inside. Imogen took note of his brisk behavior.

"My goodness, Archibald. Why so jumpy?"

"There is no need for you to peruse my desk and take the liberty of removing things from it."

"Very well. I beg your pardon for I meant no harm," Imogen said as she made her way to sit opposite his desk in a large wingback armchair upholstered in rich, brick red leather. Archibald handed her a crystal goblet amply filled with the delectable red Bordeaux wine.

"Thank you, Archibald. Such a generous pour, I hope I am able to keep my senses about me," said Imogen.

"There is a part of me that hopes you will not."

She immediately regretted making any insinuation that she might lose control of herself. *My nerves must be getting the best of me. Why did I say such a thing?*

"What did you have there? Something you needed to conceal?" Imogen inquired wondering why he had made such a hasty dash to his desk.

"It is of no concern to you."

"Nonetheless, you said we needed to have a discussion. What is the nature of this discussion?" Imogen asked as she observed Archibald's behavior and began to become concerned about his agitated state. He was pacing the floor, back and forth, back and forth, only pausing to take large sips from his goblet of wine.

"I have reached my limit. I will no longer share you with another man. You must at once cease being in any proximity to Mr. Sawyer Frye! If you do not do so, I shall have no alternative but to take matters into my own hands, at any cost, and you will be to blame!" Archibald bellowed, startling Imogen. She took a large gulp of the claret, nearly depleting her goblet. She found herself inhaling the potent liquid, which made her begin to feel its effects.

"We have been thu 'is bethore, Archi..." Imogen said as her words became slurred. She took a moment to settle herself and gain control over her speech as she stood to address him.

"Archibald, you must come to your senses and stop your unrelenting campaign to settle your differences with Sawyer through violence! It has come to my attention that a challenge exists between the two of you."

"How are you aware of such a thing?"

"When one stands in the streets of Georgetown making loud threats meant to harass and intimate another, people take notice. Word travels very quickly."

"So, there is a snitch who has come to alert you?"

Imogen was not about to mention that Tea had come to her and relayed the news of the near altercation. For all she knew, if she did, Archibald would next be threatening Tea to a duel. She was relieved that no one from *The National Intelligencer* had overheard the exchange and run the story for all to read. She knew she could halt her newspaper from printing a word about it.

"My heart is breaking with the thought of harm coming to either of you!

You must stop these threats! Can you not reconcile your differences by means other than violence? I hold no respect for you and this passion you have nurtured for dueling! Do you feel your stature is raised with a firearm in our hand? Do not fool yourself, for in my eyes you have diminished yourself yet again. And, how dare you attempt to throw the blame of your actions onto me!" Imogen's body was shaking as she shouted at Archibald, as though escalating her voice would pierce his ears with the good sense to change his course.

Archibald had heard enough of her wild rage. He was seething inside and like a full pot of boiling porridge, he could no longer hold back his overflowing anger heavily seasoned with pent-up jealousy. As his temper flared, he stepped forward and slapped her across the face hoping to end her hysterical tirade. He was at once sorry for losing control of his anger. Imogen fell back as she put her hand to her face, stunned he had taken such action toward her. Although his behavior of late had begun to border on rough, this was a volatile side of him she had not before witnessed. The slap was not only a wound to her person, it was nonetheless a wound to her emotions that would not be eased by the application of a soothing salve. No man had ever taken his hand to her. *He will pay for this! He will get his comeuppance!* Her proclamations railed in her head like the ominous foretelling of a truth – a prophecy of warning to Archibald.

"Oh my god Archibald! What in God's name is wrong with you? This extreme lack of chivalry does not become you and I shall not stand for it!" Imogen held her ground even though a part of her feared her tone might prompt him to bring additional rage upon her.

"I do apologize. I do not know what has come over me. I am not feeling myself. Perhaps it is best that you take your leave. I see no benefit from any further discussion about Mr. Frye. I shall come to terms with him in my own way."

"Well, it is something to receive an apology from you, no matter how paltry. I remember, soon after you took Talmadge's life, you went to great lengths to persuade me to forgive you. I was far from ready to do so at the time, as you will likely recall."

"Are you now prepared to say I am fully forgiven, carte blanche, for any hurt and hardship I have brought to your doorstep?"

"Do not interrupt me, Archibald. There is more to be said. My face still stings from the insult you placed upon it. I trust when you say *your own way* you will not impose violence upon Sawyer?" Imogen asked, knowing Archibald would not be forthcoming with details of his plan. "I have been privy to serious rumors, which I hope will not hold true," Imogen declared, although she wondered if pleading with Archibald would alter his mood. He waved off her concerns, poured a very generous portion of wine and consumed it in one swallow.

She felt in a perpetual tug-of-war between her strength and Archibald's desire to control her. *I will not be controlled but I must warn Sawyer to avoid contact with Archibald. His demeanor is not boding well,* she worried as she made haste to leave. As she exited the room and stepped into the hallway she heard Archibald mutter, "There is little you can do, for the plans are in place and come tomorrow all will be resolved."

"What is that you say, Archibald?" Imogen turned and inquired. "Did I hear you say tomorrow? Please tell me this is not so?" Archibald uttered no further words as he pulled close the doors to his study, shutting himself off from any intrusions the outside world cared to sling his way.

Archibald wandered aimlessly in his study, finally deciding to light upon the seat of his favorite upholstered chair. The chair sat before the firebox where its large wings enveloped him in warmth. His mind was in turmoil. He needed to find comfort from the thoughts weighing him down and in the absence of Imogen, the chair would have to suffice to embrace him. He leaned back, resting his head against the chair's plush brocade fabric. His eyelids became heavy. He was too spent to fight against the increasing urge to sleep. As he drifted into slumber, his mind's eye became clouded by a ghost-like aura swirling about him like an unrelenting wicked storm. He was caught in the middle and could not free himself. He felt his arms flailing to clear himself from the mass but his efforts were to no avail. He became more and more engulfed in the tempest threatening to engulf him until his valet startled him awake.

"Master Howard, sir. Master Howard!" Harrison shouted, hoping to arouse Archibald and have him cease his fitful movements before he slipped from the chair to the floor.

Slowly, Archibald opened his eyes. He blinked several times to bring Harrison and the room into focus. He swallowed hard and took in several deep breaths to gather his senses.

"Ken I be gettin' ya anythin' Master Howard sir? I'm tellin' ya, yaz, I'm tellin' ya. Youse sure had me worried there. Guess youse was havin' a bad dream?"

Archibald thought no truer words had been spoken. *It was indeed a bad dream,* he acknowledged in a hush, as he relived the ominous images and wondered if they portended of tomorrow's fate?

"Thank you for your concern. Not to worry, Harrison. I have everything under control," Archibald said with less than firm conviction. *The dream, although disconcerting, was nothing but a dream,* he attempted to reason. *What could possibly go wrong?*

Savanna waited outside Dr. Litle's for the arrival of Sawyer's conveyance. She heard the ever-present clopping sound of horse's hooves making their way toward her and was pleased to see Teddy and Sawyer come into view. Savanna's body tingled with anticipation. To be in Sawyer's company without Imogen present to monitor their every word and action was everything she hoped for. She knew her plans to attend the theater with him on this Friday eve were devious but she gave her concern little care. *Imogen will not be the wiser. I have every right to accept an invitation from whomever I please without seeking her approval,* Savanna concluded, using her own bold reasoning to appease her conscience.

She found ways to busy herself in Georgetown after her work at the apothecary so she would have no need to return to Woodholme before the theater. She expressly wanted to avoid incurring any questions from Imogen.

Sawyer pulled the horse to a halt, jumped from the carriage with great zeal and temporarily tethered the horse as he walked to Savanna to assist her into the carriage. He was once again captured by her beauty, grace and charm. Her radiance was infectious as he warmed in the glow of her.

"Beauty seems to follow you wherever you go. Tonight is no exception. I believe I shall be the luckiest and most envied man in the theater. It is to my benefit that the lighting will be subdued, for otherwise I would not lend one moment of my attention to the stage. My focus would be entirely upon you," Sawyer beamed as he lent a hand to Savanna for her to step up into the carriage.

He admired her gown, which was exquisite. She had gone to great care to protect it with a smock while she worked knowing she would need to keep the garment as fresh as possible into the evening. Constructed of soft, satin silk, her purple gown had short, full sleeves with flounces of lavender lace bordering their edges. Lavender netting folded into soft pleats formed the gown's bodice, which sat just above Savanna's waistline. A garland of petite purple roses clustered along the gown's tastefully scooped neckline were repeated along its hem. A strand of eight-millimeter pearls adorned her neck, its clasp set with three brilliant cut sapphires. Matching pearl drops ornamented her earlobes. Her long ivory-colored gloves were ruched just below her elbows. *Ah,* Sawyer observed, *she is a vision of elegance.*

"You are most chivalrous and most kind, Mr. Frye," Savanna nearly purred as she settled into the carriage, which sent rousing sensations throughout Sawyer's torso as he untethered Teddy, entered the carriage and held the reins.

"Step up son," Sawyer ordered Teddy as they moved along Bridge Street and made their way to Louisiana Avenue between Four and One-Half and Sixth Streets to The Washington Theatre.

"I am very much looking forward to attending *Hamlet.* This will be my first venture into the theater since I arrived here. As I mentioned, my parents, or perhaps I should refer to them as the Carlyles, were avid supporters of the arts and imbued me with the culture that naturally follows from such exposure."

"It pleasures me to be your first," responded Sawyer, realizing his words could be misinterpreted. *Or are my deepest desires playing games with my tongue?* he mused. "Perhaps I should rephrase for I meant no impropriety. It pleasures me to pleasure you…" Sawyer's words were cut short by Savanna who began to laugh.

"You make me laugh when you stumble on your words. I should not assist you by easing the distress you have created for yourself but I shall," Savanna teased. "What are some of your favorite lines from *Hamlet*?"

"Very well. This one is perfect, 'The lady doth protest too much, methinks.'"

"Touché, Mr. Frye. I shall say, 'This above all: to thine own self be true, And it must follow, as the night the day, Thou canst not then be false to any man.'"

Sawyer gave pause to the soliloquy Savanna recited. As diligently as he was trying to avoid thoughts of what tomorrow would bring, the words reminded him of what he would be facing as the night followed into the day.

"Ah, the night into the day."

"Have I said something wrong? You seem of a sudden troubled?"

"I assure it is not you, fair Savanna. I have something to face tomorrow with which I shall not burden you."

"You know you may tell me anything. I shall not think less of you."

"I know and I appreciate the way you think. I want this evening to be about you and me and enjoying our time together," Sawyer said, trying his best not to alarm Savanna about what he knew was on the horizon. A soliloquy from Act III, Scene I came to his mind, 'For in that sleep of death what dreams may come, When we have shuffled off this mortal coil, Must give us pause.' *Perhaps, if I meet my death tomorrow, it will free me from any future concerns. But, hopelessness is not my nature. I want to live! I am looking forward to my future, should that be God's will tomorrow — especially a future with Savanna. I want her to know the depth of my love for her,* Sawyer worried. He recited to himself the words from Hamlet's letter to Ophelia: 'Doubt thou the stars are fire, Doubt that the sun doth move, Doubt truth to be a liar, But never doubt I love.' *I can only pray I am given more days to live on this earth so I am able to say these words to her.*

"Have I lost you?" Savanna inquired.

Good Lord! Does she have a way to read that, which travels through my mind? It is uncanny how her words match my thoughts, thought Sawyer.

"Oh, no. My apologies. I guess my mind wandered for a moment. Here, we have arrived. Let us think of nothing else than enjoying this opportunity to be together."

Gertie took note of the handsome young couple making their way into the theater, her with her arm through his. *My, my, they are perfect together.* Her smile quickly faded as she thought of her dear friend. *Poor Imogen. It appears her concerns have merit. I think her time with Mr. Frye will be coming to an end.*

"Here my dear," said Tea. He lent a hand to Gertie as they stepped into the theater's entrance. "Your good spirit seems to have been tempered by something," he added as he looked about. He noted the couple who garnered his wife's attention as they disappeared into the dim light of the theater's house to take their seats several rows back from the stage. The man looked familiar to Tea. *Could it be that is Mr. Frye?* Tea wondered to himself.

"Gertie, do you know that couple upon whom you have such a steady stare?"

"I recognize the gentleman. I believe he is Mr. Sawyer Frye. Several weeks past I called on Imogen at *The Inquirer* and she introduced me to him."

"And the young woman?"

"About her I am not certain but, if I were to guess, I would say that is Talmadge's daughter Savanna Carlyle whom Imogen has told us about. I have yet to meet her, but seeing them together draws my concern for Imogen. I know she is fond of him beyond his good work at the newspaper."

"Is that what has caused you to lose some of your gaiety?"

"Indeed. I was thinking that Imogen's time with Mr. Frye might soon be coming to an end."

Tea almost gasped. Her words stunned him, for she knew nothing of the dispute he had witnessed between Sawyer and Archibald. It was as though her instincts could foretell the future. *I hope she senses an end is coming to Imogen's dalliances with Mr. Frye and not an end to Mr. Frye's life.* Tea shuddered at the thought.

"Well, let's not worry ourselves with such topics tonight. As the saying goes, 'There's many a slip twixt the cup and the lip.' We have little control over matters of love. What will be will be," Tea said, pursing his lips together in a smirk of resignation as he gave his head a shake side-to-side.

"Well, are you not the philosopher Mr. Smallwood? 'Tis one of the many reasons I love you so."

Gertie had no sooner prepared to lean toward Tea and give him a kiss on the cheek when her eyes spotted Lydia and Winston Cromley. She promised herself that the next time she saw the woman she would give her a piece of her mind. *She is due a severe reprimand for the shameless missives she writes. I know with very little doubt that she is the hand of the pen behind Tillie Tattler. Winston is such a kind and jolly fellow and he was such a good friend to Talmadge. I wonder how he tolerates a woman with such vile tendencies to write such horrid dribble about others? Can it be that he is ignorant of her penchant for inflicting pain? That can be the only answer, or I am certain he would put a stop to her cruel activity.*

"Tea, if you will, please engage in conversation with Winston while I have a word with Lydia." Gertie gave not a moment of hesitation for Tea to decline her suggestion as she swiftly moved to Lydia, took her by the arm and led her into a nearby alcove only pausing for a moment to give a nod of recognition to Mayor Thomas Carbery, a frequent patron of the theater.

"My goodness, Mrs. Smallwood, or should I call you Miss Taylor?"

"Lydia, you may cease your silly commentary. Call me Gertie if it helps simplify your small mind for I know it is cluttered with trite opinions and caustic innuendos." Gertie was somewhat ashamed of herself for the haughty tone that had taken over her usual grace and style, but she had had quite enough of Lydia's long-tongued chatter.

"Now, look who is throwing about barbs and accusations? I assure you I know not of what you speak."

"And, I assure you that is a falsehood. You have become quite adept at lying. You know full well you are responsible for the dribble written by you under the auspices of Tillie Tattler."

"Please keep your voice down," Lydia reprimanded, as she looked around hoping no one was listening to their conversation.

"Your sensational observations about Mrs. Simmonds must cease!"

"Why should I succumb to your demands? First, I would have to admit to being the perpetrator you claim me to be, about which you cannot be certain, and secondly, I pity Mrs. Simmonds the indulgences she has brought upon herself that have led to the compromise of her reputation in the city."

"So, you would take me for a fool?"

"How could I not?" Lydia retorted and began to turn to leave when Gertie grabbed her arm.

"What in the world is wrong with you? Unhand me this minute!" Lydia's outburst drew the attention of several entering patrons prompting Gertie to set her free.

Tea and Winston, engaged in a serious conversation about legal concerns, which Tea had with the shipping industry, had both been oblivious to Gertie and Lydia's escalating conversation until Lydia ran to Winston's side in a huff and nearly yanked him down the aisle to their seats.

"Are you so anxious to see this play that you nearly pulled off my arm? What has come over you?"

"Give it no mind, Winston. Gertie and I needed to speak no more and I, for one, need to spend my time in other pursuits, for there is much to be heard and seen on an evening such as this."

"I take it you mean the actors on the stage and their engaging dialogue?"

"Certainly that is what I mean," assured Lydia without conviction in her voice. She was pleasantly distracted when she looked at the couple seated directly in front of them and joyous recognition flooded across her face. *Hmm, if my eyes do not deceive me, that is The Inquirer's managing editor with the young woman from the apothecary. How interesting! I wonder if the widow of Woodholme is aware? If not, perhaps she needs to know.*

Gertie was sorry to have let Lydia Cromley agitate her. *It was of my own doing. I should never have approached her,* thought Gertie. *Did I truly think she would admit to being Tillie Tattler?*

Tea stood as Gertie took her seat. Gertie was pleased to find their seats on the other side of the aisle and several rows away from the Cromleys.

"It appeared you and Winston's wife were at odds with one another, is that a valid observation?"

"Valid indeed. That woman is a menace. I know she is the author of the nasty missives about Imogen, and I could not hold back one more minute in confronting her about her vile deeds she places in print."

"Well, let us think no more of her. I have looked forward to our evening out. I am always at my best when I am with you my dear."

Gertie smiled and squeezed Tea's hand. He always knew how to temper her mood. For the duration of the play she would fully absorb herself in the actors, their dialogue, their costumes and the impact of the characters on the story's plot. She could not however promise that the woman she stared at across the way would not enter her mind. *This is an evening of drama,* pondered Gertie. *I have a strong feeling there is more to come once the stage goes dark, for Lydia Cromley and her poison quill will not let the drama end here.*

Savanna was relieved to find Sawyer's mood lightened during their carriage ride after the theater. She was concerned when he became so contemplative before their arrival. Melancholy was not an air she attributed to him. They spent much of their ride back to Woodholme speaking of Junius Booth's performance and how privileged they felt to be present to watch the classic tragedian perform.

"His acting is as fine as any I ever witnessed with the Carlyles on the English stage," said Savanna.

"He is quite gifted. He has certainly cultivated his art as an actor," added Sawyer.

"I agree. I was impressed by the range of his voice too — his inflections. He carried the words he delivered with such purity and clarity."

"He did indeed. His elocution is also pleasing to the ear, which is not always the case with thespians. For him, the verse comes to his tongue so naturally."

"Yes, his oration was purely elegant, which makes me appreciate the time he has taken to hone his skills."

They were taking pleasure in their analysis of the play. They smiled and gazed at each other enjoying the mutual delight they witnessed in their eyes.

Sawyer slowed Teddy's pace as the carriage approached Woodholme. Since Imogen thus far was none the wiser, there was no need to cause a fuss with her. He and Savanna wanted their night together to remain a secret from her.

The clandestine nature of their evening was stirring romantic urges and serving as a stimulant to them both. Sawyer's longing to embrace Savanna and bring his lips to hers was meeting with a decision that left him torn between abstaining or following through with his desires. He hoped his actions, if he chose to execute them would not be repelled or deemed untoward by Savanna. Little did he know that Savanna was harboring the same desires. He knew he could not linger at Woodholme's portal for fear Imogen would appear. *If I am to make a move, I must do so now*, he announced in silence.

In the essence of time and a growing need to feel her against him, Sawyer leaned close to Savanna and placed his hand gently under her chin to turn her face toward him. She tilted her head up to accept his advances as he accommodated her by placing his lips on hers with a soft kiss. She felt she must be in heaven. Her face tingled with the delight of his face so close to hers. Their nearness erupted feelings neither could contain as they put their arms around each other and kissed again with renewed passion. Their eager kisses became more fervent until Sawyer pulled away lest he not be able to contain the urges building within.

"Savanna, dear Savanna," said Sawyer. "I shall never forget you."

"You make it sound as though you are leaving me forever, Mr. Frye. And now, how could you after we have shared a wonderful evening together, which has only grown more enriching?" Savanna cooed.

"Oh, I mean nothing by that. It is just a matter of speech. I want you to know that you are with me always even when we are apart. I have something to give you before you go," Sawyer informed Savanna as he pulled an envelope from his vest. "This may appear an odd request but I must ask that you not read this letter until tomorrow after the noon hour. You will understand my request at that time, I assure you. I am sorry for my cryptic behavior but I have no choice in the matter." Savanna gladly received the envelope Sawyer handed her. He had written her name in a beautiful script.

"To say you have aroused my curiosity is to minimize the grave concern you stir in me."

"Please do not worry. I hope to be well able to stir many things in you in the days and years ahead."

"Sawyer, how can you tease me so when your words seem like warnings of something to come, which leaves me to do nothing but worry."

"I should not have said a word. Here, let me help you from the carriage and see you to the door. Wait up Teddy, I shan't be but a moment."

Sawyer watched as Savanna slipped the envelope into the bodice of her gown for safekeeping. It comforted him to know she placed his letter close to her heart where it was also well concealed from Imogen's eyes. He imagined himself as intimate with Savanna as his letter. *I hope that day shall be a reality for me. We shall see what tomorrow ushers in.*

With Savanna safely returned to Woodholme, Sawyer and Teddy went on their way. Sawyer held a modicum of guilt for not having written a letter to Imogen. He tried to rationalize his decision but he could find no plausible reason that would either satisfy his conscience or serve to soothe Imogen's hurt if she became aware of his omission. His feelings for her had lost their luster and, if he survived the events of tomorrow, he would in all fairness have to be true to his heart no matter the cost.

He looked down the lane. Darkness having set in required him to keep his eyes on the path home. The carriage lanterns did little to light his way. *Teddy, I hope you have the keen sense to keep us on a solid path that takes us home,* Sawyer relayed to the equine while his mind went to thoughts of tomorrow and the hope that he would live to once again see the path home, to see Savanna, and never again face a challenge like the one placed before him by Archibald.

Imogen paced the drawing room, first back and forth, then in circles until she made herself dizzy. She plopped herself onto the divan, leaned back and closed her eyes until the dizziness passed. Her mind was screaming with frustration for not having been able to locate Sawyer and attempt to alter the path that he and Archibald would soon take.

Archibald said tomorrow. Oh my god, tomorrow! I have no way to stop them! Imogen wanted to scream. *Where is Sawyer? And Savanna? She has yet to return? Perhaps she went to visit Virginia. I should have sent word to Virginia for she may know where they are. The hour is now too late.*

Helplessness and the inability to control a situation were very uncomfortable feelings for Imogen. Sitting on the divan was not calming her in any way. She was preparing herself to abort her quest to locate Sawyer when she heard a rustling sound coming from the hallway.

When Savanna entered the foyer, she saw the light from an oil lamp emanating from the drawing room. She assumed Imogen must not have retired for the evening and thought it best under the circumstances of her evening to move hastily by with hushed footsteps and retreat to her bedchamber to avoid any inquiry from her stepmother. Savanna knew it would be difficult to conjure explanations that would placate Imogen and she was torn because she felt it necessary to neither report her every move to Imogen nor receive her approval. *Tonight's outing with Sawyer will be especially trying to explain, for Imogen will see it as a betrayal of her generosity to me and such revelation will flame her fires of suspicion. Sawyer was definitely not part of the offerings and amenities she wished to extend to me.*

"Savanna, is that you?" Imogen said as she raised her voice to be heard. *Why am I calling out to the girl? I have no intention of relaying Archibald and Sawyer's agreement to her. Such news will only serve to worry her, as it has me, and neither of us has any ability to alter the events of tomorrow. I can only pray their differences are settled before any weapons are brandished.*

Savanna could not in good conscience ignore Imogen's call to her. She stopped for a moment to collect her thoughts before slowly moving toward the drawing room's doorway. She studied Imogen's face and saw a look there that was not known to her. Obviously, Imogen was distraught. There was a far away look in her eyes like someone whose aged mind had begun to slip away. Concern enveloped Savanna, yet she wanted to limit her time with Imogen before she began to question her whereabouts. With Savanna's appearance in the doorway Imogen halted her fitful promenade as recognition returned to her face.

"Oh, Savanna. There you are. I have been so worried about you. It has been hours that you have been away and no one, not even Patti, was able to quell my worries. What has kept you?"

"Thank you for asking but there is no need for worry. My day took a longer turn than normal. I had a bite to eat in the city and lingered there. It is amazing how time can get away from one. But, I am here now." Savanna explained with as much evasion as her conscience would allow, as a touch of guilt began to raise its ugly head.

"But, the hour is late."

"Yes, you are quite right. On that note, I shall continue to my bedchamber. It seems a good night's rest will do us both good," concluded Savanna, as she waved her gloved hand to Imogen to signal her departure.

Imogen suspected Savanna and Sawyer were in each other's company. *There is no other explanation, for the girl was too hesitant to answer me. She is hiding the truth, although not very well.* The pain and worry of anticipated loss darted through Imogen's body as anger at being deceived welled within. She began to retrace her steps as she paced about the drawing room, mumbling the truth she knew would soon unfold. *I fear the long reach of the fingers of change will soon be knocking at my door.*

Patti hesitated to bring in the newspaper she found at the front portico the next morning. The copy of *The National Intelligencer* was folded back to a page Patti often heard talked about when she was shopping in the market in the company of other ladies' maids. She had read several of the articles by a writer who called herself Tillie Tattler. Patti assumed it was a woman who wrote the pieces because, as she had announced to the maids after reading one, "Who but a woman would write such tales? Men's got more important thin's to do then be writin' like a gossipmonger. In my experience, and limited it may be, the men want nothin' ta do with small talk and 'earsay." The maids laughed at Patti, especially enjoying her naïveté. She took their teasing all in her stride, not embarrassed by her innocence, which she saw as a virtue several of them could not boast about.

She wondered who delivered the newspaper and questioned why the particular page was selected to be in full view? She picked it up and began to read:

Dearest Readers,

The theater had an unexpected scene to be witnessed Friday evening. It would seem a certain young woman known for the potions she blends was on the arm of a young gentleman with attachments to the publishing world. His attachments, I might add, extend beyond the news he prints.

Could this be the demise of the relationship of the mistress and her younger man? Is she aware of the transgressions of the two or is she none the wiser? Will she confront him about his wandering eye or will she find a way to rid herself of the beauty who bids him hither? So many questions. Answers to come.

Poor Fickle Mistress. You may soon need to sow your aging oats elsewhere.

With dramatic concern,
Tillie Tattler

"I dun't know 'ow I can be given this to me mistress. It will only displease 'er. But someone, I be sure, is wantin' her to put 'er eyes to this," reasoned Patti as she spoke aloud. She began to fold the newspaper to discard it when Imogen rounded the corner.

"Patti, to whom were you speaking?"

"Oh, jest meself mum. Pay me no mind."

"What is that you have? Let me see," ordered Imogen, her nerves frayed from a night of worry.

"I dun't think ye be wantin' to read this now."

"That is for me to decide. Hand it over. My patience is running very thin."

Imogen snapped the paper from Patti's hands and began to read the latest rumors put in print by her nemesis Tillie Tattler. She would like to label the accusations as falsehoods but she knew truth was harbored in the paragraphs.

Chapter Forty-One

May 1822

Doctor Davenport found Imogen in the parlor intently engaged in a colorful needlework. The activity helped occupy her mind as she tried to displace frightening images of Archibald and Sawyer wielding weapons at one another. The approach of footsteps startled her, causing her to prick her finger with the needle's tip. She looked up as she pressed gently on the site of her wound offering aid to her injury. To see the doctor in her home administered an immediate sense of foreboding, which overtook her as she began to stand and found her legs less than accommodating, as her nerves got the best of her. The doctor stepped quickly to her aid and urged her to remain seated.

She knew he had been present when Talmadge met his end and assumed he was at the ready, if needed, to lend his medical skills to Archibald and Sawyer's wounds as well.

"I bear bad tidings." Slowly and directly came the doctor's words.

Imogen turned pale. The expression of fear on her face was profound. Since early morning she felt deep in her bones that Archibald and Sawyer's encounter would prove to be fatal. *Oh, my god, who is it that has met his end? Or, could it be both have succumbed to the challenge they presented one another?* She shook her head to clear the cobwebs forming in her mind. *Had the time come for both of them to die? Have they both gone to the blessed beyond?* Tears began to form in her eyes as she imagined Sawyer, injured, lying on the cold earth, drawing his last breaths, as she sat in her warm home attempting to busy herself with a piece of needlepoint. *It seems I cannot escape sadness. It appears to follow me like a dark shadow intent on stalking my every move.*

"Please doctor, I have no patience for your delay. My nerves are frayed and I fear the news you have come to share will only magnify my fragile constitution of late. You have come to deliver the fates of Mr. Howard and Mr. Frye, have you not? I begged them to find another way to settle their disputes! Both were hell bent on dueling with no hope for arbitration! Why did they have to be so stubborn? Men and pride are dangerous bedfellows!" Imogen was so distraught she was just a pitch below shouting.

"Now, now Mrs. Simmonds, it's best you try to remain calm lest you are taken ill. That will serve no purpose and certainly not help Mr. Frye as he recovers from his wound."

"Mr. Frye you say? Mr. Frye? Is he not dead? Spill it out doctor! You said you bore bad tidings, so I assumed both men were gone. What of Mr. Howard? Please tell me at once!"

"I mention Mr. Frye first because it is my understanding that he is in your employ at the newspaper."

"Indeed he is, or was, depending on the news you so reluctantly share."

"I am doing my best to reveal to you what I know without causing undo harm to your well-being."

"I assure you that your delay in spitting out your words is the matter causing me harm. What has become of Mr. Frye and Mr. Howard?"

"I fear Mr. Howard met his death at his own hands. Mr. Frye received a flesh wound to his leg from the ball fired from Mr. Howard's pistol."

"At his own hands? Mr. Howard was a moderately skilled marksman. How could he have turned it on himself?"

"I am fairly certain Mr. Howard was overcome by something he drank prior to receiving his pistol from his second."

"Something he drank? Were the men inebriated? Had they shared shots of brandy prior to pacing off?"

"It was Mr. Howard who suggested, actually insisted, he and Mr. Frye each have a chalice of whiskey before their duel, *to steady their hands* he said. He placed the cups on a silver salver and directed Mr. Frye to take the cup closest to him reserving the other for himself. They saluted one another with the cups and then drank them down fully. Their seconds handed them their pistols. The two men stood back-to-back and no sooner had they finished their pace and begun to turn when Mr. Howard's eyes began to roll and his arms began to shake, forcing his pistol-wielding hand to become unsteady. At that moment, his pistol discharged. The ball passed through the flesh of Mr. Frye's leg as Mr. Howard rapidly collapsed to the ground."

Imogen, who had been fully engaged in the story the doctor was revealing, shook her head and placed her hand over her mouth in disbelief.

"How could this be? Was Archibald suddenly taken ill? I have never known him to exhibit such erratic behavior. How do you explain what occurred?"

"At this time I have no explanation other than the knowledge that Mr. Howard's symptoms came upon him so swiftly, it appeared he had been poisoned. The authorities were summoned. The matter will reside in their hands. I am certain they will want to speak with you and any other associates of Mr. Howard's to determine what transpired. All I can offer for now is, unfortunately one man is dead and another is injured."

"Will Mr. Frye sustain any long-term ill effects from his injury?"

"I was able to remove the fragments of the pistol's ball from his leg, clean the wound and bandage it at the scene. He will need to watch it for any signs of infection. However, that said, if the wound heals properly and he exercises good judgment, he will likely not suffer any lasting physical consequences from his actions today. I cannot speak to any legal consequences that may be cast his direction."

Imogen was trying to absorb the onslaught of emotions bombarding her, which would not be quelled until she saw Sawyer with her own eyes. She trusted Doctor Davenport's account of the morning but there were questions remaining to be answered. *What could possibly have overcome Archibald? Did he have a sudden spell? A stroke? What befell him? Doc mentioned poison? Oh, my! First I lose Talmadge, now Archibald,* murmured Imogen. She felt as though time had retreated and left her in a limitless limbo pondering what could possibly happen next.

"Oh, and lest I forget, here is a letter Mr. Howard gave to me when he arrived at the dueling grounds. He asked that it be given to you regardless of the morning's outcome."

"A letter?"

"Yes, he said it was important that you receive this."

"Did he anticipate that he would not survive?"

"Perhaps he was merely insuring that whether alive, injured or, God forbid, dead, he would be able to speak to you. He was very insistent that you have this letter."

Imogen held the neatly folded parchment in her hand and slowly opened it to reveal words written in Archibald's flowing scrawl. Tears formed as she began to read what were the last words she would ever have from him:

My Darling Imogen,

Our time together has been an adventure I will always cherish. I apologize for my behaviors that have caused you pain and hope you will in time forgive me for any anger or jealousy that caused me to act in such a way.

I write this letter in hopes that I will survive to be with you again and, in that case, I will present it to you myself. However, if you are reading this in my absence I am forever gone from your life. I fear something must have gone severely wrong and not according to plan. I fully expected to survive.

And, if Mr. Frye has perished at my hands, I hope you will forgive my actions that led to his death for I was compelled to pursue the code of honor to which he and I both agreed.

You are of great importance to me. My life has been made richer with you in it and I hope I shall always remain important to you. Hopefully, you will hold me in loving memory. I will always love you.

Yours now and forever,
Archibald

The tears in Imogen's eyes were obstructing her view. Archibald's writing was becoming a blur, a jumble of words linked together by a hand, which had lent her pleasure and pain. Her heart ached and felt tattered into shreds. *Archibald has met his journey's end,* she lamented.

Doc Davenport offered her a handkerchief to blot away the tears as her weeping began to ease. Imogen turned her eyes to the parchment to once again read Archibald's parting words, 'Something must have gone severely wrong and not according to plan.' *What could he mean by this? What plan other than a duel where the outcome could not be known? Why was he so assured he would survive? Oh, Archibald, what have you done? What have you done?*

A short time after Doctor Davenport took his leave, Patti answered a knock at the door and was relieved to see Mr. Frye. She had overheard the doctor's report about the duel, yet feared the worst about his condition. He had lost the pace of his youth as he ambled in with the assistance of a cane but Patti was very pleased to see that his handsome countenance remained intact.

His walking aid was a finely tooled stick of polished mahogany with a handle carved in the shape of an equine. A narrow leather wrist strap, which Sawyer chose not to use, dangled from the handle. Patti gladly offered her services to walk beside him all the way to the drawing room where Imogen awaited his arrival. Patti was prepared to assist him if his leg pained him and he needed to pause in the hallway before proceeding. She also happily imagined the pleasure she would gain to have him rub against her. Her fantasizing came to an abrupt halt when her mistress appeared in the doorway.

"Sawyer, oh my Sawyer," Imogen sputtered out her words as she moved to his side and Patti turned and walked away. "This morning I rose to some degree confused, praying for the best yet imagining the worst. And, once again my nerves have had to endure the foolishness of men. I am so relieved to have you here. The doctor says your leg will fully heal. I hate to ask, for I am grateful you were not more seriously harmed, but what possibly could have happened to cause Archibald's *plan,* as he termed it in a letter to me, to fail so?"

"Doc Davenport suspects poison. Without casting aspersions, Mr. Howard was rather insistent that we drink a chalice of whiskey, which he prepared. As my good fortune would have it, when the seconds presented the salver to us with the drinks, the placement of the cups must have been reversed from Mr. Howard's recollection and he drank from the chalice intended for me."

"Poison? Poison? Archibald would stoop to such dire tactics?"

"Apparently yes. He was hell bent on removing me from your life."

"How can you be certain that he was responsible for the poison, if indeed he was?"

"I cannot say with all certainty except that Miss Carlyle happened to mention to me that she had a rather curious conversation with him at Dr. Litle's Drug Store. He was inquiring about poisons and, in particular, their effectiveness for eliminating rats."

"I know he had been making some concerning threats. However, I never thought he would go to such extremes," Imogen said as her memory drifted to the bottle she had observed on Archibald's desk, which he swiftly removed to a drawer when he saw her spying it. "And, look at the outcome. Archibald essentially extinguished his own life in attempting to extinguish yours," Imogen said as she began to sob, unable to contain her emotions.

Sawyer reached for Imogen as she abandoned herself in his arms. She nestled her face into his chest, which served as her haven, a safe harbor to release the tears that showed no signs of relenting. He held her close and rubbed her back trying his best to soothe her sorrow. She was at once conflicted. Sadness for the loss of Archibald continued to wash over her while relief for Sawyer's safety filled her with subdued elation.

"Thank God you have returned to me," Imogen cried as she pulled away and looked into Sawyer's eyes. Concern greeted her. She saw something different residing there. *Was it residual fear from his experience on the dueling grounds? Was it concern for legal action, which might find its way to him? Was he numb with exhaustion?* Questions were wielded about in Imogen's head.

Sawyer stepped back slowly, using the cane for support as he tried to lessen the pressure on his injured leg. He made his way to the drawing room's aubergine divan and carefully settled himself there motioning to Imogen to join him. She obliged his request taking great care not to brush against his bandaged wound. He took her hand in his and grasped it with a firm grip. Imogen was pleased, yet in the same breath wondered if his touch was an endearment, or he simply needed to warm his hands from the morning chill.

She knew he would not accept the use of a cane for support unless it was absolutely necessary to his comfort. *Perhaps he is more seriously injured than the doctor revealed? I know Sawyer would not want to be viewed as weak, as needing a crutch, and he would not use the cane to gain sympathy as the wrongfully injured party,* reasoned Imogen. *He would not bring such attention to himself.* But, as she focused her eyes on him more closely, she could see in his expression a necessity for the walking implement.

She freed her hand and reached up with her fingers to brush a stray strand of his hair back into place. He took her hand and kissed her palm. Life's little pleasures, simple and sweet, were something he appreciated. When his morning began, he could not predict the outcome. He was grateful for Imogen's touch, for her companionship and most of all for still having life in him to live. Yet, he was unsettled. He had watched a man die this day. He knew that which had been seen could never be unseen. Archibald's passing was etched in his mind and there was no letting go of it, not ever. And, there was another person to consider. He could not clear his mind from thoughts of Savanna. *Dare I ask Imogen if she be near? How possibly can I?* Sawyer was torn. His mind and heart twisted with the knowledge that two women wished him by their side, yet he knew he wanted to claim only one as his own.

When Savanna awoke she reached under her pillow to retrieve the envelope Sawyer had given her. She had placed it there after removing her gown and preparing for her night's sleep. She held it in her hand and brushed it back and forth on her palm. She looked at the mantel clock. *Eleven forty-five*, sighed Savanna. *I am surprised Patti has not come to rouse me. I must be exhausted from the theater to remain in bed until this hour. Sawyer said to read this after the noon hour. Shall I wait or read this now? Fifteen minutes should make no difference.*

Savanna broke the wax seal stamped with the letter 'F' and opened the envelope. She slid the single piece of folded parchment from its protective covering. She opened it wide and began to read from the flowing script written in Sawyer's own hand:

My Dear Savanna,

Knowing you has sweetened my life. To think we both traveled to America in search of someone only to find he had perished. And yet, we had the good fortune for our paths to cross. It is as though we were meant to be.

You know I speak of your father. I too came to see him for it was his guidance when I met him in England that persuaded me to pursue my interest in journalism. I hope he would be pleased that we found each other for, in a way, our meeting was of his doing. We have much for which to be thankful and I hope that circumstances continue in our favor in that regard.

I asked you to wait to read this letter for it may become a keepsake, something you may hold onto as my last words to you. I care so deeply for you. As I have said before, I shall never forget you. I hope the outcome of my day has worked in my favor with harm to none. With faith and God's goodwill I shall return to you with open arms.

With love and devotion,
I remain your faithful servant Sawyer Frye

Savanna felt numb. *The outcome of his day? This has all the markings of a letter of farewell. We had such a lovely evening together. What can this mean?* Savanna gripped the letter in her hands and began to reread it as tears welled in her eyes.

Patti could barely contain herself as she kept her close proximity to the drawing room to listen to Doc Davenport relay the news to her mistress of the duel and its outcome. Her eavesdropping had become more fine-tuned in recent months. *I'd be bored to me death if I didn't listen in on the talk at's been 'ad around 'ere,* Patti reasoned. She wasted no time going to Savanna's bedchamber to tell her about Mr. Howard and Mr. Frye. As Patti anticipated, Savanna became immediately distraught until Patti finally explained, "Not to worry, Miss Savanna. Mr. Frye, 'e's injured but 'e's alive an' well. The doc said so 'imself. In fact, I ken tell ye that he's 'ere in the flesh if ye want ta be seein' fer yerself. Ye best be puttin' on yer robe."

Savanna nearly pushed the girl aside as she raced from her bedchamber, out into the hallway and quickly descended the staircase to the foyer.

The sound of footsteps caught Imogen and Sawyer's attention. Within seconds, Savanna rounded the corner and stood in the doorway. Relief flooded her face. She wanted to run to him, to embrace him, to take in every part of him, but she knew restraint must be her guide for Imogen would be devastated by any such display of passion by her for Sawyer. He wanted to step away from Imogen and announce to Savanna his declaration of love for her but he could not exercise such cruelty toward Imogen.

"Mr. Frye, you have given us such cause for concern. I believe I may speak for Imogen as well that we are extremely relieved to see that you live and breathe!" Savanna declared as she wiped the tears from her eyes.

"I surely do and no one is more grateful than I," said Sawyer as he tried to subdue the elation he felt for not only surviving the duel but for another day to be with Savanna. His relief was sobered with the fact that a man had died but, by the grace of God, not at his hands.

Imogen observed the look on their faces. *I am not blind. I see the great affection they hold for one another. Sawyer is all I have left. I shall not lose him to my stepdaughter. What irony to have welcomed her into my home! A deed of courtesy on my part, only to have her usurp my kindnesses and wield them against me!* Imogen's thoughts were causing her distress. She was determined to remain strong and revel in Sawyer's good fortune.

Savanna could not hold herself back. Her emotions gave way to her relief that Sawyer survived. She knew she could not however dismiss or ignore Imogen's feelings. Carefully and deliberately she walked to Sawyer. She first put one arm behind Imogen and then her other arm behind Sawyer, orchestrating the three of them together into a human triangle. Savanna served as their instrument of peaceful coexistence, if only for this one moment, uniting them together with mutual, yet momentary pleasure.

The sudden pings of a silver spoon against the hardwood floor startled them to attention as Patti's clumsiness awakened them with the precision of a percussionist. The commotion allowed pent up emotions to release themselves as the deep affection Imogen and Savanna felt for Sawyer surfaced, and both women began to cry, leaving Sawyer to wonder what the outcome would be when they released themselves from one another.

Dearest Readers,

So sad to report that once again the widow has lost another. Beware gents, for the men in her life seem to be dropping like flies! As though the scandal of it all is not enough, this loss is rumored to be laced with foul play.

Will her young gent risk it all and remain by her side? Or, will he make the wise choice to find another to his liking?

Poor Mistress. Could it be time to mend your wayward ways?

With a degree of sympathy,
Tillie Tattler

Chapter Forty-Two

Patti pulled back the damask draperies in the drawing room welcoming a new day to Woodholme. She fastened them in place with heavy corded tassels that attached to the hooks on either side of the window moldings. Going about her duties kept her mind from the dark cloud that had been holding court over the mansion. *I find it 'ard to believe Mr. Howard's met 'is end. Seems like tragedy's findin' its way to this doorstep more then it should. Hope that be the end of it but with the mistress of this manse, there be no tellin' what might be brewin',* Patti worried as she fluffed several pillows. Her eyes caught the glimmer of a pair of earrings on a side table. *Oh, they be Miss Savanna's. I seed her wearin' 'em last night.*

"Patti, there you are. Have you seen Miss Carlyle this morn?" Imogen inquired.

"No, mum. But, I've seen somethin' of 'er, or I should say, somethin' of 'ers," Patti announced as she held out her hand to reveal the pair of earrings.

"How did you come into the possession of those?"

"They was just layin' about mum. Would you be wantin' me to take them to 'er room for safekeepin'?"

"Yes Patti, please do." Imogen answered quickly, then thought better of her response. "No, on second thought, give them to me. I shall return them to her."

"Like I said mum, I 'aven't seen 'er this morn."

"Perhaps she has gone to the apothecary. There are some concerns there since the passing of Mr. Howard." Imogen's eyes started to well with tears as she thought of Archibald. She knew it was highly suspected that Archibald stole poison from Dr. Litle's. Savanna had mentioned to Sawyer his erratic behavior and her error in allowing him to be alone with the bottles of poison when she went to the storage room. Dr. Litle received a complaint from a patron who purchased cyanide only to find it was sugar crystals. *A substitution by Mr. Howard, no doubt,* surmised Savanna when she learned of the switch. Since Archibald was a victim of his own deception, there were no charges to be placed against him. The case was as closed as his coffin.

Imogen shook her head and quickly squelched her emotions from fully forming as reasons for Savanna's earrings being in the drawing room began to take shape in her mind. *I cannot allow my worst fears to rise. No,* she worried as she shook her head to negate the images.

Sawyer had made an unannounced call to Woodholme last night after his work at *The Inquirer* to show Imogen the injury to his leg was much improved in the week since the duel. She, although pleased with his news, had little time to dote over him for she had called a meeting of her anti-slavery committee and needed to depart for several hours. *Ah, that left him in the company of Savanna! Why were her earrings free from her ears? I have suspected for some time that the two of them cannot be trusted together! Could it be that he was nibbling her ear!* The thought nearly sent Imogen into a tailspin, which she halted as she composed herself.

"Give no further concern to Miss Carlyle's earrings. I shall take them to her room."

"Of course, as you say mum."

Imogen held Savanna's earrings in her right hand as she lifted the hem of her gown to ascend the stairs. Her mind was heavy with thoughts, which made her passage up the staircase seem inordinately long. *Why do I have to have these concerns? I need some semblance of order and calm in my life,* she fretted, then chose to dismiss her concerns. *Silly me. I am just assigning worry where it has no place.*

Savanna's bedchamber was a favorite of Imogen's among the numerous spaces for guests to reside. The varying hues of lavender, green and rose offered a lovely respite from the toils of the day. She smiled and looked about the space. Everything was in perfect order. She looked to the dressing table for a vessel in which to place the earrings and saw an oak coffer with a carved top of vines and roses. For all appearances it served as a jewelry box. Imogen lifted the lid expecting to see other pieces of jewelry in the box for safekeeping.

Certainly my eyes deceive me! Imogen's face reddened as her fingers shuffled through the papers resting within the box. She held the papers before her as her eyes scanned the words that flowed upon the parchment. Her worst fears were confirmed. She stared at the beautiful script, which she readily recognized as Sawyer's. *The scoundrel, the scoundrel! How could he do this to me? And, her! How could she do this to me as well! I have been duped! I should have known when his affections for me waned that she was the cause of his roving eye.*

Feeling the victim was an emotion Imogen had born to perfection. In order to be such, she had to lay blame anywhere but upon herself. She would dare not believe herself to be the cause. There had to be someone else or others upon which to cast aspersions. *Why did I not escape the temptation of exploring her room? Whatever was I thinking? What outcome could I have imagined? Oh, now I am being duly punished for stepping where I was not invited.* Thoughts whirled in her head as she once again looked upon the parchment and began to read aloud the words that brought raging tears to her face:

> *My sweet Savanna, you are as refreshing as a summer rain and pure as a rose petal kissed by a droplet of morning dew. My thoughts fly to you like the fluttering wings of a hummingbird hovering for a taste of nectar to quench its thirst.*

Imogen thought she might take sick. She dared not read another word of Sawyer's missives for her stomach was beginning to roll. *Why am I so possessed with jealousy? I suspected something was amiss in our relationship but nary did I imagine he would be so lovelorn that he would pamper her with these endearments!*

Slowly, with shaking hands she replaced the letters and closed the lid to the coffer. She would not purloin Sawyer's notes to Savanna. The letters would remain as she had found them but she would not dismiss her knowledge of them. *He must answer for his actions! I will meet with him on the morrow.* Imogen made her declarations, knowing in her heart of hearts that revelations might be made that would not bode well for her and her relationship with Sawyer.

As soon as Imogen got word from Savanna that she would be out for the day on a visit to Virginia's, Imogen sent Patti to *The Inquirer* with a very curt note to Sawyer that he was to come to Woodholme at once. It was not unusual for Imogen to request his presence during the daytime hours when she knew her home would be free of other guests. Her staff knew their discretion was paramount to remaining in her employ, always turning a blind eye to where and how long their mistress and her gentlemen callers spent their time together.

Sawyer took the note Patti proffered, recognizing the parchment and handwriting. Patti looked at Sawyer as if to scold him then hesitated, knowing her mistress appeared distressed and as though she had spent a night with little sleep. *I best not be puttin' me opinions on 'im,* thought Patti. *The mistress would not take kindly to me meddlin' where I dun't belong.*

Sawyer quickly perused Imogen's note, which was short and to the point: *Stop what you are doing and come to Woodholme at once.* He turned to ask Patti why an audience with him was so urgent but the girl had already gone on her way. He wondered if something dire had occurred. Imogen had sent him notes in the past but they were always laced with sweet remembrances and a call for more intimate time together.

I must not delay. Curiosity alone would have me go to her posthaste, Sawyer reasoned as he made his way to his carriage not knowing what would await him.

"Why, oh why, I must ask, have you deceived me so? Another woman tickles your fancy and you forget all that we have meant to each other, not to mention the great lengths I have gone to on your behalf to raise you up in the newspaper industry? Are you so besotted with her that you are willing to forgo all alliances we have formed? Do you have no shame? How can you be so cruel?" An angry diatribe of unguarded words flowed from Imogen's mouth. "I have harvested enough evidence of your betrayal to me!" Imogen railed as she pulled Sawyer's letters from the oak coffer and waived them in the air.

"Listen to the words written in your own hand on this note, *My thoughts fly to you like the fluttering wings of a hummingbird hovering for a taste of nectar,* Imogen nearly exploded as she read the words aloud. "I am appalled that you have offered such endearments to her! Hummingbird, ha! More like the nocturnal wail of a male whip-poor-will incessantly calling for a mate!"

Sawyer stood stoically still. Embarrassment captured his facial expression to know his and Savanna's privacy had been encroached. He stared at Imogen as he formulated his thoughts, not wanting to inflict any additional distress her direction. It was certainly true that a heated attraction had existed between them, but perhaps theirs was an attraction of convenience. She was a recent widow and he was in need of an assignation that would satisfy his needs both personally and professionally.

As he hesitated to respond, Imogen became increasingly disheartened. His silence spoke volumes to her. She had readily accepted his unconditional love and adoration but now she felt like a buffoon, a victim of his attention. She had been wronged by him and victimized yet again by another of the male gender. To add to her misery, she would not easily accept there was no one to scold but herself for these outcomes.

Sawyer took a few more moments to gather his thoughts. At a time like this, the proper import of words was crucial to subduing the situation. He intended to speak in fairness to minimize any undue harm. He had cared deeply for Imogen and would always appreciate their times together. He had not anticipated meeting Savanna and becoming so enthralled by her.

His unchaste relationship with Imogen was in absolute contrast to the pure joy he had come to experience in Savanna's presence. He felt tantalized by her virtuous nature, always wanting more time with her. Holding her hand and sweet kisses she would allow him to bestow upon her tempted him to press for increased intimacy, which she was not wont to allow until they were one in marriage. He respected her wishes but he was finding it more and more difficult to abstain from pressing further. He wanted to explore and savor every part of her body and have her return the sensual pleasures. At times he imagined her lips on his, her hands rubbing his bare chest, running down his torso, gripping his buttocks, and causing arousals in him that would bring their bodies together in their own personal ecstasy. He was brought back to the present by Imogen's demanding voice.

"Have you gone into a trance? You must explain yourself!"

"Imogen, please hear me out. It has taken some time for me to recover from the ordeal with Mr. Howard."

"I can say, I am pleased to see you walk unaided."

"Yes, the cane is no longer my constant companion. The injury to my leg has fully healed however, that day was a defining one. I was thankful to be spared my life, for that experience was the closest I have ever come to losing my life. I do not wish such feelings on any man or woman. It opened my eyes to the options about me and I realized I must act now, not wait for a tomorrow I may never witness. Please do not be dismayed," said Sawyer with all the compassion he could render.

"What? Dismayed? Not I! I am overjoyed with this news! How can I be otherwise?" Imogen spoke with sarcasm dripping from her lips.

"Imogen, please understand. I have always deeply cared for you. I have no intent to distress you. It has come as much a surprise to me as to you that Miss Carlyle has had such an affect on me. I truly was unguarded by the emotions she elicited from me."

"My, my, my. You speak as though this is not of your doing."

"If the truth be told, and I am allowed to be blatantly honest, I tolerated the attraction you and Archibald held for one another. You explained to me that he was part of your life in a carnal way even when Mr. Simmonds was alive. Without sounding judgmental, you were not steadfast in your vows."

"What? You would throw accusations toward me? You, who are writing love letters to another?"

"You and I have no such vows to have abandoned. I am sorry you have found out this way. My intent was to talk with you in the coming days about Miss Carlyle."

"Miss Carlyle, ha! Spare me the formality when you clearly call her your 'sweet Savanna.' I do not recall such superlatives attached to my name by you. I have exerted every effort to please you and support your desires. Now, quite frankly, I have exhausted my will to continue what has become a charade."

"Imogen let us not forget all that we have meant to one another with and without endearments. Change is amid us in so many ways. I know some change may be difficult to understand or embrace but there is no stopping it. There are opportunities ahead for you. You are trying to influence change with your committee work, which along with the newspaper will only encompass more of your time. I am sorry for this change between us. It saddens me to see you so distraught."

"Your pity upon me is most unwelcome!" The words left Imogen's mouth like a battalion of daggers spit forth to inflict harm. "Perhaps you should make haste and take leave of my presence before I attempt to conjure ways to repay the pox you place upon me."

Sawyer glanced at the box of letters, then to Imogen who held Talmadge's handkerchief to her face to blot away the tears spilling down her cheeks. The square of linen aided her in keeping him close. She had always relied on him to comfort her and today would be no exception.

"I shall see myself to the door," he said before pausing to say more. "We have yet to discuss my position at *The Inquirer*..." Sawyer began without finishing his statement before Imogen interjected.

"You may consider this your notice of dismissal. You may retrieve your final wages from Gibs on the morrow. Not to worry, for I am certain you will have no difficulty finding a position elsewhere," Imogen stated very flatly, all warmth of emotion having escaped her. A pang of regret, which she would not acknowledge spread over her. The moment the words 'consider this your notice of dismissal' escaped her lips, she wished she could retract them. But, alas she could not. The pain of the loss of Sawyer had left her numb. *I have no other course of action at my disposal for I have been betrayed. Now, I must not dwell on what once was, for only sadness will ensue,* vowed Imogen.

Sawyer was not surprised. He knew she was deeply hurt and would not be able to abide his presence at the newspaper. He cared for her but another had stolen his heart. As Imogen's tears ceased, there were no more words to be spoken. He turned to leave the room while residual silence hung heavy in the air. A tempest was building. Sawyer knew he needed to alert Savanna. Imogen's anger was like a threatening cloud waiting to dump its swell of precipitation in a flood of fury that would either wash them apart or, with any luck, cleanse away the animosity and bring them together.

Imogen stood at the window in her bedchamber and watched the day begin its cycle into night. As twilight settled over her estate and the day's sun dissolved into darkness, she searched for a kinship with the natural progression of life and its ever-changing nature. She thought of all the days gone by and those to come. She thought of her dark days and wished to dismiss them from her mind or, at the very least, not have them dictate her future. A hopeful energy, a renewal she wished to hold close began to surge inside her. *I shall weather this dark time in my life as I have all the others. I have had many days filled with joy and shall continue to pursue that which brings me happiness.*

Chapter Forty-Three

Days had passed since Imogen confronted Sawyer. She was always one to compel respect but of late found herself lacking in such regard. *Mortified! That is how I feel! Mortified! How could I have allowed myself to be such a fool?*

Banishing Sawyer from her personal and business life had proved more difficult than she had anticipated. She missed his affection and the newspaper was struggling without him. She was hoping to recruit a managing editor from *The National Intelligencer* and was in the process of negotiating his wages. Joseph Gales and William Seaton, co-owners of the newspaper, were reluctant to let their employee breach his allegiance to them. Coming to terms with a mutually agreeable wage was taking more time than she liked. *I think I shall turn this over to Gibs. He is more than capable of hiring Sawyer's replacement. As Grandmum used to say, 'I have bigger fish to fry.'*

Imogen had spent much of her time sequestered in her room contemplating the best way to evict Savanna from Woodholme. *I must think of a way to offer her an alternative to my residence without appearing to be destitute of good manners and without portraying myself as the poor damsel who has been scorned. She simply cannot remain living under my roof, especially if I am to make any attempt to salvage my relationship with Sawyer.* Since the discovery of his letters to Savanna, the level of discord between Imogen and the girl had escalated. Neither was spending much time outside their bedchambers, nor did they want to be in each other's company.

Patti, in her own inimitable way, had overheard the intense exchange between Sawyer and her mistress. Having taken a liking to Miss Savanna, Patti felt it her duty to make her privy to the fact that her mistress had found letters written by Mr. Frye. "Love letters!" Patti exclaimed. "I best be tellin' ye, Mrs. Simmonds is madder than a 'ornet trapped in a bonnet!"

Savanna's complexion had become ashen upon Patti's revelation. She thought she had hidden Sawyer's sweet words from view and never anticipated Imogen venturing into her bedchamber and opening her jewelry box. She kept herself sequestered in her room for two days, only opening her bedchamber door to have Patti assist with her toilette and bring meals to her for sustenance. That was until Patti informed her that Imogen too had not often left her bedchamber. Savanna sent a note to Virginia and asked if she could stay with her at Rosedale for several days. Virginia had gladly accepted her request hoping days would extend to a more permanent arrangement.

A visit to Virginia Sterling immediately came to Imogen's mind. *Yes, Virginia will do quite nicely. I must call on her. She originally extended an invitation for Savanna to lodge at Rosedale and on several occasions indicted her desire to have her daughter live with her. On the morrow, I shall call on her, although it will gravel me to my very core to have to explain why I need her to vacate my home. Who am I deceiving? Myself? For certainly Virginia has been privy to the gossip spreading about the city about the poor 'Widow of Woodholme' who has lost yet another lover. That troublemaker Tillie Tattler has kept the cog turning on the gossip mill. It is not very Christian of me but at times I wish her harm!*

Gertie came to mind. *Perhaps I should take benefit of her good counsel. She usually sets me straight to right. Her teachings are very able aids for one to live by.* Imogen often told Gertie she should write a book addressing proper etiquette. She repeated some of Gertie's philosophies: '*It is important to make politeness a nature of daily life and one should avoid thoughtless self-gratification, which must be subdued. One must avoid the innate tendency to prefer self. Such tendencies must be kept in abeyance. And, she added, above all dear, a clear conscience, kindly nature and fine manners can conquer all things.*'

Hmm. I have had more than a little difficulty adhering to her edicts. Perhaps if I had, or did, I would not find myself in such predicaments.

Imogen pulled her carriage up to the front of Rosedale and was immediately greeted by Virginia's footman who aided her in disembarking and then secured her conveyance to a hitching post near a trough of water for her horse to refresh himself. Before Imogen departed Woodholme, Patti informed her that Savanna had announced she would be lodging with Mrs. Sterling for several days. That news suited Imogen just fine. *Perfect! I can kill two birds with one stone by meeting with Virginia and Savanna at the same time and discussing my reasons for Savanna to leave Woodholme. But, what are my reasons? I will need to think this through quickly.*

Imogen was still sorting reasons through her mind when she entered Rosedale and was greeted by Virginia. There was no sign of Savanna. She wondered if the girl was hesitant to be in her company and perhaps would not make an appearance.

"Welcome, Imogen. Savanna will be along shortly," said Virginia as though she had read Imogen's mind. "I must also say, you have my sincere condolences for the loss of Mr. Howard. I hope this is appropriate for me to say, for I do not wish you any displeasure with my acknowledgement of his passing."

"Thank you, Virginia. I take no offense at your reference to Mr. Howard. It would be best at this time to refrain from any mention of Mr. Frye. Now, to the business of the day. I am pleased to know Savanna will join us. I wondered if her work at the apothecary would impede her ability to meet this morning."

"She said she made arrangements with Dr. Litle to delay her arrival. She felt it important for all of us to speak. I feel compelled to tell you that Savanna has been very forthcoming with me about the circumstances that have led to her coming here."

Virginia's statement gave Imogen an idea about how she could proceed. *Trust, I shall use trust as my guidepost.*

"Do tell. What exactly has Savanna revealed?"

"I do not wish to place myself in the business of others but, that said, she mentioned the discovery you made when you intruded upon her privacy."

Embarrassment began to threaten Imogen's expression of calm. *Has Savanna expressed the content of the letters I found? If so, hearing how upset I was with their content would only serve to confirm for Virginia the rumors circulating about me. And, now she will take joy in the knowledge that Sawyer's attentions have shifted to another.* Imogen shook her head. *I cannot dwell on what Virginia might think or feel for she has no rule over my life.*

"You make a point about privacy, however I had the best of intentions when I entered her bedchamber. Did she happen to mention that I was returning her earrings, which she left in the drawing room most likely after a playful rendezvous with Mr. Frye? And, under my own roof, I might add! I doubt she shared that tidbit with you?"

Imogen's raised voice became tempered when Savanna appeared in the doorway. It was important to her to keep a civil relationship with Savanna if for no other reason than the girl's connection to Talmadge. Theirs was a bond that could neither be denied nor, deep in Imogen's heart, did she want it to be. She liked Savanna. She was very smart and had shown Imogen much warmth and interest in her anti-slavery work and the success of *The Inquirer.* Obviously, Imogen wished she had not chosen to entertain interest in Sawyer and he in her. She doubted Sawyer would find his way back to her. Such was a painful truth she would have to accept.

"Savanna."

"Imogen."

With their curt greetings out of the way, Virginia attempted to soften the tone of their visit. "Please ladies, let us sit and see if there is a mutually agreeable opinion to which we can come. I have instructed Darcy to bring refreshments."

Virginia's words had no sooner left her lips than her housemaid, Darcy, entered the room with a large salver appointed with a teapot, cups, saucers and a two-tiered tray of sweets. Darcy, petite in frame, was the antithesis of Patti whose manner and attentions Savanna had come to know so well. *Perhaps a hearty meal would do her good,* thought Savanna as she and Imogen complied with Virginia's request but took seats on divans far opposite one another. Virginia selected a large armchair between the two divans in an effort, it would seem, to buffer them from one another and act as a mediator for their visit.

Imogen was the first to speak. "Savanna it is good to see you. I know we have not been on the best of terms of late and I hope we may soon remedy that situation. I am dismayed to learn from Virginia that you cared to tell her the circumstances that have led to your coming to her home."

"So, you are saying you would discourage me from having a confidante? What better source than my mum who would see no harm comes my way? She in her own way has tried to protect me since my birth. It has taken me some time to come to terms with her decision but, as I have told you in the past, we have let forgiveness be our guide. Perhaps you would like to pursue that course?"

"I must be able to trust that someone living under my roof is neither harboring secrets from me nor taking advantage of my relationships for their own benefit."

"Is not trust something with which we should all be in compliance? I must be able to trust that certain areas I occupy are free from the public domain. I was shocked to learn you had gone into my bedchamber and felt free to look through my personal belongings. I find such activity unacceptable," retorted Savanna, remaining confident in her appraisal of Imogen's actions.

"I believe Imogen is willing to apologize for opening your jewelry box for, to my understanding, she was only intending to return your earrings to their proper place. Is that not correct?" Virginia inquired as she tried to bring Savanna and Imogen into agreement.

"Yes Virginia, you are correct. Savanna, I apologize for lifting the lid from your jewelry box with the best intentions for the safekeeping of your earrings. I further apologize for reading the letters, which came into my view. Without placing blame, you could have done a more sufficient job of concealing them rather than essentially having them in plain view. Seeing and reading the letters however has brought a truth to me that I have suspected for some while. It will take time for me to accept but, for your father's sake, we must take the utmost care and not find ourselves estranged."

"Imogen, if it suits Savanna, would you be agreeable to her leaving Woodholme and living at Rosedale? You will be more than welcome to come calling whenever mutually convenient. I sense you both do not want to break the bond you have worked hard to establish. A bond, I might add, which Talmadge would not want to see brought asunder."

Savanna, although she thought it best for her to choose Rosedale over Woodholme, was feeling like a boomerang, having arrived in America, briefly lodging at Union Tavern, then Woodholme and now Rosedale. *I can think of worse scenarios,* pondered Savanna. *I have been afforded luxury upon every threshold for which I am most thankful. It is probably best that I keep a healthy distance from Imogen lest I be disposed to endorse her moral compass.*

"Yes! Thank you to both of you for allowing me to stay in such fine accommodations. And, family is very important to me. I want to continue to know both of you better and, Imogen, I hope we can resolve our *discomfort* about Mr. Frye."

Savanna was quite eager to accept my suggestion that she reside with Virginia, thought Imogen. As much as she obtained the outcome she sought, she felt a sense of abandonment and loss that was becoming a recurring refrain in the stanzas of her life. Jealousy also raised its ugly head as it was wont to do when Imogen coveted something others had, which made envy supply bitterness to her tongue. *I best not say what I would like to say. Best to let bygones be bygones for now, until we can let the late unpleasantness pass. We shall see what tomorrow brings.*

Chapter Forty-Four

In secret we met—In silence I grieve,
That thy heart could forget, Thy spirit deceive.
If I should meet thee, After long years,
How would I greet thee? With silence and tears.
—Lord Byron

Imogen's usual determination in her step was sluggish at best. It was as though her feet were keeping pace with the emotions that weighed down her thoughts. *How is it that I find myself once again in this cemetery? How is it that I cannot refrain from visiting here?* As she walked the grid-like paths between the gravestones comprising the avenues of the dead, she looked about the marble stones marking the remains of once thriving men, women and children, now nothing more than a name, date and perhaps an epitaph added to sustain a memory of their having existed. *Memories of them are all we have left,* sighed Imogen. Her thoughts were validated as she read the inscription on a nearby memorial, "The sweet remembrances of the just shall flourish when they sleep in dust."

Oh, so many gone, she thought as she lifted the skirt of her gown and cape to gain ease of movement as she advanced through the rows of graves toward two familiar names. Here lay Talmadge and Archibald, their remains nearly side by side. The irony of their placement did not escape her. Below Archibald's name, and below the dash that connected his dates of birth and death, was inscribed, "Tho lost to sight, to memory dear." *So similar to*

Talmadge's, mused Imogen as a familiar wave of melancholy cast its shadow over her.

Evicting Savanna from Woodholme had not been a pleasant task but Imogen viewed her actions as a necessity to maintain her dignity. Virginia had kindly invited her to live with her at Rosedale, which eased Imogen's conscience. She struggled with her responsibilities to Savanna for Talmadge's sake, yet could not abide witnessing Sawyer calling on her right under her nose. Seeing the two of them together was a constant reminder of the betrayal and loss she suffered. Virginia continued to host large social gatherings and extended invitations to Imogen who attended out of the need to remain in the public eye. *One never knows whom one might meet,* she would repeat to herself to justify her attendance, although it galled her to see Savanna and Sawyer arm in arm.

Arm in arm, how I should like to be on someone's arm. How I should like to have someone care enough about me to keep me close. What say you Talmadge and Archibald? Do I not deserve happiness? Imogen queried as she looked back and forth at their headstones.

As in times past, she wanted to collapse into their arms. She imagined them thriving where they would be able to comfort and protect her from the intense sense of loss and longing enveloping her. But, such comfort did not come. *'When sorrows come, they come not single spies, but in battalions,'* thought Imogen as she quoted Claudius' soliloquy from Shakespeare's *Hamlet. The words ring true, the words ring true,* she lamented. The sky had darkened, as had her mood. The descending vapors of threatening nimbostratus clouds began to encompass her as she cast off thoughts of others and took cover and comfort within the confines of herself.

Chapter Forty-Five

June 1822

Savanna woke with great joy in her heart. *This portends to be a glorious day!* She mused as she rubbed the sleep from her eyes and awaited Darcy's arrival at her bedchamber to assist with her morning toilette. She sat up on the edge of her bed, the mattress still plump with its luxurious filling of down. She stretched her arms, then walked to one of the windows to seek confirmation that the day would indeed be ripe with promise for her outing. She pulled back one panel of the silk draperies and smiled. *Yes, the sun has risen and so have I,* she declared with unbridled enthusiasm.

Only days before, Sawyer had suggested they take a carriage ride to Red Hill. She had heard it spoken of by Virginia's lady friends as a favorite spot to picnic and take in the panoramic view of the region. One of Virginia's guests had mentioned that on a day free of fog, one could look across the river and see the cupola at General Washington's house. Savanna was very much looking forward to venturing to the site in upper Georgetown for reasons beyond a day out. *I am so looking forward to being in Sawyer's company*, she swooned as she wrapped herself in the folds of the drapery panel like a royal cloak. A gentle knock at her door broke the cadence of her rapture.

"Who is it?"

"It's me, miss. It's Darcy. Good morning to ye."

"Come in. Good morning to you. Yes, it is a good morning. The weather appears to bode a beautiful day," replied Savanna, almost giddy with anticipation.

"Will ye be wantin' one of yer fancy gowns?"

"I think one of my day gowns will suffice. I am going on a picnic and do not want to appear too fussy, although I *do* want to look my best."

"No worries there, miss. Ye could be wearin' a gunnysack and look more beautiful than the finest ladies of the court."

"How sweet and kind of you to say so. My, my, though the mere thought of scratchy old jute against my skin makes me itch. Ouch! I shall cast off such thoughts," Savanna smiled and went to her wardrobe to select a gown to wear.

"This shall do quite well," Savanna declared as she swept around in a circle, holding the chosen gown close to her chest. Constructed of cotton, the neutral oatmeal colored fabric was printed with an overall pattern of florals in muted shades of apricot, raspberry and honeydew. To its ruched bodice were attached puffed sleeves in the leg-of-mutton style, which were cinched to rest just below the elbow. Tatting bordered the edges of its wide, white collar. The intricate knotting of the cotton lace tapered to long ends to be tucked into the gown's low décolletage for a modest wink at the wearer's cleavage. The gown's gathered full skirt was in two tiered layers, one shorter overlaying the other, the longest rising just above the shoe line to discreetly hide her ankles. She held the gown away from her to give it one final look of approval before Darcy laid it on her freshly made bed and readied Savanna's morning toilette.

"Darcy, I think I shall like to wear a hat with a large brim. Preferably, one that will serve to repel the sun's rays and keep me refreshed from the heat."

Darcy went to the shelf in the wardrobe and quickly scanned the hats. She reached for a wide brimmed one with a large, soft muslin ribbon.

"How 'bout this one, miss? If there be a breeze, the ribbon will keep it from flyin' off yer head."

Savanna laughed. "You have got that right. Good of you to think of that, Darcy."

"I'm always tryin' to do me best, miss."

"I appreciate that more than you know. You have yet to fail me. I am certain Mrs. Sterling appreciates your dedicated service."

Darcy blushed. She enjoyed praise but remained humble about her work. She wondered if Mr. Frye was responsible for Savanna's exceptionally blissful mood but she was afraid any inquiry on her part would be deemed inappropriate. However, curiosity had come nagging and was beginning to get the best of her. *There must be a way of askin' without askin',* pondered Darcy.

"It makes me 'appy to see ye so 'appy, miss. Yes, this must be a day truly special that ye have planned," Darcy said as a statement, rather than a question, hoping Savanna would reveal some details to her.

"You know me for a short time, yet you know me well, Darcy. Yes, I have been looking forward to this day. You remember Mr. Frye who has been to Rosedale on several occasions at the invitation of Mrs. Sterling?"

"I do, miss. A 'andsome gentleman if I may say so."

"Well, it seems you have said so," replied Savanna with a smile. She noted the blush returning to Darcy's face as the girl proceeded to brush through Savanna's thick coal-colored hair. She pulled her hair back and up, securing it with a tortoise comb onto the crown of her head, leaving several pieces on each side spiraling down into soft curls framing Savanna's face.

"No worries. I find him quite handsome too but let's keep these thoughts to ourselves lest we fan the flames of Mr. Frye's ego," teased Savanna. "He has invited me for an outing to a place I have not yet seen since I arrived in the city. I understand it is called Red Hill for obvious reasons. I hear the area has sloping earth banks of soil composed of small amounts of iron oxide, which, I recall from my studies, forms from the minerals in rocks. As the rocks weather or decompose, the process creates red clay, which is recognizable as rust-colored soil. Thus, the site is aptly called Red Hill."

A warm smile crossed Darcy's face. She felt privileged to have Miss Savanna converse with her in such a manner. To her it was as though they shared a kinship where they might further confide with one another. Darcy lifted the gown from the bed and slipped it over Savanna's head taking care not to muss her hair. Savanna shimmied the gown into place for Darcy to fasten the back with its multiple laces. She put her hands on Savanna's shoulders and turned her toward the large cheval looking glass. An expression of extreme satisfaction came to both of their faces. Darcy brought Savanna's jewelry box to her where she selected a triple strand of pearls to wear at her neck and pearl drop earrings for her lobes.

"Will ye be wantin' me to bring ye somethin' to eat for your mornin' meal?"

"Thank you Darcy but I think not. The morning has grown late and I am too excited to eat."

"But, ye dun't want to be starvin' when the time comes to eat, now do ye?"

"I understand what you are saying but I prefer to wait, and the time is approaching for Mr. Frye to arrive." No sooner had Savanna spoken than Virginia arrived in the doorway.

"Good morning to you both. I just wanted to let you know that Mr. Frye has arrived. I guess the two of you want to get an early start before the heat of the day sets in? How lovely that Dr. Litle honored your request to be free of work on Saturdays so you may have some leisure time. Oh, and I might add Savanna, you look radiant!"

"Thank you. I owe it all to Darcy. She is always a great help to me."

"Here," said Virginia as she handed the large brimmed hat to Savanna. "The crowning touch."

"Well, here we are Teddy," Sawyer announced to his horse as Teddy pulled the carriage up to the front of Rosedale where one of Virginia's stable hands awaited their arrival. Sawyer handed over the reins and gave Teddy a pat on his snout. "I shall not be long, old boy."

Sawyer had a particular liveliness to his step as he approached the front portal. The thought of being with Savanna today was met with high anticipation. He hoped the day would go as planned for he had gone to great effort to make it a special day.

Virginia arrived in the foyer to greet Rosedale's guest within moments of his arrival. She had grown fond of Sawyer and although the rumors of his relationship with Imogen had proven to be anything but platonic, she understood his interest in her had waned. She sensed he was a man of good character and that he would not disappoint her when it came to his affections for her daughter. She also determined she was willing to forgive his relationship with Imogen as an unfortunate lapse in judgment while under the influence of Imogen's charms. Blaming Imogen was Virginia's way of brushing away any wrongdoing on Sawyer's part. She was pleased with herself for thinking in such a way.

"Well, if it isn't the handsome Mr. Frye," Virginia proclaimed as she put the top of her right hand forward hoping he would grace it with a welcoming kiss. She was thrilled when he complied.

"And you Virginia, look exceedingly lovely and well. I sense from your greeting that you have found a place of comfort with my interest in your daughter?"

"You are quite correct. I have considered everyone involved with, if I might say, the affairs of the past, and have come to the conclusion that seasons change and so must I. Harboring anger and mean thoughts only serves to dwindle the joy in my life. I must remain glad for what I have, for I have gained a daughter for whom I care deeply. If she had not released herself from the anger and betrayal she felt learning about her adoption, I would not have the opportunity to know her and embrace her."

"It goes without saying that I am relieved to hear these words. I want only the best for your daughter and will bring her no harm, of that you may rest assured."

"Very well then. We are of the same mindset. Here, I am forgetting my manners. Please come have a seat," Virginia suggested as she proffered her hand toward the drawing room.

As Sawyer began to follow her lead, a rustling sound was heard on the staircase, which caught his attention. He looked toward the sound to see Savanna holding on to the handrail as she carefully and thoughtfully ascended each step with Darcy not far behind. As she raised her foot to descend the last three steps, she lifted her eyes and became distracted by Sawyer's gaze. In her zeal to greet him, all of a sudden she was in a misstep with no control of her feet. As she began to stumble down the stairs, Sawyer quickly noted her predicament and began racing to her aid. Within seconds he captured her in his arms before she hit the foyer floor.

"Oh my god!" Virginia gasped. Sawyer wondered if her outburst was out of fear for Savanna's safety or concern that he had his hands perhaps inappropriately on her daughter.

"Whew! That was close," said Sawyer as he helped Savanna steady herself to get a firm standing on the patterned Axminster carpet, which in addition to Sawyer served to soften her fall.

Savanna took a moment to catch her breath, which due to her proximity to Sawyer's face, took her longer to accomplish. She found comfort in his arms and was enjoying lingering there, although Virginia's presence was inhibiting the flights of fancy and thoughts of rapture spinning like devilish muses in her head. She looked into his eyes, shyly smiled and stepped back to compose herself.

"How awkward of me," stated Savanna as she broke the silence.

"Thank goodness you are none the worse for wear," responded Virginia. "You startled me so."

"I beg your forgiveness. It was not my intent to come barreling down the stairs."

"Oh, I know my dear. I meant no disrespect. I am glad you suffered no injuries."

"I'd be sayin' we're all mighty glad Mr. Frye was 'ere to save Miss Savanna from an early grave!" Darcy exclaimed, her hands starting to visibly shake.

"Yes, Mr. Frye," said Savanna demurely as she dipped her head down and gave a little curtsy to Sawyer. He smiled at her playfulness, removed his hat, held it at his waist and bowed.

"My, my, you two," Virginia said as she shook her head observing the onset of a mating game like the wishful thinking of a strutting rooster in a pen with his hen. "I am amazed Savanna that you and your gown are not all ruffled up."

"Yes, Miss Savanna. Ye look as fine as when we finished gettin' ye dressed this morn."

"I agree with Darcy. You look very lovely, Savanna. I shall be the envy of everyone partaking of the view at Red Hill today." He wanted to take his fingers and run them through the ringlets of curls framing her face. He fantasized about loosening the ribbon tied under her chin, its asymmetric bow resting on her left cheek. He wanted to embrace her and run his hands along the full length of her body but he knew all of that would have to wait. If he had his way, all of this would come in good time and he knew it would be well worth the wait.

As Savanna beamed, Virginia wondered if she and Darcy should take their leave, but she decided her duties as a chaperone were needed. *Perhaps I should send Darcy along with them,* thought Virginia. *How silly of me. They will be among many others today, so I have no need to worry.*

As the carriage made its way toward the end of High Street to the heights of Georgetown, the incline, paired with the weight of the carriage and its occupants, forced Teddy to slow his pace. Sawyer took the slowdown in his stride, nary forcing his hand with a whip or shout to the horse. Savanna admired his caring ways. *He is a gentleman with man and beast,* mused Savanna.

She looked ahead as the large land formation came into view. A pair of earth banks flanked the road, dwarfing their conveyance in size. Before them was an opening — a natural vista formed of rust-colored red clay and yellow sand.

"It is as it was described to me, yet more breathtaking than I could ever have imagined," declared Savanna.

Sawyer watched her reaction with great pleasure. He was pleased to be the one to take her to this remarkable place provided by Mother Nature and guided by God's hand.

He waved to several clusters of people as they passed along and selected a spot that would provide distance between them and the others partaking of the beautiful day and exquisite setting. He tethered his horse, then assisted Savanna in her exit from the carriage.

"Here, come look," said Sawyer as he took Savanna by the hand. He watched with delight as her face took on a glorious sense of awe at the view before her. "You mentioned Mount Vernon. We are fortunate for a clear day to perhaps catch sight of its cupola. Look toward the southern horizon — across the river to Virginia and you might capture a glimpse of its location."

"You may find me mute for a few moments for the scene before me is without compare!"

"If you look down over this way, you can see sections of Georgetown. See the line of trees near that rising ground? They are Lombardy poplars that overlook the canal on the southern flank of Georgetown College's grounds." Sawyer was enjoying sharing his knowledge of the area, particularly with Savanna. In his time away from his newspaper duties, he spent his leisure hours exploring the city and studying the history of what had become his newfound home.

"They appear so majestic with their slender, columnar shape. It is as though they are standing sentry over the halls of academia," laughed Savanna at she considered the idea of trees representing a bulwark to guard the campus. She closed her eyes and took in a deep breath of air wondering if, when she reopened her eyes, she would be in the same place, with the same view, with the same man at her side.

"Oh my, Sawyer. What a bucolic setting. I can imagine the poetry, songs and paintings a scene such as this inspires from creative souls whose talents lean toward the arts. It is truly idyllic here," Savanna nearly purred as her eyes panned west to east taking in the breadth of the glistening river. She took another deep breath as a soothing breeze blanketed her in its healthy embrace.

"So much of the city's plans remain unexecuted. It may take great time but I am certain it will become a metropolis of great grandeur," noted Sawyer.

She began to imagine the city that might be as growth and prosperity came in the coming years. *I imagine it will be a place not only of government but a place of grand buildings, grand homes, commerce and industry –a testament to the talents and toil of the men and women who make it their home.*

"You seem to know this place well? Have you taken other young ladies to this very spot?" Savanna could not resist her inquiry. She felt it was a question that begged to be asked, if for no other reason than to confirm Red Hill was a destination he had saved for the two of them to enjoy together. *Perhaps I should not have limited my question to young ladies for he may indeed have ventured here with Imogen.* Savanna quickly discarded the thought lest it ruin her time with Sawyer.

"You may rest assured that you are the one and only of the opposite gender to have accompanied me here," Sawyer ensured as he continued to hold Savanna's hand. "Red Hill is a place of unsurpassed beauty, which, if I might add, is such as are you." Savanna felt prepared to swoon with delight as Sawyer gently squeezed her hand. He wanted to embrace her but was careful not to race ahead with his plans so he quickly segued their conversation toward the subject of their picnic fare. "It was Gibs from *The Inquirer* who first alerted me to Red Hill. He said it was a favorite gathering place for his family, especially on special occasions. I joined him and his wife here about one month past. We dined on delicious fish caught by Gibs himself. He told me his favorite fishing spot is just below Little Falls where the fish are quite abundant, especially in May. From what I tasted, I would say the fish are unrivaled in quantity and flavor. Come, let's return to the carriage. I have our food and a large blanket. We can 'make our camp' so to speak."

Savanna found she was not only in awe of their setting she was in awe of the man who held her hand. He was not only handsome but he exuded other qualities that were important to her. He was smart, strong, caring, talented and charismatic. She loved his smile and his sense of humor. *Yes, I believe I am forever smitten by him.*

Sawyer lifted a blanket from the carriage and placed it under his arm. Then he removed a basket. With his arms occupied, he cocked his head to indicate for Savanna to join him a short distance from the carriage. Once he had everything in place and the two of them had settled on the blanket, he opened the basket to reveal a sumptuous repast.

"Everything looks delicious!" Savanna exclaimed. "If I may ask, where in the world did you find such generous provisions?"

"You can thank Virginia for the suggestion of Gadsby's in Alexandria. I sent a courier over the river this morning to pick up our fare to assure it would be fresh. I considered our local taverns in Georgetown but I wanted something very special for this occasion."

This occasion? Savanna wondered about Sawyer's meaning. *Perhaps he simply means introducing me to this place?* She decided to focus on the contents of the basket and put aside the curiosities of her mind.

"I hope you will be pleased with my selections. Gadsby's is known for their roasted duck breast. I asked that it be thinly sliced. There was a choice of potatoes. I selected potato dumplings. The new cook there is a German immigrant whose family has established a farm in Virginia. They raise many of the vegetables offered at the tavern. A very popular dish is the pickled red cabbage, which the cook, Frieda, informed me is called rotkraut. I was curious about its preparation. Frieda said she cooks the cabbage with sweet apples and onion in a broth of vinegar, sugar and dry red wine seasoned with spices, such as cloves and bay leaves. Oh, there is corn pudding too and for something sweet, we have German crumb cake," Sawyer smiled as he presented each of the dishes to Savanna. "I hope you find everything most enjoyable."

"You sir, have outdone yourself! My mouth is watering to partake of this bountiful display! And, how thoughtful to go to the trouble to venture across the river for these provisions."

"It is my pleasure. Anything for you Miss Carlyle."

Savanna was thankful for her hat, which kept the heat of the sun from her face as she and Sawyer dined and talked. She found him to be a good listener, as was she when he shared news of his family.

"I, like you, have no siblings. My parents have sent word that they wish for me to soon return. However I have no interest in such travel. My interests lie here," said Sawyer as he put down his plate and moved closer to Savanna. She too laid her plate on the blanket, sensing their meal had come to an end and something equally as appetizing was in the offing.

Clouds had begun to form, negating the sun's rays. There appeared to be no threat of inclement weather, however Sawyer determined he would take no chances in moving forward to accomplish his mission. He inched closer to Savanna, the leg of his britches grazing the skirt of her gown. He took her hand in his and looked into her dazzling emerald eyes. Savanna willingly accepted his approach while titillating sensations began to flow through her body.

"Miss Carlyle," Sawyer began in earnest formality. "Upon one of my visits to Dr. Litle's, you once said you hoped nothing was ailing me," recalled

Sawyer as he continued with nervous anticipation. "Well, if the truth be known, yes, I am ailing. You have stolen something from me and that loss can only be rectified by an affirmative response to a question I so humbly ask."

"I, sir? I have stolen something from you and it has affected your health? What pray tell might that be?"

"As I am certain you are now well aware, it is my heart you have stolen and I shan't go on another minute without it being returned to me."

"And, how may I best come to your aid?" Savanna nearly giggled as she enjoyed their playful repartee.

"I, Sawyer Frye, ask that you accept my most humble and sincere proposal of marriage. You occupy my thoughts both day and night. I want to provide for you. I want to be with you in every way. I want us to create a family together and live our lives together into our advanced years. I love you and want you to be my wife. Will you, Savanna Carlyle, marry me?"

Savanna thought her heart would overflow with joy. Watching Sawyer's face, his sincerity, his proclamations, his obvious abundant love for her, filled her with gratitude and desire. Her loins were nearly throbbing with a need to be fulfilled yet she was committed to maintaining her vow of celibacy until marriage. *What better way to satisfy the physical needs rising in me than to accept Sawyer's proposal? I love him. I have loved him for some time now and have just needed to erase the vision of him with Imogen from my mind. Thankfully, I have put that in the past where it must remain if I am to maintain a relationship with Imogen and love Sawyer to the fullest extent.*

Sawyer was becoming concerned with her hesitancy. He thought she would readily accept his proposal and wondered why there was any delay.

"Have I stunned you?"

"My, oh no. I am just thinking that I might need reassurance that I am your sole beloved. I would nary want anyone to come between us."

"You have my word that you are the only woman I ever want in my life. As I have said, I love you beyond words and always will. I am devoted to you from now until eternity."

"Then, Mr. Frye, I must answer in the affirmative. Yes, yes, yes! I accept your proposal of marriage."

Sawyer could barely contain his excitement. He let go of her hand and gently loosened the ribbon from her hat that formed the bow under her chin. He lifted the hat from her head and as he placed it on the blanket, they leaned into one another. Sawyer placed his cheek against hers, taking in the warmth and softness of her skin. He leaned his head back. They looked at one another, finding love reflected in their eyes. He moved toward her again, this time with his lips to hers as they came together slowly, released and returned more intensely. Sawyer knew he needed to cease their amorous interplay before desire overcame reason, particularly in a public place.

"I love you so much, Savanna."

"And I you."

"I brought something to celebrate this occasion. One moment while I retrieve it from the carriage."

"Am I to assume then that you assumed you would receive an affirmative response from me today? How presumptuous," laughed Savanna, her heart filled with glee. Sawyer looked back at her and joined her in her laugh. He quickly returned from the carriage with a bottle of claret and a small box.

"I held every hope that you would honor me with a 'yes.' What better way to commemorate our pledge than a delicious glass of claret and this small token of my love," said Sawyer as he handed the box to Savanna.

She removed the lid and lifted out a pocket-sized box covered in gold brocade. She lifted its lid to reveal a beautiful ring with a 2-carat rose cut diamond surrounded by pavé diamonds set in white gold. Nestled closely together they formed a brilliant field around the center stone.

Savanna gasped. "Oh my goodness! Sawyer, this is too much! Without sounding improper, you must have had to leverage your entire salary on this!"

"Not to worry, my dear Savanna. I have been saving for a day like today and when I saw this ring at the jewelers, it spoke to me of you. Here, try it on. I think I got the size right."

Sawyer removed the ring from the box, lifted Savanna's right hand and slipped the ring onto her finger. It was a perfect fit. She looked up at him, leaned forward and put her lips to his in a brief kiss of appreciation.

"It is perfect. More than I could ever have dreamed."

"When we marry, I shall give you a shiny white gold band to match and you may move this to your left hand to guard your wedding band, that is, if you wish."

"I find that to be a lovely tradition. Thank you for suggesting it."

"I think I best be getting you back to Rosedale before nightfall and we find ourselves here when darkness settles in."

"Oh my goodness, in the dark? What would we find to do with ourselves then?" Savanna teased.

"What a leading question from one so fair and proper. Why, I can think of nothing more than looking into the night's sky with you and counting stars," Sawyer teased back knowing he could think of several ravishing things he would like to do in the dark with Savanna.

Chapter Forty-Six

As much as Imogen hated to admit it, she was relieved to learn that Sawyer had readily secured a position at *The National Intelligencer* for she wished him no harm. It was his good fortune that the managing editor decided to move his family to Philadelphia, leaving the void for Sawyer to fill. Additionally, the newspaper offered him a sizeable room above the offices for his living quarters, which he gladly accepted since, as quickly as Imogen dismissed him from his position at *The Inquirer*, she promptly announced that he would need to find an alternative living arrangement.

Imogen was trying her best to finesse the changes infiltrating her life. Loss seemed to be high among the matters she had to accept. Patti, in her own inimitable way, had been the bearer of the news that Sawyer and Savanna had become engaged. The news was quite a blow to Imogen even though she suspected that would be the next step in their relationship. Patti and Virginia's housemaid, Darcy, were purchasing provisions at the market. They were known to each other having frequently crossed paths there. Center Market on Pennsylvania Avenue between Seventh and Ninth Streets was an ideal place to pick up not only the latest produce but also the latest gossip. Darcy excitedly shared that Miss Carlyle and Mr. Frye were to be married in the coming months.

"Mum! Mum!" Patti shouted, finding her mistress in the drawing room peacefully reading the newspaper. Her tone startled Imogen and garnered her immediate attention. "Miss Savanna is to marry Mr. Frye!" Patti blurted, wasting no time upon her return to inform Imogen in a most indelicate manner.

Imogen flung the newspaper from her hand, releasing the pages in a flurry. As the swirl of pages fell to the carpet, Patti made haste to gather them up, fearing she, like the newspaper, might incur the ire of her mistress.

"I shall need to be alone, Patti. Please see to it that I am not disturbed," ordered Imogen, holding back a flood of tears like a human dam. Imogen was determined to bar her emotional display until Patti left the room.

After she had a sustained, good cry, fairly saturating Talmadge's handkerchief, which she continued to keep close at hand, she felt a sense of relief. Sawyer and Savanna were perfect together. She knew that and would rally herself to find the acceptance necessary to be joyful for them, although it would take some doing. The hurt she felt about losing him had not yet fully healed.

I must ask Gertie to make a call to Woodholme and invite Savanna as well. This will be a perfect opportunity for them to meet and for me to come to terms with their union. Perhaps I must view this as having lost Sawyer for myself but gained him as a family member, Imogen reasoned, still not certain she could rally herself to be so magnanimous.

"Gertie, thank you for taking the time to travel to Woodholme. I trust your journey took you along more well-packed roads than not so you were not excessively jostled about in your carriage."

"Pack your worries, my dear. All was well with my ride, and the anticipation of seeing you in your lovely home only served to make the trip all the more pleasant. I probably should not say but Hazel, Mabel and Tea were a bit miffed that I came along without them. "

"Oh, my. Perhaps I should have invited them as well. I would not want to disappoint them or be the architect of discord. Please assure them they may accompany you here in the future. I did invite Savanna to join us today and she accepted. She has very happy news to share, about which I am adjusting."

"Ah, happy news is the best and I look forward to meeting her. And, no worries about my siblings. They, as my mother used to say, 'have the same shoes to get glad in.' I cannot let the morning go without extending my sympathies about Mr. Howard. A pity he harbored such hatred toward another," Gertie noted, as she shook her head to dispel the unpleasant thought. "On to other topics. So, I take it you and Savanna have resolved any differences you may have had regarding yourself and Mr. Frye?"

"I was put in the unenviable position of having very little choice in the matter. Any permanence to our relationship was not to be. I additionally found guilt was becoming my constant companion where she was concerned. How could I no longer treat her kindly? Talmadge would advise me to be considerate of his daughter."

"A wise decision indeed. When one has a powerful personality such as yourself it is not always possible to accept the path of least resistance for the desired outcome. There were times I questioned whether you were conducive to my advice?"

"You are such a calming voice of reason for me. I so appreciate your guidance. I think your faith in me precedes my own. Perhaps, at times, I was not ready to partake of your advice, however I feel I can never repay you for all you have done for me."

"Ah, repayment is neither necessary nor expected. You have a passion about you Imogen, which brings me to inquire about your anti-slavery society. How are things progressing in that regard?"

"Thank you Gertie for your interest. I am feeling encouraged to a limited degree, for I met with several congressmen to request, actually to beseech them, to enact a law of Congress for the gradual emancipation of slaves. They are our citizens and must be treated as such. To deprive them of freedoms such as industry and knowledge is, to say the least, unjust."

"Your thinking is sound, Imogen. You are an important vanguard in the abolition movement. Someone must shine a light on injustice. However, you must find frustration when your calls for attention to this matter seem to go unheard?"

"You are quite right. There is much opposition but I shall continue to pursue this important mission even if at times my efforts appear to be standing in stagnate waters. The word 'pure' may not be one often associated with my name but I assure you I have the purest of intentions when it comes to this cause."

Gertie smiled, pleased with Imogen's determination and resolve. She was prepared to change the subject when Patti announced Savanna's arrival. They both stood to greet their visitor.

Savanna had a glowing aura about her, which Imogen attributed to her engagement to Sawyer. She was always beautiful but today there was a viable joy that seemed infectious as Imogen relaxed and found herself wishing all the best for Savanna. Her hair was neatly piled in curls on top of her head with several ringlets tastefully dangling down on the sides of her face. Her attire was the epitome of simple elegance. Her shoes matched her frock of pale pink cinched at the waist with a cape-like collar resting at her shoulders. Several inches of embroidery along and up the hemline added a subtle touch of color with threads forming pink roses accompanied with soft green leaves. The fairly monochromatic garment was the perfect adornment to her frame.

Gertie was speechless as she took in the sight before her. Savanna's outward appearance was everything Imogen had described. Her resemblance to Talmadge was unmistakable. *Oh, how wonderful it would have been for him to have lived to know her,* lamented Gertie.

"Gertie Taylor, may I present Savanna Carlyle."

"Miss Carlyle, it is my pleasure to finally make your introduction."

"And I yours, Mrs. Taylor" replied Savanna with a brief curtsy.

"I feel, although this is our first meeting, that we are family. Please call me Gertie. I know that would please my husband Tea for he prefers to think of me with his surname, which is Smallwood. The reason for the surname controversy is a long story, which I shall refrain from burdening you with at this time. Although, I must say, it is a sweet story of love, which has endured."

"Then Gertie it shall be, and you will please address me as Savanna for I shan't be Miss Carlyle for much longer."

"Here ladies, let us sit. Savanna has news she wishes to share," said Imogen as she rallied every morsel of grace to accept the hearing of the engagement from Savanna's mouth.

Savanna had no sooner sat down than she eagerly blurted out her news. "I am beyond thrilled to announce that Mr. Sawyer Frye has asked me to be his wife and I have accepted!" Savanna's voice nearly raised an octave as delight filled her expression.

"How wonderful, my dear," said Gertie. "It is my fervent hope that you and Mr. Frye will have a sweet story of love that endures through the years ahead."

"Thank you so very much," Savanna beamed. She looked toward Imogen to see if the same expression of delight encircled her face and was pleasantly surprised to see the look of acceptance hover there. *Ah, she has finally acquiesced,* thought Savanna.

Other thoughts began to taint Imogen's good humor as she imagined Sawyer making love to Savanna. *Will she please him as I have? I wonder if he has already had his way with her? He is a man after all and has certain needs. Perhaps she is a tease and is holding sacred her flesh? Oh, poor Sawyer if she has denied him his basic carnal pleasures.*

"Imogen, we seem to have lost you dear? I was asking Savanna about their wedding plans," said Gertie hoping to awaken Imogen from her trance.

"Oh, my. I do apologize. In a way, I was thinking about the future, the future of our tea and sweets and I was wondering what is keeping Patti from our refreshments?" Imogen lied as her mind began to drift to sweet images of herself with Sawyer. *I must put these thoughts to the past and not revisit them,* she thought as she admonished herself. *I must not continue to bring suffering across my threshold.*

"Yes, let me see to Patti and then Savanna will have ample time to share the details of her betrothal and impending marriage."

Patti entered the drawing room just as Imogen stood to search out the girl. "Well, it is high time you made your way to us, Patti. Pray tell what held up your arrival?"

"It's sorry I am mum. There was a problem in the kitchen I was needin' to tend to. When I went to the root cellar to get a fresh jar of jam fer yer biscuits, a tiny little mouse was sittin' on top of the jar. 'e may 'ave been small but 'e sure did be scarin' me in a big way! I started chasin' 'im and 'e be runnin' so fast 'e 'eaded straight fer the kitchen. I ken't say where 'e be now but I gave a good look to yer teapot and 'e's not in there..."

"Enough Patti. While I appreciate your candidness, there are some things best left unsaid. Please rest the tray over there. We will try to forget the story you have told so we may enjoy partaking of the contents on the salver. Please see to it that Cook is fully aware of the unintended invader. That will be all for now."

Gertie and Savanna released their laughter, which they had held back, not wanting to upset Imogen or make Patti feel like a fool. Imogen joined them as a refreshing moment of bonhomie overtook the drawing room.

"I never know what the girl might do or say but she means no harm, of that I am sure. Here," said Imogen as she passed around the crystal bowl filled with strawberry jam. "Thankfully, there is no evidence of mice to taint the taste," noted Imogen as she smiled and placed a hefty dollop of the jam on her scone.

Gertie and Imogen listened intently as Savanna relayed specifics of her trip with Sawyer to Red Hill. She left out nary a detail as she described the view, the delicious food from Gadsby's, and Sawyer's proposal. Imogen kept her composure as she listened, forcing herself to let go of the feelings of bliss she had with Sawyer. Gertie and Imogen asked questions about the plans for the wedding, when and where it would be held, and both offered to assist in any way Savanna felt they could fill a need.

"You both have made me feel so confident about my future. I am the happiest I have ever been, especially in light of the truth I came to know only months ago. Sometimes I want to pinch myself to be certain what I am feeling is real. I worry this joy will not sustain itself and there will be challenges to face on the morrow."

"There will always be challenges, for change is inevitable my dear and we must adapt and embrace change the best we can if we are to grow. My advice would be to take advantage of all today has to offer for tomorrow is not promised," Gertie suggested as she placed one of her hands on Imogen's hand and her other hand on Savanna's hand forming a sisterhood, a trinity, a union of three finding strength as they joined together to celebrate what was to come.

Chapter Forty-Seven

July 1822

Sawyer waited patiently in Virginia's grand foyer and kept his eyes focused on the majestic staircase hoping at any moment to see Savanna descend its steps. They were to be married the first of December and had much to decide. Savanna sent correspondence to the Carlyles informing them of her nuptials. She was pleased to know they accepted her invitation and would make their first voyage to America to see her married. She was particularly excited for them to meet Sawyer, Virginia and Imogen. So much had happened in the several months since her arrival, at times she felt overwhelmed with her good fortune.

When she first placed her feet on the ground in the City of Washington, she knew not what to expect. The seat of government was experiencing, as was the country itself, so much growth and change. Commerce, industry, building, politics and the livelihoods and activities of the social elite, amidst the functions of everyday citizens, created an ever-changing landscape. Important figures in the construction and regulation of the policies forming the union of states were visible at many of the social events, balls, theater and taverns. The power in the city was like a vibrant pulse propelling life-sustaining blood through its arteries. Savanna and Sawyer agreed they would make the City of Washington their home. It had been good to them and they hoped it would remain so.

Virginia and Imogen were fortunately able to come to an agreement that the reception following the wedding would be held at Woodholme, which was Savanna's first choice. Although she had been residing at Rosedale, Woodholme held warm thoughts of her father. It was her way of including him as a part of her special day.

Sawyer had asked her church preference for their wedding ceremony. "I should like to be married at St. John's Episcopal Church. Patrons of the apothecary have been speaking of the bell that has been commissioned from Revere's son to be placed in the steeple there, I believe in November. I understand it will rival the bell in the steeple soon to be atop the Unitarian Church. With any luck of timing, on our wedding day they will ring to the heavens in tandem at noon. Will that not be spectacular?"

"It will be a most joyful occurrence and occasion," replied Sawyer, who took the opportunity to draw her to him and place his lips to hers. "I love you so dearly, Miss Savanna Carlyle. It will be my great honor to pledge my love to you before all to hear. I shall cherish you always until death separates us to meet again in eternal life."

"I love you so very much, Mr. Frye, and soon I shall take your surname. Such thought brings me great pleasure," said Savanna, as her mind went to other activities of marriage she anticipated that would bring her great pleasure. She hoped she would find lovemaking a pleasurable experience and that Sawyer would find gratification when the time came for him to know her in every way. Her loins began to throb at the thought of being with Sawyer, free of the bondage of clothing, exploring each other's bodies, as they burst with desire.

"Here she is now," announced Virginia as Savanna appeared at the top of the landing.

Sawyer watched as she gracefully descended the staircase, holding his breath that she did not become distracted and come tumbling down as she had in the past. She smiled and grasped the handrail. He moved closer to the banister. He rested his left hand on the large newel post and placed his right foot on the first stair tread to stabilize himself should she take a spill. He took a sigh of relief when she arrived at the last step. They looked into each other's eyes where every essence of love waltzed between them. He lifted his right arm with it bent at the elbow and put it out for her to grip with her left hand. It was a natural, genteel motion with which they both felt at perfect ease.

"You must make haste," shouted Darcy, as she rushed into the foyer, breaking the magic of their moment. "A storm be in the air! Best ye be waitin' 'til it's past!"

"Good lord, Darcy! You would have us believe the wrath of God is ready to make an assault upon us," said Virginia, shaken by Darcy's sudden appearance and loud announcement. Virginia looked out the window to see the skies had darkened but no precipitation had yet fallen.

"I have the hood up on the carriage, which will serve us well should Mother Nature loosen her grip on the clouds. If you have no objection, we will take our leave. We have only a short journey to meet with Reverend Hawley, the rector at St. John's, and will be able to seek cover if it becomes necessary."

They bid Virginia and Darcy adieu and began their promenade from Rosedale. As they stepped onto the portico, Sawyer released Savanna's arm and walked to the front garden where he plucked a flower from its bush. It was a beautiful, long-stemmed rose in a deep shade of red. He checked it for thorns and finding none, walked back to Savanna.

"I present this rose to you as a symbol of my love. As lovely as it is, it however can never surpass your beauty. You are one-of-a-kind, Miss Carlyle and soon, I am most happy to say, we shall become one."

Chapter Forty-Eight

The heart will break, but broken live on.
—Lord Byron

"Patti, look how the skies have darkened. Close the drapes. There's a storm coming and I choose not to witness its fury this day. Heaven knows I have weathered many tribulations of late although, fearing the worst never serves one well. Perhaps this is God's way of cleansing my life, of handing me a fresh start, my tabula rasa." Imogen's words came forth in a stream as though she had unleashed the innermost cavern of her mind and willed it to speak aloud. She had pulled herself from the depression that had sought her out and, having succeeded, was determined she would no longer be ruled by it.

Words of scripture from Matthew 6:27 came to mind: "And who of you by worrying can add a single hour to his life?" She closed her eyes and began to recite the words, *Not to worry, not to worry. I am strong, I am strong, I am strong.* The incantation she invoked had become a frequent visitor to her tongue, especially when she adopted a meditative state. She felt more relaxed and wiser for taking the time to give herself a verbal vote of support.

A sudden flash of thunder and lightning startled her. She opened her eyes and looked about for Patti who had apparently exited the room without seeking further instructions from her mistress.

"A least the girl completed her task with the draperies. When the storm passes I shall have to have a word with her. Perhaps she has taken to hiding under a table like a frightened dog?" Imogen queried aloud, pretending to ignore her own discomfort with the pending storm.

Another rumbling clap of thunder nearly sent Imogen to the floor but she rallied her senses, determined not to allow nature's fury to have its way with her. Alone in the darkened room, her mind, as it often had of late, turned to thoughts of Talmadge and her life with him, her life with Archibald, her life with Sawyer, and the intrusions of Virginia and Savanna into her life. *What a cast of characters I have experienced on my life's stage,* Imogen silently mused as she ran her hand along a velvet throw neatly placed on a nearby chair. She sought comfort in its soft pile. Though inanimate, just the fondling of it soothed her nerves and brought her to a place of peace.

She reflected that as a child, she kept a wide strand of satin ribbon tucked away in the drawer of her dressing table. Her mother had given her the ribbon to tie on a bonnet but she elected to stow it away. Her mother said the color was representative of a shade preferred by Louis XIV, which he called *couleur de feu,* a bright flame color, which she found more appealing and exciting than soft yellow or blue hues. And certainly, she determined, if the color was suited for royalty, it was more than suitable for her.

Whenever she felt troubled she would remove the ribbon and repeatedly glide her thumb and forefinger along its smooth surface. It was a ritual she carried into her adulthood. When she told Patti the story, she kindly found a piece of satin ribbon in the sewing box and placed it in a small gilded coffer on a table in the drawing room. *Where has that girl disappeared? Must I shout to gain her attention?* Imogen blurted her questions aloud, impatient with Patti and the lingering storm, which slowly took its leave.

Imogen stepped through the threshold onto Woodholme's front portico where she hoped to find comfort. It was often the place of mixed blessings where visitors were either a welcomed or unwelcomed sight. A phrase often repeated by one of her lady friends floated through her mind: "All of our guests bring happiness. Some by coming, others by leaving." The phrase reminded her of a sage reflection attributed to Benjamin Franklin: "Guests, like fish, begin to smell after three days." The adage brought a smile to her face, as the heady scent of lavender embraced her nostrils.

The perennial, with its slender stem and multiple, pale purple florets, was a favorite along her front walkway. Its royal color lent an air of grace and elegance while its fragrance lifted her spirits. She occasionally snipped stems of lavender and brought them indoors to dry to be used in a tussie-mussie she could carry and bring up to her nose to improve the air about her if the occasion arose. Fragrant aromas from florals helped to combat less desirable societal smells that were wont to waft one's direction. She had always found it best to be prepared for such circumstances.

Cleansed by the welcoming scent, Imogen returned to the drawing room and reflected on the year past. A single tear eased its way upon her cheek as Talmadge's image came into view, then Archibald's, Virginia's, Sawyer's and, less reluctantly now, Savanna's. Each had played a role in the decisions she chose to implement in her life yet, how could she solely blame them for the outcomes? She had endured public ridicule, which despite her attempts to brush the opinions of others aside, caustic comments and judgmental glances her direction resonated like reverberating tremors on the social landscape of her life. Other than the Taylor sisters and Tea, she felt she had only one other person remaining whom she needed to give her full faith — herself. *I shall lift myself up with the buoyancy of a fine vessel enjoying fair winds and following seas,* she declared, as she stood steadfast in the center of the drawing room. She planted her feet firmly on the Axminster carpet, which lent some comfort to the mood that had beset her for the greater part of the day, which the storm did little to ease. She positioned her body directly in front of the room's large fireplace whose mantel served not only as a protective ledge should soot or flame escape the firebox but also served to form a visual baseline for her portrait Talmadge had commissioned soon after they arrived in America.

Where has time gone? Imogen pondered. She saw before her the visage of a vital woman, not one in decline as she felt of late. Every morsel of her being seemed to be waning yet, in the portrait, her skin radiated a vibrancy that perhaps was proffered by the gentle application of oil paint and soft, nearly invisible brushstrokes masterly administered by the artist Rembrandt Peale. Named for the 17th century Dutch painter, Peale was influenced by French

Neoclassicism, which was evident in Imogen's portrait that resembled the beauty of François Gérard's portrait of Madame Récamier. Moderately reclining on a throne-like chair covered in a rich tapestry, Imogen was resplendent. She was enveloped in rich yet sober colors, while well-delineated lines lent simplicity to the overall setting of the piece.

About her neck was a necklace composed of three strands of alternating large emeralds and diamonds each set in a gold bezel. Matching earrings, formed in a briolette style adorned her ears and, in addition to her four-carat diamond wedding ring on her left hand, on the middle finger of her right hand was painted a three-carat emerald surrounded by brilliant cut diamonds. She owned none of the jewels except the wedding ring. They were merely a request by her when the portrait was commissioned. When Peale asked about their inclusion in the portrait, Imogen said if she should die before Talmadge and he were to remarry, she wanted his second wife to go mad looking for the beautiful gems. It was one curse she felt she could issue from her grave.

The thought brought a smile to her face, which quickly disappeared as her mind once again raced with images of Talmadge, Archibald, Virginia, Sawyer and Savanna. Before her rose a bold assembly of lovers and acquaintances who littered her past and whose actions and fates had altered the visions she had imagined for herself. She stared at her portrait seeking solace, yet feared it would not come. *As sure as dusk precedes night, the sun will rise on yet another dawn and I shall be here, fortified by the walls of Woodholme*, Imogen mused. *I shall greet the challenges that rise before me. I am strong. I am resilient.*

Upon her words, she paused and took a long, deliberate look at her image. She stared deep into the eyes of the woman depicted there searching for her soul, searching for a window into her future. She lifted her shoulders in salute to the artist's image of a strong and influential woman and vowed to honor his depiction. *I am strong, I am resilient,* she again recited aloud in an attempt to bolster her unequivocal resolve to seek an inner strength that would encourage her to live out her final days in the mansion that had always brought her great comfort. *Past trials and tribulations may have been constant companions, which I endured, but today will bring a new dawn. Of that I am certain.*

She walked to the darkened window, pulled back the drapes and grasped the cords to pull up the ruched shade. She watched the shade rise inch-by-inch as the cords slid through the pulley and daylight reentered the room. She looked up and smiled. She imagined herself the captain of a ship monitoring a compass to keep her course. The shade was her sail as she set her sights on the new day. *I will not succumb to any rough seas ahead. I know they shall come. But, I am strong and can defend myself against them. Resilience shall be my battle cry,* Imogen avowed as she gathered the multiple swathes of fabric comprising the skirt of her gown, a creation as complex as the layers of her life. She was determined to not fall victim to despair in her waning days and she was determined to not be alone.

She reached into the gilded box adorned with a beautifully carved rose on its lid and removed the strand of satin ribbon in a delicate shade of lavender that Patti had placed there for her. Lavender was one of her favorite scents and colors. She admired the pure sheen of the long strand as she held it in her hands and continued moving the piece among her fingers, enjoying its smoothness and the healing calm it brought upon each touch. She began skillfully entwining it among her fingers as a satin web began to form.

If it were spider's silk, what prey might become entrapped by my wily ways? She pondered aloud as she watched the evolution of the web. She raised her hands and stared into her palms as a soothsayer might when interpreting the lines created there during gestation that were becoming accentuated as Imogen aged. Although not trained in palmistry, she attempted to envision her future as she searched the four lines on her right palm representing life; head; heart; and fate. She shook her head. She had no idea what she was supposed to be seeing as she studied the lines, some having grown deeper than others. *Hands, they have the ability to raise up and to break down, to build and to destroy. I have lost too many at the hands of another. This madness must end,* she exclaimed as though her declaration would bring her comfort and perhaps a degree of joy.

She recalled Gertie's words when she sought her counsel after the loss of Talmadge, Archibald and Sawyer. "Everyone has pain, my dear. It is but the suffering, which remains optional. You see there *is* choice in the matter."

Rather than dwell on sadness, Imogen closed her palms, clasped her hands together and made her way to the study as she defiantly declared, *Though my future remains a mystery, I am determined to find my path forward. There shall be nothing to hold me back. Nothing to stop me now.*

A knock came to Woodholme's front portal. Imogen had received word that Tea was coming to call with a gentleman friend he wished to introduce to Imogen. She was curious that Tea was making such a request with no mention of Gertie tagging along. Within moments, Patti rounded the corner and stopped at the door of the study to announce Woodholme's visitors.

"Thank you, Patti. Please see them into the drawing room. Tell them I shall be along shortly."

Imogen stood and smoothed the layers of her gown to remove any rumples. She put her hands to her head and felt her hair to see that all the strands were in place. She pinched her cheeks to refresh her color and gave a quick lick to her lips to moisten them before making her way to her guests.

Upon her entry into the drawing room both men immediately stood and bade her hello with a brief bow. Tea was the first to speak as he made his way to Imogen to greet her with a hug.

"Imogen, how lovely you look. Is it possible that you have found the fountain of youth? If so, I wish to bathe in the same spring water," cajoled Tea.

"Oh, Tea. How kind of you to say. You make me blush with such adoring kindnesses my direction."

"You know I mean every word," Tea continued, feeling that his flattery would help to ease their conversation. "Imogen, may I present my friend Oliver Sinclair Dewberry. We have come to know one another by way of our mutual love of the sea. Ollie, as I call him, has been anchoring his business in the City of Washington. Even though the tobacco trade is not as prolific as it has been in the past, the Potomac port has been very viable for his shipping business. The mills and factories in Georgetown, supplying flour, paper and textiles, generate more than a fair amount of trade. Due to the build up of silt, he is bringing in smaller vessels that are still able to navigate the area."

"Oh, I see," said Imogen. "I thought perhaps you were a head seaman or boatswain on one of the vessels Tea manages."

"My goodness no, Imogen," declared Tea feeling slightly embarrassed by her assumption. "Ollie is the owner of a fleet of vessels. The two of us have banded together with Captain Easby, a master shipbuilder at the Navy Yard. The captain bought the old Tunnicliff's Hotel property. I sure miss that place. It was entertaining to watch the activity with the Georgetown Stagecoach since it was a terminal for so many arrivals of travelers — some weary from travel and some jubilant to have made it safely to their destination. Word has it that passage from the City of Washington to Baltimore is a five hour ride..." Tea rattled on, only to be stopped when Dewberry broke the awkwardness.

"Mrs. Simmonds, I have looked forward to this day. Tea has told me much about you and I must say, I am intrigued. Oh, I must add that while Tea chooses to call me 'Ollie', which I accept as an endearment from him, I, for business purposes prefer to be called by my given middle name, Sinclair, and hope you will refer to me with that moniker."

"Totally understood, Sinclair. It is a pleasure to meet you and please call me by my given name, if you will. When you say I intrigue you, I question what dear Tea has relayed to you. I hope his introduction has had nothing to do with the rumors that sometimes come calling at my door. I am somewhat concerned about that, which you may have heard?"

"Quite the contrary. Public opinion is often bound by biases. I prefer to draw my own conclusions."

"I am comforted by such knowledge."

"I can tell you, I appreciate a woman of conviction who is willing to take risks no matter the cost to her personally. I would not have the success I have if I were not accepting of an occasional risk. Tea has also informed me of your advocacy work for the well-being of the enslaved. I stand behind your cause as well. Recently I was in Boston. There is a young man there with the last name I believe of Garrison, yes William Lloyd Garrison, if I properly recall, who is crusading to begin an anti-slavery periodical. He intends to title it *The Liberator*. It proves to be very informative and enlightening. I feel Mr.

Garrison will garner a good deal of support for his cause."

"How interesting. Perhaps I need to meet this Mr. Garrison."

"Just say the word and we can board one of my vessels and sail away to Boston. The city proves to become the center for the American anti-slavery movement. There's a young woman, let me think a moment, for her name is comprised of several names. Oh yes, I recall it now. Her name is Eunice Russ Ames Davis. She is two and twenty but she is building a name for herself and joining forces with Garrison. It would certainly behoove you to visit there."

Imogen was warming to this man who was so newly her acquaintance. Not only was he tall and handsome with a cheerful, reflective smile but he also had the bluest eyes, seemingly direct from the sea, and it seemed his thoughts aligned with hers.

"Your interest in abolition is clear. It appears you have done your research at every port to which you sail," said Imogen with a smile. "I admire that. I actually find very refreshing a man with an open mind. I wish there were more in society who had such freedom of thinking. One can encounter many hypocrites in the city. I have been asked by some, how I can dismiss such talk and accusations," Imogen said as she glanced at Tea. "My feeling is that I shall not be lured by their attempts to interfere with my purpose."

Dewberry listened intently to her words. "Sometimes I find, especially when hypocrites prevail, that we are victims of misunderstanding. We cannot make people be for us who do not wish to be so. There will always be those who question our motives. Another woman, a lesser woman than yourself, might say, 'of course' and forgive all in an effort to accommodate peace."

Imogen felt an immediate kinship with Dewberry. They had only just met but he seemed to know her from another life, another time. She felt a sense of genuine comfort with him that had been a longtime overdue.

"Tea also told me about your position at the helm of the impressive newspaper you own. I would imagine that you have met a multitude of interesting inhabitants of Georgetown and the city from the simplest pedestrian to those of power in the political arena."

"Indeed I have. Their stories run the gamut from mundane, to laughable, to criminal, to inspiring, to the struggles of the government and so much more."

"I can say, I do hope we have opportunities for you to reveal some of the highlights of your work. I gain great pleasure from listening to a story well told as much as I enjoy telling one myself."

"I should like that very much," replied Imogen. Her heart felt lighter than it had in months. *Mr. Dewberry appears to be just the tonic I am in need of to lift my spirits,* Imogen cooed to herself.

"Perhaps, if you take no exception to my suggestion, I might become your great vindicator. I, as it also appears to be the same for you, have never been one to shrink from adversity. We may forge our resiliency together," promised Dewberry as he moved closer to Imogen and took her hands in his.

Tea was especially entertained with their repartee, as was Imogen who smiled at Dewberry's approach and his intimate proximity.

"May I call on you again, Mrs. Simmonds?"

"That you may Mr. Dewberry," responded Imogen without hesitation.

"Consider me at your service."

Epilogue

August 1822

The Washington Inquirer ran an obituary, which captured the attention of many in the City of Washington and Georgetown:

> A team of horses ran down the wife of a very reputable and respected lawyer as she carelessly stepped into their path. The driver tried earnestly to hold the horses back to no avail. The woman was deemed dead at the scene, steps from the entrance of *The National Intelligencer*, where it has been suggested she was delivering a piece for publication.
>
> There are those among the social elite who have attributed a popular gossip column to the deceased. Two sheets of parchment were found strewn near her body but they were so badly mangled by the carriage wheels there was no way to salvage them. Some say her death was fitting for she had spent so much time running down the lives of others and curiously, upon her death, no word has again been uttered by Tillie Tattler. May Lydia Cromley rest in peace? God only knows.

Acknowledgments

Where to begin? Gratitude is the word that pops into my mind. "Gratitude is the memory of the heart," notes a French proverb. How true. I extend heartfelt gratitude to my wonderful family and friends for your unwavering inspiration and encouragement. Each of you contributes to the ideas that spin in my head and ultimately spawn the creation of another novel. I also owe a great debt of gratitude to my readers and thank each and every one of you for supporting my writing. You mean the world to me!

Many thanks to my earliest readers Mark Gilder and Sue Thorpe and to my daughter, Jacqueline Gilder Brentzel, for the light and joy she and her family bring to my life.

Historical novels require extensive research. Delving into the ever-evolving formation of the City of Washington and nearby Georgetown in the early 1800's was fascinating! Much gratitude goes to historian Hayden W. Mathews for discussing with me early maps of the Territory (District) of Columbia and guiding me to several wonderful resources, among them the books: *The City of Washington, An Illustrated History,* by The Junior League of Washington; *Early Recollections of Washington City,* by Christian Hines from the collection of The Columbia Historical Society reprinted with illustrations and notes by The Junior League of Washington; and *A Portrait of Old George Town,* by Grace Dunlop Ecker.

Additional thanks to the editors who publish my work and to the booksellers and retailers who promote my novels and keep them "top shelf."

But most of all, my heart is full of gratitude as I thank my wonderful husband, Mark, for everything.

The characters in *The Widow of Woodholme* have kept me company for many months and I hope they continue their journeys in your imagination and bring you pleasure. I also hope the joy of reading and escaping to another world never fades as you let literature inform, transform and inspire you.

Special credit and thanks to these talented individuals
Author's photo: Stone Photography, Bethesda, Maryland
Palladian window architectural rendering used with permission:
Pam Haag of Pam Heinen Haag Designs
Publisher's logo: Mark Brodsky dba Graphic Squirrel

Author's Notes

The wonderful maps available on the Library of Congress' website offer great paths to street names in 1821 in the independent port of Georgetown. Here are a few of Georgetown's main streets referenced in *The Widow of Woodholme* and their current names: Bridge Street is now M Street; High Street is now Wisconsin Avenue; Water Street is now K Street; Market Street is now 33rd Street; and Washington Street is now 30th Street.

On some maps in the late 18th and early 19th centuries, as well as in many of the writings about Georgetown during that time, Georgetown was either two separate words or hyphenated as George-Town. The town, formerly part of Maryland, was established in 1751. It wasn't until 1879 when most of the streets in Georgetown were aligned with the names of the streets in the City of Washington (District of Columbia). Additional nomenclature changes to Georgetown streets occurred in 1895.

Founded in 1791, the City of Washington, comprised of land ceded by Maryland and Virginia, was recognized as the federal district in 1801. The City of Washington and its adjacent environs of Georgetown and Alexandria were sometimes referred to as being in the Territory (District) of Columbia. In 1871, the Territory of Columbia was officially renamed District of Columbia.

A note about Columbia Foundry owner Henry Foxall and the spelling of his last name since he is briefly mentioned in *The Widow of Woodholme*. Those familiar with the Washington, D.C. area may wonder if there's a typo with his last name in the novel because the 'h' is missing. Foxall manufactured many of the armaments used in the War of 1812. Additionally, he served as mayor of Georgetown; was director of a Georgetown bank; he was a preacher; and he donated land for the building of Foundry Chapel, which became Foundry United Methodist Church. He owned property called Spring Hill Farm where the historic district of Foxhall Village now exists at Foxhall and Reservoir Roads. As often happened in the recording of names, variations in spellings occurred where the letter 'h' appeared in Foxall's surname, which years after his passing became the norm and the rest, as they say, is history.

The Widow of Woodholme

a novel

A Warren Press Readers Club Guide

1. If you were Tillie Tattler, what would you choose to write?

2. If *The Widow of Woodholme* were made into a movie, whom would you want to play Imogen? Talmadge? Archibald? Virginia? Sawyer? Savanna? Patti? Gertie? Tea?

3. Which character in *The Widow of Woodholme* is most like you? Which character would you most like to hang around?

4. Who is your favorite character? Who is your least favorite?

5. What attributes do you like to see in a woman? In a man?

6. How does Imogen Simmonds change during the course of the novel…or does she?

Photo: Stone Photography

Sharon Allen Gilder is a native Washingtonian. She resides in Maryland and South Carolina with her husband. Her debut novel was *The Rose Beyond* followed by its sequel *Beyond the Rose.* Her road map for a happy life includes time with family and friends, writing, reading, walking, relaxing on the beach, and singing her original Irish drinking song, "Oh the Whiskey," at neighborhood restaurants and wine bars.

For more information, please visit:
www.sharonallengilder.com

Made in the USA
Monee, IL
09 January 2023

24839513R00194